DARK SECRET

A MARK INGRAM ADVENTURE

Cover by: Ken Farmer

DARK SECRET

BY

DORAN INGRHAM

timbercreekpress@yahoo.com

ISBN 10: 0990438937
ISBN 13: 978-0-9904389-3-9

Printed in the United States of America
Published by:
Timber Creek Press
312 N. Commerce St.
Gainesville, Texas 76240
timbercreekpress@yahoo.com

DEDICATION

This novel is dedicated to all the men, women and WMDs who stand in harms way to defend and protect the free world. I am forever grateful for your sacrifice and service. In addition, I dedicate this book to those I worked with around the globe providing security for our clients. In your memory and to your honor I will keep the tales of our work as close to the truth as allowed by law and common sense. I promise never to divulge your true identity.

ACKNOWLEDGMENTS

I must first thank my incredible wife, Maria Mae, for her support and endless encouragement, followed by Timber Creek Press, Buck Stienke and Ken Farmer, who offered invaluable suggestions how to improve each book I have written to date. Without their offer to coauthor "Black Eagle Force: Blood Ivory" I would not be living the life-long dream of being a published writer. Finally, I want to thank all those who have read my work and spread the word about Mark Ingram Adventures.

THE AUTHOR

Doran W Ingrham – Inactive USMC – Viet Nam Veteran. Retired Risk Management/Close Security Specialist (call sign 'Zorro'). Extensive global experience dealing with terrorist threats. Has vast working knowledge of weapons, explosives, survival skills urban, jungle, desert and intel gathering methods used around the globe for covert (Black Ops) actions and Executive Protection. Combat Pistol competitor and International Sniper competitor. He has appeared in over 20 commercials, 15 television episodic and 40 films. Has written a series of film scripts based on his world-wide experiences. Doran now lives with his wife, Maria Mae, exact location undisclosed

First printing - 06/18/2014

SHORT REVIEWS

Edward E, Pare
Ex Special Forces Demolition Expert

Just finished reading Doran's third book DARK SECRET. It is a very well written and fast moving action adventure tale, on an even larger epic scale than his first two. With some bad guys far uglier than either Bond or Bourne ever dealt with and races across three different continents. The protagonist Mark 'Zorro' Ingram (an Afghan veteran US Marine) lives up to his reputation of being extraordinary personal security. No spoiler to say there is a secret...A secret that needs to be exposed.

Doug Lee

Dark Secret is the second in the series of Mark Ingram adventures. Like the first, "Blood Brothers", it's a non stop, action packed, continent jumping ride as Mark Ingram and his fellow operatives battle the forces of evil from the Taliban to the Yakuza. Follow Mark as he uncovers the dark secret. Clear your calendar because once you start reading this book you will not want to put it down!

Robert 'Slash' Thompson

I rarely read fiction that captures my imagination like Dark Secret. The formula writers popular today are too predictable and boring in my opinion. This book is a breath of fresh air. Maybe it is because I worked in the field this new author writes about. I laugh at those who attempt to portray it as glamorous or sexy. It is not. It is, as Doran Ingrham so justly wrote, a dark, ugly, dangerous world. I have not read another author who has a clue which brings me to believe he lived the experience written in Dark Secret. I will be checking out his other novels and look forward to the future adventures of Mark Ingram.

Robert 'Slash' Thompson
Former Navy SEAL
Retired Risk Management Specialist

Katherine Boyer

Doran Ingrham's novel, *Dark Secrets,* his newest Mark Ingram novel, sizzles with more intrigue, excitement and, yes, wit. When Mark Ingram takes on a contract to provide security for wealthy Joris Barnhardt and his family, he has no idea of what will be discovered. What are the secrets unearthed by Mark Ingram and his team? A must read for all readers.

As a retired librarian, I know that libraries are always looking for books that will hold the attention of the reader. *Dark Secrets* does just that. I consider Mr. Ingrham to be an author in the same class as Tom Clancy, W.E.B. Griffin and Larry Bond.

Katherine Boyer, BA, MLS
Retired Library Director

OTHER NOVELS FROM
TIMBER CREEK PRESS
www.timbercreekpress.net

MILITARY ACTION/TECHNO
BLACK EAGLE FORCE: Eye of the Storm (Book #1)
by Buck Stienke and Ken Farmer
www.tinyurl.com/storm4un
BLACK EAGLE FORCE: Sacred Mountain (Book #2)
by Buck Stienke and Ken Farmer
www.tinyurl.com/SacMtn2
RETURN of the STARFIGHTER (Book #3)
by Buck Stienke and Ken Farmer
www.tinyurl.com/StarF01
BLACK EAGLE FORCE: BLOOD IVORY (Book #4)
by Buck Stienke and Ken Farmer with Doran Ingrham
www.tinyurl.com/befivory
BLACK EAGLE FORCE: FOURTH REICH (Book #5)
By Buck Stienke and Ken Farmer
www.tinyurl.com/befreich
BLOOD BROTHERS - Doran Ingrham, Buck Stienke
and Ken Farmer
www.tinyurl.com/bloodbrothers1

SCI/FY
LEGEND of AURORA by Ken Farmer & Buck Stienke
www.tinyurl.com/LegendAurora-E

HISTORICAL FICTION WESTERN
THE NATIONS by Ken Farmer and Buck Stienke
www.tinyurl.com/thenations1
HAUNTED FALLS by Ken Farmer and Buck Stienke
www.tinyurl.com/hauntedfalls1
HELL HOLE by Ken Farmer
www.tinyurl.com/hellhole-Bass
DEVIL'S CANYON by Buck Stienke
Www.tinyurl.com/Devil-sCan

WESTERN ROMANCE
SURRENDERED by Peggy Patrick
http://tinyurl.com/Surrendered-I
SURRENDERED II by Peggy Patrick
http://tinyurl.com/Surrendered-2
SURRENDERED III by Peggy Patrick

Coming This Summer

SCI/FY
AURORA: *INVASION* by Ken Farmer & Buck Stienke

WESTERN ROMANCE
SURRENDERED IV by Peggy Patrick

MILITARY ACTION/TECHNO
BLACK STAR BAY by T.C. Miller

HISTORICAL FICTION WESTERN
ACROSS the RED by Ken Farmer & Buck Stienke

TIMBER CREEK PRESS

CHAPTER 1

AFGHANISTAN
Seven Clicks North of Day Chopan
December 9, 2001

"Alabama five to Alabama one," the wounded radioman called frantically. "Alabama five to Alabama one."

"Alabama one…go ahead Alabama five," a voice crackled back on the field radio.

"Gunny…Gunny! I have HQ on the line!"

Heavy fire—small arms mixed with RPGs—came in on the position held by the remnants of a US Marine reinforced platoon. The Taliban had run their quarry to ground atop a barren rocky mountain and had them surrounded.

Mark belly crawled from his firing position to the radio and took hold of the handset. "Gunnery Sergeant Ingram here. Where's the *fucking* air support?"

"On target in twenty Gunnz…had to reroute…"

"Reroute my ass! Calling all operators…Broken Arrow! I say again…Broken Arrow!" Mark screamed over the roaring fire fight.

"This is Sparrow three…give me your coordinates," the voice of a F-16 fighter jet radioed back.

Mark handed the handset back to the operator, flashed him a thumbs up. "Bring 'em in, Thompson."

Ingram began crawling back to his firing position. A pair of AK47 rounds ripped through his pack—knocking him onto his left side. Another of the 123 grain bullets sliced through his shoulder, missing the bone, but leaving a searing ragged wound. *Son of a bitch!* He looked down at his torn blouse as he tried to move his arm. The wound itself burned like hell—just like the other four bullet holes he had acquired earlier that day. *Ain't no time to stop now…I can still crawl.*

He cradled Betsy in his arms and scooting himself across the rocky ground, he ducked his head as a burst of full auto fire kicked up gravel and rock chips off the trail and peppered his face. His Oakley wraparound sunglasses spared his eyes, allowing him to pick up the movement as the shooter stood from behind a nearby boulder and attempted to close the distance between them.

Mark lifted his nine pound M-14 with one hand around the pistol grip, swung the muzzle at the man's midsection and yanked the trigger. The grizzled Taliban was reaching for a spare magazine when the 7.62 bullet ripped through his spine.

Can't stay here…too God damned open. He scrambled to his feet and half sprinted, half hobbled to a depression he had chosen along the perimeter and slid into it as a half dozen enemy fired at him. An RPG narrowly missed and roared overhead before it detonated harmlessly on a boulder some forty yards on the far side of their perimeter.

Other Marines yelled out a warning, "On your right, Gunnz!"

Mark picked out a pair of running Taliban and fired his rifle twice in rapid succession, left handed—wincing at the pain from the recoil. Both men tumbled face first onto the rocky ground and lay still.

"Welcome to your seventy-two virgin camels, mutha fuckers. Allah Akbar my ass," he shouted at the enemy.

Several Muslim fighters screamed back their own replies to his insults, bringing a fleeting smile to his face. He checked his last two magazines strapped in Velcro pouches on his vest. *Only forty rounds? Fuck me runnin'.*

"Set your fire to single! Air support incoming…Conserve your ammo!" Mark yelled to his remaining platoon members.

"No shit? About fuckin' time," a badly wounded lance corporal called back as he changed magazines.

Seeing a dozen enemy charging forward on his left flank Mark called out to the remaining men on that side, "Grenades!"

In unison, both men stopped firing their M16s and launched a pair of fragmentation grenades into the advancing jihadis with their M203 launchers. Mark rose up long enough to lob a pair of phosphorous grenades into their decimated ranks for good measure—being ambidextrous had its advantages. The screams of the dying and burning men added to the audible den of chaos.

Two days of chasing the elusive Osama Bin Laden after the fall of Kandahar resulted in a head-on clash with a much larger force of the Taliban fighters seven clicks north of a mud hut village no one had ever heard of before. Surrounded and about to be overrun, the words of the Marine legend General Chesty Puller kept running through Mark's head, *"We are completely surrounded...We have the enemy where we want them. God help them bastards...We're comin' outta here."*

CHAING MAI, THAILAND
Crank's Lotus Blossom Hotel
March, 2014

Mark sat bolt upright in a cold sweat in the bedroom of Crank's home. Sweat covered his torso and he was panting heavily. Nothing but the sound of the wind blowing outside and the squeaking ceiling fan greeted him. Moonlight streamed in, broken by the dancing shadows of the window curtains on the floor and walls. *Jesus...same dream...every time. Thirteen years now...Never changes.*

BANGKOK, THAILAND
Club Perdomo

What a great night thought Joris Barnhardt. He was a middle-aged Dutch national who owned numerous high-tech companies around the globe. The valet held the front door open as he stepped out onto the sidewalk—he could still feel the cold air from the exclusive club on his back as the tropical heat of

4

the street washed over him. One of his security guards, a stocky man from Denmark, stepped out of the front of the limo and moved to open the back door for the wealthy foreign investor.

A volley of gun fire raked the dark blue Mercedes killing the guard instantly as a black Mazda cab pulled up and three members of the New People's Army jumped out and rushed toward Joris waving handguns and firing into the air.

Stunned by the assault, he stood with his hands up as the men ran towards him. The valet grabbed him by the arm and pulled him back towards the club, but a series of bullets cut down the brave young man.

The French driver, Rennie, a former cop from Lyon, stepped from the limo and fired four times at the attackers, killing one and wounding another. Rennie went down from a bullet to his bald head—falling to the street in a crumpled pile. His blank eyes stared up sightlessly at the smog-filled night sky.

A pair of Bangkok Metropolitan Police ran toward the fight, firing wildly. A woman standing between them and the lone assailant was shot through the chest and her small child took a bullet to the leg. The screaming crowd panicked and ran from the melee or cowered on the sidewalk, unsure what to do.

As the lone NPA gunman grabbed at Joris, his instinct to fight finally kicked in and he wrestled with the man for control of his pistol. The two fell to the sidewalk—rolled off the curb—and struggled as several policemen arrived and disarmed the oriental man.

The Mazda cab roared off—ramming one car and sideswiping another—and disappeared into the busy traffic.

At that same moment, a motorcycle passed Barnhardt's limo. The passenger threw a lit Molotov cocktail onto the roof, engulfing the luxury car in flames. Some of the fiery liquid splashed off onto Joris and set his coat ablaze. He ripped it off, tossing it back into the street.

In a matter of seconds the attack was over. He stood shaking in fear as the police arrested the assailant.

"Please go back in club until ambulance arrives, sir," one of the uniformed officers said in broken English.

"I…I…my men…" he mumbled.

"Please, sir…go wait inside."

Turning to reenter the exclusive club, he stumbled over the body of the dead valet. "Oh, my God…What just happened?"

CHAING MAI, THAILAND
Crank's Lotus Blossom Estate

There she goes. Everyday…when she goes…someone goes with her. Mark Ingram sat on the second story balcony thinking about a line by Richard Widmark in one of his favorite western films—*Garden of Evil*. The recent events at President Mobutto's estate in Kenya put him in a retrospective mood. Much like the way the Ping River in the distance flowed endlessly to its destination, the reality of how fleeting life really was haunted him with the deaths of his fellow operatives.

Wearing only a pair of gray running shorts, due to the oppressive heat, he sipped iced Thai tea—less the sweet cream—through a straw as was the local custom. His chromed aviator sunglasses—exact replicas of those issued his father while serving in Nam—cut the glare and allowed a clear view of the radiant colors streaking the sky and reflecting on the clouds.

"When is Crank getting back bro?" Rheinhart 'Rhino' Fabain, a huge muscular man standing 6' 4" and weighing 245 pounds—hence the call sign 'Rhino'—asked in a thick South African accent as he lay face down on a massage table.

"Not sure…said he was going to cruise around looking for a new choty goty after he dropped Malakhi at the airport."

"Great…lucky to see him by mornin' then…What's for chow?"

"Name your pleasure bro…I'll let Mongkol know."

"Chicken phad puk and…tom kha soup."

Mark stood up and moved into the cool interior of the old home. Built by a former CEO of a New Zealand logging company before World War II—the architecture reflected both Thai and Western influences. The large open rooms with tall ceilings, double and triple French doors allowed for effective cross ventilation. There were ceiling fans throughout. Crank had purchased the old estate for a virtual song, but the ensuing repairs and upgrades were another story.

The walls surrounding the estate had mostly fallen down and had only been four feet tall. He had them repaired, raised to eight feet and topped with a bed of cement into which broken shards of various colored glass were buried. Most of the exterior wooden doors had been replaced. The entire electrical wiring, light fixtures and most of the plumbing had been removed and upgraded. The tile roof was replaced with modern composite tile that closely resembled the old ones in appearance.

"Tell koffie-moffie to hold the damn ghost pepper kak!" Rhino called out. "I can't be standin' 'nother fokin' day on the toilet."

Mark could not help but smile at the final request. He and Rhino had shared numerous close security operations and both had suffered injuries that came with the territory. The 7.62 round that hit him in the ass had him whining like a little girl.

The sound of Crank's four stroke high-performance crotch rocket echoed into the house from the courtyard announcing his return. A few moments later, the former Navy SEAL entered the kitchen—his long blonde hair pulled back in a pony tail under his backward baseball cap—with not one, but two beautiful Thai women. "Zorro, like you to meet Kulap and Waan."

The girls gave Mark a sly, sweet smile and said in unison, "Han loh bay bee."

"Your choice, grandpa," Crank said with his trademark grin. Standing 6' 2", he packed 225 pounds of muscle-on-muscle onto his knuckle-dragging frame. Before the SEALs he had been a All-American linebacker at UCLA, but gave it up to follow his dream of becoming a world class surfer.

"Sa wat dii khrap," Mark replied *hello* to the girls in perfect Thai. "Not feeling it, Crank. But thanks for the offer…Sure are shiny young things."

Mark turned to Mongkol and gave him Rhino's dinner request, then bowed his head slightly with hands clasped in prayer form to the women before heading to his room. "Sa wat dii tawn yen."

It was nearly midnight when Mark joined the entourage at the swimming pool. The clear sky sparkled with an array of stars as the estate sat miles from the city. Crank and all six of the female guests were playing a game of water volleyball. Rhino lay on a lounge chair—protected from the incessant mosquitos by a white daphenious canopy—cheering them on.

"Is that all ya got, ya wave runner skaapie? The girls are kickin' your donkey arse," Rheinhart called out, ribbing his buddy.

"Savin' the best for later."

Mark took a chair beside Rhino. "How's the healing comin' along?"

"Good." Rhino massaged his left thigh just below the wound as he spoke,

"Ahhh…life in paradise."

"Zorro! Come on in…we need you to even the teams," Crank yelled over the blaring rock and roll music coming from the state-of-the-art Boise sound system pounding the pool area in surround sound—with Jimi Hendrix's *Are You Experienced.*

He waved to the participants, but shook his head. Turning to Rhino, he said, "I just got off secure comm with Hal…Gonna be leaving for Honduras soon. When you're a hundred percent let me know…I'll keep an opening for you…"

"I'm thinkin' a couple of months 'til I'm back in action. Can't barely walk worth a shat yet."

"You stay here a couple of months, you may never go back to work," Mark said watching the nubile naked young women cavort in the pool.

"Ja...I was thinking the same bro. Maybe open up a Starbuck's franchise...make a killing on the expats flowin' in here...or a disco."

"What the hell would you know about running a club?"

"What's there to know...loud music, hot chicks, alcohol...air conditioning. Have to have air con...did I say hot chicks?"

One of the women walked up, water dripping off her perky breasts. "You ready go boom boom, Mister Rhino?"

HAL McCAMBELL'S OFFICE
Dallas, Texas

Hal McCambell, a Scottish-American businessman—owner of multiple companies around the globe—sat chewing an unlit Nicaraguan cigar. The inactive US Marine and former Secret Service agent was still an imposing figure despite being in his seventies. The office was decorated with a number of decidedly Texas-influenced bronze statues, paintings and furniture. On a long dark walnut credenza sat numerous photos of himself with sports heroes, politicians and his prized Longhorn cattle. Above the display, the wall was covered with photos of himself with family and close friends—his favorite being one with the Duke.

At the far end there were photos of he and Mark—the team that went into the war-torn Nigeria to extract Belgium aid workers, he and Zorro—wearing a well-worn USMC shooting jacket and holding his prized National Match grade M14, lovingly named Betsy—with a first place trophy at a international long-range shooting event. Another showed both of them on a deep-sea fishing trip off the coast of Panama with his five grandchildren—yeah, they had a history.

He considered the conversation he had just finished with Mark then called to his secretary—who was also his wife of fifty-nine years. "Maggie! Get me John Batt on the phone."

Moments later the intercom on his land-line lit up. "Mr. Batt is on line two."

"John, I have a man lined up to take care of security for you and your people in Honduras. Name is Steve Wilson," Hal lied giving the client only the name Mark would be using as he worked in Honduras.

"You come highly recommended McCambell so I'll assume Mister Wilson is well qualified…"

"The best. I call on him when governments need to fall or countries need invading. He cleans up well for social functions and speaks fluent Spanish," Hal replied grinding on his cigar. *Hate these prissy corporate panseys…always asking if my judgment is sound.*

"I will be arriving at Toncontin International Airport in Tegucigalpa in three months…Will send the itinerary by fax and have two engineers with me…We will need twenty-four hour protection…"

"Send the itinerary. Wilson and his team will meet you at the airport. I have to go." Hal hung up, his Scottish blood starting to simmer. *Dumbass! Like I don't know which country*

TGU airport is in? And why the hell would you be paying the big bucks if I wasn't providing twenty-four-seven.

He used the intercom and called Maggie, "Batt is sending a fax with his *itinerary*," he said mockingly. "Send it by secure line to Zorro as soon as it arrives."

"Calm down honey...Batt Engineering Resorces is a new client. He'll learn to deal with your..."

"Damn well better be a fast learner...too old to be wet nursing..."

CRANK'S ESTATE

A light drizzle fell covering the estate grounds in a gray fog as Mark finished his morning routine. Moisture flowed down the cold stone walls, dribbled off the roof line and splattered into the muddy pools below. *Reminds me of the rain in the forest around Mount Elgon.*

He performed his normal kata routine and finished with a light Zen meditation. The life he led required constant readiness. The twelve foot balcony outside his room provided ample space for his workout on the original teak deck—refinished during restoration and now smooth—polished a dark red with black grains accenting the wood.

He moved into the spacious bedroom and onto the comfort room where he started the cold water running in the open-walled, tile floored shower. He laid his green sweat-soaked shorts and tank top on a pile of dirty clothing in a cheap blue plastic hamper and stepped under the refreshing flow falling from a ten inch round brass shower head directly above him. The temperature and humidity in Thailand rarely called for a hot shower.

His satellite cell phone rang in the other room just as he lathered his hair. *Have to call you back, whoever you are.*

After drying off and shaving, he checked the caller ID. *Hal, ol' buddy...call you as soon as I have some breakfast.*

He entered the huge kitchen—built to provide service for the lavish dinner parties and other events the original owner held frequently—to find Mongkol, a Thai in his mid-fifties. The quiet man with long white hair and beard was watching the news while waiting for everyone to rise.

"Ham and eggs today, boss man?" Mongkol referred to Mark by the name he heard his employer, Crank, call him.

"Sounds good. Can you whip up some crepes as well...with that delicious longan preserves on top?"

"No problem. Tea or coffee today?"

"Costa Rican, black...Anybody else up and moving?" *Costa Rica...wonder how Chikako's settling in now?*

"Not yet...Mister Crank and Mister Fabian never up before noon. You know that," the cook said with a chuckle as he began rattling pots and pans to prepare Mark's meal.

The morning news played on Thailand Color Television Channel 3, the country's first commercial channel. Mark sat down as Mongkol placed his coffee cup on the table. *Great way to refresh my Thai.* A newscaster finished up the sports comments and was replaced by another with the lead story of the day.

"Last night outside the Club Perdomo assailants attempted to kidnap foreign businessman, Joris Barnhardt, owner and CEO of Barnhardt LLC. The attempt was foiled by the fast actions of the Bangkok Metropolitan police and Mister Barnhardt's two personal bodyguards. Unfortunately, both security men were killed in the exchange of gunfire that rocked the street outside the club..."

"Mongkol...could you turn that up please?"

"Yes, sir, mister boss man."

The female newscaster continued, "This is the latest example of how dangerous it is for foreigners to live and do business in Thailand. Chief Charoen Nantakam of the Bangkok Metropolitan Police made a statement this morning informing the press that he was making this sort of crime a top priority. He went on to say that his department would look in every corner for the men who attempted the kidnapping last night..."

"Thanks...Go ahead and turn it back down," Mark said as the cook set his breakfast in front of him. "Foreigner kidnappings still a problem here?"

"Last year fifty...maybe more...businessmen and women were taken. Foreingers...no telling how many Thai. Mostly by the NPA. Some never see again even though ransoms were paid in full."

Mark ate leisurely then headed to his room, intent on calling Hal back for the latest update on his contract in Honduras.

DARK SECRET

JORIS BARNHARDT RESIDENCE
Bangkok, Thailand

Located in the Khlong Toei district, the three-story luxury home with full basement—including parking garage and lift to the upper floors—was considered one of the finest residences in all of Bangkok. Situated on two acres of prime real estate, the home had eight bedrooms and full baths, a large family media room, private pool, two reception rooms and was fully air conditioned. The final touch was a immaculately landscaped rooftop garden that allowed a beautiful view of the city.

An additional house was built shortly after he purchased the property. The four bedroom with four baths were intended to house his personal security force and chauffeur. There was a full kitchen, but the men took meals in or from the main house for the most part.

Joris liked to entertain—wealthy foreigners, Thai nationals, political dignitaries and Asian entertainers—and kept a full staff of servants to do so. Gardeners, cooks, house maids and boys completed the staff totaling fifteen in all. A simple event could cost 939,825 bhat—roughly thirty thousand dollars.

His wife, Dalisay, was a classic example of a trophy wife. Younger by twenty years, attractive, seemingly very well cultured and educated. There were many rumors concerning how they met. The one that Joris preferred and alluded to when asked presented her as a former Miss Philippines in the Miss World competition. Their nine year old son, Rutger, spent most of his time in Holland with Joris' parents since he started school at age six. His absence was a point of conflict for the couple.

"I will handle it!" Joris said emphatically.

"Like you did last night?" Dalisay replied.

"Look, I was not harmed...I will hire some new security. Two for each of us...as many as necessary. Chief Nantakam agreed to keep police stationed around our home twenty-four hours a day..."

"Isn't that what he did for that poor woman from Sweden? Two days after her husband's attempted kidnapping she was abducted..."

"I won't let that happen!"

"They never found her body."

"Shut *up!*" Joris yelled. The look in his eyes gave his wife pause. "There will be new...*better* security in place soon. Until then you are not to leave the house...Is that clear?"

The two stood across the stainless steel chopping counter in the kitchen, glaring at one another. The kitchen staff waited in the pantry nervously. They had never heard the Barnhardt's argue so vehemently.

CRANK'S ESTATE

Mark walked into the spacious, though sparsely furnished, office and checked the FAX machine. A communication from McCambell Import Export, LLC lay in the tray addressed to him. He picked it up and moved to the balcony off his room before reading it. He unscrewed the plastic cap from a chilled container of mango-kiwi juice, slid a straw into the small opening and took a long slow swallow. *Ummm...have to try squeezing some lime into one of these next time.*

Laying the cover sheet down on a bamboo table he read the message…

Honduras contract. Ninety days out. Will contact ten days before expected arrival Tegucigalpa. Operatives from class of 2014 to be assigned. Train them. Hal.

Mark crumpled the paper and tossed it onto the table. *Well, crap! Three months? Not going to spend three months sitting around Crank's lotus hotel.*

***

CHAPTER TWO

CRANK'S ESTATE

Crank and Rhino sat on the verandah eating—surrounded by chattering and giggling female house guests—when Mark walked out of the house dressed in off-white cotton slacks, light blue shirt with a coat draped over his left arm that matched his pants. In his right hand he carried a Haliburton case that held his Colt Gold Cup and Smith and Wesson 5906—as well as six loaded magazines for each. He had his hair tied back in a low pony tail with a length of leather thong.

"Whoa! All duded up there boss man...Where you headed?" Crank asked.

"Bangkok. Taking the number two overnighter...Could you spare Mongkol to drive me into town?"

"No problem. What's up in Big Mango?"

"Checking on some work. Honduras is on hold for ninety days. I'll go nuts sitting around here watchin' and listening to you two sowing your seed…Be back in a couple of days," Mark replied as he walked back into the house.

"Business…business…bidness…Zorro never lets up on the pedal," Crank said as Kulap—sitting in his lap with one arm around his neck—fed him pieces of fresh fruit.

"Give him a break. Somethin's on his mind ever since I got 'ere. Train ride might do him good."

"As for what's on his mind?…Chikako's her name."

"The Yakuza assassin? *Man*…based on your pass down… can't wait to meet that little presser."

"Never happen…Hal scrubbed her. New name, papers…the works. She's friggin' history…More gone now than the witness protection program back in the states…Only way he's ever gonna see her again is if she wants to find him."

CHAING MAI, THAILAND

Mark had Mongkol take him to a long-established well respected tailor shop, the Viengping Collection, on Sridonchi Road across from the Chaing Mai Plaza hotel. He had stayed at the Plaza several times before Crank bought his home. The owners and staff at the shop knew him by name.

"Thanks. I'll catch a cab from here to the train station." He offered 2500 bhat as a tip, but the normally stoic Thai refused and drove off with a smile and a wave, leaving Mark standing on the busy sun-drenched sidewalk.

Inside the shop, Mark was met warmly by the front desk greater, "Mister Mark! Nice to see you again. Long time you no come visit. How may I assist you? Would you like some tea?"

"Iced tea would be great. I need a suit, couple pairs of slacks and shirts…and I must catch the 1800 Nakhonphink today. Can you get me done?"

The slender immaculate dressed elderly man looked at his watch and replied, "Oh most definitely, Mister Mark. For you, we get this done…Right this way. Let us select the fabric first."

Four hours later Mark stepped into a taxi, with the requested attire in a hang-up travel bag. The cab ride to the Chaing Mai Railway center allowed him an hour to kill before the Express Nakhonphink Number 2—rated the best train travel in Thailand—departed for Bangkok. The overnight journey and taxi ride would put him into the US Embassy by 1000 hours.

He stepped into a private sleeper compartment after he handed the porter a tip and closed the door behind him. *Beats the hell out of air travel here…and only forty bucks. Finally get a good night's sleep. Rhino and Crank party way too hardy for my tastes. Gettin' too old for that shit.*

The hours before dark provided some great views of the Thai countryside as the train rolled south. From inside his compartment the pastoral landscape looked like a description in a Hemingway novel. Men were tilling their rice paddies with water buffalo, others driving buffalo-powered two-wheel carts laden with bags of produce or rice and women thrashing freshly-harvested rice beside the fields or stilt homes.

As night fell, he moved to the dining car and ate a light meal of seafood and vegetable dishes from the buffet along with a mix of Thai nationals and foreign vacationers. The other travelers did not notice him other than he was alone and carried himself with an air of confidence.

He returned to his compartment to find the bed folded out, sheet and light blanket turned down and a small mint chocolate on the pillow. After securing the almost useless lock, he attached the suppressor to his S&W 5906 and laid it by the pillow. *Anyone pops in, I'd rather not let the porter or other passengers know I offed him.*

He undressed, hung his slacks and shirt in the tiny closet, and washed his face—careful not to allow any water to enter his eyes or mouth to avoid any Thai revenge—and lay down on the thin mattress. He was out like a light as the gentle rocking of the train and light clacking of the wheels lulled him to sleep.

KHLONG TOEI SLUM
Bangkok

Located on the banks of the Chao Phraya River, the Kholng Toei had a history dating back to the ninth century as port to the cities upstream. It was also known as a district of criminal elements—even more so now. The numerous improvements to the district in the last few decades did little to change the slums along the river.

Inkong, a muscular male—tall by Thai standards with a ragged scar running from his hairline across his blue-gray sightless left eye down to his chin—sat smoking a brass hooka with three of his associates. The pungent aroma of opium laced hashish filled the room and wafted out the open doorway, off the third floor balcony to the river market below. No one would notice or care, as the majority of those living in the slum smoked as well.

"Our attempt last night was a disaster." He drew in another long pull on the pipe and coughed lightly as he exhaled.

"We lost three men... Disaster seems..."

Inkong held up one finger and silenced the member of his gang. "I sent word to the south...there are nine brothers coming. They arrive soon. Until then...we wait. Study our quarry and make new plans...We *shall not* fail again."

HUA LAMPHONG STATION
Bangkok

Most Thai referred to the Hau Lamphong as the Bangkok Railway Station rather than the proper name. Located in the center of the city in the Pathum Wan District, it was always a bustling center of travel. Locals and foreigners moved like a brightly colored army of ants through the station day and night. Though well manned by the Metropolitan Police, crime was rampant.

Pickpockets and street hookers mingled with the travelers looking for an easy target. Vendors of Thai street food as well as those who sold various local trinkets lined the fringes of the walkways attempting to hawk their goods. Cab and motorcycle tuk tuk drivers jostled for position and a paying fare.

Mark walked down the extended folding stairs between train cars onto the dirty platform and briefly looked around to gain his bearings before joining the mass of humanity flowing around him. He felt the light touch of an accomplished thief on one, then the other of his rear pants pockets. *Hope you enjoyed the feel asshole. Never carry anything where you bastards could pinch it.*

Outside the terminal building he moved to the waiting line of cabs and chose one that had the windows up—indicating it had air conditioning. *Don't want to sweat like a stuck pig on the way to the embassy.*

The cab driver wove through the tightly packed throng of vehicles as Mark took out his satellite phone and dialed. The embassy operator answered. "Steve McCallister here. Could you connect me with Deputy Chief of Mission…Patrick Murry."

The woman manning the call desk spoke perfect English with a light influence of her native language, "I will connect you with his office, Mister McCallister."

"Deputy Chief of Mission Patrick Murry's office. How may I assist you?"

"Steve McCallister here, Darlin'. I'm en route to the embassy now and need Patrick to facilitate my entry as I am carrying some gardening tools."

"Gardening tools?"

"He'll understand…Here's my number, 66-555-012-7787. Have him call me back. Thank you."

He caught a glance in the rear view mirror of the driver—missing most of his left ear—studying him. *Probably sounded a little strange to him. Gardening tools?* "When we get to the embassy I may need you to keep the meter running."

"No problem. You likie giulfriend while you Bangkok? I know many young giuls. Very nice…boom boom long time…"

"No thanks…only here for the day."

BARNHARDT RESIDENCE
Bangkok, Thailand

Joris was about to enter the lift as it was commonly called in Thailand, when Dalisay called out from the kitchen, "I want to go to the MKB mall and shop for the balikbian boxes I am sending to my family this week."

The Dutchman's head tilted forward and he closed his eyes for a moment before moving to discuss the activity face to face. He was wearing his finest lightweight custom-tailored suit as he was to meet the Minister of Finance that day for lunch at the Royal Bangkok Sports Club—the most exclusive private facility in the country. *Let's get this over with…one more time.*

He entered the kitchen to find his wife sitting at the small breakfast table wearing a purple robe with a map of the Philippines on the back in gold thread. "We went over this last night dear…Until I locate qualified security personnel, you must remain here. The Metropolitan Police outside will prevent any attempt to harm you…"

"I promised to send it this week. If you do not have the personnel you want by…say, day after tomorrow?…I'll just have the police escort me to the MKB." She never looked over at Joris but continued to eat her poached eggs and toast gazing out the window at the city skyline.

"*Fine*. I'll inform Chief Nantakam to have four plainclothes officers here day after tomorrow. I hope you will be happy knowing the political expense it will cost me."

"Consider hiring someone with some social skills this time. Those last two were complete idiots."

Joris spun on his heel and departed before the conversation wound down to where he was certain it was headed.

***

CHAPTER THREE

SHENYANG, CHINA
Dadong District

Dadong—the largest industrial district—sat in the center of Shenyang. With a population of 640,000 people, it was the hub of shipping and commerce—legal and not so legal. Hundreds of manufacturing plants and thousands of small shops offered employment—though barely enough income to provide the basic necessities for the workers.

Zhi Peng Wu, first cousin to the recently deceased Chang Wu—next in line for Dragon Master of the Big Circle Triad—sat listening to the leaders of the separate gang cells. The huge warehouse used for the meeting was his and security was tight. Since the death of Chang, the organization had been thrown into chaos. Rivals jockeyed for position in a sometimes deadly game of who's the boss.

"I say it was the Wah Ching!" one man yelled.

"They are not strong enough to do what happened in Hong…" another cried.

"I agree…it was the Wah Ching. They are ever trying to encroach on our territory."

"It was the Yakuza! Chang was a fool to employ them…"

Zhi, raised one hand slightly in the heavily smoke filled room and the men fell silent. Behind him four of his largest Triad soldiers, chosen for their intimidating 6' 4" stature, stood silently with arms crossed, watching for any who might take the opportunity to harm him.

He looked around the room slowly, allowing the silence to settle in. "My cousin's decision was wise. If anyone is apprehended in Kenya smuggling ivory…let the burden fall on the Yakuza." He took a drag on a slender American cigarette from a long ivory holder. He exhaled slowly, letting the meaning of his words sink in on the agitated men.

"The Yakuza were killed in Kenya shortly before Wu…I think it is the CIA," an elder leader said.

"They would not endanger their precious flow of our money," Wu added with a knowing smile.

A nervous murmur of laughter and whispers moved around the room as everyone considered Zhi's wisdom concerning the CIA.

"One of the Yakuza is unaccounted for…a woman named Chikako," a wizened old man with flowing white beard said softly. "She may be the key to who did this."

Zhi turned to one of his soldiers. "Find me this Chikako." He looked at the general assembly. "Spread the word to our cells...Someone will see her if she is still alive."

"Our brothers in Hong Kong said they saw four people lifted off the roof in a helicopter."

"Find them as well."

US EMBASSY BANGKOK
120/22 Wireless Road

Mark had been waiting for ninety minutes when his satellite phone finally rang. "Hello."

"Steve you old rebel dog! How are you?"

"Good. I'm outside on Wireless Road in a cab...I have some tools with me and need assistance getting in the embassy."

"Of course. I'll be at the gate in ten minutes. Oh...you are talking...small tools...right?"

"Yeah. Large briefcase."

"Right...I'll get you in the gate but we will still have to let the Marines take a look once inside."

"Semper Fi."

True to his word Murry—a mid-fifties black American man with flecks of gray in his hair—had Mark in the gate and into a small isolated room inside the embassy without incident. Two Marines wearing sidearms walked them in and stood on either side of the door at parade rest as Mark and Patrick caught up on old times.

"When's the last time you were in Bogota?" the Deputy Chief asked.

"Been a while. Not very popular there of late…Took the shine off too many Path boys…Yourself?"

"Left in '09. Haven't been back…You ever talk with Captain Medina's wife? What was her name?"

"Marta Maria. Lost track of her after she and her family got out of Colombia."

"Dirty business there…What brings you to Bangkok?"

"Vacation, actually, but I saw some news last night that smelled like money."

When the Sergeant of the Guard entered the room the two Marines snapped to attention.

"What do we have here Deputy Murry?" The forty year old master sergeant asked gruffly as he moved to the table where Mark's travel bags and the Haliburton case lay. A chest covered with medals spoke volumes about the man's service in the Corps.

"Master Sergeant Lewis, meet Steve McCallister. He has the trust of President G. W. Bush…possesses a get-out-of-jail card to prove it. My trust as well…He is armed and has followed all protocol entering the embassy. I'm requesting you take possession of these items until he leaves."

"Open it," the barrel-chested sergeant ordered.

Mark dialed in the numerical code and stepped back.

"Damn…You mind?" Lewis asked as he looked at the two weapons.

"Not at all, Master Sergeant."

He picked up the Gold Cup like it was the Holy Grail, dropped the loaded mag and checked the chamber—ejecting the Glaser round—before easing the slide down gently. "Always wanted one of these...How much did it set you back?"

"Purchase price and the work done at Gunsite...four thousand."

The old Marine balanced the weapon in his huge hand then brought it up and sighted it at a framed photo of Obama on the far wall. Satisfied, he placed the pistol back in the padded case and closed the lid. "Thanks."

"Proud to have a fellow Marine appreciate it."

"You served?"

"Couple of tours in the *sand*...My card." Mark extended a business card with his fictious name and cell number. "I may be here for a couple of months. Be glad to let you pop some caps through her if you have the time." *Never know when a old devil dog might come in handy.*

"I definitely would...This case and your bag will be in my armory 'til you leave." He picked up the case and clothing bag and left the room, followed by the two guards.

Murry sat down behind his modest desk as Mark seated himself in the only other chair in the sparsely furnished office.

"So...fill me in. What brings you to me?"

"A news clip yesterday about the attempted kidnapping of a foreign businessman here in Bangkok. Said his security guys were taken out of the game...Got a couple of months to burn 'til my next assignment…Can you hook me up with this Joris Barnhardt? Like to offer my services."

"Pretty tame stuff for you…isn't it?"

"Maybe…But work is work. If I sit around for a couple of months…I get rusty. Plus, the money will be good considering Barnhardt has seen the elephant…up close and personal." He grinned.

Murry studied the silver-haired Texan for a moment, punched his intercom. "Sukhon."

"Yes, sir?" the young pleasantly attractive woman asked as she entered.

"Call our friend at the Ministry of Commerce, Mister Boonliang, put him through when you have him on the line."

"Yes, sir." As Sukhon started to leave she turned to Mark and flashed a warm inviting smile. "Would you care for something to drink while you wait?"

"Thai tea, no cream, if you have it. If not, water's fine."

"And you, sir?" she asked while still looking at Mark.

"Thai tea with cream for me, thank you."

After she left the room Patrick stood up and moved to the single window in his office and gazed out at the city as he nervously played with his keys. "I ran a report on you after you called. Seems you have not been active with the agency in some time but you are still in the system…What have you been up to?"

"Private contracts."

"If I'm going to sponsor you...so to speak, with Mister Barnhardt...I'd like to know what sort of *private* contracts we're talking about."

Mark moved next to Murry. "You keep up with the news in Kenya lately?"

"Civil war...military coup...nearly deposed President Mobutto...You were in Kenya?"

"Not officially."

"Who's side were you on?"

"Some...uh, associates and I were with President Mobutto at his estate near Mount Kenya...Hell of a rodeo...We won."

"Mister Murry, Mister Boonliang on line one."

"Hope you know what you're getting into here. The NPA are some really nasty fellows."

"Which brings up the second bit of assistance I need from you...get-out-of-jail-free cards...and carry permits."

HUA LAMPHONG STATION
Bangkok

Inkong stood across the street from the railway station in the shade of a large pradoo tree. The midday heat and humidity only increased the stench of the garbage blowing about as vehicles passed. The full glare of the sun reflected off the pavement and passing windows of the slow moving traffic—creating an oven-like effect.

He lit a Krongthip—a locally manufactured cigarette—with a cheap imitation Bic lighter. He had to strike the device several times before it worked and after lighting his smoke, he tossed it to the curb.

Spotting the men and women he waited for, he pulled a red bandana from his pants pocket and shook it twice as if to unfold it before wiping his brow. One of the six NPA members recognized the signal, motioned to the others and led them across the busy street.

"Officer Wattana sends his regards," the oldest male said with some hesitation as he handed him an envelope.

Inkong's reputation as a single minded party member preceded him—as well as his explosive temper. "We take these tuk tuks. Get in. We go now." Inkong ordered. As he entered a small motorcycle-driven taxi he opened the communication from his superior in the NPA.

The New People's Army is depending on you to achieve you appointed task. Your success will make it possible for me to promote you and allow you a thirty day pass to visit loved ones. Do not repeat the previous results.

He folded the paper and placed it inside his shirt pocket as he pulled out a sweat-soaked package of cheap Thai cigarettes. He indicated to one of the new arrivals he needed a light before raising his hand and motioning forward.

THAILAND MINISTRY OF COMMERCE
44/100 Nonthaburi 1 Road

"Hello, Mister Barnhardt's office. How may I help you?"

"This is Booliang at the Ministry of Commerce. I have some interesting news for Joris concerning possible security measures he may be seeking."

"One moment please," Joris Barnhardt's personal secretary replied.

Several minutes passed before Joris came on the line. "Mongkut, how you are today?"

"Very well, thank you. A trusted member of the US Embassy called today with some information I think…in light the incident…would be of interest to you."

"What would it be? The Dutch Marines have landed?" Joris said with a laugh.

"Not exactly. There seems to be a highly trained risk management specialist in Bangkok today and he has requested a meeting with you."

"Really? How fortuitous. I *am* in the market for just such services…And you said he is well recommended?"

"According to my source he is…how you say, over qualified, but seeking employment presently. Do you care to meet with him?"

"I do. How may this be arranged?"

"His name is Steve McCallister and you may reach him directly at the Sukhothai Bangkok any time after 1500 today."

"I appreciate your efforts to assist me. I will include you in the list of Christmas bonuses this year. Good day."

DARK SECRET

SUKHOTHAI BANGKOK HOTEL
31/3 South Sathorn Road

It was a lushly gardened oasis in the bustling heart of Bangkok—one of the cities many five star hotels. The hotel was a frequent stop for wealthy international business and leisure travelers.

Mark chose a deluxe resident suite overlooking the olympic pool—away from the busy traffic side of the hotel.

"Will you be requiring a guide while you are in Bangkok, Mister McCallister?" the front desk attendant asked with a knowing smile. *Guide* was a common term for a high-end prostitute. All the hotels in the city had a select list of women they allowed to ply their trade with their guests.

"No, I've been here before."

"Ah…in that case, welcome back. Please call if there is anything you need."

The ninety-eight square meter suite was like a private residential apartment. After tipping the departing bellman, Mark pulled his eavesdropping detector from his inner coat pocket and began a thorough scan of the suite. Satisfied the rooms were safe, he removed his coat—revealing his Gold Cup nestled in it's saddle tan Bianchi shoulder holster—and hung it in the walk-in closet next to his travel bag. He removed his shoes and walked across the cool polished teakwood floor to the wet bar and retrieved a cold Singha beer.

Ahhh…that really hits the spot. Ain't a Shiner Bock…but it'll do. The entire suite was appointed with rich, dark teakwood giving the space a sense of warmth. Sounds from outside were virtually nonexistent. He moved to the sliding-glass door and stepped out onto the rich red tiles with gold scroll of the balcony. Six stories below, the individual dark red cabana canopies and lounging chairs surrounding the crystal clear swimming pool—enclosed by a twelve foot wall covered in lush green vines—looked inviting except for the intense midday heat. *Later. Some laps would be nice.*

Next to the pool in a separate fenced enclosure a single tennis court with a powder blue surface offered the opportunity to play a few sets under the lights.

The land line rang and brought him back inside—he allowed it to ring. After a few moments the flashing light told him there was a message. *Easy way to get an unlisted number. Call 'em back if it means money.*

Listening to the recording Mark made a mental note of the number. He dialed it five minutes later.

"Joris Barnhardt's office. May I help you?"

"Steve McCallister…I just missed your call."

"Yes. One moment please."

A brief moment passed before the wealthy Dutchman came on the line. "Good afternoon Mister McCallister. I understand you wished to speak to me concerning security matters."

"Straight to it Mister Barnhardt. I saw the news yesterday. I'm in town and think I can be of service."

"FAX you resume over and I'll take a look…"

Mark could not help but laugh. "Good one, sir. I don't have a resume as such. Tell you what…call Patrick Murry at the

American Embassy…If you're interested in meeting, call me back." Mark hung up before Joris could reply. *Best I set the ground rules now. He may pay the bills…but I call the shots.*

ZAMBOANGA del SOL
Philippines

Isagani and his band of thirty-nine Moro National Liberation Front soldiers had taken refuge in the dense mountainous jungle to the north of Zamboanga City after the attack on the city water treatment plant on Pasonanca Road. The terrain worked perfectly for the experienced jungle fighters.

His ancestors had fought the infidel invaders since the first arrival of the Spanish in the mid-fifteenth century. He was trained from birth to be a warrior for his god, Allah.

After disabling the water supply to half the city he commandeered a Catholic school bus at the Saint Francis orphanage two miles south. Five of his unit took a priest and two nuns as well as a dozen children hostage. The precision with which his gang struck and carried out their assigned tasks made it easy for them to take the Pasonanca highway north before the Philippines military could react and blockade the route.

"Put the hostages in the cave. Four of you guard them. Ramil, post sentries eight hundred meters back down our trail," Isagani ordered with authority that belied his youth.

"Yes, Isagani," Ramil replied.

The twenty-two year old leader's father had been the commander at the infamous Basilan incident in 2007. Fourteen

Philippine Marines had been captured while searching for the Italian priest, Giancarlo Bossi. Eleven had been beheaded. Months later Bossi was released even though the ransom was never paid. It was Isaganis' first jihad and he had proved himself with the killing of three Marines during a firefight and the beheading of two others.

His orders were to escape and evade, eventually making his way back to the island of Jolo. But he had far grander plans. Intending to be a war chief before he reached twenty-five, he would wait until the search ended then take his band north to Zamboanga del Norte. No one had struck that far afield since they battled the Japanese during World War II. Such a raid would insure his ascent.

The priest called out, "The children are thirsty. Please may we have some water."

His daydream faded at the sound of the old man's voice. Looking into the cave he motioned for the priest to join him. When the frail man stood beside him, Isagani knocked him to his knees, drew his bolo knife and with one swift blow, removed his head. He picked it up and swung it around for his men to see as they chanted, "Allah Akbar."

The nuns began to cry hysterically as did the children witnessing the brutality of their priest's death.

Motioning to the soldiers he said, "Take the old infidel wok woks to the back of the cave. As it is written in the Qu'ran…enjoy them as your slaves."

As the nuns were lead away crying he called over a older soldier—a strong wiry man with only one hand—who had served with his father. "Jaco, take the canteens. Bring water. Let them drink. No fires."

"Yes, Isagani."

"And choose the two weakest men. Send them back to the bus. Have them drive it on north and hide it before they start home." *If they are caught I will have only lost the weak rather than any good men.*

JORIS BARNHARDT RESIDENCE
Bangkok, Thailand

Dalisay hung up the phone with tears in her eyes. Lying on the king size bed beside her was a framed photo of Rutger and her family at the beaches of Bohol. The last words of her son repeated themselves in her mind. *I miss you mommy. When can I come home?*

Her cell rang, the ring tone told her it was Joris.

"Hello."

"I will be late tonight. I am meeting with a risk management specialist after work."

"Really? You do not have time during business hours to discuss investments?"

"Not that sort of risk, Dalisay…the man's in the security business."

She could not help but show her delight at the news. "Is he…I don't know…qualified?"

"According to Patrick Murry he is…You remember him? He was at the New Year's party last year?"

"Vaguely. If it's who I think he is…he was very nice and so was his wife…Please make sure he has better social skills…"

"Our safety is the main concern…I'll call you on the way home. Love you."

SUKHOTHAI BANGKOK HOTEL
31/3 South Sathorn Road

Mark waited in the dimly lit lounge. The view through the ceiling-to-floor glass allowed a perfect view of the pool—the water reflecting the surrounding lights in shimmering waves as swimmers played. It was near dark and the oppressive heat was beginning to dissipate allowing for a refreshing dip after a long day of business or sightseeing. He had positioned himself with a view of the entrance from the lobby as well as the service door behind the bar.

"Would you care for a beverage?" asked the waitress, dressed in black slacks and a white blouse that covered her discreetly—but did little to hide her alluring figure.

"Bottled water, no ice and a couple of slices of lime."

"Anything to eat?"

"I'm meeting someone…Maybe later."

The young woman laid a white napkin on the table and placed a small red card with the number twenty-four on it in the brass holder centered on the table.

As she walked away Mark could not help but admire her. *Some things never change…The Travels of Marco Polo—actually written by a Frenchman, Rustichello da Pisa, from tales told to him by Marco while they were imprisoned together in Genova—said the women of Siam were the most beautiful and pleasurable he discovered in all his worldly travels.*

Barnhardt entered the lounge, accompanied by a pair of off-duty police officers in plain clothes. He searched the lounge, seeing and recognizing him—from the description he had been given on the phone—as he stood and raised his hand.

Mark remained standing to greet the prospective client and offered his hand as the Dutchman approached. "Steve McCallister."

"Joris Barnhardt...forgive me but I expected someone...no disrespect...someone bigger."

"I get that a lot...Have a seat."

The waitress returned with the water and limes.

"Top shelf single malt...neat," Joris ordered without a look.

"We have an old saying back in Texas...it ain't the size of the dog in the fight...it's the size of the fight in the dog."

"Very interesting Mister McCallister. You come highly recommended by Mister Murry...How do you two know one another?"

"We worked some...*events* together in South America a few years ago."

"I prefer to employ those I can due a thorough background check on. All I have on you is Murry's recommendation."

"Did your previous security detail have good resumes?"

"Exemplary. Both men had years of experience in Europe."

"How'd that work out for you?"

Barnhardt stared at the man sitting across the table from him. *This man has some damn big balls. Time to straighten him out.* Before he could speak, the waitress returned with his cocktail.

After she departed, Mark laid out his offer. "Here's the deal…I bring in *my* team. We live on the grounds…all expenses paid. You and your wife will do as we say…when we say." He squeezed a lime into the glass and poured water into it as he spoke. He took a drink before going on, "The only time either of you are not in our line of vision is in your private quarters. Twenty-four seven protection…one hundred thousand USD a month."

"You seem very sure of yourself…"

"I've never lost a client. You hire me and I will insure nothing happens to you…or your wife. You a member of any shooting club here in Bangkok?"

"Yes, I am. I shoot skeet frequently at the range not far from Wat Pho…Why do you ask?"

"The Territorial Defense Department range. I know it. Let's send a few downrange tomorrow. Oh…and I've taken the liberty to acquire some papers I'll need once you hire me." Mark pulled copies of the permit to carry and get-out-of-jail documents Murry had given him earlier.

Joris briefly scanned them. "You would not mind if I kept these overnight?"

"I made those copies in the office center here at the hotel for you. Thought you might be interested in…confirming them."

DARK SECRET

The smile on the man's face was genuine, but Barnhardt found it irritating, nonetheless.

***

CHAPTER FOUR

TERRITORIAL DEFENSE RANGE

Located in the Phra Nakhon district, Wat Pho was a Buddhist temple, known as the birth place of Thai massage and home of the reclining Buddha. At one hundred and sixty feet it was the largest image in Thailand and was covered in a thin layer of pure gold—except for the soles of the feet that were covered in mother of pearl. Adjacent to the temple itself was the range, owned and operated by the Thai military, but open to the public for a fee.

Mark sat on a low polished white stone bench viewing the reclining Buddha. The Navy SEAL Luminox EVO watch gently vibrated alerting him it was time to meet the Dutchman. A sly smile came to his face as he recalled Crank giving him the watch as a replacement for the expensive limited edition Swiss one that was damaged beyond repair in Kenya.

Stretching his neck gently to either side, then slowly rotating his head, he stood, picked up his Haliburton case and moved outside just in time to see a new jet-black BMW limo arrive. He walked to the car as the plain clothes Metropolitan officers exited and surveyed the area. As Barnhardt stepped out, Mark called, "Good morning. Beautiful day isn't it?"

"Yes…I suppose it is," Joris replied looking to the sky, then at his watch. "Glad you are on time. I have a busy schedule today."

"Understood. Let's get 'er done."

Barnhardt easily cleared the way for their entry to the range. The firing line, though showing signs of age, was immaculately maintained—a recent coat of white paint gleamed in the morning light on the range stations, the grass was freshly cut, spent brass had been swept up and deposited in the five gallon bucket at every station.

A slender Air Force officer—in a perfectly pressed pair of khaki shorts and short sleeve shirt—awaited them at station six. "Good day, Mister Barnhardt. Nice to see you again, sir. I see you have a guest with you."

"Yes. Mister McCallister is here to give a demonstration of his skills."

Mark reached inside his off white linen jacket and produced a copy of his right-to-carry papers. "You may want to take a look at these." He said as he handed the documents to the officer.

After a brief review. "They seem to be in order. Shall we proceed…Mister McCallister?"

Mark laid his case on a side table as he unlocked it. "Could you set up three silhouettes for me at seven yards?"

He opened the valise and the police men were immediately impressed. The Thai range officer let out a low whistle. None of them had ever seen a Colt Gold Cup before other than gun magazines or movies.

Mark moved the pistol to the shooting bench as well as two eight-round Devel magazines and waited for the range officer to tell him it was clear to fire.

"Shooter take your…"

Before the man could finish, he slammed a mag home and ripped off eight rounds from the hip at the targets from right to left. Before anyone could catch their breath he dropped the empty, loaded a fresh magazine and repeated the process in reverse—left to right.

"Damn!" was all the officer could say.

The two policemen exchanged looks of pure shock then grudging admiration.

Joris stood quietly in the back, not certain what he had just seen. *How could anyone be so fast…and accurate?*

"Can you reset the targets…this time three at seven, three at fifteen and one at twenty-five?"

"It is highly irregular but…yes. I would very much like to see this," the range officer replied. He lifted a small two-way radio from his belt and instructed the target setters—all dressed in matching white shorts and polo shirts—to do as Mark had requested.

Half a dozen young men hustled to place the targets as ordered while several of the other shooters along the line began to gather behind stations five, six and seven.

As he waited, Mark returned the 1911 to the padded case and picked up the Smith and Wesson 5906 and three fifteen round magazines—placing them on the firing bench. He removed his sun glasses and wiped them off with a lens cloth. *Damn humidity is fogging 'em up. The last three shots were blind luck* he thought as he waited.

"Targets are set. Shooter take…"

Again, before the man could finish, he slammed a magazine home and began firing as he moved along the seven foot wide shooting station from right to left—this time using a solid two-hand grip. He double-tapped the seven and fifteen yard targets alternately and when the mag was empty, reloaded in a smooth fluid motion to finish the last of the six targets.

Without pause he switched hands, changed mags and placed three in the twenty-five yard target then—again moving along the firing station, this time from left to right, only faster—walked his fire back in placing head shots in each seven and fifteen yard silhouette before adding three to the head of the twenty five yard target.

Up and down the line a round of applause from the other shooters could be heard. No one had ever seen a display like it before. Several men came forward wanting to shake his hand. Mark placed the weapon and magazines back in the case, closed and locked it.

"Hope you enjoyed the dog and pony show. I will be at the hotel until noon tomorrow. Let me know if you feel I could be of service." Mark shook the amazed Joris' hand. *Bet you didn't see that coming.* "Thank you gentleman. Have a good day," he said to the small crowd that surrounded the shooting station.

He picked up his case and walked off leaving the audience—still dazed at what had just happened—talking excitedly amongst themselves.

The target setters arrived with the targets and laid them on a table grouped by distance.

"If I had not seen it with my own eyes...and look...look at the groupings," the Air Force officer said as he pointed to several of the targets.

Before he could flag down a air-conditioned cab Barnhardt approached him on the street. "Mister McCallister...When can you start?"

"I'll fax over my standard agreement. I can start as soon as you sign it."

"If you do not mind I would like to deliver it this evening and have my wife meet you as well."

Ahhh...the wife. Time to be polite. "Be delighted to meet her. Would 2000 hours be acceptable?"

Joris nodded and extended his hand. "Absolutely."

O CHAO PHAYA RICE BARGE
Bangkok River Market

John and Susan Reynolds—a newlywed couple from Atlanta, Georgia—were on their dream honeymoon. They walked down the wooden gangplank onto the dock from the Rice Barge tour boat sweating in the glare of the midday sun. Both were in their late twenties and university graduates. It was the first time either had been out of the United States. John, a former All-American second baseman at University of Georgia, was an electrical engineer. Susan, blonde-haired and blue-eyed had been a cheerleader at UG, was a photographic journalist with the Atlanta Journal-Constitution. She had not told her husband that she was nine weeks pregnant with their first child.

"Oh, John it is so beautiful. I could move here today," the attractive woman said with a sweet Georgia drawl.

"Me too, baby. Aren't you glad now we scrimped and saved for this trip?" John replied with a thick southern twang.

They wore expensive watches and jewelry and flashed large amounts of money in the local markets.

Inkong's men moved in on them both as soon as they reached the street.

"Wait! What are you doing? Let go of me…" the young woman cried as two men grabbed her arms and rushed her into the waiting van—her toes barely scrapping the ground as she struggled to slow them down.

"Hey! You can't do that! Let go…Ahhh!" her husband yelled…then screamed as Inkong placed a palm-sized stun gun—producing 200,000 volts—in the small of his back and rendered him unconscious.

Their calls for help were ignored or dismissed as foreigners raising hell by the crowd. In less than thirty seconds they were whisked off into the busy traffic.

SUKHOTHAI BANGKOK HOTEL
31/3 South Sathorn Road

Mark sat in the Jacuzzi allowing the rushing jets to massage his body. On the edge of the tub, a ice bucket with a open bottle of Singha beer sat within easy reach on his right and on his left his stainless steel S&W 9mm. The news played on the thirty inch flat screen television. *Damn...this is good. Wonder what stupid business is happening.*

"Today at the river market, two western foreigners were abducted. It is speculated that elements of NPA are again behind this latest kidnapping. Their names have not been released as yet. A spokesperson for the Metropolitan Police stated in a formal announcement that all possible resources were being brought to bear to find them. We will update this report as new information..."

Done and gone they are. Mark changed the channel. A BBC British news reporter stood on the street a block from the Langham Hotel with the image of the charred upper story in view. *Oh good...a little recent history.*

"...in Hong Kong there are still more questions than answers in the case revolving around what may be a turf war between rival gangs. Interpol is confident one of the hundreds of new leads will assist them in capturing the perpetrators of the murder of Chang Wu in his penthouse. Mister Wu cosidered by some to be a well respected business man was under investigation..."

DARK SECRET

It was Bush's fault. He laughed as he switched channels. The vibrating alarm on his watch told him it was time to get ready.

BANGKOK STREET TRAFFIC

Cars, trucks, tuk tuks and busses jammed the roadway. A heavy blanket of dirty gray and orange smog covered the sky in a lung-burning cloud. The lights of the city were just starting to illuminate the street as the sun set. The driver—an off duty member of the police—honked the horn incessantly as he weaved the new BMW limousine through the crowded thoroughfare. The excessive weight of the bullet proofing made the vehicle far less responsive than he was accustomed to. A second officer sat in the front seat beside him—ever scanning the surrounding traffic.

In the luxurious passenger compartment—with the glass closed between the Barnhardts and the officers—Joris talked uncharacteristically excited, "This is the guy. You would *not* believe the exhibition he put on today...every target at every distance..."

"You said that already. I know it is important...but we attend so many functions and the last two were morons." Dalisay stared at the passing skyline.

"He seems very polished though a bit arrogant. I'll put up with it as long as our safety is assured..."

"Do not forget, Rutger will be here soon *and* you are scheduled to visit the new orphanage in Cebu when it opens."

"He promised to have a team in place quickly. I feel confident..."

"I want to go see my parents while we are in the Philippines. It has been a year now."

"But of course dear. I am looking forward to the opening of a new home for the unfortunate children. I will spend some time with them while you visit with your family." Truth be known, Joris cared little for her family as they were simple people and lived in what he considered a remote third world squatter's village.

CHAING MAI, THAILAND
Crank's Estate

Rhino—wearing a loose-fitting pair of brown silk Thai boxing shorts and a tank top—walked up and down the verandah with a pair of crutches. Crank—clad in dark red surf trunks—lay on a lounge chair with a young girl reclining beside him and two others close by. One was feeding him fresh fruit the other giving him a foot massage.

"Any word from Zorro?"

"This afternoon. He's meeting some Dutchman about a contract tonight." Crank took another piece of pineapple off a fork held out for him by one of the girls. "Ummm...nearly as sweet as you are, little one."

"If he takes it...you goin' to join him?"

"Oh, *hell* no! Grandpa taught me too well...never...ever work where you live. He takes it...he's on his own in the Big Mango."

DARK SECRET

SUKHOTHAI BANGKOK HOTEL
31/3 South Sathorn Road

The Barnhardts entered the lobby with one plainclothes officer behind them. The driver of the BMW was outside, detailed to remain with the vehicle to deter any foul play.

Mark, wore his new hand-tailored dark blue Thai silk suit and waited in plain view. The dark plum silk tie accented his suit as much the light blue shirt set off his clear blue eyes. He had his longer-than-shoulder-length hair neatly pulled back in a low pony tail with an elastic tie, which he concealed with a one inch wide silver band that sported a dark blue lapis stone mounted on it. *Wives always like a well-dressed man.*

Though not expecting any problems in the busy hotel he wore a pair of vertical Bianchi shoulder rig holsters carrying his Colt and S&W. He had asked the tailor to cut the suit slightly wider in the chest to assist in concealing the weapons.

"Mister and Missus Barnhardt." Mark extended his hand to Dalisay first—out of respect. "I took the liberty of making a reservation for dinner here in the hotel. I prefer one of the hole in the wall local sites but…safety first."

"Fine. I have your contract signed. When can you start?" Joris said as he held out a white envelope with his logo—BI, LLC—in the upper left corner.

"Let's take our table first, if you don't mind. We can discuss the arrangements over cocktails or dinner…Lovely dress, Ma'am." Mark motioned the two to follow him.

Once seated, he ordered a full course of finger foods and drinks in perfect Thai.

Joris and Dalisay exchanged surprised looks as the waiter departed.

"I can start tonight."

"What about your team?"

"They'll be on the ground within forty-eight hours now that I have the contract. Until then…you will need to continue retaining the off-duty policemen."

"You're not as I expected," she said.

"Yeah…I get that a lot." He shared a look with Joris.

"Honey, it is not the size of the dog in the fight but rather the size of the fight in the dog. Isn't that right Mister McCallister?"

Showing off your newfound knowledge, you are. Mark turned to the Filipina and smiled. He spoke in good—though not perfect—Visayan, "I appreciate your concerns…I assure you I've never lost a client. You will be safer here than you have ever been…Safer than you ever were in the Philippines."

Dalisay's eyes went wide with surprise hearing him speak so well in her native tongue—a very difficult Philippines language with over thirty different dialects.

"How did you know I was a Filipina?" she asked in Visayan.

"Due diligence, Ma'am. I need to know my clients to provide the best protection. But…we leave your husband out now. May we continue in English? I don't speak a word of Dutch." *I won't tell them I'm fluent in Dutch. Who knows what intel I may pick up?*

Joris, never learned more than a few common phrases in his wife's native tongue and sat befuddled at the conversation.

"My husband tells me you are a wizard with your pistols," she said returning to English.

"He is...too kind. I know some who are much better...Do you shoot?"

"No...I abhor guns."

The waiter returned with the platter of appetizers and drinks. "Are you ready to order now?"

"Give us a few minutes. Thank you."

"I had a four bedroom house built on the grounds for a security force. How many men will you be bringing?"

"Three men and one woman. As I said earlier...neither of you will be out of our line of sight with the exception of when you are in your private quarters. I suspect Missus Barnhardt will..."

"Please...call me Dalisay, Mister McCallister."

Done deal. Offered her first name. "Of course...and thank you...Dalisay...I suspect you will want to go shopping from time to time. Tola...she's Thai...will accompany you...in case you want to try on some clothing or visit the comfort room...*Never* out of our line of site."

"My chef can prepare us dinner at home. Shall we get on with it?" Joris suggested.

"Certainly. Take care of the tab while I get my bags. See you in the lobby...say ten minutes?" Mark rose to his feet after Joris nodded his agreement and walked briskly to the elevator.

She watched him all the way. *He moves like cat...No, not a cat...A panther.*

KHLONG TOEI SLUM
Bangkok

Inkong sat on the tiny balcony over looking the river when his cell phone rang. "What is it?"

"The Dutchman and his wife just left the Sukhothai hotel. The westerner he met at the gun range today is with them."

"Continue your duties. Keep me informed," Inkong said before hanging up. *Umm...Yet Kae...a new player in the game.* He moved back into the squalid three-story rusted tin-roofed shack and into a windowless room. The overbearing stench of the river was thick in the night air. The only light was a weak bulb hanging by its electric cord from the ceiling. He pulled down the dirty string to reveal the Reynolds couple.

John—gagged and blindfolded—stood with his hands tied over his head to a rafter by a coarse hemp rope. Where his right ear had been was a bloody gaping wound—now covered in a swarm of hungry flies. Susan lay on a thin sweat stained, badly soiled brown sleeping pad on the floor. Her hands were tied to a rusty eye bolt in the wall. She was gagged, but not blindfoled.

Susan began to whimper when the light came on. She starred at her shirtless captor with fear in her eyes. The large tattoo of a cobra ready to strike on his chest, glistened with sweat under the dim light. She rolled over on her stomach then onto her knees and struggled to free herself once again. Her wrists were raw and bleeding from her previous attempts.

"I sent a ransom note to the authorities. Your passports will identify you...the ear will convience them I am serious." He began to unbuckle his belt as he walked slowly toward the cowering woman. "Until the money arrives..."

Susan tried to scream, but the duct tape muffled the sound—not that anyone close enough to hear them would care—then she attempted to kick at him.

Inkong grabbed her ankle as he continued to speak. "...you and I entertain ourselves...I suggest you relax and *enjoy*...my sweet little capitalist princess."

John moaned then growled as he struggled to free himself—certain that his bride was about to be violated. He was right. Over the course of time Inkong had them in his clutches he would listen as Susan was repeatedly raped by Inkong, his men and even his women. He was not exempt from the sexual abuse. Their dream vacation had become a living hell on earth...

JORIS BARNHARDT RESIDENCE

Mark woke at 0530 hours, performed his daily ritual, showered, shaved and walked the short distance to the main house. The smaller bungalow was furnished simply in common Thai decor.

Inside the main house he moved to the spotless modern kitchen and found Dalisay sitting at the breakfast table reading a copy of the Mindanao Star—a newspaper from her home island. On the table next to her blue cup and saucer was an empty pair of three-in-one packages—a favorite morning drink in the Philippines—a mixture of powdered milk, coffee and sugar.

"Good morning, Mister McCallister."

"Thought we agreed on Steve and Dalisay last night. What's for breakfast?"

"Our cook has gone to the office with Joris today. He caters a proper lunch for him and some visiting business associates. Val will not be back until five or so."

Mark opened the stainless steel refrigerator door. "Any eggs and bacon?"

She set the paper down and joined him. "Val will be shopping today. Make a list of what you like and I'll fax it to the office. Do you like Filipino foods? Panset? Shrimp egg rolls? Lechone?"

"Actually, I do...but it's a little early for them. Where do you keep the teas?

She moved to a cabinet and removed several boxes. "How did you learn Visayan?"

"I've worked some contracts in the PI. Got injured on one...my ICC took me to his home for a couple of months to recover. I mostly picked it up from his children."

"ICC?"

"In country consultant. Always hire one wherever I work. Reminds me, Keit and Tola will be arriving today. I mentioned her last night, she will be your shadow once she arrives. He will take over driving duties. He's a long time associate. Knows his way around Bangkok and has an extensive network of other consultants as well."

"What exactly do you mean by consultant?"

"Covers a vast number of duties. Driving, intel gathering, heavy lifting if necessary, translating…"

"But you speak fluent Thai."

Mark grinned. "I…hardly ever let on that I do. I spoke to the waiter last night to show you and Joris one of my skills. Keit will do all things revolving around a liasion role."

"I see…Very clever. What else is required to do your job?" She sat back down at the table and studied him.

He poured the near-boiling water over the stainless steel tea bulb—set in a delicate white fine China tea pot—and sat down facing her. "It's a pretty long list…How did you and Joris meet?"

She looked out the window, avoiding eye contact—a fact not lost on Mark. "We met at the Philippines finals for the Miss Universe competition. Joris was a judge."

"Really? *Interesting*. And your family…where do they live?"

"On the island of Mindanao. Near Dipolog…have you heard of it?"

"Yup. Zamboanga del Norte. Sister city to Dipitan."

She turned to him. There was a warm but sad look in her eyes. "Would you mind taking me to the MKB mall? I need to buy some things for a balikbian box."

While she got dressed for the shopping trip, Mark used his electronics eavesdropping device and swept the first two floors of the residence. Sure enough he discovered one in Joris' study and another in the living room. *Hundred bucks to a dime I'll find one in their bedroom.*

He disabled both devices—making sure to leave them in place for a later time. Whoever placed them would be showing up to find out why. *Look forward to meeting you. Should give us a chance to discuss your employer.*

HAL McCAMBELL'S OFFICE
Dallas, Texas

Two men stood in front of Hal's desk. Roger Mantle, standing 6' 3" and tipping the scales at 250 pounds was a former Secret Service agent Hal had given the call sign *Blaster*. Mike Sloan, slightly smaller at 6' 2" and 210 pounds was a sixteen year Army Ranger now know simply as *Dog*.

"You can pick up your pocket litter and tickets from Maggie on your way out...I'm sending you to Thailand to work for Zorro. He will get your boots dirty. Don't screw up...There aren't any do-overs. Understood?" Hal rattled on as he flipped through the pages of the Dallas Morning News.

"Yes, sir," the two said in unison, then stood for a moment unsure of what to do next.

Hal settled on the sports page and read the headlines, *Jerry Jones at it again*. "Ahh Jesus! When is that Arkansas razorback gonna stop fiddling around..." He looked at the two men. "What? You dick head fannybaws need me to hold your hands?" Hal barked, glaring over the top of his reading glasses.

"No, sir," they chimed in unison once again. At the door Blaster turned.

"This the same Zorro you talked about the first day of orientation?" Roger asked.

"There's only one Zorro. You owe me for setting you up with the best damn Op I ever had. Don't screw up…if he doesn't kill you, I will."

After getting three new passports, drivers licenses, other identification documents and airline tickets Blaster and Dog stood on the sidewalk outside the McCambell Import/Export home office building.

"Can you believe it? Zorro!" Dog asked.

"Not yet. Do you think he will…ease us in 'til we get collected?"

"Man, I don't know. Hal said he beat the hell out of an Op that screwed up in Peru…"

Blaster pumped up his chest and flexed his muscles. "I'd like to see him try that with me. Ain't no one ever beat me down."

"Yeah?…Well, we better get moving…plane takes off in three hours."

METROPOLITAN POLICE HEADQUATERS
Bangkok, Thailand

Lead investigator on the Reynolds kidnapping case, Virote Pradchaphet, a man of slight build—lightweight champion for the last ten years on the police Thai kick boxing team—stood looking at a dozen photos of abducted persons on a shabby worn cork bulletin board. Behind him in the small smoke-filled room members of the CAF—Crimes Against Foreigners—tactical team waited for his orders.

A sergeant entered the room hurriedly. "Virote, we have received the ransom note…and this." He placed a bloody white rag on the table.

The tired Virote turned around, placed his cigarette in an ash tray already full of butts and opened the cloth, exposing a human ear. "Yet Bpet! Get this down to forensics immediately."

The officer rewrapped John's ear and departed.

After reading the scrawled message on a piece of meat wrapping paper and viewing the passports, Virote addressed the men, "The Reynolds are Americans. This will be a high profile case, gentlemen. I will contact the embassy and start the ball rolling to the families. I want you to get out there and toss every informant you have. *Get* me some intelligence."

The group of experienced men gathered their gear and headed out the door, leaving their boss to the unpleasant business of passing the bad news on to the Americans.

MKB MALL
Bangkok, Thailand

Dalisay and Mark exited a blue and white Nissan cab on the street in front of the mall. It was the third cab they had ridden in. There were eight floors packed with 2,000 shops that sold everything from clothing to furniture to the latest electrical devices. You want it they sell it.

"Okay…explain the three cabs?"

"Harder to follow us. Someone wanted Joris bad enough to pull a snatch-and-grab in front of the Pedromo club…they're unlikely to miss an opportunity to pick you off."

"How do you know that man…or that one…or those men for that matter are not going to do it?" She pointed at some of the passersby.

"Don't see it in their eyes. Too soft."

"Too soft? So you can…"

Mark took her arm above the elbow and pulled her behind him as he extended his left hand at a pair of young men walking, texting and talking to one another as they approached. The two looked surprised by his actions.

"What did their eyes say?"

"Nothing. They were locked in on their electronics…but they were going to bump into you…That's not acceptable."

She noted he was always scanning the throng of people, even glancing behind them frequently. As they stepped on to the escalator, "What would you have done if those two were going to harm me?"

"Whatever it takes…Where we going?"

"Eighth floor. There is a shop that sells lotions and such my mother loves." The scent of her perfume floated past him as they rode up. *Umm…very nice.*

Four hours later they stood on the street with three carts filled with goods. Three mall staff stood holding the merchandise as Mark hailed a van cab. He put her inside and saw to the loading of her purchases, all the while holding the front passenger door open with a eye on the driver. Once the back doors closed, he handed the young men a thousand baht each and got in next to Dalisay.

"Must be very tiring for you…always looking around for trouble."

"Easy money…so far."

***

CHAPTER FIVE

BARNHARDT'S OFFICE

Most of the staff had departed, leaving only the company security guards and janitorial staff. The lights had been turned off in most of the building and only the necessary security lights illuminated the building. Joris walked toward the elevator with the two police officers behind him.

"Gelul Godverdomme! What do you mean the construction will not be finished? The opening is in two weeks."

Rico, his main man in the Philippines, replied, "The permits were just issued yesterday…"

"Yesterday? I paid Cobato three months ago to smooth the permits. Damn Filipino time…never mind. I'll deal with that lul kutwijf later. How much will be completed when I arrive?"

"The first phase is complete now. The second is very close. It is the sleeping wings that will be incomplete…"

"Kutzooi! We can not have the press all over the grand opening if there is not a proper place for the children to sleep. I want you to hire more people. Work three shifts…round the clock, you understand me?"

"Yes, sir."

As he entered the elevator he spoke to no one in particular—though the two officers nervously entered with him, "Just can not hire good help any more."

His limo drove out of the first floor parking garage into the traffic. A pair of non-discript motorbike waiting at the curb half a block away pulled out and followed. In the busy traffic, a normal observer would not notice them amongst the throng of other cycles.

KHLONG TOEI SLUM

Inkong sat on the floor alone smoking hashish from his hooka. His cell phone rang a dozen times before he realized it was not part of his dream. He answered, his voice foggy and thick from the drug, "What?"

"The westerner and the wife just left MKB."

"Continue…your…du…ties."

As he hung up, he had another call. He lifted a bottle of warm cheap Thai beer and rinsed it around his mouth before swallowing. "What?"

"He has left his office."

"Stay with…him."

In the drug-induced fog that filled his mind, he was vaguely aware of moans coming from the next room. He got up, staggered against the wall and made his way to where the

Reynolds were held. The smell of their body fluids in combination with the river stench would make a person unused to the squalor lose their lunch.

Sitting on a low three legged green wooden stool, one of the NPA females dialed the knobs on a small electronic apparatus. Wires ran from the device to crude metal clamps attached to the sensitive parts of John and Susan's bodies. The woman laughed as she turned the controls up and down, sending waves of pain through each of them.

Inkong said with slurred speech, "Get...*out*!"

The surprised female—dressed only in dirty orange shorts and a black headband—jumped from her stool and eased past him, apprehensive he might strike her.

Leaning against the wall, he gazed at the brutalized pair. He stumbled as he moved closer, falling on his face, and then he crawled on his knees to the gagged and secured Susan Reynolds. Now completely nude, her left eye swollen shut from a blow by another assailant, she moaned as he climbed on top of her. He roughly groped her breasts before he raped her for the third time that day—the eighth such ravaging in all. Unable to resist his assault she endured his desires as she moaned and cried quietly.

SURVARNABHUMI AIRPORT
Bangkok, Thailand

Located sixteen miles from downtown Bangkok in Racha Thewa in the Bang Phli district, Survarnabhumi Airport was the fourteenth busiest in the world with ninety-six airline companies arriving and departing twenty-four hours a day.

Roger Mantle and Mike Sloan walked off the Cathay-Pacific 747 jetliner into the busy terminal with the rest of the first class passengers. Keit stood quietly in the crowd of people awaiting passengers, holding a small sign that read McCambell Import/Export above his head.

"Damn good to see somebody to meet us," Roger said as the two approached their in-country contact.

"Zorro said get you...arrive house pretty damn quick. We go now...get luggage," Keit replied with a strong Thai influence in his English, then moved into the mass of travelers.

"We go now," Sloan said with a chuckle and followed the Asian, who was weaving quickly through the crowd.

"Jesus, don't lose the little bastard." Roger nudged Mike and struggled to keep him in view.

JORIS BARNHARDT RESIDENCE

Keit drove the white Land Rover into the underground garage, after a brief stop to allow the policeman on duty to check the papers of the two passengers. He parked in one of the five spaces marked guest, moved to the back cargo door and opened it.

"Zorro waits. We go."

The two men removed their luggage and followed to the elevator as Keit hit the car's remote control, locking it and setting the alarm, before pushing the button for the lift to arrive.

Roger yawned. "Shit…I'm exhausted, stiff as hell…my head is pounding. Now it's a sprint to…"

"Boss man say PDQ…we go PDQ," Keit said calmly as the three waited for the elevator.

"You work with Zorro before?" Mike asked.

"Many times. Number one boss man."

Dog and Blaster exchanged looks as the lift arrived and the doors opened.

Inside the elevator Keit punched the first floor button and turned to the two new arrivals. "You new boys. Small suggestion…no disrespect please. Do what Zorro say…you be okie dokie. No do…you maybe dead."

When the doors opened, the small but thickly muscled Thai exited first. "This way. Leave things in house. Then meet boss on roof."

Ten minutes later, Keit led them onto the rooftop of the residence. Sitting under a dark blue canvas canopy Mark, Missus Barnhardt and Tola were finishing lunch. Close by, two boy servants stood, each wearing freshly pressed pants that matched the color of the canopy and embroidered white long sleeve shirts. As the men approached the wait staff collected the dishes and utensils and departed.

Mark stood up and extended his hand as the men approached. "Steve McCallister. Who's who?"

"I'm Roger Mantle and this is Mike Sloan."

"We'll orientate at 1600 hours. Keit will show you to the kitchen…Chow down. Get some rest."

Inside the elevator the three rode without speaking back to the first floor. In the kitchen they were met by Val—Joris' personal chef—and the staff.

"What do you like for lunch, gentleman?" Val—dressed in proper chef attire, including a puffy hat—asked without looking up from the huge cut of pork he was preparing for the evening meal. His hands were covered in blood and he did not offer to shake.

"Steak and eggs," Blaster said.

"Same for me, thanks," Dog added.

"No steak today. Ham and eggs," the chef replied. "Kulap, two ham…" he started to order one of his staff, and then looking up at the two big men, "Four ham…one dozen eggs."

"Coffee?" Blaster asked.

"Lawan, two coffees," Val ordered never halting his work.

Both women jumped to perform. Lawan had the coffee in their hands in a minute and returned to her station awaiting her next order. Kulap placed four of the half inch thick slices of ham on a large griddle and began to break a dozen eggs into a stainless steel bowl.

"I go. You finish…you return other house. Zorro see you there…sixteen hundred." Keit walked off without time for the either man to reply.

"Efficient little bastard," Blaster remarked.

"Hey, watch it," Dog replied, nodding at the departing Keit. "He's just doing his job."

"I didn't join up to be goose steppin' like a monkey on a chain."

"Me either but 'til you get the lay of the land…"

"You call me bastad one mo time…you sing sapano in choir. My parents honoable people." Keit's English reflected his anger.

Neither man had noticed him walk back to them. Standing next to the 6' 3" Blaster, the 5' 6" Asian looked comical to the unsuspecting viewer. He had dealt with bigger men many times and had no fear of doing so again.

"Easy there little guy. I…"

"One mo time," the smaller man said staring directly into Roger's eyes before turning and walking off.

"You seem to have a way with making new friends." Mike chuckled.

"Shit…"

"There will be no cursing in the presence of the client or their staff."

Roger and Mike turned to find Mark standing behind them.

"Yes, sir," both responded.

"Hal's orientation must have changed since I went through…Social skills 101…polite, courteous, respectful *and* professional…at all times."

"Yes, sir."

"Mark turned to the chef. "May I have a platter of mixed fruits for the ladies, Val?"

"Lawan, fresh fruits," the man ordered as he wielded a large meat cleaver, hacking the pork into individual portions. "She will deliver it to you."

"Thanks." Mark looked at them, tilted his head and moved to the stairs.

Mike and Roger again exchanged glances.

"Way to go, ace," Dog said with a smile.

SECURITY QUARTERS
Barnhardt Estate

Mark entered with Tola—a 5' 6" and 145 pound master of three martial arts styles and well accomplished with small arms. Waiting in the living area, Keit, Roger and Mike sat watching American basketball by satellite on a sixty inch flat screen.

Neither Dog or Blaster saw or heard them enter but when Keit turned off the screen and stood facing the entry hall both men followed suit.

"Gentlemen, I'd like to introduce you to Tola. Don't let her looks fool you. She could probably whip all our asses…except Keit's."

"Afternoon. Good to meet you," Mike said.

"Likewise," Roger added.

Mark began his own brand of orientation. "Have a seat. I received your jackets from Hal. Impressive stateside resume, Roger. Outstanding duty, Mike. Now…forget all that. This is the shadow world. Nothing is as it seems…and everything changes by the heartbeat."

Mark paused to allow the information to sink in. "Every thing you learned in Hal's training does apply...with modifications...My modifications." He smiled broadly before continuing, "You work with me...and anyone and everyone who seeks to harm our clients...*dies*. There are no exceptions. Understood?"

The two men nodded in agreement.

"Understood?"

"Yes, sir."

"Keit will take both of you out tonight after you meet Mister Barnhardt and familiarize you with the terrain...the office...the club...everywhere Joris normally goes. Our main source of intel in Thailand...Keit...will fill you in on the winds of war as he sees it...Pay attention."

Mark's cell rang. He checked the caller ID. "The Scotsman calling to see if you arrived. Where was I? Oh...Keit will be our driver. If you get in a tight spot follow his lead. You'll get the hang of it."

Mark noticed Mike shift his weight. "Questions?"

"No, sir."

"There aren't any *old* operatives. Some retire...tired. Some get out because the business is too tough or they become disabled. Some...die. Keep your eyes open and your head out of your ass so you don't become the latter."

"I, ahh...have a question," Mike asked tentatively.

"Shoot."

"If...you know...we get into a situation...what's up with the local police?"

"Good question. I have acquired a carry permit for both of you and a limited get out of jail free card…"

"Limited?" Roger asked.

"If you're performing your duties, you get a pass. If you're off in some seedy girlie bar and get in trouble…you're on your own. I strongly suggest you focus on business and not your dick while you work a contract."

Both men glanced nervously at Tola sitting in the corner. A sly smile passed over her face.

"The four of you will live in this house until the contract is up…Meals delivered from the main house. With the exception of Tola, unless I assign you otherwise, you will steer clear of Missus Barnhardt. On the occasion I assign you to cover her…you will avoid all unnecessary conversations. Clear?"

"Yes, sir."

"Hal must think pretty highly of you two or you wouldn't be here. Do your job…Screw up and you are out of here."

The meeting concluded two hours later when a staff boy called over the intercom that Barnhardt had returned from work.

"Let's go meet your client. Put on a suit, there's a Armor500 vest in that box for each of you…it works, I guarantee you. And wear your piece…High-end clients like to see their security wearing weapons."

METROPOLITAN POLICE HEADQUATERS
Bangkok, Thailand

A field officer of the CAF entered as Virote talked on the phone. He backed out and waited in the hall.

"Chief, we have few leads. The couple were abducted in a delivery-type van with no identifying signs. We found one that met the description today abandoned just outside the Toei slums. Forensics is going over it now. I'll let you know what is found." Virote hung up and motioned the officer inside.

"What do you have?...Please tell me it is some good news," he said wearily as the officer stepped to his desk.

"A reliable source told me that word on the street is, it was Inkong and his gang."

"Any idea where they are hiding?"

"Khlong Toei slum, sir."

"Great, that narrowed it down. There's what...two hundred thousand thieves and beggars living there now?" Virote swiveled his beat-up wooden chair and gazed at the large map of Bangkok on the wall behind him. "All right...get the task force together. I'll call Major Praphasirirat at the Ministry of Defense. See if he can allocate a detail to assist us."

"Yes, sir. What about the river, sir? Word will spread quickly that a force has entered the slum looking for Inkong. They will slip away on a launch if..."

"I'll request back-up with the River Patrol as well...and some air support. A couple of helicopters overhead will be very useful. Tell the men to expect a jump-off at dawn."

JORIS BARNHARDT RESIDENCE

Fifteen minutes after the staff boy informed Mark the client had arrived, he led the three men and Tola into the spacious living area to meet the client. None of the team lost note of the expensive European furnishings, oil paintings by several of the Dutch masters hung in heavy gold frames, each with its own individual lighting.

"McCallister, I see your team has arrived."

"Yes, sir. Allow me to introduce Tola, she'll be Missus Barnhardt's constant companion. If I had a wife, I would entrust her to Tola's care. Keit, our driver, is a longtime associate and knows Bangkok like the back of his hand. Roger Mantle and Mike Sloan just arrived today from the states. At least one of them will be with you every minute when you are not home."

Joris shook hands all around. "My wife and I thank you for coming. Feel free to let Val know of any dining preferences you may have. He's a master chef and very proficient at western and eastern fare."

"You can inform the police they will no longer be needed twenty-four seven. We will take over all security concerns as of 0600 tomorrow."

"Yes, I will do it first thing in the morning. May we have a word just…you and I?" Joris asked Mark.

"Absolutely. Keit…give 'em the nickel tour. Gentlemen, Tola…tomorrow morning…ready to roll at 0500."

After the team departed, Joris led Mark into his study and closed the door. A floor to ceiling rich teakwood bookcase covered one wall—filled with classics and a smattering of new author's work. On his desk was new novel titled *Haunted Falls*—about Bass Reeves, the first black Deputy US Marshal west of the Mississippi—by two heralded Texas authors.

Many people all over the world were fans of the old west. Joris had complete collections of several well known western authors but his newest obsession was the works of Ken Farmer and Buck Stienke. The desk—a seventeenth century antique handmade of Dutch walnut—had been imported from Holland.

Joris moved a corner cabinet, opened it to reveal his private stock and began to pour sixty year old Scotch into a finely cut crystal glass. "A drink, Mister McCallister?"

"No thank you, sir. Never while on duty," he lied to build the assurance of his client. He had been known to drink himself into a stupor when the images of his lost wife and child plagued him—both killed in a Mexican drug cartel drive-by incident in Texas, several years earlier while deployed in Afghanistan.

"Dalisay informed me you moved your things into one of our rooms rather than in the house I have provided for you and your team."

"Yes, sir. I have no intentions of interring with your private lives. But to do my job I will need to be close to where you sleep. You have a problem with that?"

"We sometimes have parties and invite overnight guests, in which case we may need the room you selected."

"You will need to invite one less overnighter. Until I have a handle on the threat level, I'll be sleeping in the smaller room on the second floor."

"I understand but…"

"There are no buts. The first month's payment cleared my account this morning as promised. If you have second thoughts…we will consider it a non-refundable retainer and I'll pack the team up and get out in the morning."

"No…no…we will do as you insist." Joris turned to the window, his back to Mark to hide his anger.

"Good to know. I will inspect your home security system thoroughly tomorrow. Please arrange to have a representative call me so we can set a time to meet. Early day tomorrow…if there is nothing else…I'd like to turn in."

"No, nothing else. Good night."

KHLONG KOEI SLUM

One of the NPA soldiers ran onto the balcony where Inkong sat watching the sunset with one of the female members of his gang. He was out of breath and sweating in the heat of the days end.

"Inkong…the CAF intend to sweep the slum tomorrow looking for the Americans," the man blurted out.

"Yet Kae…Alert everyone. Tonight we move up river to Pak Kret. Inform Mookjai he is to blow up his tour boat at 2200 hours. It will be our cover. The river patrols will be busy with the event while we go."

At precisely 2200 hours the fully loaded Pink Pearl tour boat exploded under the clear star-studded night sky as it approached its dock with a full cargo of tourists. Mookjai, having given the helm to his unwitting second, had slipped over the stern into the dark muddy water three minutes prior to the explosion and had already reached the shore. He sat, dripping wet on a low pier, watching the fiery blast with perverted glee.

The response of the river patrol boats in the area was immediate. All forces that normally cruised the river inspecting suspicious craft were completely oblivious to the thirty foot launch carrying Inkong, his NPA cell and the Americans up river away from the burning boat.

To further obscure his tracks, a time delay bomb exploded in the three story shack they had inhabited at 2230. The ensuing fire—fueled by several plastic five gallon containers of petrol—destroyed the structure as well as several surrounding shanties.

BANGKOK TRAFFIC

Keit drove the limo with Mantle riding up front with him. In the passenger compartment, Mark and Sloan rode with Joris.

"I appreciate your professional efforts Chief Nantakam. Your men did a fine job. I will see you are on the list of Christmas gift recipients. Good day." Barnhardt hung up and turned to Mark. "I will be having lunch with business associates at the Sporting Club today."

"Understood. I need a list of all your upcoming events for the next month so I can schedule the team."

"You shall have it today. There will be several hundred people at the lunch event. Will that be a problem?"

"Not at all," Mark replied as his cell rang. "Excuse me. It's Tola." Without waiting for approval he took the call. "Zorro."

"Missus Barnhardt just informed me she is to meet her husband for lunch today. How do you want this?"

"I'll have Keit pick you both up. We'll all go together."

Mark hung up. "Missus Barnhardt will be attending the luncheon?"

"Yes...yes she will," he replied.

"I'll need her schedule as well. For today, once you are in the building, Keit and I will return and pick her up."

"Is this a problem?"

"No, sir. Once I have the schedules we'll operate more efficiently." He looked to Mike. *That's how you handle it.*

Sloan gave a barely discernible nod to acknowledge.

As they exited the vehicle in the parking garage Mark gave his final instructions, "One of you is with the client every second. He needs to drain his lizard...one of you inspects the head, the other waits outside the door...Understood?"

"Yes, sir," they answered.

"Mister Barnhardt, we will be waiting for you when you're ready."

"Very good...Until then," he said as he started to the elevator flanked by the two operatives.

"Off they go," Keit said with a hint of laughter.

"Yeah...Give me a day or so. I'll get this cluster straightened out. Let's get back to the house and pick up the girls," Mark's tone indicated the disorganized start to the day did not meet with his approval. *Easy now. The first few days are always the most complicated.*

His cell rang. "McCallister."

"I am Isra Charoenkul with Master Safety Enterprises Ltd., Mister McCallister. Joris Barnhardt requested I call you as soon as possible. How may I assist you."

Well…he's quick on the draw if nothing else. Mark thought as he listened to the young woman introduce herself. "I need your best technician to come out to the residence in the morning."

"Is there anything wrong with the system today?"

"Don't know yet. I just took over the security for the family and I need some orientation. Based on the video links I viewed yesterday…some upgrades may be needed."

"He is one of our best customers. I will be there with a technician at 0900 tomorrow."

"That will work. Good-bye." Mark hung up and dialed the secure link to McCambell Import/Export, the recorder picked up. "Maggie. Zorro. I need to talk to Hans Schoepke right away. Give him my number. Wish you all the best…especially dealing with Hal."

JORIS BARNHARDT RESIDENCE

Tola and Missus Barnhardt were sitting in the upstairs living room when Mark entered. There were several photo albums on a large walnut coffee table and the two women were going through one of them.

"He is a beautiful boy, Dalisay," Tola said.

Already on a first name basis I see. Mark thought as he stood in the doorway. "We will be leaving in one hour. Best get ready. Tola, you need to go change into social event attire."

"Yes, boss."

"I'll be ready in thirty minutes," Dalisay said as she closed the album and proceeded to put all of them back inside a large cabinet.

Mark sat talking with Val when Tola entered the kitchen.

"Joris is a pillar of the community here and back in Holland. I have worked for him now...twenty years. He started with nothing and look what he has built," Val said.

"Very impressive. Ahh...Tola you look splendid," Mark replied as walked across the room.

"Thanks. We should talk," she replied.

"Okay...right after the luncheon." His interest was peaked by her comment.

"I'm ready," Dalisay announced as she joined them, dressed in a brightly patterned Fred Sabatier French designer silk dress and pink high heels.

"Beautiful," Tola could not help saying.

"You can borrow it sometime if you like. We are about the same size."

Tola looked to Mark before answering, "Thank you but..."

"No buts...if you do not agree to borrow it I will simply give it to you."

"You two work it out on the way. Tola, I suggest you take her up on the offer," Mark said as he headed for the elevator.

BARNHARDT'S OFFICE

Mark and Keit waited beside the limousine—motor running for the comfort of the two women inside—when Blaster, followed by Joris and Dog, exited the elevator.

"I want you to get this vehicle checked out, Keit. Body, glass and tires."

"I call my uncle. He can do."

"Sooner than later. I don't recognize the company that sold this *hard* limo to Joris. Until you get it approved, I feel like we're driving around like pop-up targets."

Mark opened the rear passenger door as Keit took his place in the driver's seat. Roger took up shotgun again as Mike and Zorro entered the passenger compartment with the Dutchman.

As the limo pulled out of the parking area a pair of motorcycles parked not far away moved into traffic and followed them...

***

CHAPTER SIX

ROYAL BANGKOK SPORTING CLUB

The century old member's-only club—who's patrons either owned or ran the country—was the place to go for the stressed-out wealthy, diplomats and politicians in Bangkok. The guest list for the luncheon was a who's who list as the royal family was in attendance—a rare occurrence but not unheard of.

"Mister Ambassador, how are you today?" Joris asked the portly career German politician—using perfect Deutsche since residents of European countries normally learned multiple languages—as he and his entourage moved through the crowd.

"Quiet well, Joris. Good afternoon Missus Barnhardt," the man replied. He was surprised to see so many new faces surrounding the couple. He exhaled from a long dark cigar and turned to his wife and three others. "Looks like Barnhardt is taking the kidnap attempt seriously this time."

"Gunter, darling, it is only the prudent thing to do. I wish the embassy had sent more than one man as our escort," his wife replied as she fanned the cloud of thick gray smoke away from her face. She turned to one of the other women. "Those are two really handsome boys…I haven't seen them before," she whispered behind a gold-colored event list before waving it like a small fan as she smiled.

Once into the mix of the crowd, Tola and Mike flanked Dalisay as she mingled with the wives of Bangkok's rich and famous, while Mark and Roger stood with Joris. The duty of protecting a client was very similar to the work Roger had performed while a Secret Service agent back in the states and he fell in to his new situation easily. Mike, on the other hand, was a little off-center with all the humanity swirling—resembling chaos in his opinion—around his client.

Mark stood close—but not too close—to Barnhardt ready to move in at any moment. He did not expect any danger in the crowd, which had been carefully screened upon entering the large reception room by uniformed Thai soldiers due to the king and queen's presence. "Blaster, step in here for a moment. I'm gonna check on Missus Barnhardt."

Once Mantle stood in his position Mark began to weave across the room. Halfway through the crowd, he met Patrick Murry and his wife who were in conversation with embassy officials from various countries.

"Steve, you remember my wife, Athelia?"

"Yes I do. Very nice to see you again. How are you today Ma'am?"

"Wonderful. Good to see you too. Patrick really surprised me when he mentioned you were in Bangkok."

"How's the contract going?" he asked.

"Good so far…Thanks again for acting as a middle man…"

"Glad to do it. Us old dogs have to stick together."

Mark could see that the crowd around Dalisay was growing. Tola had moved beside her but Mike had not moved closer as he should. "Absolutely. Give me a minute please? Missus Murry," he said with a nod to Athelia.

He moved as quickly as he could through the crowd without drawing undue attention, not because he felt there was immanent threat but wanted to advise the new operative in a timely fashion so as not to have a lack of cover if necessary in the future.

He arrived to find a large circle of women—dressed in a rainbow of expensive attire—seven deep surrounding Missus Barnhardt and the Queen of Siam. "Excuse me. Thank you. Excuse me. Sorry." He addressed each of the women in his path until he was at Dalisay's side.

"Oh, Hello, Steve. Your highness…ladies, this is Steve McCallister. Our new head of security."

"Hello, everyone. Your highness…a privilege to meet you. Missus Barnhardt please come with me." Mark took her gently by the arm and with Tola's help began to lead her out of the crowd.

"Is there something wrong?" she asked furtively looking around.

"This way Ma'am…Mike," he said with a look and a nod.

Once clear and in a more open area he released her. "Okay now…There's a large crowd here today. I want you to keep

Missus Barnhardt out of any groups like we just left. Always have an open path to a safe zone…Got it?" Mark stared at Mike the whole time he was speaking.

"Yes, sir."

"Oh, really now, Steve…those were all friends…"

"Even so…no more crowds." Mark leveled his gaze on her.

The women in the group stood looking at Mark, Tola, Mike and Dalisay from a distance chatting amongst themselves.

"That was rude," one said.

"Totally. Who does he think he is?"

"He just whisked Dalisay off like a dog on a leash. Our security would never do that."

Joris watched the move of his wife while listening to a business rival pontificate about his new microprocessor product line. A smile crossed his face. He looked to Roger who acknowledged his glance with a slight nod, never taking his eyes off the group surrounding his charge. His experience allowed him to keep an eye on Joris, the crowd and Mark's actions. *Smooth move boss.*

The event lasted two and a half hours and other than the extraction of Dalisay, it went smoothly. As the Barnhardt's and the team stepped outside the main clubhouse, Keit drove the limo under the white covered awning and remained behind the wheel.

A dozen staff attendants—dressed in black slacks, red shirts and white jackets trimmed in gold at the collar and cuff—directed traffic. The surrounding grounds, parking area and the street were heavily manned by armed Royal Thai Army soldiers. Mark, ever scanning the area for a threat, ushered the couple into the passenger compartment. *It's good to be King. Must be four hundred troops here today.*

"Blaster, shotgun. Mike…on me."

Once everyone was seated, the limo pulled out and onto the crowded street. The pair of motorbikes pulled from the curb and began to follow.

Mark opened the glass wall between the passenger area and the driver's compartment and spoke to Keit. "You recognize those trailers?"

"Yeah, boss."

"Give 'em a couple of u-turns."

"Coming up now, boss," Keit replied as he turned the extended vehicle effortlessly into the oncoming traffic and joined it.

"What's happening?" Joris asked.

"Practicing evasive driving. Nothing to be alarmed about, sir," Mark answered.

The two bikes made turns as well, but fell behind the limo and weaved quickly through the traffic to regain a position two cars behind.

Keit repeated the process then turned back into the entrance of the sporting club and stopped. The two bike riders pulled to the curb and parked.

"I'm stepping out. Keit…give me your stick."

Keit reached under his seat and retrieved a two foot long two inch thick length of polished mahgony—with a natural knurled ball on the end—and handed it back.

"Go in sixty seconds. I'll see you at the residence." Mark did not wait for a reply but stepped out of the vehicle and then with his cell phone to his ear—the mahogany baton hidden close to his body away from the cyclists—walked to the sidewalk. He choose a spot halfway between the entrance and exit of the private club to avoid close proximity to the armed troops.

"What's going on here?" Joris called out as the door slammed. "Where's he going?"

"We go home now," Keit said as he viewed his watch. At exactly one minute he put the car in gear and drove onto the street as instructed.

The two cyclists started to follow. The first driver, a smallish male wearing dark wraparound shades, a black ball cap on backwards and shoulder to hand fingerless gloves drove past Mark and looked at him but continued on. As the second driver approached, Mark stepped off the curb, threw out his arm and clothslined the driver with the wooden weapon then leapt back to the curb quickly.

"Uggg!" The woman—wearing a black helmet with the visor down and a light bike jacket—rolled down the street like a rag doll.

A white van rolled over the fallen woman with a sickening thump before it came to a stop. A subsequent vehicle slammed into the back, followed by the next one as well. Traffic squealed to a horn-blasting stop from the muti-car pileup.

Damn! Not going to get any intel out of that one Mark thought, seeing the helmet crushed and blood oozing out onto the dirty street. He ran to the fallen Suzuki cycle, jumped on and in three quick kicks, started the engine. He raced off after the other rider with smoke boiling off the rear tire.

Hearing the wreck behind him, the NPA looked back just in time to see the silver-haired man start the bike and get on. He quickly began to accelerate and sped past the limo.

Moments later Joris and Dalisay were surprised to see their head of security fly by as well—looking like a wild man on a mission—his long hair flowing in the breeze and his jacket flapping behind him exposing his shoulder rigs and pistols.

"What the hell is going on?"

"Boss man take motorcycle ride," Keit answered.

Mark chased the fleeing NPA through the traffic, weaving around the jostling vehicles. More than once he slid the bike sideways to avoid impact with a car or truck, and then fishtailed around them. *Shit! Wish I had the proper boots on.* He kept his thumb on the horn and blew it repeatedly to alert drivers he was passing. A large grasshopper impacted the right lens of his Bausch and Lomb sunglasses smashing them hard against his face and cracking the lens—leaving a golden smear of goo impairing his vision. *Crap!*

It was evident the man he pursued was an excellent driver by his evasive manuvers—twice pulling onto the sidewalk, racing through the pedestrians, knocking several off their feet.

At a intersection that circled a large fountain, he jumped his bike onto the trunk of a stopped car, drove over the top and front hood and continued his flight.

Unable to gain any ground Mark eased off the throttle just as a siren wailed. He looked back to see a squad car in pursuit. With a sly grin he moved to the curb and stepped off the bike. He removed his damaged sunglasses and gently touched the now swelling cheek bone and eyebrow. *Gonna be a hell of a shiner.*

As the police vehicle pulled to a stop, Mark took copies of his carry permit and get out of jail card from his inner jacket pocket and tapped them gently on his other palm. *Here we go. Better me than the boys. Gonna be interesting to see how these street cops deal with this goat rope.*

JORIS BARNHARDT'S RESIDENCE

Mark arrived in a Metropolitan squad car. He stepped out, entered the estate through the garage and walked to the lift. He paused to make sure the gates closed before he punched the call button. He found everyone waiting for him in the living room.

"I apologize for the confusion. Sometimes there's no time to explain things as they're unfolding," he said as he removed his jacket.

"What happened to your eye?" Dalisay asked a note of concern in her voice.

"Bug attack."

"Do you have time now?" Joris asked, a bit sarcastically.

"Yup. Keit and I noticed two motorcycles from the time we left your office. No reason to be tailing us unless they were up to no good. I wanted to…uh, question one of them."

"Did you?"

"Unfortunately, no. I dropped the second driver, but she was hit by a truck. The first driver got away as I was stopped by the local gendarmes."

"So all the dramatics for nothing. I've already received several calls from friends and associates asking if we are all right. Your actions created quiet a stir. I'm sure it will be the talk of the town by tomorrow morning," Barnhardt said tersely.

"Maybe we should continue this discussion in private, sir. I need to debrief with the team…"

"That won't be necessary. I assume your actions were valid. I only ask you consider our image before you create another incident," the Dutchman said before taking his wife by the arm and leading her to the elevator.

KWAI TSING CONTAINER TERMINALS 6
Hong Kong

Kwai Tsing was the main port facility in the reclamation along Rambler Channel between Kwai Chung and Tsing Yi Island, Hong Kong, and the third busiest in the world. The sheer volume of sea shipping containers that pass through terminal six daily was a perfect cover for the numerous illicit Triad activities.

Lu Sun sat in his top floor executive suite signing shipping documents that would take hundreds of containers to Vietnam, Shanghai, Singapore, Indonesia and the port of Davo in the Philippines. Twenty percent of the containers contained illegal contraband ranging from drugs, ivory, horn and human slaves.

Dressed in a custom-tailored three-piece suit he looked nothing like the image of a Triad gang leader—not one tattoo was visible. Two other Chinese men, dressed in black suits, stood on either side of his office door. A stunning blonde female who bore a striking resemblance to a twenty-five year old Sharon Stone—thanks to the booming plastic surgery business in Hong Kong—sat on a leather couch reading a copy of Cosmopolitan magazine, smacking her gum vigorously.

"There is a Mister Zhu asking to see you," his personal secretary called over the intercom.

"Send him up. Have him wait in the conference room. Once he is there, come in and get the shipping documents customs requested today."

"Yes, Mister Sun."

Lu collected the stack of documents and placed them in a 11x14 envelope as he spoke, "Sharon, I want you to go shopping. *No* more shoes…understood? Xin will accompany you. I will see you for dinner at eight."

"Yes, dear," the tall, slender, breast-enhanced woman responded as she stood and collected her black and white Chanel purse. She walked to his desk and kissed him dispassionately on the cheek before leaving.

"I want both of you waiting in the conference room when Zhu enters."

"Yes, master Lu," the two men responded.

The Triad leader kept Zhu waiting for an hour before he entered the room. Not that he had any other business, but to enforce his position as the man of importance.

"Zhu, very good to see you. What do you have for me today?"

"I have some information about the helicopter our brothers saw flying from Ching Wu's suite the night he was killed."

"It is about time…How many blue and white helicopters can there be in Hong Kong?"

"Thirty-five to be exact. Of those, thirty were quickly eliminated due to various reasons. The one of most interest has been identified and confirmed. It belongs to an American owned Import/Export business."

"Confirmed? You are now certain it is the one?"

"Yes, a mid-level transportation worker at the business informed one of our brothers the helicopter was used twice during the time frame for flights other than business. I will not bother you with the details, but we are now holding an Australian pilot who flew the aircraft on the night of Wu's death."

"This pilot…he has confirmed his participation?" Sun asked with a keen interest.

"Not yet…But he will. Our specialist from the mainland will be here tonight and conclude our investigation."

"Report your findings directly to me. No one else."

"Yes, Master Sun."

METROPOLITAN POLICE HEADQUATERS
Bangkok, Thailand

Chief of Police Charoen Nantakam, entered the CAF meeting room as Virote was concluding the morning briefing.

"Good morning, Chief," he said with a bit of surprise. The chief rarely came down to the rank and file meetings.

"What's the latest on the John and Susan Reynolds case?" he asked coolly.

"All intelligence seems to indicate it was the Inkong gang that abducted them. We had a tip they were being held in the Khlong Toei slum. I set up a joint search and rescue attempt but the night before we going in one of the tour boats exploded and diverted the river patrol from their position in the net. I suspect the cell escaped during the sweep."

"What leads do you have now?"

"We are squeezing every contact we have and I expect to have new intel today."

"When this meeting is adjourned I would like a word with you in private," Charoen said.

He nodded. "Dismissed men. Get out there and get something we can use."

The last man out closed the door with a knowing look to his superior. Whatever the chief had to say, it would not be good for the CAF department.

"The press, the US embassy and now a international human rights group are breathing down my neck...Not to mention the Minster of Tourism. If you do not have results in the next forty-eight hours I will be forced to turn this over to the military...You know what that will mean."

"Yes, sir. I am confident we will have new leads today."

"All right then. On another subject...You have any information linking the Reynolds case with the attempt to kidnap Joris Barnhardt?"

"Not at this time, sir...Do you?"

"No, but if you suspect the NPA in the Reynolds case there may be. Barnhardt has a new security team. A man named Steve McCallister heads it up. He applied for and received a PTC and a damned high-level get-out-of-any-jail card as well from the Ministry of Law a couple of days ago."

"Either of those usually takes weeks if not months to obtain. How did he do that?" Viktor asked, his interest slightly peaked.

"Patrick Murry at the US embassy made the call. I ran some background checks on this McCallister...he's a ghost."

"Really? You thinking...CIA?"

"No idea...but there is nothing on him. Why don't you arrange a meeting? Suggest a get-together to disclose current threats for foreigners living in Thailand. Whatever...use your imagination. Keep me posted on what you discover."

CRANK'S ESTATE

Crank was asleep when Kongkut knocked on his door. He rolled over one of the three sleeping Thai girls and stumbled to the door in his birthday suit. He picked up his S&W Model 29 from the bedside stand as he moved. *What would Zorro do?* He grinned at the thought as his ingrained training kicked in.

"Yeah?" he asked, standing to the side of the heavy teak door—his revolver held ready.

"Mister boss man is on the land line. Say he call you on your cell many time…No answer…Say it important."

Crank rubbed his eyes and yawned as he looked at his watch. *0600. Jesus, must be important if he's calling this early.* "Tell him I'm up now. Call me on the cell."

"Yes, Mister Crank…I tell him."

The big man crossed to the dresser where his cell phone lay in a jumble of other items, picked it up and turned it on. Sure enough there were four missed calls. Before he could return to the bed, it rang.

"Zorro…shit man…I'm tryin' to sleep here…"

"Yeah, yeah…I need you to get on the train today. Bring me four H&K subs, a twelve gauge pump and my over-and-under. Ammo all around…"

"You thinkin' of startin' a *little* war here?"

"Nope. But if one comes my way I want more than pistols. Jump the overnight at 1800. Meet you at the station. You can turn around and be back home in a day."

"How's the contract otherwise?"

"Easy money so far. Oh…tell that South Afrikaan brak to rhino up and get his ass healed."

"He's making progress…Walks the porch couple of times a day now and the wound's good enough to get in the pool."

"If he laid off the pressers you have romping about he'd be well by now."

"You're *really* startin' to sound like a grandpa now. See you tomorrow."

SECURITY HOUSE

The team sat around the living area when Mark entered. Everyone was dressed and ready to go about the day's duties.

"Tola, you and I are on Dalisay today. She's attending a fundraiser at the church. Blaster, Dog...on Joris. He's scheduled all day at the office...Anything changes call me. Keit...drop the client off, see your uncle about the car. Call me when you are up and moving again...Any questions?"

"Me," Mike said. "You laid out the event with the street cops yesterday during our debrief. How did they act when you gave them the papers?"

"They're in good order...evidently. If for some unforeseen reason you have a different experience...I have an iron clad rule...Never give up your weapon to *any* law enforcement officers...*ever*. Be nice, but be firm..."

"But what if they insist? Draw down on us?" Roger asked.

"Every situation is a judgment call. The card should be all you need...if you stay collected. I can tell you from experience...and that of other Ops...give up your piece... you risk entering a world of pain."

Tola stood up and put on her jacket. "Police uniforms used by bad guys every day. Last time I work with Zorro we stopped by impostors down south wearing Phuket police uniforms."

"What happened?" Mike asked.

"We shot them," she said. "Well…actually…Zorro shot them."

"Time to roll. Call me if anything looks off. See you back here tonight. Oh…the schedules Joris gave me indicate an down day tomorrow. Anyone wants to tour the town is cleared to do so. Back on duty 0600 the next day."

"All right! I definitely want to see some sites," Roger exclaimed jubilantly.

"Just remember…the get out of jail free card only applies to on duty activities. Get in a jam down at the Soi Cowboy district and you're on your own."

"Thanks for the tip…Any clubs you recommend?"

Tola and Keit exchanged a look and rolled their eyes.

"Tola get with Missus Barnhardt and Keit get the limo ready…complete sweep. Use the new electronics just like I showed you. The boys will be down with Joris in fifteen minutes"

After the two had left, Mark turned to Roger and Mike. "Nana plaza has several joints that are not too pricey. An inactive Marine buddy of my dad's owns the Rawhide club. You can tell Rocky I sent you."

"Which one has the best looking girls?" Blaster asked.

"They're all the same. The girls that work for Rocky are a little more…up scale…maybe. Better English if it matters to you. Let's get this day rolling."

HUA LAMPHONG STATION
Bangkok

Mark and Keit walked out of the station, each carrying a pair of large black cordura bags delivered by Crank. As they placed them in the trunk his cell phone rang.

"McCallister."

"Mister McCallister, this is Isra Charoenkul. Are we still on schedule to review the security system for the residency today?"

"Thanks for calling. The Barnhardt's have made a change in plans today and I will not be able to meet you. Also, I've changed my mind."

"I see. So the system is acceptable?"

"Thanks for calling. I have to go now."

Mark hung up. *Cluster after cluster. Have to get the system upgraded before any pop-ups come calling.*

"Difficulty?" Keit asked noting the look of dissatisfaction.

"Little one. No biggie…yet. You will have to stay with the vehicle 'til your uncle gets this ride checked out.."

"Okay, boss."

Inside the limo, Mark turned to his Filipina client. "Now we can go to the mall. Sorry for the delay."

"What's in the bags?"

"Tools of the trade." he responded with a look to Tola.

PAK KRET, THAILAND

Inkong lay on a woven mat on the wraparound porch of the stilt house three miles outside Pak Kret. Located in the middle of a coconut groove with visibility for a quarter mile in any direction it was a good place to hide for the gang while waiting for the ransom demands to be met. The thatch roof deflected most of the light rain that was falling and the cool breeze drifted through the house offering relief from the oppressive heat.

In a tiny room normally used to store provisions, Sharon and John Reynolds lay on several of the hundred pound bags of rice secured hand and foot, but no longer gagged or blindfolded. Both had long since stopped crying and lay exhausted and defeated…Their clothing was now a torn filthy rice bag infested with lice. A large Asian rat sat on a shelf above watching them with bright red eyes while gnawing on a sugar cane stalk.

The gang either slept in hammocks on the porch or, like Inkong, lay on woven mats. It had been a long night moving from the slum to the stilt house and all were exhausted.

Inkong's cell phone alerted him to a incoming text message.

Response to classified ad received. Money coming. Expect exchange in forty-eight hours.

The NPA cell leader smiled as he responded.

Acknowledged. Reply as ordered.

ZAMBOANGA del SUR
Philippines

The MNLF was on the move. They only had the oldest four children with them and the youngest Nun. The other hostages had been stoned to death or beheaded in the cave. Those left behind were deemed too old or too young to keep up.

"If any infidel falls behind...kill them," Isagni shouted to the men leading them.

Whomp, whomp, whomp—the sound of a distant helicopter caused everyone to fall to the side of an animal trail they were using to traverse the rough mountainside. It was the third they had heard that day and only reinforced the reality that the Philippine Army was still searching for them.

After the sound of the aircraft subsided to the east, the Muslims resumed their travel to the north.

***

CHAPTER SEVEN

MANDANGO RESTAURANT
Bangkok

The little hole-in-the-wall sari sari store and restaurant was empty other than the staff when the three entered. The shelves and counters were filled with food goods and items from the Philippines. Like most Filipino shops around the world it was a buffet and served a variety of dishes popular in the Philippines.

"Good afternoon, Dalisay. So good to see you. Thank you for coming today," the plump jovial Filipina bubbled in Visayan as she seated them. "Long time we no see you."

"I am sorry, Reginia. I rarely get out these days. How is your family?"

"They are good. Everyone is good. Thank you so much for asking...Toma...the usual for Até Dalisay," Regina called to a short, round Filipino behind the buffet bar. "What would you two like?"

"I'll take a look at the buffet. Tola stay with Missus Barnhardt," Mark answered to the owner then to Tola in Thai.

"On it," she replied as she sat down facing the entry door.

"You speak our language good. You know Philippines?"

"A little. Be right back."

Once Mark was out of hearing range, Reginia addressed Tola. "He very handsome man. He you boyfriend?"

"No. My boss...I'll just have whatever Missus Barnhardt is having, thanks."

Three middle-aged Filipino men entered from the street, throwing a sharp ray of sunlight across the dark cool room. Tola immediately stood up and stepped between them and Dalisay.

"Reginia, is our lechon ready yet?" one man asked.

"Yes...five minutes to wrap it up."

Mark had turned when the door opened and had his left hand under his jacket resting on the butt of his pistol. Realizing the men were known to the owner, he returned to placing his order with her daughter as well as taking a closer look at a possible exit route.

Tola remained standing but relaxed her grip on the Walther 9mm she carried in the small of her back.

Mark's cell rang as the three were finishing their meal. He did not recognize the local number but decided to answer it. "Hello."

"Hello, is this Mister McCallister?"

"Who is this?"

"Virote Pradchaphet, head of the crimes against foreigners with the Metropolitan police. Am I speaking with Steve McCallister?"

"Yes."

"I got your number from a mutual friend, Patrick Murry. I was wondering if you and I could meet today."

"I'm working. If you care to come by the Assumption Cathedral…say between 1400 and 1600, I'll be glad to visit with you."

"Very good. I'll be there, Mister McCallister."

"What's this about?"

"I would like to bring you up to date on some crimes against foreigners here in Bangkok."

"Thanks. Could use all the help we can get. Good-bye."

Tola and Dalisay's expressions showed their interest in the call.

"Let's get moving." Mark checked his watch.

ASSUMPTION CATHEDRAL

Nestled in a historic area off Charoen Krung Road near the Chao Phraya River, the Assumption Cathedral was the oldest Catholic church in Thailand. Built in the late seventeen hundreds—when the capital was moved from Ayutthaya to Bangkok—and designed by a French architect the structure exemplified the cathedral's of Europe though not as lavish in detail. Inside, the cathedral had a sloped ceiling leading to a classic sanctuary beneath frescoes reminiscent of the Italian Renaissance. Outside extensive open grounds, were a convent and two huge bronze statutes—one of Saint Peter, the other of Pope John Paul II—stood at the main entrance.

They had taken a cab from the sari sari store—again changing cabs along the route. Dalisay paid the last driver and offered a generous tip for his service.

Mark stepped out first, followed by Tola then Missus Barnhardt. After removing the items purchased at the mall they walked into the cathedral through a side door that led directly into a large meeting hall. Though not air-conditioned the dark interior was pleasantly cool compared to the humid afternoon heat outside. Mark noted the iron metal floor grates along the walls. *Cool air? Who ever designed this place used some good ol' common sense. Bet there's a basement with outside ducts sucking in hot air, then cooling it before it rises into this room.* He looked up and spotted a row of open windows along each wall near the ceiling.

As the women mingled about—attending to duties necessary for the annual upcoming bizarre and auction—Mark noticed a Russian operative he had competed against some years before. They had vied for first place at a international long-range shooting event. In the end they both lost to a female Chinese competitor who later defected and went to work for Hal McCambell.

"Tola, I see someone I need to speak with…Back in five."

"Good to go, boss."

As Mark approached, Urie turned, extended his hand and greeted him with a thick Russian accent, "Zorro, good to see you old friend."

"You as well, Urie. Wondered where you ended up."

"I be here now three years. Very good duty…rich German industrialist. You new security for the Barnhardts?"

"For a couple of months. So…what's the lay of the land? Who are the number ones?"

"Mostly the NPA. Some troubles with the muslims. Always the troubles with them…My card," he said as he handed a dark gold one with black lettering to him. "You should call me. We drink some good vodka."

Mark dialed Urie's number.

The burly Russian's cell rang.

"Now you have my number. I may visit an old buddy of my dad's…he owns a club here. Depends on how things go…If I do I'll call you."

"The Rawhide? I know it…Rocky is good man…for a Texan. You know those Texans pindos…always a little crazy," Urie said with a wry smile.

"Good to know. Look…I gotta get back."

"You call me…we go see Rocky…you tell me all about Kenya."

"Kenya?"

"Oh yez…Malikhi come to see me last week before he go home. He said you have a big time in Kenya."

"Not that big, old friend…Later."

Virote Pradchaphet entered the room wearing a rumpled tan suit that had seen better days. He removed his cheap Ray Ban knockoff sunglasses and scanned the room. Seeing only one man that fit the description given to him by Patrick Murry, he made his way through the crowd of laughing, chattering women as they prepared items for the upcoming blind auction.

Mark stood a few feet from his client conversing with a priest of French and Thai descent, "How long have you been at this parish?"

"Thirty-three years now. I am surprised at your grasp of our language. The last two men who would come with Dalisay to mass were not versed at all."

"I hope to improve my skills while I am here…"

"Mister McCallister? I am Virote Parddchaphet."

Mark had watched the man approach and was surprised to see the him arrive so promptly. *A man on a mission I suspect.* Switching to English, "Good to meet you…Father, if you will excuse me."

"Of course my son. Come back any time. You are always welcome in the house of the Lord."

Mark and Virote moved to a position directly behind Dalisay. Tola—seeing her boss' move—rotated between the client and the entry door.

"You have any leads on who attempted to kidnap Barnhardt yet?"

"Nothing substantial but we have strong suspicions it was a NPA cell led by a man called Inkong."

"Any idea where this guy is hiding out?"

"We had a lead that he was in Khlong Toei, but he eluded a joint task force sweep of the slum...so at present...no. I was informed by the Chief of Police that you acquired several documents for you and your staff that normally take some time to get."

Mark kept his eyes on the entrance door and a small side door. "Patrick Murry assisted me."

"Yes, Minister Murry confirmed that he did. The Chief is...curious, though...it seems he was unable to find any details about you."

"Is that a problem?"

"Ah...well not in and of itself...but you must admit it is disconcerting for the Chief. He's a very thorough sort of man..."

"When you called you said you wanted to fill me in on details pertaining to threats for foreigners," Mark said as he turned his eyes to Virote.

The policeman was taken back for a moment. He had seen plenty of blue eyed westerners over the years but none had such a piercing gaze. "Yes...yes of course. I suggest you come down to my office...at your convenience of course and let me show you what we are dealing with."

"I just got boots on the ground. Give me a couple of days. Need to get the kinks worked out before I take any time away from the Barnhardts."

"I understand. Feel free to call me any time," Virote extended his hand with a business card.

"Thanks. I'll do that," Mark replied still holding a steady gaze into the officer's eyes. *Measures up to be okay...so far. Stinks of cigarette smoke though. Always good to have someone in the LEO community on standby.* "Do you have the means to get myself and my team onto a quiet range? I like to blow a few hundred rounds a week, at least."

"That would explain the little exhibition you put on at the Wat Pho range the other day."

Mark was a little taken aback but quickly looked around the room to disguise it. "Word travels fast. So...do you have a range where we can practice?"

"I do. Call me when you are ready." Virote started to walk away. He turned as he spoke, "Oh...my bother-in-law was the master range officer the day you gave the demonstration. I look forward to...popping a few caps with you...That is how you Americans say it?...Right?"

A smile crossed Mark's face. *Not sure why yet...but I like this guy.* "I'll be bringing other operatives with me."

Virote did not look back, but waved as he walked off.

YACHT CLUB ISLE de SOL
St. Maarten/St. Martin

Situated 150 miles east of Puerto Rico, the Dutch island Saint Maarten fell under the government of Netherlands Antilles and the Kingdom of the Netherlands. Its diversity and the strong influence of West-Indian traditions made its culture anything but exclusively Dutch. St. Maarten's atmosphere was a winning blend of Caribbean hospitality and European sophistication.

DARK SECRET

The Yacht Club at Isle de Sol was ideally situated near the Simpson Bay Bridge. The St. Maarten marina had a highly secure and private ambiance, not to mention impressive facilities and professional staff on-hand seven days a week to help provision and provide most services, amenities, or requirements desired by those rich enough to dock there. Unlike other St. Maarten marinas, this one catered exclusively to mega yachts and the reputation of the Isle de Sol was second to none in the world.

Thijs Vandeputte lay on a deck lounge chair on his 252 foot Smeralda Motor Yacht, custom built in 2012 by Hanseatic Marine. With accommodation for up to eight guests in four suites—comprising one owner cabin, three VIP cabins, plus eight additional cabins—all retrofitted to accommodate his recording and duplication of high quality child pornography.

His phone rang interrupting his noonday nap. "Hello," he answered with a deep Netherlands's roll.

"I have not received the figures from the last quarter. Send them to me via secure line by noon tomorrow your time," the familiar voice of his business partner said.

"Of course. You will be very pleased...as I recall your share is a little over fifty million."

"Yes, the funds are in my account. I would like to see the details. Not that I don't trust you old friend...but you know me...always a stickler for the details."

"Consider it done. How soon can you send me some new raw footage? I have pre-orders in the thousands for our next *Little Ones Go to Heaven* releases."

111

"Shipped them yesterday. I will send you the tracking number as soon as we are off the line. Should be there in three days at the latest. What other titles are selling well?"

"*Sweet Baby Blondes* is holding steady in Japan and in the middle-east. *Chocolates From Around the World* is very disappointing again last quarter...mostly sold in the US, Canada and western Europe. *Asian Delights* is doing well around the market place over all...I am receiving hundreds of requests from the camel jockeys for more redheads...and donkeys...Those guys are seriously sick you know?"

"Ha Thijs...all our clients are seriously sick...at least by the morally right. I cannot assist you with the redheads. Talk to our woman in Ireland. As for *Asian Delights,* I expect some exciting new footage within three weeks."

"One other thing, the magistrate here is asking for a five percent increase. Claims he is dealing with more and more Interpol and US FBI investigators of late."

"Uh-uh! Offer him...a two percent increase. If he doesn't take it, we move the operation."

"Hate for that to happen. Saint Maartin is as close to heaven as one can get. I will proffer the offer and get back to you. Oh...how are your wife and son?"

"I have told you repeatedly Thijs...no personal conversations when we are on the phone."

"I apoligize..." Thijs looked at his cell when he realized the line was dead. "So damn anal."

NAIROBI, KENYA

A gentle vibration alerted the owner a call was coming in on her covert cell phone. The elegantly dressed black woman excused herself from the wives she was listening to brag about how important their husbands were and walked out onto to the patio of the Muthaiga Country Club.

"Yes," she answered.

"Our new manager arrived today. He will contact you tomorrow at the latest," the voice said with a light Chinese accent in his English.

"Good. He can deliver the cash to the new drop box and we will get started again."

"Did you have a chance to collect the shipping documents I requested the last time we spoke?"

"They are in the drop box now. I have to get back…"

"One more thing, Madame X. Our last two managers met untimely deaths. Would you happen to know who arranged it?"

"No."

"If you happen to hear anything…our mutual friends would be very generous."

"How generous?"

"Say…two hundred thousand pounds."

"I'll let you know if I hear anything. Good-bye," Lutto said before hanging up. *Tidy sum. Have to find out what Mobutto knows about this* she thought as she headed back into the gala event celebrating the return of calm in Kenya after the violent coup attempt by rogue elements of the Kenyan army.

MALPAIS, COSTA RICA

Kari—formerly Chikako before Hal McCambell scubbed her identity—lay in a mosquito net hammock, high above a long secluded beach below wearing only a pair of blue running shorts and a yellow tank top. Half a world away from Bangkok it was midnight. Behind her, a dark green and black eight-person family tent stood in a small opening she had hired cleared by hand the first day she arrived.

Her meager supplies of food hung from branches in a large Pochote tree—the thorns of which she had carefully trimmed off with a machete. The sweet aroma of the tree's delicate flower wafted over her campsite. Near the tent a pair of Grain surf boards—constructed from Maine cedar by hand then covered with a layer of fiberglass and three coats of epoxy resin—waited for her next wave adventure.

She chose Malpais for it's isolation and natural beauty as a place to regroup and start her life anew. Finally free of the Yakuza, she gazed at the world-class surf below shimmering in the moonlight and thought of the last days in Hong Kong. *I'm free…no more looking over my shoulder. No more contracts. Build a little bungalow…open a surf shop up the beach…maybe just…live till the savings run out and see what comes.*

A hundred and thirty kilometers to the nearest airport in San Jose, accessible by a dirt road noted as highway 160 and eighteen kilometers from Montezuma—closest town of any size where supplies could be purchased. She had chosen wisely as a place to disappear.

The lush green jungle around her ran down to the beach and behind the twenty acres atop a low knoll she purchased—all the way to the Cabo Blanco Absolute Reserve—itself a vast uninhabited area that encompassed three thousand acres. The sound of the diverse wildlife was all she heard other than the breaking of the waves below on the normally deserted beach.

The deep wound in her shoulder—delivered by Zhang during the assault on Ching Wu's fortress in Hong Kong with Zorro and Crank—was mostly healed, but still tender when she overtaxed it like when she helped clear the campsite or earlier in the day when she surfed. She rubbed a light coat of coconut oil mixed with aloa vera gel on the scar as she viewed the open night sky. *I could get use to this. No cars, trains or airplanes...no guns, knives or swords...Maybe a dog...I've seen videos of surfing dogs.*

As she drifted off to sleep under the sky filled with stars her thoughts turned to the man who had saved her—only one night in his arms, but one never to be forgotten. *If only I had met you now rather than then.* Then a deep sleep swept all thoughts aside and Kari became a part of the jungle that surrounded her.

THE PEAKS
Hong Kong

Lu Sun sat on the patio of his luxurious 3,200 square foot townhouse located on what was known as The Peaks—the most exclusive location in Hong Kong. The address was both prestigious and peaceful, located amidst green surroundings with facilities including a pool and tennis court. Reclining on a lounge chair, his movie-star look-alike mistress sunbathed in the nude. *This bitch is starting to bore me. Have to replace her soon. Maybe a younger model...like a Lindsay Lohan type.*

His thoughts were interrupted by his cell. He looked at the caller ID. "Hello, Zhu."

"The Australian died before he could tell us who he flew off Chang's rooftop..."

"How could that happen? Our interrogator has never lost a subject."

"The Aussie bit his tongue off and bled out between interview sessions."

"Damn!...Keep searching...Raid the offices of the import/export business. Find me a name!" Lu yelled.

"Yes, master..." He was cut off as Lu Sun disconnected the call.

JORIS BARNHARDT RESIDENCE

Joris entered the living area to find Dalisay and Tola watching a popular Filipino talk show—Kris TV. Both women were laughing uncontrollably at the antics of the host and her guests.

"Please turn that down," the tired Dutchman said as he made his way to the kitchen.

Dalisay quickly turned the television off. Tola stood up out of respect for her client. Joris continued on without another word.

"He doesn't like my shows much," Dalisay said.

"I understand..."

"Dalisay, come in the kitchen."

116

Mark exited the lift just as he called to his wife. "Tola, take a break. The boys are going to do some self-defense work on the lawn. Join them…and don't hurt or embarrass them too much before I get there…Okay?"

"Yes, boss."

As his wife started to the door, Joris returned to the living area. "Ah…McCallister…glad you're here. I want to lay down some ground rules concerning my wife's activities."

Neither Mark nor Dalisay spoke, both waiting to hear what was on his mind.

"We will be going to Cebu next week. While I am attending to the opening of a new orphanage, Dalisay wants to visit her family. Do you need to hire more people?"

"I will need two additional men. I've already contacted a ICC in…"

"Our son, Rutger will be accompanying us as well. You will have to provide for their safety as well as mine in two completely different locations."

"Not a problem. I will detail the ICC to stay with you, Roger and Mike. I'll take Tola and visit the family."

"It's Muslim country down there. I'd feel a lot better if you had more men."

"I'll see to it immediately. I'm certain Berto will not mind having one of his sons join us. I've worked with both in the past. I've found them very reliable…Well versed in the local difficulties…Anything else, sir?"

"Not for now." Joris took his wife by the arm and lead her into the kitchen.

SECURITY HOUSE

Mark stood looking out the glass doors at Blaster, Dog and Tola working out. It was evident Blaster relied on his size and strength, while Dog appeared better adapt at his self-defense skills using speed.

Tola stood to the side stretching as the two men sparred. To the untrained eye it appeared as if she was ignoring them. In fact, she was watching and evaluating every move they made.

Zorro removed his coat and draped it on one of the recliners before joining them outside. He unsnapped the belt loops on his two shoulder rigs, removed them and laid them on the glass table under the patio awning. He stepped out of his shoes, socks and emptied his pockets before beginning to stretch—well aware the two new operatives were watching him.

"Going to join us?" Dog asked.

"Nope. Have my own routine. Just thought I'd referee for you three."

"Three?" Blaster asked with a sideways glance to the woman as she twisted and turned through a Muay Thai form with such effortless grace it looked like ballet.

"Let me know when you're ready, Tola," Mark said with a sly smile crossing his face.

"Oh...I don't know...wouldn't be fair...she's got no chance Zorro..." Mike said hesitantly.

"Ready."

"Okay, then. We'll start with a little two on one. Whenever you guys are ready...begin," Zorro stated matter of factly.

Roger and Mike looked to each other with disbelief, shrugged their shoulders, did a fist bump and turned towards her just as she landed a flying roundhouse kick on the side of Blaster's head as she flew by—the ball of her foot impacting him behind the left ear.

Before he hit the ground, she flipped 180 degrees— landing on her hands—whirled and stuck Dog with a powerful falling roundhouse back heel to the jaw—knocking him to the deck with stars blurring his vision.

Both men feebly rolled to their knees, shook their heads and staggered to their feet. They turned toward her as she leapt in the air, cocking both feet and delivered a lightening fast front snap kick to each man's solar plexus. The two hulking giants went down like a sack of rocks—landing hard on their backs.

As deftly as she had leapt to strike, she landed between them and was about to plant a palm smash in their defenseless faces.

"Hold!" Mark called out quietly before he extended a hand to each man. "Never judge a book by it's cover, gentlemen. Truth be known...she could open a can of whoop-ass on all three of us and never break a sweat."

"Jesus man...I didn't know it was going to be full contact," Dog replied as he grabbed Zorro's hand and stood up on wobbly legs.

"Enough of the nice guy. Let's go again," Blaster said angrily as he rolled over and pushed up on hands and knees.

Mark looked to Tola, who nodded yes. "Go."

Before Roger could stand she landed a full-on side kick to his head, literally knocking him unconscious—the sound of his neck popping gave Mark cause for concern—before she jumped over him intent on landing a whirling elbow smash to Mike's face.

"Shit!" Dog exclaimed as he fell and rolled way, then quickly bounced back to his feet in a defensive position. Looking down on his buddy he realized he was in it alone.

"I tie hands behind my back if you like?" Tola said with a wicked grin.

Mike circled to his left then back to his right before feinting a move to his left again but instead spun and rushed forward with a series of rapid hand blows and strikes. Tola dropped to her right knee, placed her right hand on the ground and drove her left foot—heel first—into his balls.

"Ahhh…," was all he could say as his breath rushed out and he face-planted on the lawn, holding the damaged family jewels.

"Wanta play some Chinese checkers?" Mark asked.

"What about boys?"

Mark glanced at the two men laid out on the well-manicured lawn in the late evening sun. "They can join us when they're ready…Oh…well done, young lady."

"I was wonder why you wait so long?" Tola asked as they entered the cool air-conditioned living room.

"It's all in the timing…you know? Always best to let a man get acclimatized before you school 'em."

Seeing his smile, she broke out laughing. "You one clever man, Zorro."

"How's your daughter doing?"

"She is good. Thank you for ask...Doctor say one more operation and her lip all good."

"Let me know when..."

"I pay this one, Zorro. You give me work now. I pay."

"I...ah...*inherited* some money from my last gig. Let me help you one more time..."

"I pay." The tone of her voice let him know it was not up for discussion.

"You have someone she can stay with while we are in the Philippines?"

"Stay with my family. Like last time...like now. You should come see her. She like you very much."

"I would enjoy that, Tola. Let's get this contract running smooth and I will. How about after we get back from the land of no planning."

"Where that?"

"Inside joke. Everyone who has worked in the seven thousand islands learns pretty quick...the Filipinos have no word for *plan* in any of their dialects. Hence...The land of no planning."

"You not like live there my friend...you always have plan."

"Prefer to...and always good to have a backup...Have you been able to keep up your weapons training?"

"Two time each week. Why?"

"Mindanao is like...well, you know, like the old west sometimes."

"How that?"

"Wild and wooly...A time in America...back in the eighteen hundreds. No real law except what a person could make for themselves. Much like down south here in Thailand now. The mussies are running amuck...whacking off heads like there's no tomorrow."

Tola considered his comment for a moment, "You know the Muslims are devils? Pure evil."

"Agreed. Still living in the seventh century...but ya get 'em in a crowd...egging each other on...it gets ugly quick."

"Or as I hear you say many times...a target rich environment," she said with a laugh.

***

CHAPTER EIGHT

AYSEN REGION, CHILE
Hans Schoepke's Ranch

The one thousand acre home place was everything he had ever wanted. Vast panoramic views of the towering Andes, world-class fly fishing in the many rivers and streams both on the ranch and nearby three miles of shoreline on glacier-fed Lake Riesco allowed for his passion for sailing. It was remote, secluded, pristine—all paid for with cash.

He had married a native woman, Francisca—twenty-three years younger than he, from a prominent well-connected family. She had borne him two sons and a daughter—all were home-schooled and in the top five percent of their peers scholastically.

Hans sat on the deck of his boathouse enjoying a leisurely breakfast with Francisca when he received Maggie's text message concerning Mark's request to speak to him.

"Who is it, love?" Francisca asked in English with a lyrical touch of her native language.

"Zorro...you remember him? He was at the McCambell event in Miami a couple of years ago."

"I do. Handsome rugged cowboy sort. Angelica was very taken with him."

"I've been told he has that effect on women. I should return his call, darling...Excuse me," he said as he stood and started walking down the pier to his Oyster 625 yacht. When he was not working, the electronics genius would spend days sailing on the sixty-one foot ship that afforded any luxury he desired as he had it custom built. Getting it to Lake Riesco had cost a small fortune in itself.

As he waited for Mark to answer, he stepped onto the deck and moved to the stern.

"Zorro."

"Hans, hola, mi amigo."

"What can I do for you today?" He continued to walk the perimeter of his ship inspecting every detail with loving care.

"I need some heavy security for a client...Upgrade his old system. Need sixteen cameras, multiple entry code keypads, elevator lock down, entry gate access, twenty-four-seven data recording system...And any new gadgets you have laying around."

"How soon?"

"Last week."

"Ha ha ha...the price just jumped. Where?"

"Bangkok...Wealthy Dutchman survived a kidnapping attempt and I've taken over his security. How much for you to install it personally?"

"Ha...the price just jumped again...I would only consider it if Francisca agrees to come with me...All expenses on the client's dime...of course."

"Absolutely. How soon can you get here...and how long to complete?"

Hans stopped his inspection of the ship and gazed out at the crystal clear lake. A Chilean black-chested eagle—considered the largest eagle species in the world—swooped down and pulled a trout from the water for breakfast. They shared a moment as the eagle passed over the stern looking him in the eye as drops of ice cold lake water dripped down and struck the slender white-haired computer guru on the shoulder. "If my wife agrees...we could be at the airport in...two days. I'll order the components from a manufacturer after I see the site. Most likely take a couple more days to receive the items. Say...two weeks max."

"If the client is agreeable, you two can stay at his place. There's more than enough room. If not...there are several five star accommodations that would make for a nice getaway."

"I have very specific dining requirements..."

"Master Chef lives and dies to please here. Send me the checklist."

"Bangkok...It's been what ?...Thirty years since I saw the Big Mango." Hans thought of his last visit. "Just estimating but

I suspect what you are seeking will cost...a hundred thousand. Plus expenses."

"Pocket change here. Get Francisca excited about the trip and call me back. Later, old friend."

The Mensa society computer wizard pocketed his cell phone and began adjusting the tie-downs to his mainsail. Not that they needed it but because he was beyond fixated on perfection—so much so he weighed his cereal in the morning each day and only wore clothing tailored to his specifications.

Some considered him odd for all his idiosyncrasies, but none denied his superiority when it came to anything electronic. With a master's degree from MIT and one from Columbia University in electrical engineering—as well as hundreds of patents on devices used around the world by security firms and operatives, he was the go-to guy—hands down.

SECURITY HOUSE

Tola and Mark sat playing Chinese checkers while listening to the *Best of The Bird*—Charlie Parker—when Roger and Mike finally entered the house. Both men gave a look to her that said volumes about the short lesson she had given—and a new sense of respect.

"We have been invited to eat in the big house tonight. Get clean up. Business casual...wear your piece on the ankle," Mark said without looking up from the board game. "Plenty of ice in the freezer if you need it."

Roger held the side of his head in one hand as he spoke, "I'll pass. Rather go into town..."

"Not an option. Tonight we all dine with the Barnhardts. You can hit the streets when we're finished," Mark replied with a look to both men.

"No parties start before midnight on Soi Cowboy," Tola said. "Man show up early...too needy. Girls no take them serious...just take their money, honey."

Blaster and Dog were taken back by her statement. It was the most she had said to either since they met her.

"And you know this...*how*?" Blaster asked.

"Tola use to work for Rocky."

"You worked in one of the clubs?" Mike asked incredulously.

"Oh yeah...she was his number one in security. Saw her toss four drunken Italian sailors around like ping pong balls one night. Made her an offer she couldn't refuse...Get shaking, we go in twenty," Mark relayed as he stood up and stretched. "Tola, wear something...refined tonight. The jade dress will do."

"No bring it, boss. But I have dark blue one that is cut same same. You see...you like it."

PAK KRET, THAILAND

Members of the Inkong NPA gang sat in a circle eating a meager meal of dog and rice. Their leader was reading from a short pamphlet by Karl Marx and Friedrich Engles titled *The Communist Manifesto*—first published in 1848. Just as Inkong finished, his cell rang.

"Yes."

"Everyone is at the residence. Can we secure our vigil?"

"One must stay. Everyone else can stand down until 0500." He disconnected and looked around at the men and women in the small room. "If we do not hear from the Americans soon...we will remove one ear from the woman. That way they will be truly...balanced."

The group laughed hard at his joke about the ying and yang.

One of the younger men stood up and said, "It's my turn...one last poke before she has only one ear."

The group laughed even harder as the nineteen year old walked from the room and into the dimly lit storage space where Susan and John Reynolds lay bound.

JORIS BARNHARDT RESIDENCE

Val himself brought in the main dish—Rookworst he had prepared personally to Joris' liking—followed by the staff, each with a side dish of stampot as well as smoked eel and raw herring. He placed the food on the long white linen-covered table. Fine cut-crystal glasses were filled with spring water imported by the case from Holland and stout steins with the Barnhardt family crest were filled with light Grolsch Dutch pale lager.

Once the table was properly set, the chef and his staff returned to the kitchen to make ready the desert.

"Dalisay, would you please say grace before we begin enjoying this fine meal?" Joris asked.

"Dear heavenly father, please bless this food to the nourishment of our bodies and minds. Give us the strength to do your will at all times. Lead us not into temptation but protect us from all evil. In Jesus Christ's name we pray," she prayed softly.

"I asked Val to prepare a traditional Dutch meal tonight to celebrate the joining of our lives. We are very grateful that you are here to protect us from those who seek to harm us. I say this now as I am sometimes a bit headstrong and it may not seem like I appreciate your efforts at all times…Shall we begin?" Joris nodded to the three young boy wait staff who immediately began to serve portions of every dish.

"Mister McCallister where are you from originally?" the Dutchman asked cordially.

Mark glanced at the other operatives before he spoke, "It's standard policy not to give out too much personal information, sir. In certain situations, the wrong people can get hold of it and be a threat to our families back home…I hope you understand."

The team sat quietly observing the exchange—Roger and Mike absorbing a new rule for the future. Keit and Tola continued to eat unconcernedly.

"Are you a Christian?" Joris continued to probe.

"Yes. Though I don't attend any service on a regular basis…How about yourself?"

"Most certainly. I am Roman Catholic as is Dalisay. Which reminds me…it is not on the schedules we gave you, but we attend mass frequently. In fact the mass this Sunday is one we would like to attend…Is that a problem?"

"Not at all. Tola and I will go with you. The boys are going out for some night life after dinner and I doubt they will be back in time to join us."

"Night life in Bangkok is sometimes very…lurid. I hope you will not succumb to the flesh pots on Soi Cowboy," Dalisay remarked.

"Ahh…no ma'am. Just want to see some sights," Mike said too quickly.

The general conversation continued without further awkwardness, mostly revolving around the meal, sports and world events. Once the main meal was complete the chef led the staff in with bowls of dessert for everyone.

"Wow…This is rich…what is it?" Mike asked.

"It is an old Dutch treat called hangop. Full fat yogurt, heavy cream, raw sugar with vanilla beans. Care for some fresh fruits?" Joris responded.

"It's delicious," Roger added. "I'll take some strawberries."

Another half hour passed before Mark said, "Time for us to go. Thank you both for the fine meal and hospitality. What time is the mass tomorrow?"

"We attend the 11 am mass normally," Dalisay replied.

"Keit will have the limo ready by 1030 hours then. Goodnight and thanks again." Zorro got up and nodded to the team.

SOI COWBOY DISTRICT

Roger and Mike stepped out of a cab near the entrance to the Nana Plaza entrance. After paying the driver, both men stood wide-eyed staring at the glitz and glitter of the flashing neon lights. The mingled sounds of a dozen different styles of music created a undefinable blend of noise. A dozen of the more than hundreds of street girls approached hawking their services.

"You number one. Me number one. We boom boom all night long," a slender woman who barely looked fifteen said.

"Me tongue you long time. Fifty dolla," another chimed in as she grabbed Mike's arm.

"I make you foget wife and gulfwind right away. Fifty dolla all night you neva foget," a older woman yelled. It was evident she had worked many a night and now was grasping at any trick she could turn.

"No thanks…let go of me," Mike responded as he made his way down the street.

"Beat it, bitch," Roger said as he pushed the older woman aside.

"You gurlie boys…right?" another young girl yelled. "No like gurls. You suckie dick."

"Aggressive little cunts," Roger remarked as the two began to stroll the mile long avenue of go-go bars and strip clubs.

Each club had it's own style and the loud music that blared over the exterior speakers alerting the passerby what might await inside. One named the Red Horse had sixties American rock and roll—another named Slick Willie's had country and western. Several had hard-driving euro techno music pulsing to the flashing lights.

At every entrance were the enticers—women dressed in scanty attire, mostly far younger and better looking than the ones inside. Some clubs had pedestals with a pole on each side of the entrance and young girls gyrated to the music with far away vacant looks in their eyes. Most were on some drug or the other to kill the pain of their existence.

"Hey! There's the Rawhide…I say we start there," Mike yelled to be heard over the noise.

"Works for me. Should have asked what the going rate was. Fifty on the street could mean a hundred in the club,"

"Those girls back there were rough as rusty nails and probably jerked you off on the price."

Inside, the two were hustled toward a table by a older female hostess. Mike noticed two stools at the bar and shook her off and lead Roger to the long dark, well-worn mahogany bar. "Better view from here. And the flies don't seem as thick," he said nodding at the girls moving from table to table offering to sit with the patrons.

"Man there's some smoking hot girls on the stage."

"Two beers," Mike yelled to the bartender, a thirtish woman wearing black short shorts and a black bikini top.

"Daft oh bottle?"

"What draft do you have?"

"You fom USA? We have any USA daft you want."

"Miller lite?"

"Two Milla lite coming up."

"I'd do her in a heart beat," Blaster said as he watched her walk away.

When she returned with the beers Mike leaned in and asked, "Is the owner in tonight? A friend of his said to look him up."

"I don't know Wocky had any fwiends," the woman replied with a devilish smile. "What you fwiend's name? I see if Wocky in office. Maybe not yet."

"Tell him Steve McCallister recommended his place to us."

"I see. You wait," she said again with a smile.

"Oh, man…a night with her and a steaming hot bowl of Wolf Brand chili…I could die and go to heaven a happy man," Blaster said as he leered at the disappearing bartender.

Suddenly the lights dimmed and the disc jockey announced, "Stand by hard dicks. The amazing Sheila is next on the stage."

A single spot lit the side entrance to the raised stage and a stunning beauty danced out to the sounds of Led Zeppelin's Stairway to Heaven.

"Holy shit!" Roger exclaimed.

Both men were mesmerized by the exotic beauty performing on the center stage solo. All the other girls were off in the crowd working their admirers.

"Wocky say he no know you fwiend," the woman behind the bar said as she tugged on Mikes arm.

"No way…His dad and Rocky were in the Marines together," Mark replied unable to take his eyes of the dancer.

"Solly."

"Hey…just a minute. Ask him if he knows Zorro," the young operative asked as he turned to the bar keep.

"Zowwo? Zowwo is here?" she asked looking around the club furtively.

"No, he's not here tonight. We work with him…"

"You tell him come see Tatana. He no leave Bangkok he no come see me."

"Yeah, sure," Mike replied as he turned back to the stage and remarked, "Seems the old dog beat you to it, Blaster."

"Hell...one night with me and she would forget all about Zowwo."

Both laughed as they sipped their beer.

A few minutes later a big Caucasian with a long gray biker mustache and a black patch over his left eye approached the two. "Tatana says you know Zorro," he asked with a strong Texas drawl.

"Yes, sir. We work with him," Mike replied taking his eyes off the performer long enough to see a late sixties six footer—wearing a olive drab T-shirt, black leather vest, jeans and exotic snakeskin cowboy boots—standing beside him.

"Tatana...beers on my tab," he yelled as he pointed at Roger and Mike. "You like?" he asked as he looked to the dancer.

"Oh, hell yeah." Roger blurted out.

"She's a he," Rocky responded with a hearty laugh.

"What? No friggin' way, man!"

"Oh...way. Voted most beautiful dancer in Bangkok three years runnin'. Costs me three hundred a performance, but he... she draws 'em in every night."

"Damn," Mike muttered.

"Plenty of other girls, boys. See any one else you like, let Tatana know. All the girls in the red outfits are seventy-five a night...plus bar fine. The ones in blue or white are only fifty."

"Bar fine?"

"If you want to take 'em out of the club you have to pay me for loss of drink money…Same in every club. The fine is twenty-five."

"So…a hundred bucks?"

"Can be…Then there's the tip. Most of the girls consider ten to twenty acceptable. But hey…compared to a date back in the states, it's a bargin…and you know you're gonna get laid."

"Rooms on site?" Mike asked.

"Hell no. Big problem. You have to take the girls some where else to do the deed. I recommend the White Lily. Not too pricey and the sheets are clean…Air conditioned, too."

"Jezz…looking at over a hundred bucks easy," Blaster said disappointedly.

"There's always the street girls…but I wouldn't recommend it. AIDS is pretty prevalent around here and she may just have a boyfriend or a pimp that will storm in while you're getting your whistle blown and roll you."

"Tatana! Two more Miller lites," Mike called out over the blaring end to the Zeppelin song.

"Gotta get back to being the boss around here. Tell Zorro to come see me."

"Will do, Rocky. And thanks for the beers," Dog answered. "If that's a man…we're going to have to check the package on any girl we think of taking out of here," he said as he took a long swig of the cold beer.

"Ten four that…I'm liking the little spinner at the end of the bar. She's been eyeballing me ever since we came in. I'll be baack," Blaster said in his best Arnold Schwarzenegger impersonation.

VIROTE'S APARTMENT

The head of the CAF sat staring out the window as the sun broke through the early morning rain showers and sent golden glimmers off the wet buildings and street below. He was up early, even though it was Sunday, as he had to meet the parents of John and Susan Reynolds at the airport on a flight arriving at 1120 hours. *Hard enough to get this sorted out without angry parents storming about. Oh, well...it could be worse...they could be here to pick the bodies. For now...still a strand of hope.*

After a long, cold shower and shave, he skipped down the stairs two at a time and was out the door to find his second in command waiting for him with the department's lone SUV. It had seen better days but Virote had ordered it washed and cleaned thoroughly for the transport of the four Americans to their hotel.

SURVARNABHUMI AIRPORT
Bangkok, Thailand

Arriving at the terminal a half hour early, the chief and his second left the GMC parked in a location marked Airport Security and entered the terminal building. It took twenty minutes to get clearance from the airport's head of security for them to walk armed through the concourse as they needed to be.

"Ten minutes to spare," the second said with some relief.

"Coffee? They have a Starbuck's over there."

"Yes, sir. I'll get them."

Virote pulled a package of nicotine gum from his coat pocket and after peeling the paper and foil covering back placed the mint coated gum in his mouth and began to chew vigorously. *One more inconvenience...if they do not smoke I'll be reduced to this nasty gum.*

"Here you go, chief. Two sugars and cream."

"Thanks. If they ask about our progress let me do the talking. No sense in giving any conflicting reports."

"No problem. I hope I do not have to talk to them at all."

As the passengers arrived, Virote pulled a pair of 4x6 photos from his inside coat pocket and began using them to identify the two couples he was expecting. The Reynolds, followed by Jacksons came out with the first group as they had flown in first class all the way from Georgia. They looked worse for wear after catching the redeye from San Francisco to Tokyo with a short layover before continuing on to Bangkok.

"Reynolds...Jackson...over here!" Virote called out.

In the traffic to the hotel Virote laid out the chain of events and brought the parents up to speed. "And that's where we are today. If you are set on paying the ransom...I will inform the kidnappers immediately. It will be in tomorrow's morning addition of the Bangkok Post."

"Then what?" William Reynolds asked.

"Then…we wait for their response. Once we are assured the couple is still alive we will make arrangements for the exchange." *Not going to mention the missing ears now. Not going to do it.*

"I can have the cash Monday morning as soon as the banks open for business…"

"All in good time, sir. We suspect your loved ones have been moved outside of Bangkok. If so it will take a day or two for the kidnappers to return. Best keep the money in the bank 'til we have set a date and time."

"Oh, Bill…we should have never allowed them to come…" Sandra Reynolds said as she broke into tears.

"There…there, honey…we're going to get them back," he replied as he placed his arm around her. "Isn't that right inspector?"

"With God's will…yes. Until they are safe, we must be ready for any difficulty that could deter us."

"How will we know they are still alive?" Robbie Jackson asked.

"Normally the captors will take a photograph of the kidnap victims with a newspaper showing the current date."

"And we will be able to see them? See that they are not harmed?" his wife asked.

"Yes. But do not be alarmed if they do not look like the last time you saw them. Often kidnap victims appear to have lost weight, not been allowed to bath, things of that nature."

ASSUMPTION CATHEDRAL

Mass had ended a half hour earlier but the Barnhardts and many of the parishioners were gathered in the meeting room where the bazaar would occur. The church had provided refreshments for those who stayed and the group wandered about visiting with one another while looking at the items to be sold and auctioned.

"I hope this is not too much for you and Tola. I know it would have been nice to have a day off…"

"Not a problem, Dalisay. We work twenty-four-seven, three-sixty-five. Tola and I will get some down time this afternoon. The boys can hold down the fort," Mark replied.

"Those two are new are they not?"

"Both have extensive experience in other fields and were top of their class with my previous employer or he would not have sent them here."

"Do you have a employer now?"

Mark chuckled, then snorted before he answered, "No."

"You snorted," Dalisay said with a laugh.

Mark felt a bit of color coming to his cheeks and turned away slightly. "Yeah…every now and then…when something strikes me as really funny."

"And that was funny to you?"

"Looks like Joris is about ready to go. We should join him."

She looked at him with a new sense of interest. *So calm…cool…collected, then out of nowhere…he snorts.*

The ride home passed with little incident other than a fender bender ahead of them that caused Keit to pull an evasive maneuver to avoid being stalled in traffic. He whipped the vehicle in a one hundred eighty degree turn—tires squealing as smoke burned off the hot rubber—and joined the traffic flowing away from the wreck.

"Ahhh..." Joris exclaimed.

"Oh, my God!" Dalisay screamed as her body pressed against the shoulder harness.

Mark and Tola took the turn in stride—only reaching up to grab the hand holds above them to steady themselves.

"I uh...I, uh never rode in a maneuver quite like that," Joris said after caught his breath.

"Keit's a good driver. Completed a course for special service agents in the US many years ago."

"I believe it," a shaken Dalisay added.

VIROTE'S APARTMENT

A pounding migraine prompted the use of a ice pack and shades drawn, though the pain continued for the head of the CAF. He had made the pickup at the airport and delivery to the hotel of the American parents while holding back the urge to throw up practically every minute of the trip.

Now he lay on the couch, praying the pounding in his head would pass before the next day's unpleasant events were to unfold. His cell rang and he peeked out from under the cold compress to see it was Patrick Murry calling.

"Hello, Patrick. What can I do for you?" he said softly.

"Just checking on the Reynolds and Jackson's state of mind before I call them."

"Exhausted and frantic."

"One could only imagine. How will you handle the delivery?"

"Not certain as yet. The instructions were very clear...no police involved. I haven't crossed that bridge yet. Any suggestions?" Virote replied as he felt another surge of blinding pain and the white sparkling lights blurred his vision.

"I don't know...maybe...just maybe. Did you meet with McCallister yet?"

Virote sat up slowly, causing a new wave of nausea, and thought carefully for a moment. "Yes. Yesterday at the Assumption Cathedral."

"He made a drop some years ago in Colombia. Showed some major balls going into FARC territory to do so."

"Why would he even consider it?"

"Steve's a different breed of cat, Virote. Has some...don't really know how else to describe it...a personal sense of right and wrong. And not afraid to go in harm's way to right indiscretions...be it against man or beast." Patrick paused before going on, "You don't sound so good. Are you all right?"

"Migraine...Bad one this time."

"Let me call McCallister for you. We have some history. I could feel him out and get back with you."

"That would be sterling. Let me know as soon as you find out his position on assisting us."

"Will do. Get some rest. Tomorrow is shaping up to be some serious discomfort for all of us now that the families are here."

"Thanks again for your efforts. Good-bye." After hanging up he crawled to the comfort room and threw up. As he sat beside the porcelain throne he pondered his options as best he could through the mind-numbing misery. *Have to be a madman to do this...but I pray he does.*

ZAMBOANGA del NORTE
Philippines

The weary members of Inagsi's group stumbled into the remains of a long-lost village in the jungle. The Nipa huts were still structurally intact, but the palm leaf roofs had mostly fallen in, leaving a ghostly appearance to the once bustling community.

"We rest. Secure the children in the building near the well. Check and see if there is water. Ramil, set the perimeter," Inagsi shouted. *We make good time but we must move faster. I want to hit Dipolog and Dipitan during their annual festivals. Destroy the port and the airport. Then fade into the jungle like ghosts.* He sat down and was asleep in a matter of moments.

***

CHAPTER NINE

SECURITY HOUSE

Mark and the team sat on the patio working with the weapons Crank had delivered. Each cleaned, lubricated and reassembled the weapon that they would be using personally. It was hot and humid, but the time off from the daily grind was appreciated. Roger and Mike bantered back and forth with tales of adventures. Keit and Tola ignored them for the most part.

Mark had decided to carry a Remington 12 gauge pump shotgun—thinking with two handguns he did not need the H&K 9mm submachine gun. The 870 had a black synthetic pistol grip and forend as well as a eight shot extension tube. He laid out the various rounds and began sorting them.

"Pretty exotic looking stuff. What all do you have?" Roger asked while reassembling his H&K MP5KA1—designed as a variant of the MP5 with no protrusions so that it can be carried under clothing without detection by the untrained observer.

"Four ought buck…much rather have twenty-seven pellets flying downrange than nine double," Mark replied holding up a round. "Then there's the Macho Gaucho…"

"Macho Gaucho?" Mike asked with a huge grin while cleaning the bore of his H&K subgun. He placed a couple of drops of Tetra oil on it and worked it through the barrel and chamber thoroughly as he listened to Mark.

"Yup…a pair of fifty-eight caliber balls connected by a six inch seven-strand braided steel wire. The cable keeps the balls close together in flight and on impact, adds to the wound path…Usually six inches or so."

"Holy shit! Where did you get those?" Roger blurted out.

"Quiet sources…These I like to call…Satan's toothpicks." He held up another round. "Nineteen or so steel finned darts, normally referred to as flechettes, that…well use your imagination…"

"Is any of this shit legal? I mean…what about the Geneva Convention?" Mike asked incredulously while assembling his weapon.

"Look around, sunshine…does this look like Switzerland to you?"

Blaster and Dog exchanged looks of amused confusion.

"These little babies are API. Not as effective as 7.62 but will blow through both car doors…and after initial impact on the first, it continues on with a phosphorous trail burning at three thousand degrees…Sucks to be anyone in the path."

"What's that one?" Mike asked, now completely focused on the exotic ammo.

"I like to call it...*da* terminator. A plain ol' lead slug with hollow base...filled with number four shot. On impact, the slug mushrooms and expands to nearly two inches, stopping it from exiting your target. The rapid expansion forces the dozens of tiny pellets to spread laterally through your opponent like a cancerous disease...opening an area just inside the impact point equal to a softball. The cavity created has a shock effect of 95%. That means only 5% of any living being could survive a hit...on any point of the body," Mark said as he held the round up and rotated it in his fingers with a wicked gleam in his eyes.

"The last one...what friggin' magical powers does it have?" Roger asked with a hearty laugh.

"Got this one from a active-duty SWAT guy I know in Brazil. Flash grenade. Highly effective stun/diversion effect using a blinding flash with an extremely powerful concussion. Produces a 182dB bang with a two million candle flash. A real crowd pleaser...especially in closed quarters."

"That over and under you have there...that's not legal either is it?" Mike questioned nodding at Mark's modified Benelli over and under twelve gauge—with a barrel length of only seven inches and the buttstock cut down to a pistol grip—tightly wrapped with rich dark brown steer hide while still wet and allowed to dry to fit.

"Sure it is...Unless you get caught by the law with it," Mark replyed with a snorting laugh.

The entire group looked surprised by his action. Tola smiled as she placed her H&K sub back in its case and Keit just shook his head as he placed a lightly oiled rag over the exterior of his well-worn Walther P38 pistol. He had carried it for years and preferred it due to the size—easy to carry while working, especially while driving—and it had a threaded barrel for his suppressor. *Hush puppies are still golden.*

Mark's cell rang and seeing the caller he excused himself, leaving the two new operatives to fondle the twelve gauge ammo.

"Patrick, to what do I owe the pleasure of your call this fine Sunday afternoon?"

"You saw the news about the American couple kidnapped a few days ago?"

"Yup. Probably done and gone by now."

"Possibly. The parents of both John and Susan Reynolds arrived today. They are ready to pay the ransom demand as soon as the arrangements can be made."

"Where you going with this, Murry?" he asked as he took a piece of vitamin C cherry candy from his pocket and peeled off the wrapper.

"Inspector Pradchapet informs me the kidnappers have demanded two million dollars American and that someone other than law enforcement make the drop…"

"What's in it for the horse?" he questioned as he tossed the candy into his mouth.

"The horse?"

"He who makes the drop."

"No idea, Steve. But I would appreciate it if you give Pradchapt a call. You don't have to take the run…maybe just advise him. After the drop you made in Colombia you at least have some real time experience…"

"All right, I'll call him, but I'm not promising anything else…Understood?" he said, noting the degree of anxiety in Patrick's voice.

"Thanks, Steve. Got to go…hell of a lot of paperwork to deal with concerning this damn circus."

Mark hung up without saying good-bye. *Well hell…that about screws the pooch.*

When he rejoined the team everyone had completed their weapons readiness and sat staring at him as he approached.

"Bad news?" Dog asked.

"Don't know yet. Certainly it's not good. Tola…let's take a ride."

"You want me drive, boss?" Keit asked while placing his pistol into his shoulder holster.

"No. You hang out here…check the security camera data. We'll take the rental. Check your network…I want you to get some intel for me. Find out all you can about the Reynolds abduction the other day."

"I do PDQ. Anything else?"

"Stow my weapons in the big house. Second floor…Bedroom to the left of the lift."

PAK KRET

Inkong finished his pleasure with Susan Reynolds and sat on a bamboo mat next to her sharpening a old style straight razor. A sheen of sweat covered his body and a drop fell from his chin onto his belly. The fear in her eye—she could only see with one as the other was still swollen shut from a blow by another cell member when she tried to bite him—intensified with every grinding stroke he made.

He held up a piece of dirty brown paper and sliced it cleanly with a swift stroke and smiled. His eyes turned to the helpless American woman. "Tomorrow...police get new ear. Which do you prefer?"

"No!" She whimpered to no avail.

The NPA leader moved to the battered woman. He gently moved the matted filthy hair away. Grabbing her ear firmly, he sliced it off and laughed in her face.

"Ahhhheee!" The woman wailed as her body shuddered with waves of pain. She lost her bladder before passing out.

Inkong entered the main room and tossed the ear to a underling, "Wrap this in a banana leaf and take it to town. Have one of our tuk tuk drivers deliver it tomorrow morning with this note."

He handed the young man a folded piece of paper with a description of what would happen next to one of the Reynolds if his demands were not met within forty-eight hours.

BANGKOK TRAFFIC

Tola drove as Mark called Virote. When he answered, he got straight to the point, "Murry called today. Asked if I'd contact you. What's going on?"

"I have basket full of cobras and…hope that you might be able to help me charm them."

"How so?"

"It's complicated. Could you meet with me tomorrow morning…around 1000 hours at the station?"

"Nope. Not coming down to the station for a pow-wow. If you're going to ask what I think you are, we should not be seen together at the station."

"And what do you think I am going to…"

"Drop two million bucks and get the Reynolds out alive." Mark gazed out the side window at the passing cityscape.

The phone was silent as Virote processed the directness of Mark's statement for several moments.

"You still there?"

"Yes. Where can we meet?"

"Pak Klong Talad, 1230 hours tomorrow. The orchid vendor. You know it?"

"I will be there…"

"Come alone. Don't use any department vehicle. Dress native…no suit…definitely nothing to attract attention to yourself."

"All right…1230 tomorrow."

They passed a crowd of tourists standing at a bus stop outside a hotel waiting for a tour bus to arrive. A Caucasian couple in their late twenties or early thirties stood a bit apart from the others. The father had a small boy on his shoulders and the child had his hands wrapped around his father's forehead. The three were laughing and appeared to be having the time of their lives. A look of sadness passed over Mark's face as he studied them. *Lydia...Josh...*

Tola, after listening only to his side of the conversation, finally asked in Thai, "You do this?"

Mark responded in Thai as well, "I need you to get some of the old band back together. As many as you can. If I do this, I want some serious backup standing by to blow the hell out of the mutha fuckers."

"What if..."

"No what ifs...we do this like we did in Indonesia. No one on their team gets out alive."

The two rode in silence for several minutes. Both considering the danger in doing such a deed.

Tola again broke the silence, "Boss...about the Barnhardts."

"Yeah. Sorry I didn't make time before. What's up?"

"Something's not right. When Dalisay showed me pictures of her family...just something...not right with Mister Barnhardt."

"Yeah. Joris seems...too...too damned perfect to me. Too upstanding...Know what I mean?"

"No."

"It's been my experience if someone is too shiny...there's a dull finish underneath somewhere. Haven't had enough time to put my finger on it but...too damn shiny."

"You want I ask around?"

"Definitely."

"Where we going anyway? You not say where...just drive."

"Surprise me. I needed some space to clear my thoughts. Oh…what do you think of the two new boys?"

"Hope shoot better than they fight."

They laughed hard after a moment of reflection on her comment.

SOI COWBOY DISTRICT

Mark paid little attention as his female ICC drove through the city. His mind was racing with thoughts concerning the retrieval of the captured American couple. It was only when she parked in a covered area did he realize her intentions.

"Very clever."

"You see Rocky. Have a drink…Make some laughs."

"Damn good idea."

RAWHIDE CLUB
Soi Cowboy District

Once inside the dimly lit club, Mark and Tola moved to a table at the back wall. It was the VIP section and sat on a two foot raised deck—allowing for better vision of the interior. Still early by bar standards in Bangkok and only a dozen or so men sat drinking and watching the girls dance on stage.

Tola bent down halfway through the club and picked up a hundred dollar bill lodged under the leg of a table and slipped it into her pocket with barely a pause.

"I should come in more often," she said with a sly smile.

"Money for nothin'…but the chicks are not free," Mark replied as he stepped over a pool of vomit.

The smell of cigarette smoke and stale beer hung heavy in the room as the cleanup crew hustled to complete their duties before the evening crowd arrived. Rocky had several huge flat-screen televisions around the room and normally they featured one or more of the working girls dancing, but on Sunday nights it was American sports on pay-per-view. NBA basketball was in season and later, the place would be packed with expatriates, American businessmen and tourists.

A Thai woman in her forties wearing enough makeup to paint a house, arrived to take their drink orders and recognized Tola. "Oh my God…Tola…I no see you so long time," she said excitedly as she laid her tray down on the table and leaned over to give her friend a hug.

"Good to see you too, Kikku."

"You have new boyfriend?" the waitress asked as she eyed Mark.

"No…Boss man. Rocky here yet?"

"Hour too early. You need him?"

"Call him, please. Tell him I am here…but don't mention I have anyone with me. Big surprise…okay?

"Sure…sure me understand. You want drink?"

"Coke for me but for my boss Tequila and limes."

"I be back and I get Tatana to call Rocky."

After she had left Mark leaned in. "Don't leave without me. Is that clear?"

152

"What...you think Tatana kidnap you go all night long?" she replied with a laugh.

"Just do it."

Before the waitress could return, they both heard Tatana scream in bad English, "Zowwo! You back!"

Looking across the room they saw the Thai bartender running—her ample breasts bouncing and threatening to fly out of her skimpy top—through the tables and chairs headed directly toward them.

"Here we go," Mark said sarcastically as he stood up.

When she arrived, she leapt into the air and wrapped her arms and legs around him. "I know you come back one day. You no can live without me," she exclaimed as she planted a wet kiss on his closed lips.

The commotion caused everyone in the club to look around at the three in the back.

"Easy girl. Came to see Rocky. But it is nice to see you again. How's the family?"

"Family all good," she said as she pulled back to look into his eyes. "You have beautiful eyes...Me no foget you blue eyes, Zowwo."

"Care to join us while I wait for Rocky?"

"Oh...yeah...me go call Wocky. I so excited when I see you I foget call. I be wight back," she bubbled as she slid down onto her feet and started to leave. She turned back. "Hi to you Tola. You lookie good gulfwiend."

"Hello, Tatana. So do you."

After she had run off to the back office, Tola threw a verbal jab, "I think she like you *too* much...you go boom boom all night one more time?"

"Give me a break. I was...I made a bad decision..."

"Yeah...you go bang the gong...make her crazy...one night stand," she said as she laughed at his discomfort.

"Hey...it wasn't a one nighter. It was a week..."

"Oh you in big trouble now boss man. One week same same as marriage proposal..."

"Kiss my skinny white ass."

An hour later Rocky came in to the club from the back and made a beeline for Mark. "I'll be a son-of-a-bitch! You are a site for a sore eye, you ol' Jarhead!"

The two men held a long embrace while slapping each other on the back. Rocky picked Mark up and swung him in a circle before putting him down.

"Easy old dog. Folks are going to talk..."

"To hell with 'em...to hell with all of 'em. It's great to see you. Hey? A couple of kids came in last night and said they were working with you. So...you taking on pups now?"

"Long story...Any place private we could talk?"

"Hell yeah. Come on." Rocky started to his office.

"I stay here Zorro."

"Thanks...if you're not here when I come back...you're fired."

"I be here, boss."

The two had consumed most of a bottle of Cuervo 1800 tequila, a bowl of crushed limes sat between them and what had been long Cuban cigars were short by the time they had caught up on old times. The big room reflected the tastes of the owner. Several pieces of western art hung on the walls, a large Texas flag covered the single window, as well as black and white photos of he and members of his Marine units in Vietnam.

Behind his desk a poster of the 1963 National Champion football team at the University of Texas. They had gone 11-0 and beat Navy—with Roger Staubach at quarterback—in the Cotton Bowl. First row, kneeling was number thirty-five James 'Rocky' Cole, considered by many the best fullback in college football at the time—and it was a time when there were many tough hard-hitting players at that position.

A 8x10 framed photo of Rocky and Mark's father, Jesse, stood center stage in the gallery of photographs. They sat quietly for a few moments before Mark broached the subject he considered important.

"Can you contact Daiyu?"

"Maybe," Rocky said as he squinted his eyes with a serious question behind them.

"I think I'm going to need her help."

"Really? Who you gonna whack?" He poured two more shots.

Mark got up and moved to the photo of his father. "Ha ha...very funny." He picked it up and studied the two young men in their UT football uniforms.

"Last time I heard, that's what she does now. She's a shooter for hire and pretty damn good at it."

"Well…she smoked my ass and everyone else's one year in a sniper competition." Mark moved back to the desk, poured salt on the back of his hand, bit into a lime before licking it off, then threw the burning tequila back in one motion. "You heard about the American couple that got themselves picked off a couple of days ago?"

"Sure. All over the news," Rocky said before he burped. "Stupid ass tourist move in my opinion. What about 'em?"

"I may…be doing the drop for them."

"Oh, that would be *really* stupid. Word has it the NPA grabbed 'em. You walk in with money and they will off you and be gone."

"Thinking the same thing. That's where Daiyu comes in. A little life insurance coverage."

"I'll make a call. When you thinkin' about making this dumb ass move?"

"Not sure yet. Know more tomorrow. Remind her she owes me."

"Daiyu owes *you*? Damn…Can't wait to hear that story."

Mark checked his watch and saw that it was now ten minutes to midnight. *Time flies.* "Crap…gotta roll. Have to deal with clients in a few hours. Took over the security for a family here. Joris and Dalisay Barnhardt. You know of them?"

"Hard not to. Big time player here. In the news a lot what with orphanage or children's benefits."

The old Leatherneck started to pour another round of shots but Mark held up his hand and shook his head.

"What do you hear about them personally?"

"Nothing. Don't run in their circles down here in the ghetto. He's a player though."

"Snoop around for me. Tola has a bad feeling…"

"Hey, if she has a gut feeling…you can bet on it. I'll do some asking. Great to see you again." He paused for a moment. "How's your dad?"

"Don't know. Haven't heard from him in a couple of years. Last time I did he was on a unsecured line and wouldn't tell me where he was. How about you? You heard from him?"

Rocky leaned over and stood up to avoid eye contact as he answered, "Not lately…I have your number now. I'll call you if Daiyu responds."

Mark noted the avoidance of his question but made nothing of it. *What does he know? Not like Rocky to avoid eye contact.*

PAK KLONG TALAD
The Flower Market

Mark had followed the Barnhardt limo to the office before going on to the flower market to meet Inspector Pradchapet. Confident the two rookie operatives could handle any problems that arose in the secure site, he had Keit return to the residence to stand duty with Tola. Dalisay was going to be busy all day preparing the balikbayan boxes.

While in the underground parking of Barnhardt's office he took a black carry bag from the back of his vehicle and changed his clothing to a pale blue Thai loose fitting long sleeve shirt and dark blue pants. Under the shirt he put on a body band and slid his 9mm into the preformed holster and two spare magazines into the pouches. He then removed his working shoes, put on a pair of rubber sandals and secured the nylon bands to fit. Satisfied all fit properly, he used his reflection in the vehicle's side window to put his hair up on top of his head with push pins. Once confident no loose strands were visible he took a black wig—called the Sony Bono wig in the store at MKB mall—and pulled it on and down snugly over his head.

He removed a gray nylon shaving kit bag, removed a bottle of gum spirits and using a makeup sponge, applied the sticky substance to his upper lip and along the sides of his mouth. He pressed a black wiry mustache to the glue and held it firmly until it set.

To insure the hair piece was not too recognizable as such, he donned a dark blue safari hat with mesh venting. Finally he replaced his signature aviator sunglasses with a pair of cheap wraparound Ray-Bans with a flame logo on the ear pieces. *Just another western tourist I am.*

He used the elevator to reach the first floor and walked out past the two Thai security guards to the street and hailed a cab. *Have to address that later. Never saw me come in and asked nothing when I walked out.*

To the casual observer, he looked like any other western tourist—or valley porno star. He had the driver drop him two blocks from the east side of the market and walked to the north for a block before turning to gain entrance to the busy flower market. He had not seen any motorcycle or tuk tuks following him but the short walk insured there was not.

The smell of fresh-cut flowers filled the air and was a pleasant change from the normal stench of the city. Mark stopped occasionally to inspect merchandise—always scanning 360 degrees to identify anyone that might possibly be following him. Twice, he paused in front of buildings and used the window reflections to check his six. He also pretended to take pictures with his cell phone to add to the illusion he was just another tourist. Once absolutely certain he was unobserved or followed he moved to the booth of a old friend—Tola's father—who ran the largest orchid shop.

"Maju...how are you?" Mark asked in Thai.

"Me good. How you? *Zorro*...is that you?"

"Shhh..." he said softly as he touched his finger to his lips. "I'm good. Could you arrange a dozen orchids for me...make that two arrangements?"

"Oh, most certainly. What color you like?"

"Surprise me. Never been much good at color arranging."

"Where they go? What color room?"

"Ummm...mostly blue and white."

"Okay I do now."

Virote arrived and though dressed casually, still carried the telltale presence of a law enforcement officer—too rigid, wearing his duty shoes and his pistol created a distinctive bulge in his back pocket. He casually inspected the orchids, all the while looking for Mark.

Mark never looked over at the policeman but moved around, him to a selection of yellow flowers. "Anything new?"

Stepping back initially in surprise the policeman quickly relaxed and focused on the display of delicate orchids. "Unfortunately yes. We received another ear this morning."

"*Ouch*. Male of female?"

"Forensics has it now but…I think female. I have posted a advertisement today in the Post informing the kidnappers the ransom will be paid…"

"Tell the parents it will cost 'em a hundred thousand for me to do the drop."

The inspector drew his breath but continued to inspect the merchandise without looking to the Texan. "That's a lot of money."

"If they have two million…another hundred K will not break the bank. There will be expenses…"

"Expenses?"

"Not going to go into details. Once I have the drop bag with the money…I go alone. Don't have any of your men follow me. The bad guys will be watching every minute."

"Patrick said you have…experience at this sort of thing."

"Yup."

"Have you been successful?"

"Also, tell the families if I get the couple out and retain the money there's a two hundred thousand bonus."

"You sound very sure of yourself, Mister Mc…"

Mark turned and bumped into Virote as he passed. "No names!" he hissed.

"Yes, of course...sorry."

"Make sure the drop is at night. Call when you have something," Mark said as he moved to Maju and paid him for the flower arrangements. Without looking back he walked off into the jostling crowd.

Very strange man. God I hope he can pull this off...but then what other options do I have? Virote pondered as he continued to look at the beautiful flowers.

Twenty feet away and across the busy walk way a slender Thai woman stood with her cell phone to her face as if viewing the screen. She was actually videotaping Virote. When the policeman began to walk away she followed him as she emailed the video to her boss, Inkong.

HAL McCAMBELL'S OFFICE
Dallas, Texas

Hal paced around his office reading a FAX.

Tiger missing. Have not seen or heard from him for several days. Apartment has been tossed. Vehicle tossed. Suspect foul play. Advise course of action.

It was late but the disconcerting news had the security company owner concerned, hence his visit to the office in the early morning hour.

He sat down and used his secure line to make a call. As he waited, he took a cigar from his desktop humidor and began to chew on it.

"Big dog! What's up?" Zorro answered.

"Tiger is AWOL. Hasn't been heard from or seen for days. I thought you should know."

"Hey…don't know the guy very well. Only worked with him once…"

"You think I don't know that. That crazy cowboy act of yours in HK was the last work he did. I told him to take some time off…make himself small. But he has not checked in…"

"He's an Aussie, Hal. Probably off on a drunken…"

"Bull*shit*! He has never failed to follow orders…unlike someone I know. I suggest you tighten up the ship. If the bad guys got him, they could be on to you."

"If the Triad got him they could be on to you as well…"

"Well, no *sheet* Sherlock! Goes to prove *one* more time…never get in bed with one of your harebrained schemes."

The phone was silent for several moments.

"Did you contact Kari yet?"

"Hell no."

"I'll alert Crank. I'd appreciate it if you would let her…"

"No idea where she is. Damn it Zorro…you owe me big time now! So big you will *never* dig out."

"You'd like that. But training up these two puppies for you clears…"

"In your lame-ass dreams…and if they get killed over this Hong Kong mess…I will own you 'till hell freezes over. You hear me?" Hal shouted as he slammed his left hand down on hard on his desk.

"Yeah, yeah…I hear you. Find a way to get word to Chikako…I mean Kari. She's running solo…I got backup. Thanks for the breaking news. Gotta get back to work here."

"Don't you hang up…" Hal slammed the phone down once he realized Mark was gone. *Goddamn cowboy. Just like his father. Rides in guns a blazing…never thinking about the big picture.*

He opened a safe behind a false book case and retrieved a small black book. After thumbing through, it he made another call all the while chewing rigorously on his cigar.

The call went to voice mail and he heard the voice of a woman, "Poppie go fishing. Leave message."

"Crap!" Hal exclaimed before he realized the message tone had beeped, starting the recording. "This is Lobo. Call me…yesterday. Big trouble Little China. *Big!*"

He hung up in a state of anger and confusion. The anger was normal for the big Scotsman but the confusion was definitely not. Of the many enemies he had incurred over the years he had been careful not to get crosswise with the Triad.

He thumbed through the black book, chose another number and dialed. *Oh…he's gonna owe me now.*

On the third ring, the silky voice of a Asian woman answered. "Black Jade. If this call means money leave a message. If not…you have the wrong number."

At the beep Hal left his message, "Four words… Zorro…Triad…call me."

CRANK'S ESTATE

Rhino walked around the grounds using only a cane. Periodically he stopped and did a few slow, very controlled squats. "Ah, shit...this has got to end." *Zorro was right...again...I'm going stir crazy.*

He heard the ring tone on his cell and his spirits soared. "Moon pie...I was just thinking 'bout you," he answered—his thick South African accent noting his joy at hearing from his best friend—his blood brother.

"How's the hip?"

"Better...good...it's good."

"Think you could do some fixed position duty yet?"

"Fokin'a. When and where bro..."

"Jump the overnight train to Bangkok. I'll have Keit pick you up. Bring tools."

"All right. Likin' the sound of it already. What is it this time mate? I know it's not poachers..."

"Fill you in when you get here. Oh...and bring the Israeli briefcase."

"Can I bring one of the lotus...?"

"No. This is high society contract so clean up your brak act and look presentable. Suit and tie." Mark hung up.

"Hey goat humper...I clean up with the best of 'em..." Rhino realized he was talking to a dead line. *Ah...duty calls.*

***

164

CHAPTER TEN

PHUKET, THAILAND

The dark green Ducati Diavel motorcycle raced down the winding mountain road at speeds up to seventy miles per hour, weaving in and out of traffic like a blur as it whipped around slower traffic. Several times the driver of a vehicle laid on the horn and hit the brakes to avoid impact with the cyclist.

A light drizzle began to fall and the rider, dressed entirely in dark green REV'IT CR One-Piece Racing and matching helmet with a black visor, slowed down to fifty.

The satellite cell phone vibrated indicating a new message had arrived. Daiyu pulled to the side of the road, removed the phone from her jacket pocket and flipped the dark visor up. The former Red Guard sniper smiled upon reading the message from Hal McCambell. *Zorro. Triad. What fun.* She quickly typed in a text reply.

Phone number? Zorro.

The Chinese woman—at 5'10" and weighing a 165 pounds of solid muscle—was a former Olympic three-position rifle competitor. She defected and spent four years working for McCambell Import/Export before going private contractor. She replaced the cell in her pocket then removed the helmet—shaking her long black hair out and allowing it to fall free down her back. Reaching into a custom-made saddle bag, she pulled out a bottle of water and took a long drink.

She wound her damp hair up and put the helmet back on. She started the bike and let the engine run at idle for a moment, and then, seeing a small opening laid on the gas and raced back into the traffic—passing four vehicles before swerving back into her lane.

JORIS BARNHARDT RESIDENCE

Upon entering the residence Mark immediately went to his bedroom on the second floor and stowed the bag of clothes and disguise props in the back of the closet. After thoroughly removing the gum spirit glue with rubbing alcohol, he went to the kitchen—passing Dalisay and Tola as they packed boxes.

"Afternoon, ladies. Any leftovers?...Oh, I went to Pak Klong Talad today and picked up these flowers."

"They are lovely. How thoughtful," Dalisay said as she saw the two flower arrangements. "We had pulled pork sandwiches earlier. There's everything you need in the refrigerator."

Tola gave Mark a look that said *see me* but did not speak.

After quelling his hunger he stopped to see what was being packed. "How many folks did you buy for?"

"Fifty with all the cousins, nieces, uncles and aunts."

"Will they arrive before we do?" Mark asked motioning to the boxes.

The slender woman brushed a strand of loose black hair back, stood up, placing both hands on the small of her back and arched it forward—easing the tired muscles from their labor. "I hope so. If not, it should arrive while we are there. I talked to my mother today on Skype. Introduced Tola to everyone. The whole village is planning a big celebration. I need to go buy some more things, I think."

"Tola and one of the boys will have to go with you. Something's come up and I may need to attend to preparations...for the event."

"Really? What sort of event?"

"Personal business. Won't take but one night to conclude."

"Let me know if I can help. I love planning events."

Mark and Tola shared a look.

Seeing the exchange, Dalisay spoke quickly, "What? No, really...event planning is fun for me."

"I'll keep that in mind."

Mark was in his bedroom stretching in preparation for a exercise session when there was a quiet knock on the door. He opened to find Tola in the hall.

"Come in...What' up?"

Once inside and the door was shut she answered in a whisper, "She tell me she want me to stay close to son when he is here."

"Okay…understandable."

"Not to let son alone with Mister Barnhardt."

Mark paused. "Did she say why?"

"No."

"Speculate."

"No say. But something not right. Son be here before we go Philippines. She say…maybe…he stay some time with her family."

"That's right. You, me and Berto's son, Michele, are going with her to visit her family while Joris attends to the opening of a new orphanage in Cebu…"

"Not like that, Zorro. Son stay when we leave."

"Ah…the plot thickens."

"What?"

"Never mind." Mark frowned. "Have to mull this one over a bit. The Dutchman would *not* be happy if we left his son behind. Latest intel indicates the mussies are on the prowl on Mindanao. Mostly further south but…the last time the MNLF went on the warpath the whole island went up in flames."

SHENYANG, CHINA
Dadong District

Zhi Peng Wu did his accounting using a Chinese Suanpan—an ancient device that predated the abacus. It consists of wooden rods and beads. His was constructed of four ivory beads—once white now a rich golden color from age and use—and black rhino horn beads on each of the seven rods. Before him he had a large computer printout of his accounts but he always ran the numbers again the old-fashioned way.

His phone rang and he lifted the receiver. "Zhi Wu."

"Master, I have some information about the murder of Ching Wu."

Leaning back in his chair the Dragon Master lit a American cigarette and took a long draw through his carved ivory holder before replying. "Go on."

"Our Madam X in Kenya claims she has intelligence that could lead us to the killers."

"I do not pay until the information is confirmed."

"Yes, I told her but…she will only give it up if a down payment is made."

"How much?" Wu replied before he blew a large smoke ring that lingered before rising and growing larger.

"Half…"

"Unacceptable. Tell her…one quarter. If her tip leads us to those responsible we will pay her in full."

"I made the offer already, Master. All she would tell me is an American was in Kenya at the time both of the Yakuza brothers were killed."

"Get the name then make the transfer. Once you have the name, follow it."

"Yes, Master Wu."

"What of the Yakuza woman?"

"Nothing. It is as if she vanished."

"Increase the reward. Find her," Wu said before he gently replaced the receiver in its holder. *Chia rolled the bones. He swears she is alive and holds the answer to my quest.* He had been the trusted reader of bones for Ching Wu in Hong Kong. His readings were correct—many deaths. Unfortunately for Wu and his men it was their own deaths.

BARNHARDT'S OFFICE

Joris dialed the number of his man Rico in the Philippines then placed the phone on speaker. While waiting for the answer, he put his feet up on the desk and leaned back in his chair. He looked over at Mike Sloan standing beside the door with his hands crossed in front of him. *Bet he was a beautiful child. Blonde hair...blue eyes...must have some Nordic blood.*

"Yes, Mister Barnhardt." The sounds of construction in the background caused Rico to shout.

"How is the progress on the children's sleeping quarters coming?" he asked as he doodled on a sheet of paper covered with similar nonsensical designs.

"Excellent. The crews are working around the clock now."

"We will be ready for the grand opening? And I mean everything will be ready?"

"Yes, sir. Maybe a few details on the exterior...paint or landscaping...but everything else will be completed."

"Good. I have made arrangements with the ABC 21 televison station and several radio stations to attend. President Benigno Aquino, Mayor Michale Rama and some other dignitaries have confirmed they will attend as well."

"Impressive list. I have arranged for special security with Police Chief Superindentent Danilo Constantino…He seemed very pleased to assist us."

"Probably because of the permits I filed to open a new manufacturing plant in Cebu. A couple of thousand new jobs will be a feather in all their caps," Joris replied with a hearty laugh.

"Of course. I…ahh…my apologies but I need to go, sir. The building superintendent has arrived. We are to discuss the finishing touches to your private quarters today."

"All right then. Make sure it is acceptable for my needs."

"Yes, sir. I will attend to it myself, I assure you."

"Call me if you need my assistance."

The Dutchman hung up and seemed to be in as good a mood as Mike had seen him in the short time he worked his security.

"Sounds like a pretty big deal, Mister Barnhardt."

"Yes…this new orphanage will be the largest and most modern one in the Philippines. We will be able to care for over five hundred children."

"Whoa…that is huge."

"Most definitely. I've invested nearly two million dollars in this one. But it will be worth it…for the children."

JORIS BARNHARDT RESIDENCE

Mark completed his workout and had the water running in the shower when his cell rang. "Zorro."

"Black Jade."

He recognized the voice and his energy level went up. "Jade...are you in the land of Buddha?"

"Maybe."

"I have a drop coming up. Need some insurance."

"When?"

"Soon. I'm in the Big Mango. Can we meet?"

"Your nickel, Zorro. Five K. Tomorrow night."

"Where and when?"

"I'll call you. Some place public. One hour...Oh...and the five is due if I'm in or out."

"Always admire your attention to the bottom line, Darlin'."

The phone went dead. The conversation had taken less than twenty seconds. *Damn she's good. No way to trace that call even if I wanted to.*

PAK KRET

The one-eyed cell leader kicked a sleeping member in the leg and yelled at the others, "We go! Ransom is here. Get ready. One hour...You and you...prepare the Americans. Take them out and wash them. Put on new clothes. Bandage ears."

The men and women hustled to follow his orders. A new sense of excitement filled them thinking of their cut of the money and the rewards from the NPA for accomplishing their task. Little thought was given to failure—it was not an option.

Inkong walked out onto the balcony and surveyed the coconut grove that had been their safe zone since fleeing Bangkok. Rays of sunlight filtered through the trees and cast an eerie surreal lighting all around the pole-house. A pair of common treeshrews—startled by his surprise appearance—ran along the balcony railing, jumped onto the trunk of a nearby tree and quickly disappeared up into the foliage. *Soon I will see my family. How I long to hold my children in my arms again.*

VIROTE PRADCHAPET'S OFFICE

The head of the CAF sat behind his desk with the Reynolds and Jackson parents seated in front. The room was charged with tension—as could be expected, considering the circumstances.

"When do we meet this...delivery man?" William Reynolds asked impatiently.

"I just received conformation that the exchange will take place in forty-eight hours. I have not informed the man yet..."

"We want to meet him before the exchange...get a feel for his integrity...You know?" Bill said with an angry edge to his voice as he lit another Marlboro.

"I'm not sure..."

"You're not sure? Let me tell you right now...we will not just hand over two million dollars..."

"Honey...calm down. If Mister Pradchapet trusts this man then we should too. And Mister Murry at the embassy said himself we are fortunate he is going to help us. I mean...what options do we really have?" Sandra said as she took her husband's arm and attempted to cool him down.

"I can call him. See if he is agreeable to a meeting," Virote replied.

"You do that, inspector," Reynolds said as he got up and stormed out of the room.

SECURITY HOUSE

The day had gone smoothly for a change. Roger and Mike watched a recorded NBA game on the flat screen. Neither had a favorite team playing but the connection back to the states provided some much-needed down time.

Mark entered through the back door and was in the room before either man could react. "Well done. You're both dead. Where are your weapons?"

The two looked surprised and embarrassed as they stood and faced him.

Roger replied first, "Keit's monitoring the cameras…"

"What if he missed something? What if he's dead?"

"Will not happen again," Mike said.

"Damn skippy it won't. I find either of you without a firearm again you're both go on the street. Find your own way back to Hal…"

His cell rang and seeing the number, he knew it was Daiyu. Without a word to the sheepish rookies, he walked out the door and on to the lawn. "Ready?"

"Midnight…Rawhide," he said before hanging up.

Damn. Tomorrow's gonna be a long day. Mark thought as he looked up at the sky. *Double damn…it's getting ready to rain. Good news…only shooter I know I'd bet my life on is here.*

With a low rumble of thunder the sky opened up and a torrential down pour fell on Bangkok.

Inside, Mark picked up a towel from the rack next to the door—intended for use at the pool—and began to dry off. "Blaster I want you to go to the main house. Stay there till we get back. Tell Tola and Keit I'm off property."

"Yes, sir," he said as he headed for his bedroom to retrieve his weapons.

"What about me, boss?" Mike asked hesitantly.

"You're going with me. Bring a gun, pilgrim."

"Ready in five."

"Oh…you got a stun device?"

"Yeah…Two hundred thousand volts."

"Bring it. Meet me in the garage."

BANGKOK TRAFFIC

"How come you picked me to go with you?" Dog asked.

"Gotta get your feet wet sooner or later. You and Blaster went to the Rawhide the other night…right?"

"Yeah. Met your friend…"

"We enter separately. You don't know me…Understand?"

"Got it. Anything else?"

"Look like the same hoe dog you were the other night…Chat up some girls. Buy some drinks. But be quiet about it, though. Don't draw too much attention to yourself. Blend in."

"Are we expecting trouble?"

"Always," he said with a glance at his underling.

"What if I move around a bit? Talk with a girl away from the bar…"

"No. I'll pick someone away from the bar to chat with. I need you set up to cover me. Bars are great places for folks to go and get drunk…to see and be seen…pick up intel. That's why it makes a great cover for guys like us."

"Hal never covered that in orientation."

"Pay attention, kid. Hal sent you here to learn something. You follow me out. Not too fast…five minutes should do about right."

RAWHIDE CLUB
Soi Cowboy District

When Mark entered the club he saw Dog at the bar as instructed. Though he was only ten minutes behind him the young operative already had two girls with him. *Good start kid.*

Making his way to the far end of the bar—allowing for a complete view of the club floor and stage—he ordered a Tequila shot. Fortunately Tatana was not working, so there was not a joyous repeat of the previous visit.

Rocky was behind the bar, but as he started over to greet his friend he picked up the look and slight head shake that told him they did not know each other. Having seen Dog further down the bar he turned about and greeted him instead. The two stood, quickly surrounded by five girls, and drank beer while conversing.

Daiyu entered and surveyed the room quickly. She moved through the crowd to the VIP section where she conversed with the two keepers of the gate.

One of them looked over to Rocky for conformation to allow a single female to enter the reserved for high rollers area. Seeing a nod of agreement they allowed her to take a table with her back to the wall.

Besides her unusual height, the Chinese woman was wearing attire that caused most of the men present to follow her as she moved. The bright pink tube top and green knee-length skirt split up each side to expose her lean muscular legs hid only enough of her sensuous figure to allow her out in public. Wearing a pair of aviator-style day/night polarized sun glasses—ones that obscured her eyes to others yet allowed her to see perfectly—only enhanced her mystic.

"God...*who* is that? Does she come here often?" Mike asked.

"Never seen her before. You like?" Rocky smiled at his own joke. "Why don't you go introduce yourself."

No sooner had Daiyu sat down when men started moving to her table and making attempts to join her. One after another was rejected in turn.

"Doesn't look interested in company to me."

Though Mark had seen her as soon as she walked in, he made no move to join her. He continued to focus on the flat screen behind the bar that had the BBC soccer game streaming.

"Tell you what...I'll bet you fifty bucks your boss can join her...and one night with any girl here you like on the house."

Mike turned to the club owner with a look of surprise that quickly turned interested. "Yeah? You're on."

Rocky called one of the bartenders over and gave him a cocktail napkin with a written message to take to Mark. As the message was being delivered he said, "You haven't known Zorro long have you?"

"First time to work with him, actually. He's a hard ass..." Dog paused as he saw Mark pick up his drink and start for the VIP section. "He's moving."

Most of those in the club were aware of another man headed to her table. They were certain he would meet the same fate as the others. They were wrong.

"Hello. May I join you?"

"Champagne?"

"Of course...May I sit down?"

"Why not? I'm bored...Maybe you can entertain me," she said without ever looking directly at him. Rather she seemed to look around the room with complete disinterest.

"Ahh...hell," Dog said as he reached for his wallet. "What did you write on that napkin?"

"That we had a fifty dollar bet on his success or failure."

"I get the feeling you've done this before."

"Some...If I bet on him all the time...I'd be a rich man."

After the champagne was delivered, the two got down to business. Mark had moved a chair so as to be seated beside her for two reasons. One, they could converse without being overheard. Two, he could see the room. *Never sit or stand with your back to the door.*

"Money?"

"Here you go," Mark said as he touched his jacket. "Where the heck you going to hide it in that outfit?"

"Not here…Outside. What's the deal?"

"Kidnapped American couple. Deliver the money. Get 'em out alive," he answered while scanning the room discreetly.

"You are such a shmuck, Mark. Have you done any homework? Word is…Inkong has them."

"Heard that. Who is he?"

"The best of the worst sons-of-a-bitches in Thailand. Suspected of a hundred or more kidnappings and never been caught. You *are* definitely the biggest sucker for the defenseless…women, kids and dogs. Heard about the pachyderm adventures in Kenya. When are you going to grow up?" she replied, all the while giving the appearance she had little interest in his company.

"Big fan of you, too…I need a shooter. You in?"

"Time for refill, cowboy," she said holding up her glass. "What's the payday?"

"You tell me," he replied as he poured more bubbly into her glass, being careful not to touch the bottle to the rim.

"First…fifty thousand…and that's the *good* friend rate. Plus expenses of course."

"Done. What else?"

Rocky ordered another round of beer and slapped Mike on the shoulder. "If I was you I'd stop staring and figure out which of the girls you want to pay for tonight."

"Have to take a rain check, I'm working…hey…wait a minute. You set me up."

"Wasn't that hard," the old inactive Marine said as he blew the foam off his beer.

"Who is she?" Mike asked.

"You'll have to ask your boss…Not my place to give out trade secrets."

"You take me to the next McCambell event in Miami *as* your companion…all expenses paid," Daiyu continued as she looked over her glasses at Mark for the first time.

"Who could refuse a woman with those eyes."

"Walk me out. Give these losers a thrill," she said before draining her glass.

"Not any one waiting for you out side is there?" Mark joked as he stood up and pulled her chair back.

"One of the first things you taught me…there is always someone waiting…or looking. Let's go find out," she said as she took his arm and placed a kiss on his cheek then his neck.

"You keep that up and half the club is gonna follow us out. Seriously, Daiyu…you look smokin' hot tonight."

"Always do. That's how I sneak up on half the bad guys. The other half, I just reach out and touch with a hundred seventy-five grain .308."

***

CHAPTER ELEVEN

BARNHARDT'S OFFICE

Sloan and Mantle stood outside Joris' executive rest room while the client relieved himself. They presented the image of two large statues that could not be passed without the password or a serious struggle.

"I am not kidding man. He hooked up with a...a contractor...or something last night that was...*scorching* hot," Mark whispered.

"Did you watch?"

"Not like that, dickhead. They left and by the time I followed, she was gone."

"Is she coming to work with us?" Roger asked.

"No idea. He wouldn't tell me anything. I was just along to cover his six."

"I'm starting to get the impression he has a whole lotta secrets."

"You think his name is really Steve McCallister?"

Barnhardt exited the comfort room and the two curtailed their conversation. Roger only shrugged his shoulders.

US EMBASSY BANGKOK
120 - 122 Wireless Road

The Reynolds and Williams parents were on their way to the embassy and sounded very unhappy on the phone. McCallister had not returned his calls all morning. *Damn...it only takes one incident like this to go bad and a entire career could be ruined.*

"Mister Murry...Steve McCallister is on line four," his secretary announced over the private intercom.

"Steve! Thanks for calling. I've been trying to reach you..."

"Bad start this morning. What do you need?"

"Well...I was hoping you would come to the embassy...say in thirty minutes..."

"You sound off-center, my friend."

Patrick ran his hand over his forehead and across the top of his head, then down to massage the back of his neck. "The parents are headed this way. I was hoping you could come in and...you know...put some of their fears to rest."

The phone line was quiet.

"You there?" he asked as he pulled a white handkerchief from his left rear pocket and wiped his forehead.

"Yeah. I'm here. This deal is getting more screwed up by the minute. So...what?...You want me to quote stuff like...forty percent of kidnap victims are returned? Or...twenty-three percent are returned unharmed?"

"Jesus, Steve…work with me here. Think how you would feel if you were in their place?"

After another long pause, "All right…Tell Master Sergeant Lewis I'm coming in loaded and looking like Sony Bono."

"What?"

"Bono…you remember…Sony and Cher?"

"Yes, I do but why?…"

"Just do it. I"ll explain when I get there." *How the hell do I let myself get dragged in to this insanity?*

SAN JOSE, COSTA RICA

Kari relaxed in the tropical garden of the Casa Lima Bed & Breakfast. Mark had suggested she stay at the quaint facility. She was in the capital city to take care of some money transfers.

The small waterfall in the courtyard splashed softly as it ran down to the pool below. Exotic fish of varying sizes and colors swam lazily about in the moonlight. No one else was up at that hour and she had the patio to herself. *What are you up to now Zorro?*

Across town in a seedy district of red-light houses, shady gambling establishments and drug dens, Wong Chi, a Chinese man in his sixties sat listening to his eldest son.

"It is her…she has the long scar on her thigh, father."

"And you followed her?" He continually moved a gold coin around and over his fingers as he considered the news his martial arts instructor son delivered enthusiastically.

"Yes, of course…All day."

"Where is she now?"

"At the Casa Lima Bed & Breakfast in the Rohrmoser district. I left youngest brother there to keep watch."

"Return there. Keep her in constant observation when she leaves. Be careful...If this is truly Chikako...she is *very* dangerous. Do you understand me?"

"Yes, father. I...we will be careful. Do you think Zhi Wu will be pleased?"

"If this is the Yakuza he seeks...*very* pleased. So will I, as the reward will pay for all my children's university education and more. Use your cell phone and get photos. Wu will want proof of my claim. Go...Report to me her every move."

US EMBASSY BANGKOK
120/22 Wireless Road

Mark stood in the 10x10 cubicle facing a metal counter and the heavy steel mesh grill that ran all the way to the ceiling and from wall to wall. He had turned in his weapons to Gunnery Sergeant Lewis upon arrival and now awaited their return. The air conditioning seemed inadequate and a light glaze of moisture formed on his forehead due to the insulation of the Prince Valiant cut brown wig.

Gunny Lewis entered from the armory, closed the steel door behind him and locked it before laying the pair of holstered pistols on the counter. He unlatched the sliding gate and pushed the weapons out to Mark.

"What's up with the goofy disguise?"

"Fooled you didn't it?"

"Would have if Murry hadn't told me what to look for. So, what gives?"

"Loose lips…"

"Yeah, I know…sink ships. Seriously, it ain't Halloween. Throw the old dawg a bone."

Ah hell…the poor guy is here to reach his twenty-five. Probably bored out of his mind judging by that chest of ribbons. That's some serious weight there. "I'm making a drop to extract the Reynolds couple."

"No shit? Oh…you are one *crazy* Jarhead."

"So I've been told." Mark studied the gleam in the old sergeant's eyes. "I could use some backup…"

"I'm in!" Lewis blurted out excitedly. "I got two weeks of leave coming. When's the party?"

"Not sure yet…Soon. It's only a one night stand. But there will be a team briefing…"

"You just let me know when. I'm going stir-nuts-fuckin' crazy here with all the spit and polish bullshit. I got a arsenal here that is…"

"Just bring your own to this one Gunny. A sidearm and a M4 will do."

"Ha ha…This is the back-waters here, McCallister. But I do have some M16s and a couple of Thompsons."

"Your choice…I'll let you know. I have your number and will call you when the meet is set."

HAL McCAMBELL'S RANCH

Hal drove a dark gray diesel GMC crew-cab dually slowly across a hundred-acre pasture inspecting his Longhorn cattle. He had been doing the same patrol every night for a month. It was close to calving season and he was being proactive about keeping predators away—not that it was necessary for this breed.

His satellite phone rang and seeing who the caller was, he pulled over and shut the engine off. "How goes the world wherever you are?"

"Life is good big dog. How's Maggie and the grand kids?"

"Everyone is healthy and mean as hell. Want to tell me what exotic shit hole you are hiding in now?"

"Not a chance. What's going on? You never call unless you want something."

"Your pup is about to fall in a black hole...Got himself crosswise with the Big Circle..."

"That about tears it...where is he?"

"Bangkok. Took a contract there baby-sitting some wooden shoe mega wealthy microchip manufacturer."

"Does he know you called me?"

"Not yet."

Hal sat in the dark watching the Longhorns graze the belly-deep grass or lay quietly chewing their cud. *I hate making this damn call. Neither father nor son will be happy I did.*

"I'm in the middle of nowhere...BFE south Pacific. It will take a day to get to a piss ant airport."

"Saddle up, cowboy. I have eyes in every corner of Asia reporting on the Triad's activities. Nothing looks like ignition right now, but when the fuse sparks…"

"How the hell did he get tangled up with them?"

"Hell…he's just a chip off the ol' block. Worked a contract in Kenya saving elephants…Thought he shut it down. Took a little trip to DC to see some split tail. Ran back to pull Rhino out of a shit storm…Did you read about Kenya?"

"No. Very little news reaches here. That's why I like it."

"Zorro was in the thick of it. Son of a bitch tried to reenact the Alamo. Anyway…he found out the ivory trade was back up and running. So…just like his old man…he twisted off and invaded Hong Kong…"

"Jesus Christ!"

"Sound like anyone you know?"

"Up your ass, Hal…Deployed any backup?"

"I called you. Two crazy ass Ingrams should be enough to deal with the Triad girls."

"I'll call you when…when I hit an international airport."

"Cut the smoke and mirrors crap. I could make a flight happen for you."

"In good time…I'll need some tools."

"Stop dicking around…If I know where you are I could get you into a safe vault and in the sky…"

"Arrange Cebu. On second thought…Dumaguete."

"Done. Cello is working the vault on Negros Oriental. You remember Cello? Call sign was Badger before he lost an eye. Take this number…I'll tell him your coming."

187

Hal hung up after giving Jesse Ingram the number to his safe vault guardian.

BANGKOK TRAFFIC

Mark drove aimlessly around the city. The traffic was dense and frantic but it allowed him time to consider his plan for the drop. He pulled over and parked near the Assumption Cathedral and called Rhino's number.

"Hieta! Ya psychic or somethin' moofie pie? Keit an I just left tha train station."

"Get settled in at the Barnhardt's. I cleared it with the client for you to take a room on the second floor. Tola will show you which one."

"Tola? Love me some Tola…"

"What's not to love? You get the lay of the estate. Keit will show you around. I'll be there in a couple of hours and fill you in on the details."

"Bakgat ag bru. Hey…I'm a bit swak at present. How's the bank baas?"

"Five thousand a week."

"Kief moofie…"

"Call me moofie pie one more time…I'll stick a boot up your vrot ass shot…"

"Jo eina…Zorro. Take it down a notch."

"Yeah…Things…are getting complicated. Just get the layout, bro. Hang 'til I get there."

***

CHAPTER TWELVE

ROYAL ELEPHANT CAFE

Virote sat in his faded yellow Honda Civic waiting. He anxiously checked the time on his cheap wrist watch. *Where is he? Did he change his mind?*

Mark tapped on the passenger door window. He bent over for the policeman to see him as he lowered his cheap sunglasses—allowing the officer to recognize him without giving away his disguise to anyone else.

Virote unlocked the door and allowed the Catholic priest to join him. "You seem to have more than one disguise?"

"Yup…What's the latest on the drop?"

"We have a time and place for the exchange…0200 tomorrow night."

"Figured as much. Easier to slip away in the dark."

"The place is going to be difficult…A wharf in the middle of the Khlong Toei district," the chain smoker replied as he flipped a butt out the window and pulled a pack from his shirt pocket. With a flick of his wrist, he shook a new smoke up, took it between his lips and pulled it free.

"Didn't expect it to be easy. Probably change it once I'm moving," Mark said as he rolled the window down. "You need to smoke in here?"

Virote looked at him, and then placed the cigarette back in the package before returning it to his pocket. "I could have a helicopter…"

"The *hell* you will…I do this my way…or you find another sucker to deliver for you."

"There are certain to be plans to eliminate you…"

"Ya think? Let me worry about the drop…Just keep your dogs on a *real* short chain. Any police show up and you're signing the Reynold's death certificate. I see a cop…I'll shoot 'im myself."

Virote's eyes narrowed. "How do you want to pick up the money?"

"You and only you will deliver it to me."

"Of course. What if…"

"Virote…just hand me the money…Stay clear 'til I call you."

SHENYANG, CHINA
Zhi Peng Wu's Office

Wu sat watching a pornographic DVD. It was nearing the final two minutes—his favorite part as the nine year old boy and twelve year old girl were about to be hung by their wrists and then gutted by the large naked blond-haired man wearing a black leather mask. His depravity had been so lowered after years of watching child porn that only the snuff films now gave him the adrenaline rush he needed. A light drool slid down from the corner of his mouth.

His number one assistant entered and handed a folded note over the desk to him. Zhi took the note and dismissed his subordinate with a limp wave of his hand. After finishing the film and scrolling back to the beginning of the last scene Wu paused the DVD and read the message.

He immediately stood up and shouted, "Su! Get Feng."

Reading the message again a sinister smile crossed his face.

Master Wu. Chikako is in San Jose, Costa Rica. I have her under twenty-four hour surveillance. See photographs in email. Title subject...lost dove. Advise as to your wishes.

Feng entered the office and bowed. "You called, Master?" the stocky six foot henchman asked.

"Take your best men. Go to San Jose, Costa Rica. You will contact Wong Chi when you arrive. He has found the missing Yakuza woman."

"As you wish, Master."

"Feng...I want her alive."

Wu and his number one enforcer exchanged a knowing look before he departed. The answer to the riddle of Dragon Master Ching Wu's death was at hand.

Zhi sat down and picked up his cell phone and dialed. When a woman answered he said, "Bring me the little one with the red hair."

CUYO ISLAND, PHILIPPINES

Jesse stood under the PVC shower head—constructed himself from common cheap Korean plumbing parts. The pressure was minimal as the water gravity fed from the two hundred fifty gallon polypropylene tank—sitting above the Nipa hut on a low hill. It ran a mere a hundred yards to the dwelling. He let the fresh spring water—filtered by a system he customized and built himself from plans found on the internet—course over him. The floral pattern cotton curtain to the comfort room opened and Chique came in, pulled off her tank top, shorts and panties before moving to him. She wrapped her slender brown arms around him and rested her head on his chest.

"You must go?"

"I'll be back...I promise. You should go visit your mom while I am gone."

A pair of Philippine Tarsier monkeys—brought to the island by a collector and escaped captivity to run free with no natural preditors—squabbled outside the window. Their shrill voices caused Jesse to hit the bamboo wall with his open palm heel and send them scrambling for higher branches.

She let out a soft sigh. "Maybe you not come back Poppie. Then what becomes of Chique?"

Jesse held her close, turned his head up and let the cool water run over his face. "I'll be back, baby. Promise"

"What about the chickens and the pigs? Who will take care of them if we both go?"

"Give them to Father Thomas. He will know who needs

them. Now…" He kissed her softly on the shoulder. "Now we hold each other all night."

"You sexy time me, Poppie," she said as she turned her beautiful round face up to his and kissed him on the neck. "You no come back…I kill you."

Jesse started laughing.

Chique slapped him on the buttocks. "What's so funny?"

"I'll be back," he said as he tenderly kissed her forehead and then her lips. "But if I didn't…how would you kill me?"

BARNHARDT, LLC FACTORY
Bangkok, Thailand

Joris Barnhardt toured his manufacturing facility randomly several times a month. This visit was a little different than most as he had ordered production shut down and all the employees invited to a free meal with local entertainment providing the music and traditional Thai dance shows.

Mark spent several hours with the plant security team upgrading access to the event and even called in off-duty police officers to man the access points and perimeter. Seeing the event as a perfect opportunity for the bad guys to make another move on Joris he even positioned Rhino in the plant's highest structure with a scoped Remington 700 rifle overlooking the grounds where the feast was to take place.

"Mister Barnhardt, thank you for you consideration of us," a worker shouted in broken English to be heard over the music.

"You are most welcome, Piyawat," Joris paused and shook the man's hand.

It was a security nightmare considering the recent kidnapping attempt, but Mark and the team kept Joris as safe as he could be with over two thousand workers in attendance.

"Joris...it is nearly time for you to make your speech," a department manager said as he approached.

"In a moment, Settawut. Let me mingle with our people for a few more minutes."

"Dog...eyes on the two in black shirt and pants by the food service," Mark called over his voice activated two-way headset.

"Got 'em."

Mark stood beside the Dutchman and Roger behind with their heads on 360 degree swivels. Mark reached out and blocked a employee approaching with a gift wrapped package. "No boxes. Leave it at the security table."

"Oh, really Mister McCallister. Aungkana has been with me for nearly seven years now," Joris said with a smug smile to Mark before responding the woman, "Thank you so much. I will not be able to carry this around. Please do leave it with the security people." Joris shook the woman's hand while pointing in the direction of the security booth near the entrance to the festivities.

"Of course, Mister Barnhardt. The workers in the sanitation department just want to show our appreciation with a small token of our gratitude," the elderly woman said.

"Aungkana...you and everyone who work so hard to keep our plant clean are a vital part of the company. Thank you, again," Joris said as he moved on to the next person seeking his attention.

"Jesus…this is a friggin' nightmare," Roger said.

"Keep you wits about you, Blaster. Only another hour and we're out of here. Get between Joris and that man eating with the knife. In the blue shirt…Rhino…" Mark directed.

"On it," the South Africans answered. "If I have to tap him…someone behind him will go down as well."

"So be it…Keit…report."

"All good here, boss. Four policemen here checking every vehicle that enters."

"Stay with the limo…"

"I stay…motor running."

"Damn good man, Keit," Mark replied as he moved three people with their backs to Joris between the team moving to the stage. "Stay alert guys. Nearly over."

BANGKOK TRAFFIC

The event went without any real incident, but drained the team. The number of possibilities for harm to their client was endless. Finally on the road, Mark felt a sense of relief, but kept vigilant, knowing a hit on a target often happens as it leaves a fixed position. Mark had Mike and Rhino in the Toyota rental shadowing the limousine.

Remembering a tail had followed them from the Bangkok Sports Club, Mark kept an eye on the traffic behind and left the dangers ahead to Keit and Roger.

"Dog…cut off the motorcycles moving up on your left."

"On it." He slipped into the left lane and blocked the cyclists from pulling alongside the limo. When they both attempted to pass him on the right he pulled back in front of them again.

The two riders looked to one another, nodded and then separated to pass the Toyota on both sides. Mike waited till they were on his back quarter panel then whipped left causing the rider on that side to turn his red Yamaha bike into the twelve inch high cement curbing that separated the opposing lanes of traffic. The front tire hit the curbing at a ninety degree angle, bent hard and flipped the rider over the handle bars before the bike landed on him then bounced into oncoming traffic.

As soon as the vehicle grazed the first biker, Mike swerved right severely, causing the second rider to impact the car in the rear passenger door and fall sliding down the roadway. He corrected quickly, but not before running over the back tire of the skidding motorcycle and the rider's left foot.

"Nice work, Dog," Mark commented.

"Thanks...thought you would like that."

"We could have used this kid in Peru," Rhino chimed in.

"I concur. Keep your eyes open...back at the nest in fifteen."

"What if those two were not meaning us any harm?" Joris asked visibly shaken by the impact with the two bikes.

"They were offered the option of backing off...refused to take it. When in doubt...take 'em out."

"That seems a little overzealous to me, Mister McCallister."

"Appreciate your opinion, sir..."

"While I am at it…I am not accustomed to employees addressing me as you do," Joris said, his face beginning to flush with color.

"Been waiting for you to bow up…"

"*That* is a perfect example of what I am talking about. I pay you to provide security. Not to make sarcastic remarks…"

"Let's get one thing perfectly clear…I…we are here to protect your ass…not kiss it."

Roger looked to Keit as the exchange came over their ear pieces. Keit sensing the look returned it with a sly smile and a slow lifting of one of his eyebrows.

"Boss gonna teach him now."

Mike and Rhino following behind were also privy to the exchange.

"Here we go…school time by professor Zorro," Rhino remarked for all to hear.

Hearing his friend's remark, Mark could not help but smile.

Seeing the expression only infuriated the Dutchman more. "What are you smiling at? I'm paying you more than I've ever paid before…"

"And, again…how did that work out for you? Oh…that's *right*…you ended up in rolling around in the gutter fighting for your life."

"Tell the driver to pull over! You are *fired*!"

"Keit…you heard the man. Pull over."

"What? How did he hear…"

"Soon as you can, Keit."

The limo pulled abruptly to the side of the roadway and stopped. Traffic passed by, horns honking as the vehicles maneuvered around the vehicle now partially in their lane of traffic.

"Let's go," Mark called to Keit and Roger.

The young operative looked to the experienced driver. Keit shrugged his shoulders and opened his door.

"We go."

Both men stepped from the parked limo and walked to the Toyota parked behind them.

"What the *hell* is this? I fired *you*…not them."

"They work for me Barnhardt. Remember? You may want to call your friends at Metro and get some police over here. I'd bet a hundred bucks to a dime those two punks were not alone."

Mark opened the door to get out. Joris grabbed his arm. With a twisting move faster than a west Texas rattlesnake, the Texan whipped out of his grasp and placed Joris' hand in a wrist lock.

"Ahhh…My hand! My *hand*…"

"I have to ask myself…when a man puts his hands on me…is he in love with me?…Or just looking to wear a cast for a month?" Mark released his grasp ever so slightly to reduce the discomfort, but kept it secure enough to resume the numbing agony if necessary.

"I'll have you arrested for this…Ahhh…" Joris said then wailed in agony as the pressure returned.

"No you won't…I know where you live. The men and I are going pick up our belongings…"

"Okay…okay…just let go of my hand."

Mark released his grip completely and proceeded to get out.

"Stop. I apologize. I…I am under a lot of pressure…I said at the dinner the other night I am sometimes hard to get along with. Just call your men back."

"Good a place as any to get the sails set and the course determined. Neither I nor anyone on my team is here to bow down to you…Is that clear?"

"Yes. Yes, of course," he said as he massaged his aching wrist.

"We will continue to show you the same respect as before. After all…you are the *client*. But you will contain your alpha needs to the others you employ…Clear?"

"Yes," he answered grudgingly.

"Getting your first lesson in Zorroism today boys…iron clad rule number twenty-six. Never piss him off. I've seen people die who pissed him off less than jack wad just did," Rhino said with a wicked laugh.

"What happened to *be polite*?" Mike asked.

"Oh…this *was* polite."

"Cut the chatter," Mark said forcefully. He could hear every word they said in his earpiece while dealing with Joris. "Are we good now Mister Barnhardt? You pay us to keep you and your family alive and unharmed. That's it…Any questions?"

"No. No…I understand. Again, I apologize."

"Keit, Roger…back in the limo." Mark sat back in his seat.

While they walked back to the limo, Mike put his hand over his microphone and asked, "What the hell was that all about?"

Rhino sat staring straight ahead for a moment, then blocked his mic as well. "No idea. He's...pretty level headed most of the time...I call him...*bakgat bro*...the iceman when shit hits the fan. Something set him off...not sure what...but something."

"Rhino...switch places with me."

"Moving, Zorro," he replied. He covered his mic again and turned to Mike, "Silence is golden, kid. Unless Zorro says somethin'...make the rest of this ride quiet."

ZAMBOANGA del SUR

Isagani and the gang of MNLF raiders lay on the side of the mountain, looking down on a long narrow valley. The dense jungle obscured their presence to anyone without infrared devices. A small village—no more than twenty huts, shacks, a sari sari store and a little church—sat on the far end, nestled against the mountain, bordered by a small swift stream and the rice paddies.

"We go in from the west and south. Push all those working in the fields into the village. Everyone goes in the church," Isagani ordered. With that, he got up and led half the men along the small game trail toward the village. The other half of the men began the arduous journey down the side of the steep tangled jungle mountain at the south end of the valley.

The only hostages still with them were the two oldest girls. Both had their hands bound behind them, a length of bamboo behind their backs with arms tied to it at the elbows and strung together by a length of rope around their necks—by which one of the men led them at the rear of Isagani's group.

Once the two groups were in position, the leader of the men approaching from the south blew a shrill whistle just as he and the others stepped out of the jungle. They splashed through the calf-deep water of the first rice paddy as snow white egrets flew skyward startled by their presence. A pair of elderly men working a paddy with a Philippines water buffalo looked over. The men immediately ran away, leaving the confused beast standing alone in the shallow water.

Isagani and his men were only a few yards from the west side of the village and had spread out to sweep in a skirmish line. They waited in the dense matted undergrowth swatting mesquitoes off their filthy sweating bodies. They to began to advance upon hearing the signal.

A young woman collecting water in a pair of five gallon plastic containers from the stream was the first to see the advancing men. Her screams alerted everyone that danger approached as she grabbed her child and ran toward her home. Most darted into their huts and closed the shutters, but that would prove little defense.

One woman—who was weaving palm fronds for the repair of her roof—grabbed her baby to her chest and a four year old child by the hand and ran north past the church and into the jungle on a two lane track the villagers used to go to market with their crops. Her decision would prove to be the saving grace for her and the children.

Several of the brown village curs barked and growled at the approaching enemy, but ran with curled tails tucked when one was shot.

"House to house! Get them out…take them to the church!" Isagani shouted as he encouraged his weary men on.

Once all the villagers were inside the small chapel—with guards at the front and back doors—the remaining men began to systematically search the huts for food, medicine and other supplies they sorely needed. Everything of value was brought to the small square and stacked around the rock fountain. The only weapon was a single-shot twenty-gauge shotgun with a cracked buttstock held together by duct tape. But the food and medical supplies more than made up for that.

Touching one follower on the shoulder the Muslim leader said, "Go in the church. Find us the keys to the trucks."

The man nodded then turned to a companion. "Come with me." At that, both men trotted to the building and entered to the screams of the villagers.

Three minutes later they came back out holding two sets of keys up for all to see as they ran back to their leader.

"Only two trucks are running, Isagani."

"Start them. Bring them to the fountain. Load the supplies. You, you and you…come with me."

The young battle-hardened leader marched to the chapel and ordered all the men and boys outside. Once there he lined them up and forced them to kneel. "If you are Muslim recite for me from the Koran."

No one spoke. The Liberation Front soldiers laughed and prodded the scared men and children with the barrels of their rifles. One older male—a priest—started to stand in protest. A machete sliced through him from behind cutting him from shoulder to hip. He fell with a agonizing cry and convulsed in front of his fellow villagers as he bled out. The others began to pray out loud and kiss the simple silver crosses hanging around their necks.

The slaughter lasted four hours. Each male was first mutilated then decapitated by the frenzied Muslims while they screamed praises to Allah. The women watched through the door and windows crying in anguish.

"Bring out the women," Isagani ordered as he lit a cheap Filipino cigarette—freshly confiscated from one of the huts. A bit of tobacco stuck to his tongue from the unfiltered smoke and he deftly spat it onto the face of a three year old boy—his eyes wide open staring at the blue sky without seeing.

The females—women and children—were lined up behind their fallen loved ones and forced to kneel on the blood-soaked ground. Flies already swarmed over the newfound meal. The stench of death filled the women's nostrils as they wept and prayed, calling to God for mercy. Their prayers would go unanswered.

After inspecting and pulling several women—four teenagers and two in their twenties—all the others were butchered. No one was spared—not even the youngest—all had their breasts hacked off then filthy sharpened stakes shoved into their vaginas or rectums before their heads rolled onto the ground with those of their fathers, sons and brothers.

"Take these into the church," Isagani said as he nodded to the women still alive. "Use them for your pleasure slaves...as per Allah's teachings...except for that one. She is mine," he said as he pointed to the most attractive teenager.

The sun set behind the mountains as the members of the gang began to celebrate their good luck with food, drink and women. Two soldiers—unable to wait their turn with one of the females—used a donkey to relieve their desires.

A young Carabao was butchered and suspended over a fire pit on a steel spit. Several chickens were killed, defeathered and after gutting, were thrown into pots of boiling water around the edges of the pit with clumps of water spinach, garlic and onions.

As the festivities went on, the bodies began to swell under the blazing sun. The stench permeated the village with a blanket of death. It was not long before the flies covered the bodies in swarming black clouds.

SHANGHAI MANSION HOTEL
Samphantawong, China Town, Bangkok

Daiyu always stayed at the Shanghai when in Bangkok. It was not a five star by any means, but the hotel was comfortable and the Chinese flavor as well as it's proximity to the Chinese district suited her. The amenities were few, other than free wi-fi and dining that was in keeping with Chinese traditional fare, but it was home when she was in the Big Mango.

The staff knew her by a name other than Daiyu—one of many she used in her line of work—and as a high tech sales representative for a firm located on the mainland. All this allowed her the annonimity she needed to maintain her lifestyle without fear of anyone discovering her lair.

She worked slowly, methodically cleaning her favored rifle, a Norwegian VS-94 PS .308 caliber built on the reliable Mauser Gewehr 98 bolt action. With the Schmidt & Bender 3x12x50 telescopic sight and the exceptionally heavy barrel she had delivered precise kill shots out to nine hundred yards on more than one contract since going private.

Wearing only a pair of jogging shorts and bra, the cleaning solution and lubricant had splashed on her hands and body. She looked and smelled like a gun lover's dream. *Get this done I have to take shower then a long bath. Wonder what Zorro's doing right now? Why is it that he's the only man that's never shown interest in me? Damn sure he isn't queer.*

She placed the disassembled rifle and scope back inside its hard case, stowed it up in the drop down ceiling and replaced the insulated panels. Daiyu brushed up the debris that had fallen when she removed the panels and flushed them down the toilet.

After checking the door locks and the security bar that rested at a forty degree angle against the door knob, she picked up her Walther PPK and entered the comfort room. She started the water in the shower and stepped under the soothing flow.

Waiting for room service delivery Daiyu opened her laptop and checked for messages. One caught her eye immediately from a group innocuously titled Professional Shooter's News. It was a site used by many around the globe that made a living in her profession—not for sport but in a contract manner.

Opening the message she scanned the obligatory disclaimer and began to read the text. It was in code that was specific to her as Black Jade.

Contract. White male. Late 30's early 40's. Last known location Kenya. High risk. Five hundred thousand pounds. Interested contact Snow Leopard.

Daiyu sat quietly for several minutes staring at the message then out the window of her suite. The message from Hal McCambell playing over and over again in her mind. *Zorro...Triad...call me.*

If her instincts were right, the contract was out. If she did not take it someone else would. *Fèi a ma-o a go càodàn cao ni ma. This NPA cluster is not going to be the biggest problem, Zorro.*

***

CHAPTER THIRTEEN

BANYAN TREE BANGKOK
21/100 South Sathon Road

Mark assembled the rescue team—minus Daiyu and Rhino—at a modest business traveler's hotel to avoid notice of the diverse members coming and going from the briefing. When gunnery sergeant Lewis arrived, he introduced him only as Gunny.

The twins—Ice and Ton—were the first to arrive. Ton was a experienced driver and Mark often used his services when Keit was unavailable. Ice was deadly with sharp weapons and could sneak up on anyone, cut an artery before they knew he was there and slip away undetected. Both were experienced operators and Tola's first cousins.

Tanipat—former Metropolitan SWAT team sergeant—was home on leave from security duty on a major oil corporation tanker. Hearing Zorro was looking for guns, he jumped at the chance to work with him again.

Slash—retired Navy SEAL living in Shanghai—answered the call from Tola with a firm, "Oh, hell yeah! When's the party?"

Mark started the briefing, "It's been a while since some of you worked with me...so keep this in mind...Zorro's rule number one...Everyone on the other team...dies."

A ripple of agreement passed through the men. Only gunny seemed a bit surprised but said nothing.

"I go in with the money. I will have a suitcase and an Israeli case..."

"Israeli case?" Ton asked.

"There's a Uzi inside a large briefcase with a firing port. Trigger is built into the handle...The port opens and the sub starts spraying 9 mm."

The men looked to one another with grins and a gleam in their eyes.

"Where's the dance?" Gunny asked.

"For now, a pier in the slum district. I expect the drop site to change once I am en route. Everyone will have one of these." Mark laid his Motorola GP644 radio and headset on the coffee table. "Keep the chatter to a minimum. Too much jibber jabber confuses everyone...Clear?"

"Inkong has never been captured..."

"See rule number one...he ain't gonna be captured this time either. Now...I'm going to assign you in teams of two. One's a shooter and covers my ass...and the other is cover for the shooter. Keep your heads on a swivel. Don't know how many will show up but I can guarandamntee you...they will come in three hundred sixty when the shit hits the fan..."

"Any police back up?" Ton asked.

"You see any police...shoot 'em. Anyone not on our team is the enemy." Mark paused for his words to sink in. "I have some maps of the slum district. Let's go over every pier that might be used."

Three hours later, the men had their assignments down, the NVGs issued and they were ready to roll. Everyone knew that once the drop started anything and everything could go wrong—*Murphy's Law*. Each felt a sense of devotion to Zorro as all had worked with him before except Lewis. His alliance was to a fellow Marine going in harm's way.

"I will call you when the race begins. As noted earlier, it will be around 0200...Be ready. Once I have the Reynolds secured, we fan out...Find all NPA mofos that are in the area..."

Gunny raised his hand before speaking, "What about civilians?"

"Anyone with a gun...is the enemy, Gunny. ROEs on this fandango are simple. You think someone is a threat...kill 'em... Let God sort it out."

"Oorah!" Lewis replied.

As the men departed Mark's cell rang. He recognized the tone to be Keit's. "Yeah?"

"I have Hans and his wife. Going to the Barnhardt's."

"Be there in forty." *Gonna get this rodeo runnin' right now. Hans will have the security so tight a mouse can't get in without notice.*

COCA COLA BUS TERMINAL
San Jose, Costa Rica

Chikako bought her ticket at a travel outlet near the bed and breakfast and took a cab to the station. Located in the Zona Rosa district—the notorious red light district of San Jose and sitting on the location previously occupied by the first Coca Cola bottling plant in Costa Rica—the area and the station itself were a rough-and-tumble place. Pickpockets, thieves of all sorts, drug dealers and street whores lived and worked the area twenty-four hours a day.

The most dangerous group for ordinary travelers were the Stick Boys—groups of never less than four and sometimes as many as a dozen teenage males walking about with canes. If anyone defied their demands they would immediately beat them down with the walking sticks. Even the police gave them a wide berth in most instances.

She was not concerned about the local thugs. But she was concerned about the Asian men she recognized following her since departing the hotel. *Don't know them but I recognize Triad tattoos when I see them.*

Once seated behind the driver, she pretended not to notice the three men that boarded after her. Rather, she feigned applying makeup—something she rarely wore but often seemed to be doing to use her mirror for observation. As the bus pulled out Chikako could see the other two men standing at a Hertz car rental desk engaged with the staff. *Three on board...two on tail.*

HIGHWAY 121
Costa Rica

Once out of the city, the luxury bus made its way along the four lane blacktop for several miles until the road narrowed to two lanes. The traffic slowed considerably. The high-backed seats made it hard to view the men behind her without making it obvious. She held her mirror so as to be able to see the aisle way just behind her in case they moved forward while the bus was moving.

As the narrow road turned on a mountain she placed the shoulder strap to her travel pack over her left shoulder and stood up. Quickly stepping into the aisle she grabbed the door locking handle and pulled it back hard.

"No correcto! ¡Alto! Siéntese!" The driver yelled as she rushed through the open door and landed on the shoulder, deftly rolling forward to easy the impact.

With practiced skill, she came to her feet, jumped the metal guard rail and started down the side of the mountain. Reaching a drop that would obscure her from the road a bullet cracked past her head. Another pair hit a cow tree—so named for the white sap that flows just below the bark—next to her. Dropping to a knee, she pulled her .45 caliber pistol from the pack and wheeled. *Bamm! Bamm!*

Her first round took one of the pursuers in the chest and threw him back into the stopped bus. The second hit another

Triad squarely in the forehead and he dropped to the ground losing his weapon that clattered down the hillside past her.

A dark gray Honda SUV swerved to the shoulder and another Asian man jumped out and cycled the bolt on his Ingram 9mm Mac 11.

Before he could bring the weapon to bear Chikako dropped over the edge of the ravine. The incline was not vertical but very steep and she slid rapidly feet first—using her small pack to shield her upper body from the ground. Her left foot struck a startled Iguana in the back hips throwing him up in a lazy circle as she passed beneath him. Unable to regain its footing, it too slid towards the stream below.

She braced herself and used her feet to deflect her body from a ceiba tree that grew on the slope. The impact twisted her sideways and she began to roll. Five feet above the stream the bank ended and Chikako fell into ten foot wide stream rushing down the mountainside.

She landed face first—feet down stream—and was swept along by the moving water. The now angry Iguana landed a moment later and when he surfaced began to swim with the current angling for the far bank as he hissed at her. At the first bend she looked up to see two of the Triad sliding down the hill following her. Once out of sight, she grabbed an overhanging vine of a strangler fig and pulled herself out of the stream on the far side and moved rapidly into a bed of resurrection ferns. *Damn...hope I don't crawl onto a poisonous snake in here. That would really suck.*

Watching the far bank it did not take long for the two men trailing her to appear. They moved swiftly down the side of the stream and were out of sight in less than a minute. *Gotta keep moving. Half hour north then I'll stop and check the map.*

In a low crouch, she carefully started moving through the fern bed and realized that she had injured her right knee—now throbbing and swelling from her slide or fall.

Once out of the waist-high ferns she entered a tangled mass of brush. Finding a small game trail with a covering of vines and trees she sat down and inspected the damage. A two inch long thorn from a pochote tree protruded from the inside of her right knee. The wound bled only slightly, but the swelling was already impairing her ability to put weight on the leg. Gritting her teeth, she gripped the exposed end and extracted it in one smooth swift action.

"Ahhh..." she groaned softly then drew in several quick breaths as she recovered from the pain.

Looking around she spied a five foot long two inch thick branch off a milk tree laying just off the trail. The oddly shaped branch had a ninety degree turn at three and a half feet—a perfect walking cane for someone with her injury. *Small wonders never cease.*

She removed a one liter bottle of water from the pack and took a long slow drink before rinsing the wound and stowing it back in the pack. In another of the front pouches she found a plastic zip lock bag with first aid items. Removing an alcohol wipe pad she gently cleaned the wound. Next she added a one inch square piece of Mepilex AG—a gray foam material treated with silver salt—on the wound. *Came through again you did Zorro. Worked great on the shoulder. Sure to help on this.*

She removed a pair of black Nike stretch exercise pants from the main pocket and wrapped them around the injured knee and secured it as tightly as she could bear with a length of self-adhesive elastic bandaging. Using the walking stick she gingerly stood up and tested the strength of her leg. *Well this sucks...but at least I can move. Have to get back to my tent and rest of my weapons. I doubt those bonkuras know where it is or they would not have been following me.*

The injured Chikako hobbled off slowly—moving up the trail and away from the stream. It would be a long journey on foot before she could find suitable transportation back to her hide.

SAN JOSE, COSTA RICA
Wong Chi's Lair

The elder man sat in total fear as Feng ranted about losing Chikako. He was used to being the one in control, but the angry Triad hit man was several steps up the ladder with the organization and his agitated demeanor was threatening.

"Someone warned her. It had to be someone in your organization," Feng yelled as he slammed his fist down on the desk that separated them.

"It was not one of mine. Only my two sons and I knew of her."

Feng turned and paced about the room. He eyed the two younger Chi boys with a ugly glint in his eye. "I lost two good men today...Eliminated like school boys."

"She was on a bus to the coast," the older one said hesitantly. "Maybe..."

"Maybe? *Maybe*!...I do not deal in maybes!" Feng thundered as he approached the younger man.

"Let me contact our people on the coast. She may still be headed there...or perhaps she was there before coming to San Jose," Wong said firmly.

The stare Feng had locked on Chi's son softened slightly as he turned to the father. "Yes. Do that...Do it now."

As the members of the Triad exited the room Wong flipped through a rolodex card wheel until he reached a number he sought. Picking up his land line, he dialed.

"Wong...How may I serve you?"

"Spread the word up and down the coast. I am seeking a Japanese woman. She is attractive and tall. There is a long scar on her left thigh..."

"I know her. She sometimes visits the fish market in Montezuma. And you are right...she is very beautiful."

"When did you last see her?" Chi asked as he lit a ivory pipe and exhaled.

"It has been several days...Someone said she is a surfer. Let me ask around and call you back if I find anything else. Why do you seek this one?"

"It is business. Call me immediately if you have anything worthy and do not approach her. She must not know I am looking for her."

"Business?"

"Yes...Homeland business," Wong Chi replied before hanging up. He puffed slowly on his pipe as he considered the turn of events. He added a small yellow ball of opium to enhance the experience. *I came here to be far from the drama at home. Now it has followed me here. The reward will be nice but I would trade it all away if this she devil departed this heaven on earth.*

LUMINI PARK
Bangkok, Thailand

Established in the 1920's the park was near the center of Bangkok. Lush tropical gardens and a large lake made it a center for those who appreciate a little outdoors and a small haven of natural beauty in the large city of cement, steel and glass.

"I hope you know what you are doing, McCallister," Virote said a he approached the disguised American—again wearing the Bono wig and mustache, but wearing a long loose-fitting lightweight black raincoat.

"So do I. What's in the smaller bag?"

The two paused as a group of joggers passed near by.

"The hundred thousand you requested to make the drop."

"You hold on to it. If this goes down the toilet and I'm done...a woman will contact you. She will identify herself as Tola."

"I will see she gets it. I can still call in some of my men..."

"Anyone my team sees with a gun will be shot on sight..."

"Your team?"

"Jesus, Virote...you *think* I'm doing this solo?"

"Well...you never gave me any details."

"Damn skippy. Taking no chances anyone is on the take. Last thing I want is the bad guys to expect what's comin'."

"May I ask what's in the briefcase?" Virote asked as he studied the Israeli case.

"You may. How are the bad boys going to run me around?"

"Ah...right. They sent this disposable cell phone. Said they would call you..." the inspector checked his watch. "...in seven minutes."

"All righty then. It's off we go. I'll call you when I have the Reynolds couple. 'Til then...go help Patrick keep the parents occupied."

"Okay...Good luck."

"No luck in it...Either you live...or you don't."

Seven minutes later—as Mark strode casually through the park—the cell phone rang.

"Go," he answered.

"Make your way to the Khlog Toei district. Pier number two. You have ten minutes."

"Never going to happen. I'm on foot."

"You not say what will happen! Your do…"

"When I catch a cab I'll be…"

"You no here ten minutes…they die!"

"Tell ya what…I call you when I get to pier two and you tell me where I go next."

"I will kill them…"

"Bull fucking shit…your boss wants the two million dollars. So…take the knot out of your panties. Sit tight. I'll call you." Mark smiled as he placed the cell in his coat pocket. *Yeah yeah… Kill 'em like a monkey humping coconuts.*

He used his throat mic. "Pier number two. Set up. Rhino…find some place up on the north side. Everyone else find a hide like we planned. Remember…Slow is smooth…smooth is fast."

Each of the teams acknowledged his instructions including Rhino. All except Daiyu. She heard but did not answer. It was enough to know that Mark had set another sniper to the north. *Damn he's good. Two shooters? Ain't nobody getting out alive.*

KHLONG TOEI RIVER DISTRICT

Twenty minutes later, Mark stepped out of a cab onto pier number two. He paid the driver and turned to walk down to the river. The cell rang. *There ya go mofo. See how easy that was?*

"Go," he said as he casually strolled along. In fact, his eyes scanned every possible hide—windows, doorways, stacks of barrels, piles of pallets and rooftops.

"Halt! You go now…pier number nine. You have…"

"Screw the *you have,* monkey breath. You're sure to be eyeballing me. When I get there, call me," Mark replied as he turned and hailed the departing cab. Before getting in he alerted the team, "Number nine."

Again the men acknowledged his call and began to move.

"Easy enough for you braks on the ground. I gotta climb down five stories…"

"Cut the chatter. Hump yourself down and get moving."

The cab stopped at pier nine and Mark stepped out, but held the driver. Sure enough, the cell phone rang.

"Pier five." The line went dead.

Yup! Exactly what I would do. Run me past the drop to see how many are with me. Not bad, bozos.

"Back to five. Keep it quiet…They ran us by to see who's in the game. Separate…Hook up again when you get to five, if you can. If not…every hunter for themselves."

The teams clicked in acknowledgment. He made a chirping sound. Daiyu answered with one. *Well worth the money and the escort to Hal's shindig to have her on my six.*

At wharf five, Mark waited for three minutes then sent the cab on. He could barely see a pair of long boats approaching in the river—their small outboard motors chugging away in the dark water. Both appeared to be carrying produce to the market upstream for tomorrow's sale. *But then, appearances can be deceiving.* Another five minutes passed before the phone rang.

"We there yet?" he quipped.

"You go end of pier. Wait."

Mark lifted the suitcase with the money in his right hand and with the Israeli briefcase in his left—flipping the safety off—he began the long walk down the teakwood structure. The smell of human waste in the septic waterway was almost overpowering.

Light from several widely-spaced forty watt bulbs hanging from rusty fixtures hung on the tall gray pilings dimly lit the planks of the deserted pier. Every stack of discarded vegetable crates cast dark shadows from which a lethal attack could spring at any second. He could sense a dozen sets of eyes on him but could not see a single person as he walked slowly and quietly down the wharf. The hair stood up on the back of his neck as he felt the blood begin to pound in his temples.

"Gimme dat old time religon...dat ol' time religion," Mark sang softly to alert the team this was it. He mentally repeated...*stay low...go fast...kill first...die last...*as he focused on his heartbeat and began slowing his breathing.

Nearing the end of the wharf he noticed both boats began to make a circle. He stopped, leaving a good thirty feet to the end.

"On your six, Zorro," Rhino called.

Mark glanced back over his shoulder to see four figures approaching from the land side. "Four tangos. Six o'clock."

He returned his gaze to the boats. One headed in for a landing the other continued to circle. *So...here comes misdirection down the stretch. Reynolds holding on the far turn.* "Americans are on the circle boat. Scope it, Rhino."

He studied the greenish-gray world as seen through his night vision scope attached to his rifle's receiver. "Driver...two other men. Subjects must be under the produce."

"Motor first..."

"No fokin' shit, brak. Brilliant thinkin'," he answered. "Gonna be tight."

"All the faith in the world in you, bro. Easy as one, two, three..."

"Four more on your six," Ton called. "Two on the building at three o'clock."

"Three on the nine," Gunny added.

"Eyes three-sixty. May be more of 'em," Mark replied as the boat stopped and one of the three men tied it off to a piling. *That makes sixteen. Very doable...so far.*

"You have money?" the tallest NPA asked as he and his compatriots spread out across the end of the pier.

"Right here. Where are the Americans?"

"What in little bag?"

"The money Inkong requested for his bonus," Mark lied, knowing the news would create division among the gang.

Sure enough, the one doing the talking looked up and to his right—indicating Inkong's hide. Mark chirped twice. Daiyu answered, indicating she was aware.

She swung her Generation 4 night vision scope onto the third floor of the slum apartment. Three males were clearly visible inside the window of a room. Two had rifles aimed down at the pier. One had a cell phone in his hand and was holding to his head. *Bingo...*

JORIS BARNHARDT'S RESIDENCE

Dalisay and Tola watched a Filipino comedy show in the third floor sitting room.

"I am sad Steve didn't not ask me to assist with planning the event."

"It's not what you think Dalisay. He goes to deliver the ransom for the American couple..."

"What? No...and he left you and the others here?"

"Zorro has other team with him now. More experienced men for this..."

"But what will happen if he is hurt...or God forbid...dies? Who will take over here?"

"Rheinhart Fabian. He and Mark go back long way. They think like."

"We should pray, Tola."

"Cannot hurt...You pray Jesus. I pray Buddha."

PIER NUMBER FIVE

The three NPA gang members looked at each other with confusion in their eyes. The smallest man's cell rang and he answered in Thai.

"Yes." A long moment passed as he listened. "He says it is your money. The money you requested as a bonus."

It was evident the voice on the other end of the line was angry. The small NPA soldier held the phone slightly away from his head. Mark could make out a few of the words, but not enough to know what was being said completely.

Time began to enter the twilight zone—that place where everything moved like it was caught in cold molasses. He noted that the NPA on the right was the most nervous—his eyes darting around from Mark to his fellow kidnappers. *Target one marked. If anyone makes the first move…it will be him. Wait a minute…that's a woman. And she went through the ugly line more than once.*

Without hanging up, the man on the phone said, "Inkong say he no ask for other money…"

"Then I'll just keep it. Where are the Americans?"

The largest man started waving his SKS rifle as he spoke, "You shut up! Put money down. You go…"

"No can do big ugly. No Reynolds…no money."

"You one stupid man! Look behind you…You are surrounded."

"Yeah, I am…eight back there. Nevertheless…no Americans…no money."

The circling boat began to approach slowly.

"Oh…look, number two boat comes now," Mark said with a nod towards the river.

The three communist insurgents glanced back at the same time. Mark pulled the trigger on the Israeli case handle, the firing port clicked opened and a steady stream of 9 mm rounds sprayed them. The rapid fire blasts of the subgun shattered the near silence of the waterfront. The lightweight Glaser Safety slugs blasted chucks of flesh from the unprepared kidnappers as the 9mm projectiles shed their copper jackets and released hundreds of tiny lead shot inside the wound channels.

Ballistic energy transfer was immediate and horrifying in its effectiveness. Underneath their clothes, the gang member's bodies were rocked with wave after wave of hydrostatic shock as their internal organs were ripped asunder. The three staggered back for only a step or two before they collapsed without firing a single shot in return. Two fell from the plank deck and splashed in the Mekong.

Here we go...shit's in the fan now. He dropped the suitcase with the money behind him and fell down behind it just as bullets began to crack past. *Hope they packed this bag tight. Boat load of money will stop some lead and what it doesn't will be partially expended.*

The night exploded in a wild firefight as the NPA and the team opened fire on one another. A round hit Mark in the right side, but was deflected by the body armor side panel. Another hit him in the lower back on the right side. *Armor500...don't fail me now.* "Uggh," he said as the rounds knocked the breath out of him. He rolled onto his left side as he pulled his S&W 5906 from its shoulder rig and returned fire at one of the four men on the far end of the wharf. A bullet hit his right thigh and swung it out wide of the suitcase and into the line of fire. Mark grabbed the numbed leg and pulled it back with his right hand just as a fully automatic burst from an AK ripped the wooden planks beside him. *If Tola had not sewed pockets in these pants for trauma plates I'd be in big ass trouble now.*

Weapons roared all around him. Bullets chewed up the old wooden planks. Splinters from one round struck him in the shoulder. Another sent splinters into his left calf. A dozen rounds hit the suitcase with the money knocking it back into him as they impacted.

Down the pier, Ice moved up behind one shooter and deftly slid his blade across the man's neck—severing the artery. He rolled behind a stack of wooden barrels and grabbed another from behind and drove the blade down his throat above the sternum. He twisted the knife blade hard increasing the damage to the throat, heart and lungs. As silently as he had appeared, he moved off toward his next victim leaving two dead that never saw or heard him coming.

On the opposite side of the pier his twin brother, Ton, placed a single round into the back of the head of a NPA soldier. The front of his face exploded—ripping his left cheekbone off in shattered bits and dislodging both eyeballs. He dropped like a wet sack.

Ton turned his weapon on a shooter to his right. As he aimed, the intended target's head exploded in a spray of pink mist. *Who did that? It did not come from the north.* He dropped to cover and looked around for the mystery shooter.

Rhino placed a round squarely in the outboard motor, instantly disabling it. As the engine ceased to operate, a cloud of white smoke billowed upwards and swirled off behind the disabled craft. The boat drifted to the wharf at first, but the current began to take it downstream. He put another round in the driver's chest—knocking him overboard into the murky water.

Operating the bolt on his suppressed rifle as fast as humanly possible—all the while keeping the butt to his shoulder—he placed the illuminated red center receptacle of the ATN Night Force scope on the NPA in the center of the boat. The man turned the muzzle of his AK-47 toward the canvas tarp between the baskets of produce. As Rhino let out his breath and began to squeeze the trigger the man's head exploded. *What the...fok? Who the hell made that shot?*

The South African moved on to the NPA standing on the bow of the craft. He stood spraying the wharf—bullets coming closer and closer to his blood brother trapped out in the open. Before he could attain a solid sight picture, a round to the shooter's chest lifted him up and threw him onto the baskets of produce. *Damn! That's some hellacious shootin'!* He quickly scanned the rooftops, but was unable to see anyone other than the enemy throwing lead down at Mark. He picked another target.

Gunny Lewis aimed for the flash of a rifle across the pier coming from a second-story window. He laid a short five round burst into the target area with his M16. Satisfied his fire was effective, he moved to a series of flashes on the rooftop and repeated the process, emptying his magazine. Unsure of his success, he held his weapon on target as he smoothly dropped the empty mag and reloaded. Another burst of fire occurred but before he could return it the shooter lurched up and fell forward into the water. The old Marine ducked behind his cover as a burst of automatic fire sought him as a target. *Oorah, Mutha Fucker! Got your position fixed now. Gonna light your skinny brown ass up.*

As he did a quick peek from a kneeling position, he saw the man who had fired on him take a hit to the face and fall back. *Shooter out there…somewhere…and I'm glad they're on our side.*

Tanipat had worked his way up the stairs and was easing out onto the roof when both NPA in front of him went down in succession—both with shots to the head. He ducked back into the doorway quickly and hugged the wall. *Damn! Three seconds sooner and I could have joined them.* He performed a series of quick looks. Seeing no other shooters on the roof, he made his way back down to the street. *This whole friggin' dance will be over before I get to kill anyone.*

A pair of NPA came running straight for the door he was exiting. Intent on escaping, they inadvertently ran right into his blazing M16 and dropped in a heap at his feet. *Yeah! That's more like it.* As the retired SWAT officer began to turn, his legs went soft. He staggered forward before falling into the street. Looking down he saw the dark red——nearly black—stain growing on his right thigh. *Damn…one of those pieces of shit got lucky. I gotta get a tourna…* Tanipat passed out before he could finish his thought. The 7.62 round from his adversary's AK had clipped a femoral artery and he bled out in the gutter.

Slash had been working his way along the riverbank. Swimming with only an occasional surfacing to keep his bearings, he made for the second boat. Seeing it was drifting toward him, he slid under the surface and swam to it. He grabbed the stern before slipping out of the water and into the boat with the ease of a man—a SEAL—who had done it so many times before. Laying flat to maintain a low profile he crawled forward to the canvas cover and pulled it back.

John and Susan Reynolds—their hands and feet tied and mouths gagged with black duck tape—stared at him with terrified eyes. The face they saw was painted with streaks of dark green and black camo grease and a US Navy SEALs dive mask. Only the whites of his eyes shown in the moonlight. Slash put his index finger to his lips and lowered the tarp. He slipped over the gunwales and moved quickly to the stern and kicked the boat forward with long powerful strokes.

The gunfire ended almost as quickly as it had erupted. Mark held his position knowing any survivor on the bad guy's team would love to pick him off as a parting shot. *Damnation! I think I got a broken rib here.* He started to laugh softly then stopped with a low moan. *Ain't bad considering all the lead flyin' my way.* He peeked over the case full of money and saw Ice and Ton inspecting the bodies at the far end of the wharf.

Gunny Lewis was striding toward him like a true Marine walking the battlefield after a firefight. "Hey, Jarhead! You okay?" the burly sergeant called out.

"Yeah, Gunny. All's good here."

"You are one *crazy* son-of-a-bitch, McCallister."

"So I've been told," Mark replied as he got to his feet. He called Rhino, "Keep us covered, fat man."

"Who you callin' fat man, you brak-ass skinny runt?"

Into the headpiece of every operative. came the silky voice of Daiyu, "I'm gone, Zorro. I'll call you about the money...I promise the drop will be less...frenetic."

"Who the hell is this?" Rhino chimed in.

"Black Jade...Oh, by the way...there are three bodies in the building under you, fat man...Third floor. One was on the phone with dingleberry on the wharf...I want half the reward if it turns out to be Inkong."

"It's *all* yours Jade...You earned it," Mark replied.

"I knew it...I knew there was another fokin' long rifle out there. Hey Jade...how 'bout you and I meet a for a beer?"

Nothing but silence answered him.

"Jade? Oh come on...don't be like that...Jade?"

Again, the channel was dead.

The bow of the long boat skidded against the slime-covered pier with an audible thud. Slash reached up to grab hold of the transom. With one fluid movement, he pulled himself over the stern and flopped onto the bottom of the narrow boat. He quickly yanked his black swim fins off and got to his feet as he removed his goggles and snorkel. Wasting no time, he made his way forward and flipped back the tarp that had covered the Reynolds couple.

"You are safe now. Let's get this tape off of you."

Both began to cry as he cut their bonds with his dive knife

Slash carefully peeled the duct tape off John Reynolds' jawbone. "This might sting a little bit." He needn't have worried.

John grabbed the excess with his hand and gave it a yank. "Who are you?" he asked breathlessly.

"A friend," Slash replied. "That's all you need to know. Let's get you two off this garbage scow. Don't have much time."

He helped Susan up to her knees as she sobbed in relief that their ordeal was almost over. Her husband pulled the tape from her mouth as her body shook.

Slash tied off the boat quickly and helped the two barefoot hostages climb the well-worn wooden ladder up the dock. Mark checked out the windows and rooftops for any remaining tangos. He walked to the ladder to offer a hand to the couple. "Watch your step. These planks are kinda rough," he cautioned, as he helped John up the last step.

Slash steadied Susan as she made her way up. He made eye contact with Mark momentarily and then flashed a big grin to his friend. Seeing a thumbs-up sign from him, he turned and retrieved his dive mask and fins.

Susan staggered a couple steps on the wharf. She heard a splash in he river behind her and spun around. Their savior was already gone.

"This way," Mark said as John assisted his wife. He reached down and grabbed the ransom money and Uzi case. "We'll get you to a hospital."

John saw the sole remaining NPA kidnapper's body lying face up on the dock—her mouth open as if she was trying to say something. She was the ugly one who had brutalized them most.

He couldn't contain the rage he had built up inside him. He stepped quickly over to her and kicked her head with his bare foot, causing her neck to snap over at an unnatural angle. He screamed at her and kept kicking the body viciously until it rolled off the pier into the water and sank. John's body shook with rage and he stared at the spot as he tried to catch his breath.

In the distance, the sound of sirens could be heard approaching.

Mark spoke to the team via his headset, "Sound off."

In turn, everyone checked in but Tanipat.

"Tanipat...You hit?" Mark called. Silence confirmed his fear. "Find him. If he's down...take him out of here. Everybody get gone. I don't want Metro to find any of you." He set the suitcase with the ransom money on the dock and placed his hand on Reynold's shoulder. "Come on my friend...We gotta move."

John spun around and looked at him. Mark could sympathize with the uncontrollable rage the young man felt—years later, the loss of his wife and child to a Mexican cartel's drive-by shooting still haunted him.

Gunny Lewis walked up and extended his hand. "Come on...let's take you guys home."

The voice of yet another American seemed to momentarily break the fevered hatred flowing in John's veins. He reached for his wife and wrapped his arms around her as the rescuers herded them toward the parking lot.

***

CHAPTER FOURTEEN

PIER FIVE AFTERMATH

Virote looked on as a paramedic attended to Mark's wounded calf—removing numerous ragged wooden splinters. A white bandage was already wrapped around his rib cage and iodine stains marked the splinter wounds on his face, hands and shoulder.

Nearby other medics tended to John and Susan Reynolds. Each had a fresh clean bandage around their heads and appeared to be in shock. As the doors closed on the ambulance they looked to Mark with a haunted distant look of thankfulness.

"You did it," Virote exclaimed joyfully.

"Yeah, yeah…piece of cake."

"If one of the bodies is Inkong. There's a three million baht reward…dead or alive."

"Give it to the Reynolds couple. Ain't near enough for what they been through…but hey…it's what?…fifty grand US per ear, right?"

"You have a good heart McCallister…but a sick sense of humor," Virote said. "I will put in my report that you accomplished this task at great risk to yourself."

"I had some good help…"

"Ahh…but I cannot attest to that. No one here but you when I arrived," he said with a sly smile.

"Gonna be a little hard to fly that with all the bad guys laying around." Mark slowly stood up. "Ohhh…this sucks. Gonna to cut into my break dancing," he said softly as he held his injured ribs.

"Only add to the legend, McCallister. Only add to the legend."

Mark took a step forward then paused to let the rush of pain pass. *Gotta get some kick ass meds.* "And what…legend is that Virote?"

"Our mutual friend, Patrick Murry, told me about your exploits in Kenya…Saving the President and all."

Mark fixed the policeman with a steady gaze. "Yeah…well I had some good help then as well. How about you just exclude my name all together?"

"Oh no. Can not do that. The Chief will want a name. And the press…"

"Yeah, yeah…the press is what I'm worried about. I'd prefer to remain anonymous."

"Too late. We have them behind the crime scene tape back there, but their cameras have been running for some time. Better get your statement ready."

"Well, *hell*…this cluster just gets worse by the minute."

DARK SECRET

JORIS BANRHARDT'S RESIDENCE

Mark stepped out of the elevator just as Joris, Roger and Mike approached from the living area.

"I see we have the hero of the year amongst us," Joris said with a bit of jealousy as he waved a copy of the morning newspaper.

Mark continued to the kitchen without stopping. "Ya'll call me when you land at the office," he said with a look to Roger and Mike.

"Will do boss," Roger replied.

"You need anything?" Mike asked.

"Coffee black…two new ribs…and I'll be good."

The three entered the lift and as the doors closed Joris called out, "Look forward to hearing the inside story tonight."

Mark ignored him. As he entered the kitchen Dalisay, Tola, Val and the staff started clapping. "Ahh jeez…what's a guy have to do to get a cup of coffee around here?"

"Coffee for Mister McCallister. I have a ten ounce sirloin ready to grill for you. What else would you like this morning?" Val replied.

"Eggs…some sweet breads…maybe some fresh squeezed orange juice."

"Coming right up. Get to it girls. Breakfast for the hero."

Mark shook his head and sat down gingerly at the breakfast table with Dalisay and Tola. He eased his injured leg out and gently relaxed it.

"I…we…were worried for you last night, Steve. Tola and I both prayed for your safe return," Dalisay said as she took his uninjured hand in hers and sat down.

"Must of worked." He looked to Tola.

"Your coffee, Mister McCallister. My sister gives good professional massage. You want I call her?" the young Thai servant said as she placed the cup and saucer on the table.

"Ain't nobody rubbing any part of me 'til these ribs heal." Mark lifted the cup and took a long swallow. "Oh, that's good…Thanks anyway for the thought."

Hans and Francisca walked in at that moment. "Up to your old tricks I see," Hans chided.

"Hans…great to see you again," Mark exclaimed as he started to get up, but sat back down with a groan. He extended his hand. "Francisca you are as beautiful as ever."

"Zorro, you are such a charmer," Francisca said with a warm smile as she sat down at the table across from him.

"I reviewed the security system while you were out playing cowboy with the locals. I have a list of components and think I could have this whole mess cleaned out and replaced in seven to ten days…depending on how long it takes for the items to arrive." Hans accepted a glass of fresh orange juice.

"Let's get 'er done ol buddy. Most of us are off to Cebu in a couple of days. But I'm detailing Rhino to stay here. He's not much with electronics, but he'll insure your safety 'til we get back."

"How long will you be gone?"

"A week for Joris, Roger and Mike. Tola and I are going south to Mindanao…Be back in two."

"Mindanao? No go Mindanao…isn't that what you said the last time you went?"

"Yeah I did. But…that was a couple of years ago. Missus Barnhardt's family lives near Dipolog…Pretty quiet there compared to down further south."

"I will need someone to approve the expenses before I place the orders."

"Give me the list. I'll fax it over to the office," Dalisay replied.

"Your steak, sir. Medium rare…no bleeding." Val placed it on the table.

LILOY, PHILIPPINES
Mindanao Island

The MNLF made much better time in the two rattletrap Isuzu pickup trucks procured at the small village and pulled into the fringes of Liloy—a small fishing community that worked the Sulu Sea on the northwest coast of Mindanao.

Isagani motioned the men into a deserted shack and the drivers to move the trucks around to the back. "Everyone stay here. I will go and see my cousin to arrange for the boats."

"What do we do with the women when we get on the boats?"

"We…take the oldest three. Use the young ones 'til we leave…Behead them. Use them again if you wish."

Isagani handed his stolen M16, magazine pouches and a blood-soaked Philippines Army jacket to one of the men and walked off without another word. Now dressed in simple Filipino peasant attire he blended in with the locals nicely—his purloined Beretta 9 mm pistol hidden beneath his shirt. *Two boats will do. We can be near Dipolog before the festivals.*

Locating the modest dwelling of his relative he entered the small courtyard and approached the front door. Before he could knock, the door opened.

"Isagani? How...what are you doing here?" His cousin looked furtively around and motioned to enter.

"I walked. I need you help..."

"Yes of course...but why are you here?"

"I am going to Dipolog...with thirty-seven of Allah's finest warriors. We will strike a great blow..."

"Dipolog?"

"Yes. No one will expect us to hit them so far north. The Catholic festivals are coming."

"I see...but, what can I do? I am but a fisherman," the man asked with some hesitation.

"Boats...I need two boats."

SECURITY HOUSE

Mark had the entire team collected to go over the Philippines travel plans. He sat on a barstool with his injured leg extended.

"Rhino...you will remain here with Hans. Do whatever you can to assist him."

"Done."

"Roger…Mike…Tola…we go with the Barnhardts. First to Cebu. Once settled in, Tola and I will escort Dalisay to her home on Mindanao."

"What about me?" Keit asked.

"You remain here. Provide transport for Hans and Rhino."

"So…you're going to leave us in Cebu? Just the two of us?" Mike questioned.

"There will be a experienced ICC with you, Berto, and another operative…call sign Crank…who will meet us at the airport. Give you boys a chance to get to know each other before boots hit the ground."

"Crank?…The surfer dude Hal was ragging on about?"

"Ja…there's only one loskop Crank, kid," Rhino interjected.

Another four hours of details concluded after relentless review. Mark felt very comfortable with the plan—especially knowing Crank would be the foundation of the team left in Cebu with Joris.

Mark stood up slowly and carefully stretched. "That about wraps it up boys and girls…"

"Question," Blaster said.

"Batter up…what is it?"

"About last night…"

"There wasn't any last night. We all just landed here from outer space ten minutes ago."

"No, seriously…the photos in the paper and on the news clips…what the hell was the goofy disguise all about?"

Mark exchanged looks with Rhino and Tola. "Who was that guy?"

"Well…it was you. The police inspector said it was…gave your name," Mike answered uncomfortably—much like the kid in fifth grade who raised his hand but was unsure of his answer.

"Yeah…unfortunately he did. So…now any more bad guys looking for Steve McCallister are looking for…"

"A cheap arse knockoff of a long dead domkop brak pop singer…once married to a mompie loskop cuiter," Rhino said.

The entire team laughed at his comment. Good natured ribbing ensued with everyone throwing a jab or two about the disguise.

"I thought he was going for the Burt Reynolds look in those Bandit movies," Roger said.

"Smoky an de Bandits? I love those moobies," Keit added. "I likie the Smoky guy."

"Jackie Gleason, Keit. I thought he was going for the John Holmes thing…minus the tripod," Mike said.

"Tripod?" Tola questioned.

"He was a porn star back in the seventies. Carried a big stick…big," Roger remarked as he laughed and held his hands up spreading them wider and wider.

"Wonderland murders," Mark said.

"That one of his films?" Mike asked.

"No…John put a gang together and robbed one of the biggest crime bosses in lala land…Early eighties. Ended up going south…Four people died," Mark answered.

COSTA RICA
Jungle

Chikako paused on the side of Highway 3 at the outskirts of the town of Jesus. It had taken considerable time to get back to the small village with her injured knee. *If the Triad is waiting here I'm done. But logically…they would have cleared out after the incident at the bus. If not? Have to deal with it. Got to get another ride back to camp and my weapons.*

After a short rest break, she walked onto the shoulder of the road and began to hobble into the sleeping village. *Catch a ride on whatever is going west. Hop the bus again in San Mateo. Jump the ferry at Puntarenas. Home free.*

A vintage 1957 Chevrolet pickup—with faded blue paint—honked and began to pull over as it passed. A elderly Costa Rican woman opened the passenger door and stepped out.

"You hurt? You look hurt," Roseta said in broken English.

"Yes…yes I am."

"Gorgio…you come help us," the woman said in Spanish.

A man in his late sixties climbed out of the cab. They took Chikako by the arms and helped her to the truck.

"What happen to you? What you do out here alone? Where you go?" she asked.

"Montezuma. But anywhere west you can take me."

He and his wife started talking in Spanish far too fast for her to understand, having only begun to study the language. They continued their discussion as they lifted her into the truck and got back in themselves.

"We go to see our grandchildren in Puntarenas Canton. We take you that far. Get you to the ferry dock," the elderly woman finally said. "You leg broken? You need doctor…no?"

"No. I fell and a thorn…"

Gorgio pulled over at a small road side soda—a family run restaruant, convenience store that often doubles as a bar or disco after dark. While the woman stayed in the truck, the man got out and went inside.

"Gorgio go…get some…some…medicos. No say in English. Medicos…usted comprende?"

"Yes. I can pay…"

"No pay. We fix."

Gorgio returned with two large plastic bags and handed them through the window to his wife. Without a word he entered the truck and drove back onto the highway.

"Me see," the Roseta said as she began to remove the Nike pants wrapped around the swollen knee. "Oh chika…maybe just in time," she said once the pants were removed. "Por que esta?" She asked looking at the Mepilex patch.

"Medicina patch. For healing…Ahh," Chikako exclaimed at the old woman lifted the patch. "It kills infection…Oow!"

The woman poured some rubbing alcohol over the wound and bumped the edge of the plastic bottle against the knee as the truck bounced along the roadway.

"Ugh…mas cuidado, por favor," Chikako said through clenched teeth.

"Si...si...¡lo siento mucho! Comida...food...you eat," she said as she handed the second bag her.

Not recognizing what the foods were, the famished Chikako selected the item on top, unwrapped it and without pause, devoured the pastry filled with pork. She opened the bottle of water and washed it down before taking another one out and ate it as well. All the while she watched as her leg was cared for. *Good luck for me. Perfect cover all the way to Pantarenas. Ice? Oh my god...ice! The old man is a lifesaver.*

Rosita placed a small zip lock bag filled with ice on the injury and wrapped it gently with the soiled Nike pants. "Necesitamos más hielo que consigamos algo cuando se funde." Seeing Chikako's questioning look she said, "We get more...more hielo when this melt."

The weary Japanese woman laid her head back on the top of the bench seat, closed her eyes and fell into a deep sleep. *So tired. Just close my eyes...for a minute.*

SHENYANG, CHINA
Dadong District

Zhi Peng Wu's number one assistant entered the room without knocking and rushed to the man he served ignoring protocol.

"Master...there has been a breakthrough..."

Wu turned to the excited underling and fixed him with a hard look. He did not appreciate being interrupted without warning while viewing one of his pornographic films.

The man paused and bowed deeply. "My apologies Master Wu. I am so sorry," he said with a tremble in his voice.

"What is it that causes you to ignore my rule of privacy?"

The now concerned underling remained bowed. "The killers of Dragon Master Wu in Hong Kong. There is a...a new development."

Zhi leaned forward and placed his elbows on the desk. His eyes narrowed with interest. "Go on."

"The computers in the suite were destroyed in the fire. But the off-site backups have revealed there were three killers."

"Why has it taken this long to discover this?"

"I only thought of it last night. I spent all night reviewing them. It is clear that one is a woman. Maybe two...they all have long hair...one black another is gray...and one has blonde but is too big to be a woman."

"You want me to believe an old woman was involved in the slaughter? You jest."

"It is hard to say...they wore equipment that hides their faces...helmets, nightvision...until the end. The old one must be a lesbian if a woman...moves like a man and is...masculine looking. And there is a third...definitely a man."

"Print me images of these killers. As much detail as possible. I will inspect them and decide which ones to send our cell leaders."

"I have done so already Master," the assistant said as he extended his left hand and offered a large envelope. He remained bowed during the entire exchange and only looked up to ensure his offering was properly directed.

DARK SECRET

"I will want you to send copies to Madam X in Kenya," Wu said as he accepted the envelope. "Stand up. I am pleased with your efforts."

A look of relief washed over the man's face as he stood erect. "Thank you, Master Wu. I crossed the images with those in our catalog of employees. The missing Yakuza woman…I am certain she is one of them."

DUMAGUETE CITY, PHILIPPINES

Jesse Ingram stepped off the twenty foot fishing boat onto a wooden pier just north of the Rizal Boulevard park. Simply called the boulevard by the locals, it was a two mile long eight foot wide cement boardwalk that fronted the ocean. Between the boulevard and Rizal Blouvard was a thirty yard wide park with numerous bandstands, park benches, coconut trees and flower beds.

He walked leisurely so as not to attract any unnecessary attention. Jesse carried only a faded blue backpack and a large dark brown shoulder bag—inside was his Colt Mk IV 1911 and spare magazines. It took less than three minutes to be on the concrete boardwalk and only another twenty to be at the intersection of Rizal and Bishop Epifanio Suburban Street. Turning left he walked the long block to the Santa Maria Luisa Hotel.

"Jesse…so glad to see you," Mia, the young front desk girl, said warmly. "You stay with us again?"

"Is the honeymoon suite available?" Jesse replied as he moved to the counter. "Whew…the aircon feels good."

"Most certainly it is...on both counts. How long will you stay this time?"

"Mia, I need a shower...then I'm going down to the Why Knot and have a steak. Could you arrange for a driver and a aircon cab for me? Say...around 1700?"

"For certain I can. Here is the key. You know the way...I tell housekeeping to make sure all is good in the honeymoon suite."

He paid for three days in advance and rather than take the elevator, started up the stairs. On his left he passed the Internet cafe area—nothing more than six computer monitors and keyboards set up back to back on a long table.

"How much to Internet now?"

"Forty pesos one hour."

On the third floor he passed the elevator and opened the door to room 302—the honeymoon suite. Located on the front of the hotel it afforded a excellent view of the park and the coming and going of all who entered the hotel.

He locked the door, placed the desk chair under the knob, and then turned on the air conditioner. *Musky smelling it is in here.* He stripped off his sweat soaked clothing and took a cold shower.

Later he lay down on the thick foam mattress and considered the coming difficulties. *Get with Cello and weapon up. Contact Hal and find out where Mark is now. Get there before the Triad. Piece of cake...as Hal always says when a operation that is going south was in progress.*

Two hours later the elder Ingram walked into the Why Knot. The restaurand was owned by a Swiss man and served the only really true steak in town—grass-raised beef from New Zealand—calling it pricey was putting it mildly. A eight ounce sirloin went for a thousand pesos or twenty-five dollars and a twelve ounce rib eye was nearly twice that.

Facing the boulevard and the sea, the view was like something out of an adventure or romance novel. He had lived here for a time but noticed the flow of foreigners growing every year he had moved on to a quieter location and began the process of going native.

After placing his order, he heard a commotion outside on the patio and moved to see what was going on. Four local street toughs were harassing a elderly white man and his young Filipino girlfriend. He was his seventies and rather frail of build, and was surrounded. Although he was yelling loudly, it was obvious he was afraid. The young girl stood behind him swinging her knockoff designer purse at one of the young males when he came too close.

Damn...all I wanted was a quiet steak dinner. Jesse, still holding a glass bottle of Coca Cola, picked up a large umbrella as he walked out into the street. The thugs where so engrossed in harassing the old foreigner they did not immediately notice him approaching. That did not work out well for the first one he walked up to and he went down like a bag of wet cement when the bottle impacted the back of his head.

All three of the others pulled butterfly knives and shouting and cursing, they turned on the new threat.

"You don't have to do this. Just pick up your buddy and move on," Jesse said quietly.

"I cut you like a buaga, old man," the taller Filipino said as he advanced.

"You sorry soon, you gay chicken shit," another said as he danced around excitedly.

"Last chance boys…Pick up sleeping beauty and move on while you can."

The older gentleman had collected his young girlfriend and now huddled against the iron railing to the outside sitting area of the Why Knot. Though appreciative of the help, he was not going to be of any assistance—especially seeing the boys flip open their knives and twirl them with the sunlight glinting off the blades.

The first one to make a move received a sharp whack to the side of his head with the umbrella followed by a knee to the face as he bent over. Without pausing, Jesse spun and hit another one on his upraised arm breaking the umbrella's stem—and the young man's forearm.

"Ahhh!" he screamed as he dropped to his knees. His cries ended when Jesse's roundhouse kick landed on his jaw and broke it as well.

The third and taller of the assailants turned and fled, leaving his buddies laying on the street. Unfortunately for him he ran right into the arms of two local policeman approaching the scene. He wisely dropped his knife when he saw they had pistolseled at this chest.

"Mister Ingram…I see you are back…and up to your old tricks," the older officer said. "On the ground, Silico…Hands behind your head. Cuff him, Danno."

"Just in time Corporal Quzon. I was waiting for a steak here and heard a disturbance…"

"He saved our lives," the old Australian interjected. "These ruffians were trying to rob me. And they threatened Alicia as well."

"I suggest you go enjoy your dinner, Mister Ingram. I'll get your statement later," the corporal said.

"Sounds good," Jesse replied. As he turned to enter the restaurant, with a smile he spoke to the foreigner, "I recommend you consider carrying an umbrella in the future."

One hour later Corporal Quzon walked up to the table, sat down and placed his hat on the chair next to him. "What's your version of the event?…"

"…I understand. Where are you staying?"

"Santa Maria Louisa. Same as always."

"I must insist you do not leave town until the hearing. A few days at most. Do I have your word that you will not leave?"

"I'm just here for a day or two…"

"Do I have your word?"

"Damn, Quzon…I can't promise to stick around here for a hearing. A couple of days in your country can be weeks."

"I'll have an officer posted at the Maria Louisa then. Welcome back to Dumaguete, Mister Ingram."

Ingrham

Great. No way I can hang around here...and skipping out will probably make Dumaguete a no-go destination in the future. Well...at least the steak and baked potato were great. Jesse watched the officer leave and smiled.

***

CHAPTER FIFTEEN

DON MUEANG AIRPORT
Bangkok, Thailand

Mark, Dalisay and Tola stood several feet from the limousine while Roger and Mike, positioned further out to the front and back, stood post. Kiet sat in the driver's seat with the motor running and the air conditioning blowing full on while Joris remained in the passenger compartment attending to business on his laptop.

The large custom painted jet with the Barnhardt logo landed and taxied to the waiting vehicle.

"With me, Roger…Tola, stay with Missus Barnhardt and collect Rutger," Mark said. Without waiting for a reply he walked off. *Damn it's hot. I need to invent a business suit that ventilates. Could make a fortune on 'em.*

"That's a expensive ride," Roger noted as Mark joined him.

"Yeah, Bombardier 7000. Probably cost more than you or I will ever earn. I think they start at sixty-five mil."

"Didn't know there were two airports in Bangkok."

"Yup. This was the original…Used to be a military base. When they opened Suvarnabhumi, everybody rushed in to the new and improved international airport. Couple of years later they reopened Don Mueang because of the fees and issues with the runway crackin' and bucklin' at Suvarnabhumi."

"Once we hit Cebu…how many days will you be with us before you head out?"

"Day…maybe two. Once I'm gone you and Dog just need to follow Crank and Berto's lead. Both are the real deal."

"Any chance we'll get to see him surf?"

"Not likely. The fandango surrounding the opening of the new orphanage will be a 24/7 cluster, most likely." Seeing Joris exit the vehicle, he nodded to Blaster and returned to the family and Tola.

Once the jet shut down its two engines and the ramp lowered, Rutger charged down the stairs and ran into his mother's open arms. Dressed in his private school's mandatory attire—a suit and tie—he looked like a miniature businessman.

"Mommie!" he yelled as he ran.

"My little man…I missed you," Dalisay said as tears ran down her cheeks.

Once the reunion hugs and kisses concluded, Joris stepped up and extended his right hand. "Welcome home, son."

"Hello, father," the young boy said solemnly as he shook the elder man's hand.

"Let's get home now. I have a video conference in two hours with an associate in the islands. Don't want to be late."

Joris turned and walked to the car without another word to his newly arrived son—only pausing long enough to hand an envelope to each of the two security personnel who deplaned, then dismissing them to fend for themselves until they arranged transportation back to Holland.

That's odd. Don't think I've ever seen a father less interested in his child's return after months away. Mark watched as Dalisay and Rutger followed Joris. He motioned to Roger and Mike to return to the limo and joined them. "Mike…you take shotgun this time. Roger…in back with me."

While Dalisay and Rutger talked excitedly about what had happened at school while he was away, Joris seemed intent on the business he conducted on his laptop, never once smiling or indicating he heard a word his wife and son said.

I thought my father was distant but this is a whole new level of disconnect right here. I'd like to shut that laptop on his fingers but…better hold off rockn' the boat any more than I already have.

PUNTARENAS, COSTA RICA

The literal translation of Puntarenas from Spanish to English is sand point. It was first discovered by Hernán Ponce de León in 1519. Long used by the Spanish to enter the interior of Costa Rica, the port itself was not improved for shipping until 1840 when coffee production in the highlands reached exportable volumes—the two ports shared the town of 100,000 residents.

One was used predominately by the cruise industry for the thousands of visitors landing each year to explore the eco-industry opportunities and sex trade—both of which Costa Rica is known worldwide. The smaller port was mostly home to the local fishing ships and the ferry that connected Paquera and Puntarenas across the Gulf of Nicoya.

Chikako woke to the gentle nudging of Gorgio and his wife. She was covered in sweat and felt feverish from her wound even though a cool pre-dawn breeze blew through the cab. The old Tica offered her a bottle of chilled water, which she drank without pausing.

"We are here. There is the ferry office. It open in two hour. We wait you," the woman said.

"Thank you for your kindness," she replied as she carefully scanned the deserted dock. *If I can get on the ferry without any Triad seeing me...I still have a chance to get back to my hide.*

"She is very sick, mamma," Gorgio said to his wife in Spanish. "Maybe she needs to see a doctor?"

"No...no mucho malo," Chikako answered. "I will be good once I get home." She flexed her injured leg and let out a low moan. *Ah shit. It's really swollen now.* "Maybe you...could help me. I need a crutch or a walking cane...stick...sticko?" She made gestures with her hands.

"We stay here. Gorgio go find for you. I help you to the ferry officina he is not back in time. Then we wait you for time to cross. First boat go nine each morning," she said measuring her words in English as she motioned her husband to go.

"My second nephew has a pharmacy here. I will be back soon with what you need," Gorgio said in Spanish too rapidly for her to understand as he departed.

Chikako eased up on the seat and peered out the back window of the old truck, and then made a 360 degree scan of the dock area. She checked her cell phone to get the time. *Going south faster every minute. Sure as hell wasn't as waterproof as advertised. The little river ride did it in.* She lay back on the seat and closed her eyes. *Get back to the hide. Get back to the hide.* She continued to repeat the thought as she slipped back into an exhausted sleep.

DUMAGUETE CITY, PHILIPPINES

Jesse waited in the central park. He could see the police officer assigned to keep an eye on him sitting in the McDonalds sipping coffee. *I hate to do it to you buddy...but when Cello calls...I'm gone.*

Hearing his cell phone ring, the elder Ingram picked up his day pack and started to the entrance of the fast-food diner. The police officer tried to look interested in a copy of the Sun Star newspaper as he approached. As Jesse neared the door he pulled a short length of olive drab paracord from his pack, wrapped it around the two long U shaped door handles and secured it—effectively sealing it until someone outside removed it. He flagged down one of the many passing trike cabs and waved to the officer as he jumped up and ran to the door.

The officer did a hard face plant on the glass door, turned and raced to the opposite side of the restaurant—Jesse was already lost in the flow of traffic.

VALENCIA, PHILIPPINES

Once outside Dumagute the 125 HP Kawasaki bike strained to climb the hills on Jose Romero Road then coasted too fast on the downhill runs as it made its way to Valencia—the site of the final battle between the Japanese, the Filipino resistance fighters and US Army forces near the end of World War II on the island of Negros Occidental.

Jesse dismissed the cab driver in the Valencia Plaza, and once he had departed, he waved down a local.

"How much to Casaroro Waterfalls?"

"Five hundred pesos."

"Hell...I can rent a trike all day for that...How about two hundred and I buy your lunch?"

"Two fifty plus lunch," the man said after sizing up his potential fare.

"Done. Where do you want to eat?"

"Miguels. It is on the way. Very good food. American chips and salsa...enchiladas...other American Mescan foods." He started his bike.

"American Mescan, hey? This should be interesting," Jesse replied as he climbed into the trike side car.

"No, is good. Owner from Texas…well, wife is owner but the asawa Texan…he Mescan…he cook. Gets all his foods from the states by balikbayan box."

"I'm starving…let's go get some American Mescan." Jesse laughed.

Three hours later, two orders of cheese enchiladas and a huge plate of beef fajitas, double beans and rice, several bowls of chips and salsa and four beers, Jesse sat stuffed and contented.

Rosi came in and asked, "You want more? We make more if you want?"

"I am too full to eat another chip. Thank you though… What do I owe you?"

"Asawa said you get Texas discount…so fifteen hundred pesos to you."

"Worth every centavo," Jesse replied as he paid her and included a two hundred peso tip. *Seven bucks? Can't beat that.*

As he entered the cab Tex came out with a small styrofoam chest. "A six pack for the road my friend," he said as he handed it to Jesse.

"A big Texas thank you," Jesse said with a huge smile.

"You should know that there's a search going on now. I just heard it on the scanner. Sounds like the Dumaguete cops done lost a suspect…and the suspect they described sounds just like you."

"'Preciate it. You got an old cap or hat around here I could borrow?" Jesse asked as he removed his shirt and began digging through his day pack for another.

"I have a New York Yankees hat an expat left here couple of months ago. Been using it for target practice…but you're welcome to it."

"Sounds perfect, I guess you let anyone eat here…if you were home in Texas, you would have stretched some rope with the Yankee."

CASARORO WATERFALLS

Hidden deep in the crevices of the rough Valencia mountains, Casaroro Falls can only be seen after taking 360 concrete steps down into the ravine—not a bad hike going in but a real bitch coming out. Definitely not a place to visit in the rainy season as the additional moisture can make the climb in or out slick and dangerous to those not in excellent shape.

Jesse paid the driver for the ride and agreed to another two hundred pesos for him to wait and haul him back to Valencia. He shoved four of the Lone Star beer bottles into his pack and left the remaining two with the driver.

Once on the long climb down, he could not help but notice the eerie similarity to the jungle in Vietnam. Even knowing there were not any punji sticks, wild hog traps or lurking VC, he was still glad he had his 1911 nestled in the small of his back under the loose fitting floral cotton shirt. *Never leave home without it.*

Halfway down the trail, a voice called softly from the jungle on his right. "Hal says to give you a hand."

Jesse stopped and slowly turned. "Piece of cake."

Cello, a lean six foot black man with full beard and a high-end glass eye, pulled back the jungle foliage exposing himself partially. "The three most dreaded words the man ever spoke." He stepped onto the trail and extended his hand. "No sense in hikin' all da way down. It's a mutha fucka climbin' back out. You have a ride waiting up der?"

"I do."

"Let's get goin'. I has a small Nipa hut up da coast. Use it fer fishin' mostly…and an occasional lost weekend wit some little brown skin pleasure."

"How far to some toys?" Jesse asked.

"Depends. I broughts some to da Nipa camp, based on what Hal told me. If nots 'nough, den it's a day to da safe vault."

"I need some forty-five ammo and a long rifle…" Jesse paused as two couples appeared on the trail ahead of them.

"I waz thinkin' we should set some crab cages tonight…Maybes throws some nets in da mornin' for bangus…" Cello started back as the group passed, "What else?"

"A 308. Preferably an M14 or a M1A if you have it. A dozen grenades…phosphorus and frag mix…three or four claymores…"

"Shit man. You goin' on some warpath ain't ya? Hal said ya just needed some regular ass firepowers. Haveta spend da night at Nipa and gets to da vault for da explosives."

"Works for me. You have a satellite cell? I need to talk to Hal. Get an update on the target."

"Yeah. Back at the hut."

BARNHARDT'S PRIVATE JET
Air Space Over the South China Sea

Joris secluded himself in the private quarters at the rear of the aircraft claiming a need to deal with numerous business activities. Val busied himself in the front cabin—custom designed for his culinary activities—with practically a full kitchen.

Dalisay, Rutger and Tola sat in the second cabin playing cards. Mark, Crank, Roger and Mike occupied the third compartment specifically designed as the entertainment center. Crank, Blaster and Dog watched a basketball game on a forty inch flat screen. Mark busied himself with last minute details for the arrival of the group in Cebu City.

"Berto, our ETA is now 1100 due to unforeseen delays out of Bangkok. Same drill upon arrival," Mark said using his satellite cell phone.

"I look forward to seeing and working with you again," he replied.

"Likewise. What's the latest on the mussie activities on Mindanao?"

"The assault on Zamboanga City seems to have ended. Some mopping up going on by the Philippines Army and the US Marines who…of course are not there." Berto laughed.

"Same old, same old…but nothing else? No other hot spots?"

"None reported. If you would consider my second eldest son, Michele, to assist you in Dipolog I would be grateful. You could take his pay out of mine…"

"How old is he now?"

"Twenty-one last month. I have trained him myself. Good with weapons and very good in the field. Still inexperienced in urban…"

"Consider it done. No need to short your pay. Everyone works…everyone gets paid according to their value. How about one thousand for a week? If he's good I'll give him a bonus to bump it up a bit…and of course the standard bump if there's any real threat."

"Why are you so good to me, Zorro? That is very generous offer for a new operative."

"Well let's see now…you saved my ass in Cotabato in 09? Then there's the *hump my ass* out of Polomoko jungle in 2010…"

"Neither of which repay your efforts on Sulu island my friend. I would not be here today to play with my children and grandchildren if you had not…"

"Let's play who owes who the most when I see you, Berto. I have some details to attend to right now. Regards to your better half. I'll call thirty before we land." Mark hung up and noticed the three operatives seemed to be hitting it off well. *Crank will be a good change of pace for the puppies.*

Crank caught Mark studying them. "Time for the seminar?"

"Good a time as any. The ICC will have carry permits for us when we land. No such thing as get-out-of-jail cards in the land of no planning."

"No planning?" Mike asked.

Ingrham

"No word for planning in any of the languages in the Philippines. Not much concept of it either...even after decades of US protection," Mark replied as he shuffled through several satellite images of the area around Dipolog.

"You worked with this ICC Berto before, I assume?" Blaster inquired.

"Assume nothing...but yes, several times. Good guy. Whatever you do don't put him in a position that appears to make him lose face. Losing face is a huge deal in the Philippines."

"Like what? I mean...what looks like losing face there?"

"Jesus...the possibilities are endless. Consider this..." Mark paused to craft his answer. "There's this...macho thing in the RP. I think it comes from the four hundred years of Spanish rule. If you've been around any of the Hispanic cultures it's pretty much the same thing. Losing face is a big deal."

"I served with some Hispanics in the Rangers. Lots of *rooster strutting* we called it," Mike added.

"To avoid any unnecessary difficulties I always make sure there's a way for the Filipinos to move on without looking stupid or insulted. I suggest you do the same."

"Example?" Roger asked.

"Let 'em think they're more important or...manly than they are. Does you no harm and gives 'em a bit of braggin' rights."

Crank leaned back and put his hands behind his back while trying to conceal a sly smile.

"You want to add something Crank?" Mark asked.

"Nah, boss...I'm good."

"Maybe share your experience in Zamboagna...you know the Blue Tuna bar?" Mark prodded.

"I...ah...no, not really, boss," Crank said as he shifted his weight a bit.

"Come on Crank. What happened?" Roger asked.

"Well...Zorro and I...Berto and another op named Cello were working a contract with some mining engineers from Australia. There was a misunderstanding with some Philippine Marines...That's about it," Crank said as he reached out and picked a cold beer off the table and proceeded to down it.

Mike and Roger waited for the story to continue and when Crank leaned back in his chair without doing so they looked to Mark.

"Tell 'em how the...difficulty came up, Crank. Don't be shy...We're among friends here," Mark threw out with a wry smile.

"Shit, Zorro, never gonna let me live it down are you?...So, there was this LBMF that didn't want the affections of a drunken Philippine Marine captain...Zorro stepped in and extracted her. When the other Marines jumped up to back their leader I...well I...sort of challenged them...And then the fight started."

"How many Marines?" Blaster asked.

"Don't remember..."

"Twenty," Mark added.

"Twenty?" Dog said with a unbelieving smile. "And it was just what?...What?...The four of you?"

"Hell *no*! Zorro and Berto slipped out the back door and left me and Cello to it. Man, we trashed that bar big time. I came to in the lockup with some real ugly mofos a few hours later."

"And here's the lesson to be learned…I told the captain, the girl was my niece and I was there to take her home. Filipinos have a strong sense of family and that was enough to extract her without any loss of face with his men."

"Well, hell, you didn't tell me that until you posted my bail. I jumped in to cover your ass…"

"Covering my ass is always much appreciated…but unless I'm down or I call for backup…be nice. Crank knows that now and you two are forewarned. Unless you hear me say *Lakota Moon*, keep your can of whoop-ass ready, but unopened. When you do hear it…there are no rules of engagement. It's open season…down and dirty."

Crank decided to change the subject by bringing up the coil rifle that the Black Eagle Force had given Mark after the battle at Mubotto's Estate, "I brought that new weapon you wanted. Any chance we'll get a demo?"

"Not likely. But I hope to fire some test rounds while in the sticks with Dalisay and Rutger."

"New weapon? What kind of new weapon?" Mike asked with heightened interest.

"Top secret. So top secret…it doesn't exist. End of discussion," Mark said with a stern look to Crank.

Joris opened the door to his quarters and entered the cabin. "I'm hungry…You men hungry?"

"I could eat, sir," Crank replied as he got up and started for the galley behind the big Dutchman. As he passed, he gave Mark a look for *sorry I brought it up.*

Mike and Roger joined the procession leaving Mark to himself. *The way those two are falling in with Crank gives some comfort leaving them to Joris' care in Cebu. The crazy surfer has some quirks but with Berto in the mix he'll keep 'em in place and Mister Potato Head should be safe.*

SULU SEA

Isagani could see the village of Sindangan on the coast of Mindanao as he sat eating a meal of rice and ginamoose—a dish of dried fish popular with the lower class in the Philippines. The blue sky was only punctuated by a few fluffy white clouds drifting lazily by. He looked back at the second ship trailing his. The terrorist group had required two boats to carry them all and their limited equipment.

"Isagani, we need to stop and refuel in Sindangan," the boat's captain said, breaking the tranquil moment for the leader of the rogue MNLF group.

"My men and I will stay below decks. Make it quick…And buy some bangus. I'm growing weary of this dried fish."

"Yes. I will do so," he nodded. "Also, some fresh fruit." Turning to his navigator he spoke quickly, "Steer for Sindangan. Radio the Dolphin to follow us into port."

Both ships turned slowly toward landfall. To the inexperienced eye it was just two fishing trawlers working for a day's catch.

SAN JOSE, COSTA RICA
Wong Chi's Office

Feng paced the room as he spoke, "I am growing tired of the delay. What word from your sources?"

"Nothing, but that the woman has been seen before near Montezuma on the coast. I am waiting for further…"

"What is the fastest way to get to Montezuma?"

"To best serve your efforts I could have my eldest son drive you there. It would allow you to have transportation for your search. The coast is a big area," Chi replied.

"Make the arrangements. I want to leave ten minutes ago."

***

CHAPTER SIXTEEN

LOS DELFINES, COSTA RICA
Golf Course & Country Club

Chikako chose to take a longer ferry ride than the short trip from Punteras to Bakia de Paquerra in hopes it would throw anyone following her off-track. Once off the ferry, she made her way to the end of the dock and the local bus station—nothing more than four poles and a thatch roof. She boarded a dilapidated former US school bus painted in bright colors with images of birds and fish. It had a hand-scrawled sign indicating its destination.

The ride seemed endless as the bus bounced along the rough roadway at thirty miles an hour and her leg still ached, even with the pain meds. *Thank you God I have a chair to myself so I can stretch out. Can't seem to bend it much now.*

At Cobano she disembarked last—a clumsy experience due to the day pack and crutches—and stood watching as it pulled off in a cloud of blue exhaust smoke. She hobbled to a local shop and ordered, "Pilsen…coldest one you have."

The icy bitter beverage felt good going down. As a booster she took another couple of Celecoxib—a generic form of Celebrex given to her by the Tica woman—considered a nonprescription drug in Costa Rica.

Seeing a battered cab pull up, she hailed the driver.

"How much to Montezuma?"

"Fifty dollars, American," the middle-aged driver called back as he headed to the men's room.

"When?"

"I eat my lunch. Then we go."

"Is there a pharmacy in Cobino? I need some medications."

"Si, we go there. First my lunch."

"I'll wait," the exhausted Chikako replied. *One good thing about third-world countries…lots of great meds for sale without a prescription. Some penn-strep and some more pain killers…and I'm good to go.*

The road from Cobano to Montazuma was little more than a rock and dirt track winding through the mountains. At every water crossing, the battered cab seemed doomed to be stuck or flooded out in the rushing stream but somehow the driver made it through each one with practiced ease. The local Costa Rican tunes blaring from his portable CD player sitting on the front seat offered little comfort.

"Could we travel without the music? Just for awhile…I like the silence of the countryside."

"Yes, of course. You live Montezuma?"

"No."

"Where you live?"

Chikako's inner warning bell rang. "Nowhere for now. Just visiting."

The driver looked into the rear view mirror studying his fare, "Not so many peoples visit Montezuma. Mostly surfers. You a surfer?"

"No."

"I see your leg. I think maybe you hurt self when surfing."

"No."

"You...where from you?"

"Nowhere in particular. What part of *I like the silence* did you not understand?"

"Yes...yes of course. Very sorry," the driver said, all the while watching her with more than normal interest.

Something's not right with this guy. Always go with your gut. Have to lose this driver...now. "Could you pull over? I need to relieve myself."

"Yes, of course. There is a turn out up ahead."

Once the cab stopped Chikako climbed out on the passenger door on driver's side and as the driver stepped out she pointed her .45 at his head. "Far as you go, mister. Step away from the car."

"You rob me of my cab?" the man said hesitantly as he stared down gaping muzzle.

"Shut up...take off your shoes. Hand me your cell phone."

"My shoes…my cell phone?" the distraught driver replied. "I cannot walk on this rocky road barefoot."

"Sure you can…slowly."

"And my cell phone? I…"

"Precisely. You can't call anyone. You're wasting time. Hurry it up or you'll be walking on one foot like me," she said, lowering her aim toward his feet. "Do it *now*."

She could see him waving his arms and yelling as she drove off. The five thousand colones—local Costa Rican currency—she had tossed out the window swirled in the wake of her departure. *Thank goodness this is an automatic. No way I could operate a clutch and a brake.*

In Montezuma, she turned off of Hwy 624 onto 160—nothing more than a small dirt road—and headed south. Dark circles had formed under her eyes and the stress of her flight drained her leaving a drawn haggard look. *I'll make it before night. Find somewhere to lose this vehicle…hunker down 'til the leg heals and the search blows over.*

MALPAIS, COSTA RICA
CHIKAKO'S HIDE

Before entering her camp, Chikako sat for twenty minutes in the jungle—observing. Once assured nothing was amiss she hobbled into the site. The view of the Pacific Ocean in the late afternoon sun was soothing. The waves rolled in one after another—each adding its own musical note to the serenity of the remote location. A mile up the beach a bonfire flared up indicating a group of surf bums were spending the night to catch the first morning breakers.

An hour later, as the last rays of light reflected off the ocean—turning the sky red and the scattered clouds pink and purple—she added twigs to her BioLite Wood Burning CampStove. It was new technology stove that combined the benefits of a backpacking stove and an off-grid power charger so one can cook a meal while charging their gadgets. *Zorro's advice on this was good...how the hell does he know so much about...everything?*

Just before the water reached boiling, she poured the prescribed amount into a package of Backpacker's Pantry freeze-dried Kung Pao rice with chicken and a Natural High Pad Thai. She folded the foil packages closed at the top and set them aside to re-hydrate, and then poured a generous amount into a small stainless steel tea pot with a bulb containing a blend of Japanese teas.

The sounds of the surrounding jungle stopped abruptly. In a fluid motion Chikako pulled her .45 from its cross-draw holster and fell to the ground—her vision blurred briefly by the impact to her knee. When her sight cleared she carefully scanned the area, and then crawled to find cover behind a large tree trunk. *Sudden silence means someone or something spooked the creatures nearby. Surely no one has found my hide already.*

Several tense minutes passed before the jungle came back to life—birds and insects resumed the various sounds of life.

She waited an additional ten minutes before downing the two meals in rapid succession and drinking the pot of tea. Her hunger sated, she entered the tent, zipped the screen door shut and lay down on the aluminum framed cot. Noting the one inch REI air mattress was too soft, she loosened the valve and blew a half dozen breaths inside before closing it. Satisfied with the loft, she pulled the light nylon American military poncho liner over her and laid her head back on the small pillow—the one household luxury she had allowed when selecting and purchasing her camp supplies. *I have to call Mark, warn him the...Yakuza have...tracked...me.* A feverish sleep washed over her.

Silently a female Fer-de-Lance pit viper—larger and more aggressive than the males—slithered by the screen door, pausing only long enough to find there was no opening.

ZAMBANQUITA, PHILIPPINES

Jesse and Cello had taken a local bus from Valencia to Zambanquita. The ride was without incident, but the smells of the passengers—dried fish, fried pork wrapped in brown paper, live chickens and general body odor—gave the experience a true third world flavor. The bus swerved around debris strewn about the road way—deposited by a brief thunderstorm—and only slowed down to pass children walking home from school.

In Zambanquita they hired a local trike cab to take them to the Heaven on Earth beach resort—owned by a Filipina from Dumaguete, but run by her asawa Chicago Ron.

Arriving at the resort was a full-scale celebration for the staff. Cello was much liked by the owner and admired by the female staff who hoped to snare him as their meal ticket.

"Cello…great to see you again. I got your message and we prepared your Nipa for you. I see you have a friend," Ron said with a distinct Chicago accent. Most of the guests at his place were Filipinos and he always enjoyed the company of a fellow American to break the monotony.

"Let me introduce you to an old buddy Jesse," Cello replied.

"Great to meet you…Where you from?"

"Texas."

"Why don't you two clean up. Dinner will be served in an hour. Grab a beer…I'll have one of the girls deliver some more to your hut." Ron headed to the kitchen.

Without prompting, all the women ran off laughing and arguing about who would be the one to make the delivery.

"Follow me. My hut's de one up on de hill. It's a climb, buts worth de effort. De breeze keeps it cooler dan de ones down here near de beach," Cello remarked as he headed to a set of stairs that lead up a hundred feet to his personal Nipa.

"I could use the exercise after that bus ride."

Once the men had cleaned up, they met on the open porch and downed the last of the beers in silence. Cello reached for a small brass bell mounted on a support post and gave it two rings.

"Dat's de call for more beer. When deys rings a bell down at da kitchen three times…we'll gos on down an haves some fine eatin'."

"I could eat."

"Hal tolds me yous waza comin' cause of Mark. Somethin' 'bouts he's in a tight spot wit de Triad. Damn, I sure don't envy dat."

"Me neither. Never had any dealings with them myself and not looking forward to any."

"Well, we gets yous weaponed up an ons your way. I'll haves Ron charter a fast boat ta deliver us ta Iloilo. Where's Mark now?"

"No idea. That's why I need to talk to Hal. Is that cell charged up yet?"

"It will be by de time we eats. 'Til den it's sit back an chill out ol' buddy. Hey…here comes Zilda wit de beers"

CEBU, PHILIPPINES
Crown Regency Hotel & Towers

The normal thirty minute ride from the Mactan International Airport had taken an hour and a half due to heavy traffic and construction repairs to the bridge that connects Cebu island to Mactan. Fortunately for the Barnhardt family and the security group Berto—at Mark's instruction—had acquired a stretch limo that carried everyone but Crank, Roger and Mike in comfort. The three operatives followed in a dark blue Chevrolet SUV with Crank at the wheel and the most of the tools of the trade stored in the cargo space covered with a tarp.

Once in the hotel, Crank and the team moved the weapons up to the thirty-eighth floor luxury suite adjoining the presidential suite occupied by the Barnhardt family—while the hotel staff took care of the luggage.

Mark briefed the family on security measures. "There will be a man outside the door twenty-four seven and another one at the elevator. Visits to the pool or exercise facility will require someone on the security team to accompany you. In fact, any trip outside this suite will require one of us…What's the timetable on the orphanage event?"

"I will have a complete itinerary within the next hour," Joris responded.

"All right then. I suggest everyone kick back and relax. Tola, you stay here with Dalisay and Rutger…"

"That won't be necessary. I would prefer some quality family time," Joris said.

"Then you can converse in Dutch," Mark replied firmly. "Tola is the last line of defense and she stays." Mark gave her a knowing look which she returned with a slight head nod.

It was evident Joris was not pleased but he held back a response—remembering the last challenge he made to Mark's authority.

"Mike you take first watch at the elevator. Roger on the door. Berto come with me. I want to go over some details you will need to be aware of before Dipolog."

The team gathered in the hallway. "You two have your H&Ks?"

"Not yet, boss," Roger responded.

"Haven't unpacked yet," Mike answered.

"Berto and I will stand the station 'til you do. And use the extra mag pouches. If or when shit hits the fan…one mag won't get 'er done."

"Yeah, boss," they responded in unison.

After they had departed Zorro turned to Berto, "New guys. Sorry to leave 'em with you but Crank will more than make up the difference."

"Where is he?"

"I had him recon the hotel. Should be back any time."

"I appreciate this contract, Zorro. It will look good on my resume…"

"Yeah…well thank me when it's over. When are your sons showing up?"

"Tonight. Their plane lands at 1700."

"I'll schedule a full briefing around 2000 then. Since the Barnhardts have the entire thirty-eighth floor we will do it in the hallway. I don't want any lapses in coverage of the elevator or the door."

"Are you expecting trouble?"

"Always."

SHENYANG, CHINA
Dadong District

Chang Wu had just finished another session with his fourteen year old redheaded Irish girl and stepped out of the shower. The young child lay curled up on the bed and studied the elderly man with fear and loathing. A knock at the outer door directed his attention from her and he grabbed a bright red silk robe from a chair. Putting it on, he left the room.

"Enter," Chang called as he seated himself behind the ornate desk.

"I have news. Fang has lost the Yakuza woman in Costa Rica but sends word he is on her trail and expects to have her in his possession soon."

"I am certain he will. Fang has never failed before."

"Also, some really good news. One of our contacts inside the CIA has identified the person with the silver hair that raided your cousin's penthouse in Hong Kong. He is ninety-five percent certain it is a man known as Steve McCallister."

"Is he admitting it was a hit by the CIA?"

"No. Absolutely not, master. He says McCallister has worked for them but has been inactive for several years. He is now a contract operative...A killer for hire."

"Do we have new photos?"

"Yes, master," the assistant said as he handed Chang a trio of CIA 8x10 black and white photos. "I will send them to our contacts as soon as you order."

Chang sat studying the photos quietly. *Now I have you. No matter where you are...no matter where you go...I will find you.*

"Send them. Inform our contacts there is also a fifty thousand pound reward for him...alive. I wish to entertain myself with him before he dies."

BENT TREE COUNTRY CLUB
Dallas, Texas

Hal sat alone at the bar—having finished a round of golf with several businessmen who wanted to ship items to other countries without any paper trail. His phone rang. He recognized the ring tone to be Cello.

"The chair is behind the door," he said with humor in his voice.

"De door's closed," Cello replied playing along with Hal's joke. *You can take the spook out of the game...but you can never take the game out of the spook.* "Jesse wants a word."

"I'm calling to get an update on Zorro's whereabouts," he said after taking the cell from Cello.

"I'll check and get back to you. Last I heard he was headed to Cebu."

"We're going to Iloilo tomorrow. Need some things from the safe vault. Let me know as soon as you can. May make a difference in what tools I draw."

"Don't forget...borrowing from a vault puts you in debt. Just because you're retired doesn't change that rule."

"Hal, you *are* the tightest Scottsman I ever met."

"Just business. Cello will advise me of what you took. I'll access a fee based on his checklist."

"Yeah...yeah. Dinner time here. Later."

Hal smiled as he placed the phone in it's carrier. *Like father like son. Hell...they even talk alike.*

After ordering another double shot of twenty-five year old Scotch neat, he moved out onto the terrace and called Mark.

"What's up devil dog?"

"Where's your scrawny ass now?"

"Cebu. Why?"

"Just checking. I have some resources there you may need."

"Really? Why's that?"

"Three words…Big Circle Gang."

"You have somethin' new?"

"No. But I want to know where to find you if I do. Don't get bigheaded on me just because you pulled off the hit in Hong Kong. These guys make the Terminator look like a girl scout. They will hunt you from now…"

"Yeah…yeah. Heads up then. I'm shoving off for Dipolog in a couple of days. Taking the client's wife to see her family…"

"Hope you have an army with you. The Muslim goat fuckers are still out-of-control on Mindanao."

"Run some data for me…Find out if the uprising is still contained to the Zamboanga area. Dipolog is a long way from there."

"Done. I'll add it to your account. Which reminds me…the contract in Nicaragua is still on schedule. How're the two pups working out?"

"They'll make you a hand in a year or two…assuming they live that long. Blaster is all testosterone and Dog…seems to have the better of the two heads."

"Have you heard from your dad lately?" Hal asked as casually as he could.

What's up with all the chatter about my father? First, Rocky, now Hal. "Not a word. You?"

"No. Nothing lately. Last time I heard from him he was in your neck of the woods."

"You talkin' 'bout the Philippines or just southeast Asia in general?"

"Philippines."

There was a long pause. Hal refused to break it. Finally Mark did, "How was he doing?"

"No idea other than shacked up with some little brownie on an island…which he refused to divulge. Sounded okay."

"That narrowed it down. Only seven thousand islands over here. Gotta go. Get me the intel on Mindanao as soon as you can. Last thing I want is a run-in with raghead goat fuckers."

"Just a warm-up for the Triad, Zorro. Nothing but a warm-up."

"I'm outta here…just landed and there's a ton of shit to get organized."

***

CHAPTER SEVENTEEN

MANUKAN, PHILIPPINES

Isagani and the MNLF disembarked the two fishing boats in relays using row boats to reach the shore north of Manukan, a third-class municipality best known for its long history as a producer of chickens—the name literally translated to *chicken farm* in English. The cover of night allowed for a perfect incursion without discovery along the lonely stretch of beach.

"We must cross the Zamboanga National highway before dawn," Isagni ordered in a hushed voice.

The men moved out in a well-practiced formation. Two men advanced as the point team followed by five others, then Isagani followed by the other men—all spaced at five yard intervals.

All goes well and it's only another forty kilometers to Dipolog. Well ahead of the annual festival...plenty of time to recon our targets. Isagani smiled at the brilliance of his plan and the ease at which he and his men were approaching the surprise assault on Dipolog's airport and Dipitan's port. *Father would be proud of me. All Moros will be proud me. I spread the flame of Islam to the island of Mindanao...and beyond.*

The men sat above the highway watching the meager flow of traffic. As an opening presented itself, six men scrambled down the incline, rushed across the road and melted into the jungle on the opposite side. Isagani crossed shortly afterwards with the remaining men. Reaching the center of the paved, though badly pockmarked road, he paused and raised his M16 over his head in one hand while gazing at the starlit sky.

"Allah Akbar!" he called out, repeating the chant three times before jogging into the jungle to join the others.

CEBU, PHILIPPINES
Crown Regency Hotel & Towers

Mark and the extended security team stood in the hall outside the Presidential Suite. Both of Berto's sons, Rodel and Michele, completed the group.

"Crank's the lead here in Cebu. Berto you're number two. Roger, Mike, Rodel...Michele fall in as ordered where needed. Tola stays on Dalisay and the kid twenty-four seven...Day after tomorrow Michele and I will accompany Tola on the trip to Dipolog..."

"Sources tell me the Muslim uprising has been quelled on Mindanao. But I wonder if three is enough, Zorro?" Berto asked while slicing an apple and then eating it off his KaBar—a gift to him by Mark several years earlier.

"Don't see why not. It's a family celebration…just a little village with only a fifty or so inhabitants. According to the map, it's seventy miles south east of Dipolog with one road in or out," Mark replied.

"How long do we stay in Cebu after you're gone?" Crank asked.

"According to the itinerary, three days. We'll all be here for the big show…the opening and dedication of the new orphanage. Then he wants to spend a couple of days getting to know the staff and kids." Mark paused seeing Roger looking at his iphone. "You still with us, Blaster?"

Roger placed the cell in his pocket. "Yes sir."

"Then keep your head in the game. From now 'til you land back at the Barnhardt's residence, you only use gadgets for business."

Crank could not help but smile. *Love watching grandpa herding these new guys. Wonder which one he's going to break it off in?*

"After I'm gone someone is with Joris every minute…"

"I overheard him talking with one of his people in his office. Seems he has a residence at the orphanage. If he moves in there…do we move in with him?" Mike asked.

"First I've heard of this. *Simple Jack in wooden shoes just can't get with the program.* I'll let you know after I view the place. Probably set up outside twenty-four seven. Rotating shifts…five of you should be able to cover it," Mark replied as he thought through the new intel.

"The permits to carry. You want them now?" Berto asked.

"Yup. Hand 'em out...Crank and Berto already know this but for the rest of you...anyone and everyone who stands against us...*dies* in the course of protecting the client—Zorro Rule one. Keep your weapons on you at all times. Carry quiet...but if there *is* a need...don't stop shooting 'til every possible threat is down. Understood?"

The men responded affirmatively in unison. Only Rodel and Michele seemed somewhat uneasy.

"Berto, take some time and assure the boys why this ROE is necessary. Mike you're on the elevator 'til...0200," Mark said checking his watch. "Roger...on the door. Berto and I will replace you...The rest of you, hit the sack. Got a big day ahead of us."

TANON STRAIT, PHILIPPINES

Jesse and Cello stood on the bow of a Ocean Jet fast ferry. No one seemed interested in their luggage when they boarded—which was also arranged by the resort owner for a small fee to the cargo steward. Good thing, as Jesse did not have a national permit to carry and his 1911 would result in a decade in the infamous Cebu Provincial Detention and Rehabilitation Center, a certified third-world shit hole.

"Thanks to Ron...we'll be in Iloilo late today. By this time tomorrow you should have everything you need and ready to roll," Cello said quietly.

BARNHARDT'S ORPHANAGE
Cebu, Philippines

The crowd was larger than Mark expected upon arrival. Several weeks of relentless newscasts proclaiming the event not only brought out dignitaries, but a throng of locals with little else to do—mostly hoping for a free meal.

As the stretch limo—followed by the SUV with the rest of the team—approached on a fly-over stretch of highway, the entire event was laid out below them. The dark blue awning was surrounded by Philippine Marines standing shoulder to shoulder at port arms.

Visible under the awning were a hundred or so dignitaries milling about. A few wore suit and tie but, for the most part, they wore the accepted Philippines dress attire of slacks and a loose-fitting long sleeve embroidered white cotton shirt. The women wore bright-colored dresses and many had handmade hats with flowers as well.

"Damn…How many people show up for the opening of orphanages here?" Mike asked in awe.

Several hundred children—new residents of the orphanage—clad in dark blue skirts or shorts and white shirts waved small flags with the Barnhardt Orphanage logo. A band from the University of the Philippines Cebu—wearing green and gold uniforms—marched back and forth in front of the main entrance playing the National Anthem.

"This is a big very deal gentleman. The President, the Governor of Cebu province, the Mayor and several other notable officials are here today for this momentous occasion," Joris replied.

Mark gave orders to the team over their ear buds, "Roger...Mike step out with Rodel and Michele. Come up and post on the limo four square. We'll follow with the client. Once the local law enforcement sets up a cordon for us to get through to the reception area, we go," Mark gave his orders in even tones—belying his sense of concern at the number of potential threats. *Damn sure hope the NPA here are not tracking Joris. Only takes one motivated fool with a death wish.*

The vehicles stopped on the new concrete roadway and the unit moved into place in front and back of the limo. "Crank...take twelve o'clock and lead us in. Everyone on his command," Mark instructed.

Crank nodded to Berto. "On it boss. Surfs up boys...lets roll."

With the proper aisle through the crowd established by the uniformed law enforcement officers. Barnhardt and his family made a conquer's entrance surrounded by the team. Waiting in a large open area at the front of the new facility was the President of the Philippines and a dozen other officials.

Moving forward, he waved to the crowd as did Dalisay. Rutger held tightly to her hand and waved as well. The mass of people cheered as if the second coming was in progress.

Halfway from the limo to the waiting dignitaries a short middle aged Filipino—wearing tattered green shorts, a equally worn black t-shirt and canvas shoes without laces—broke through the police line and ran toward Joris.

DARK SECRET

Mark reacted first and stepped between Missus Barnhardt, Rutger and the advancing man. Crank grabbed Joris and secured him—placing his hand on his client's head and forcing him to bend over at the waist to reduce his target signature. Roger turned and retreated to Crank in a swift fluid motion gleaned from years in the secret service. Berto and his sons turned to cover everyone's back.

"Ikaw ang diyablo at ako dito upang i-off mo!" The man screamed in Visayan as he approached.

Mark saw the knife as the man pulled it from his pant's waist band. He instinctively snaked his Colt with his left hand from the Bianchi shoulder holster with practiced ease. "Knife!"

BAM! BAM! BAM!

Well before any of the other members of the security team could react, Zorro placed a pair of 185 grain polymer-tipped .45 rounds to the chest and one to the head.

The running man fell backwards from the impacts. The round to the head entered below his chin as the man fell, sliced through his tongue and traveled upward through his forehead—blowing out his facial features in a spray of brain matter and pink mist. His lifeless body slid to a stop at the Berto's feet—the front of his skull gone.

"Move. Get to the tent now!" Mark ordered as he scooped up Rutger and begin to walk briskly forward—his weapon still at the ready.

"Who was that man Tio? Look his shoe is still there," Rutger said pointing back at it still laying where he had taken his last forward step. "Why did you shoot him?" he asked anxiously wrapping his arms around Mark's neck.

"Look at me, Rutger. Don't look down...look at me."

Tola grabbed Dalisay by the arm and followed. Crank and Berto likewise rushed Joris forward, sandwiched between them. Crank still had the Dutchman by the back of his neck and bent over. Roger and Mike lead the way with weapons drawn covering the move. Rodel and Michele, both shaken by the event followed hesitantly, but managed to maintain protocol—walking backwards with eyes on the crowd behind them.

A half-dozen policemen rushed to the downed Filipino and the rest struggled to control the crowd. News cameras filming the grand entry caught the chaos as it unfolded—going out live on the airwaves.

"Holster!" Crank called out as he placed his pistol inside his jacket and held his hands at shoulder lever.

"What?" Mike asked.

"Put your gun away and show your hands...dumb ass," Mark said calmly as he followed Crank's lead. "There's a couple hundred guns on us now."

Roger and Mike looked to Mark and after watching him holster his weapon and show his hands, followed suit—Rodel and Michele too.

Mark, the team and the Barnhardts were met by members of the Marines before they reached the covered reception area. It took several minutes for the pandemonium to die down and a state of semi-calm returned to the crowd. Finally, after several tense moments with the Marines, the Chief of Police and a Marine major sorted it out allowing the team to enter.

"What the hell was that?" Joris said with no small amount of fear mixed with adrenaline.

"You tell me…He was headed straight for you…screaming you're the devil," Mark replied calmly as he lowered his hands. "You have enemies over here as well?"

"Absolutely not. I have never seen that man…"

"We need to start the ceremony, Mister Barnhardt. The President has another event to attend this evening," a slender well-dressed man wearing large black-rimmed glasses interrupted. "This way please."

"Yes…yes of course." He gave an angry look to Mark as he turned and followed the man to the podium.

"Crank…take the team and stay on Joris. Tola, Michele…on Dalisay and Rutger," Mark ordered as he set the boy down. "I'm sorry you had to see that. Any idea who he was?"

Dalisay was visibly shaken. "No. I…I don't." She instinctively picked her son up and held him close. "Rutger…are you all right?"

"Yeah, Tio Steve had me," the boy responded with a look to Mark. "You are fast, Tio."

"You stay close now, son. Any more bad men and we may be running next time," Mark said as he scanned the crowd.

"You…shot him…Couldn't you have just…disarmed him?" Dalisay asked.

"No."

"But…"

"No buts…Whatever it takes. Remember?"

The Chief of Police walked up. "I was watching when the man broke through. That was quick thinking."

"Just doing my job…Steve McCallister," Mark said as he extended his hand. "The team and I all have permits to carry…"

"Yes, I know. I issued them to Roberto personally. There will be a hearing of course, but as a witness, I can assure you nothing will come of it."

"I'm scheduled to take Missus Barnhardt and her son to Dipolog tomorrow."

"I'll have an officer take your official statement today. With all the witnesses…including the press…I…don't see any reason for a change of plans."

"How do you know Berto?"

"We served together in the military. I was his commanding officer…Good man. And you? How do you know him?"

"Worked some contracts on Mindanao over the years. That reminds me…what's the latest on the Moros down there?"

"All over now. The insurgents have been killed or dispersed and run back to their stronghold on Sulu. Besides, Dipolog is a long way from Zamboanga City."

"I was thinking the same thing…Before this fandango is over I'd like to introduce you to my number one. He will remain here with Joris until he departs."

BARNHARDT'S PRIVATE QUARTERS
Cebu Orphanage

Six hours later Joris led the group through the private quarters. "I apologize for not informing you about this earlier…"

"I'll put it on the list," Mark said as he checked the door to the patio and inspected the enclosed courtyard.

"What list?"

"The Joris list."

Joris eyed Mark coolly before replying, "At any rate…I will be moving here tomorrow and remain at this residence until I return to Bangkok. Is there a problem?"

"Not at all. Crank will work out the arrangements to provide for your security here. The team will require living arrangements on site."

"I will have the headmaster make some of the staff quarters available. I do not intend to leave the orphanage until I depart… which should simplify your needs."

"Crank, you and Berto do a thorough survey of the orphanage grounds. Note all entrances and assess their threat. Roger…Mark…Rodel…Michele set up outside and secure. No one in or out without a complete pat-down."

"On it boss," Crank replied as he and Berto departed.

"No one in or out boss," Mike confirmed as he and the others exited.

"Rutger is tired now. I'm taking him to his room," Dalisay said to her husband.

"Of course, dear. Get some rest. We will visit with some of the children after dinner."

"Tola, go with them," Mark ordered. *Why does this guy seem more interested in the orphans than his own son?* "Show me your bedroom. About the only part of this place I haven't seen yet."

"Certainly. Right this way."

The entire private residence was well constructed and lavishly appointed. Mark noted that the decorating trend was all typical of the Philippines and had nothing like the old world touches in the residence in Bangkok. The master bedroom was modest in size but well laid out, including the substantial workstation complete with multiple computer locations and screens.

"I must keep in touch with my business ventures even while here," he said, noting Mark's interest.

"Understood. Is any of this linked into the security system?"

"No. All that is monitored by the on-site security team in the main building. Only cameras around the exterior feed them information. I prefer to have at least some privacy…"

"Your call. If I intended to stay on longer than the three months I would advise otherwise." Mark opened the door to the comfort room and viewed the area before closing the door. "I don't see any reason for concern during your visit here as long as you remain on site. Crank and Berto will have a solid plan in place by tonight to keep you safe."

"I…I want to thank you for the quick action you took today…I will include a bonus…"

"As per our agreement…ten thousand per man if a threat occurs that requires force to deter."

"I'll have a check made out when we return home. Will that include the Filipino..."

"Absolutely."

Crank, Berto and the rest of the team stood outside the private quarters next to the limo and SUV as they waited for Mark.

"I've seen some shooters before, but nothing like today," Roger said.

"Shit...he downed that mofo before I could get my hand inside my coat," Mike added.

"If you ever want to throw some cash on the ground and walk away...challenge him to a little shooting contest." Crank grinned.

"Once...near Cobatato...I saw him take out a dozen men with his Colt while we extracted our clients. His actions cleared a path for us to reach a boat on the river."

"How many men has he killed?" Blaster asked.

"Have to ask him sometime...but I wouldn't recommend it. He's not big on keeping count and doesn't care much for those that do," Crank said. "Couple of months ago...in Kenya...I'd say at least a hundred rebel mutha fuckers. Maybe more."

"More what?" Mark asked as he approached.

The men turned to find Zorro standing behind them.

"The new guys were wondering about body counts," Berto replied with a grin.

"Highly overrated in my opinion. Looks like the front door the patio are the only entry points here. The way it's constructed, the east and north sides are attached to the main

293

building. Crank, work out the posting assignments. Rodel, you take up station on the patio for now. Mike…front door. The rest of you derilects…back to the hotel. Round up our gear and get back here ten minutes ago. Oh…Berto…find out all you can about the man I shot… Especially any details on why he attacked Joris."

"On it. I'll have something by the time you get back from Mindanao."

COSTA RICA
Chikako's Hide

Moonlight bathed the Pacific Ocean, beach and the campsite in a soft glow. She sat up, covered in a light sweat, rubbed her eyes, rotated her head and flexed her shoulders. *What time is it? What day is it?*

Carefully moving her injured knee she let out a low moan. The swelling had subsided significantly, but the limb as still tender. *Okay…I got this. Couple of days and I'll be good.*

Using a large Igloo ice chest in the corner of her tent and the cot she carefully moved to a standing position and tested the limitations of placing weight on her leg. *Better…much better.* A smile crossed her lips.

The sound of a jam box playing wafted up from the surfer hangout on the beach. The song was indistinguishable, but audible. Moving to the door, she unzipped it and stepped out onto the sand barefooted. The cool surface felt good as she flexed her toes. She zipped the door closed before hobbling to her crutches. *Get the stove going. Some hot tea. Couple more meals. Get down to the beach and soak this leg in the salt water. This would be a great time for Crank to show up. I could us a nice strong dude to carry me around.*

When the sun came up, she was sitting in the first few feet of the breaking tide—the salt water gently washing over her legs and hips. Up the beach the surfers were awake. She could smell the coffee and cooking bacon, see the campfire and several figures moving around. A pair of surfers were already out on the breakers catching the early waves. A group of sea gulls, terns and other birds wandered about on her left, looking for breakfast.

Made it. Didn't think I would but…I made it. Hang out here 'til the knee is working then…drop down to Panama. Wonder where the Zorro is now? Wonder if he even cares where I am?

ILOILO, PHILIPPINES

Cello lead the way up a narrow winding footpath to the front of his Nipa hut. Sitting back a hundred yards from the road made the house undetectable from the traffic below.

"Home sweets home. I'll gets Jasmine to cooks us some chow whiles we checks out da vault," Cello said without looking back.

"And give Hal a call," Jesse replied.

A Filipina stepped out onto the porch. "Baby! I miss you so much," Jasmine said as she rushed forward and threw her arms around Cello's neck.

"Missed yous more, baby. How's 'bout some chicken adobo ans pancet? We's really hungry."

"Who's your friend?"

"Jasmine…Jesse. He's a retired buddy. Needs some things from da vault. Only be's here tonight."

"Hi, Jesse."

"Hello. Cello forgot to tell me you were so pretty," Jesse replied, playing to what every Filipina wanted to hear—an insatiable need to be told they are beautiful and sexy being a common characteristic of the Philippine woman.

Jasmine blushed with joy. "You so nice Mister Jesse. Okay…I go cook now. Maybe one hour. Then ready."

"Perfect baby. Rings da bell in's da vault when you's ready for us."

Inside the safe vault—a pair of forty-foot sea shipping containers side by side and connected by a single double door—Jesse moved about collecting the tools he wanted. "I'm going light. This M14…three hundred rounds. Hello old friend," he said as he lifted a battle worn wooden-stocked Winchester rifle from the wall rack housing a dozen other big bore rifles. In one fluid motion, he slammed the operating rod rearward and using his thumb, set the locking lever to hold the bolt open. Moving for better light, he inspected the chamber. "Scope?"

"I has dis one," Cello replied taking a steel Square B mount fitted with a Leupold ten power scope that had seen its days on some field of battle or another.

"Is it zeroed?"

"Sights it in my own self,"

"Probably too much to ask…but…how about a can?"

The black man pulled a drawer under a big work bench. There were numerous suppressers laid out neatly in rows. "I gots a Fisher direct connect ans ah Smith Windtalker."

"Don't know either one. Which is the quietest?"

"I'd says dat woulds be da Windtalker."

"I'll take it." Jesse inspected the suppresser then mounted it onto the rifle and began to tighten down the locking ring.

"Take the M79." Jesse opened the breech and looked at the chamber.

"Only has thirty rounds for da seventy-nine but you's welcome to 'em. You's wants National Match fer da fourteen?"

"Yeah. Any API?"

"Couple hundred."

"Twenty should do."

They worked gathering the weapons, the ammunition and placing them in incolas travel bags. Jesse separated the trigger assembly and stock from the receiver and barrel of the M14 and put them in a round plastic tube designed to carry a photographic tripod.

Cello slid the M79 in a padded olive drab canvas case before putting it and the ammo in the main compartment of a gray seabag. Jesse loaded four magazines for the M14 with National Match and another one with API before storing them in the pouches of a shoulder bag.

The bell rang on the right side of the door and a small red light begin flashing.

"Chow time. Let's eat dens give ol Hal a jingle," Cello said as he headed out the door flipping a switch that shut off the ringer and the light.

Once both men were outside the black man closed the door and used a seven digit numerical key pad to lock it. He slid a bamboo planter across the doorway effectively hiding the entrance to the vault buried in the side of the hill behind the Nipa hut. "Longs as I keeps da bamboo watered it's a perfect cover...don't ya think?"

"I've only seen two other vaults...one in Brazil and one in South Africa. Both bigger, but yours is well stocked. Speaking of South Africa...did you know Bear before he became Banjo?"

"Yeah...I knews him. God rest his soul."

"He's gone?"

"Yous don't knows? He paid da piper overs in Kenya."

"Damn good man he was...How'd he go?"

"Story I heards waz he waz wit your pup protecting da president. 'Cording to da grapevine...dey was goin' inta extracts Rhino ans ends up in a real shit storm."

The two sat in silence for several minutes—each reflecting on the operative and friend who had died.

Cello's satellite phone started ringing.

"Well heres ya go. It's da devil his own self." He answered the call. "Yes, sir. He's rights here."

Jesse took the phone from Cello. "Jesse here."

"Your kid is going to Dipitan tomorrow. ETA 1600. Going by way of Dumaguete," Hal clipped off rapidly.

"Got it. Dipitan 1600 tomorrow."

"He's hired a van to take him and his clients on to some backwoods bump-in-the-road named Sagnoi. Said it's about seventy miles outside Dipolog…You got the tools you need?"

"Yeah. Traveling light…Thanks. I gotta get going here and figure out how to get to…"

"I booked you on a boat out of Iloilo at 0745 tomorrow morning. Should land you around 1300 in Dipitan. Put it on your bill."

Jesse sat for a moment considering Hal's efficiency. "Thanks. Not sure how I'm going to repay you for all this."

"We'll work that out after the rodeo. I may have a contract coming up in Java. Short term. Texaco needs some eyes on a couple of executives going in to inspect oil rigs in the back country. Piece of cake."

"Last time I heard you say piece of cake was the Borneo cluster," Jesse said before hanging up.

"What's the deal," Cello asked as he opened another beer.

"Out of here in the morning. Need to be down at the pier by 0600."

"Done deal."

***

CHAPTER EIGHTEEN

BARNHARDT'S ORPHANAGE
Cebu, Philippines

Mark settled in with the off-duty team members in the break room. None of the orphanage staff was present, having retired after a full day of activities. He wore a pair of dark blue jogging pants, an olive drab tank top and flip flops. With his arms exposed, the scars were plainly visible—the wounds received in Afghanistan as well as a wicked scar where a Shining Path soldier had driven a bayonet through his forearm.

"Zorro, how'd you come to work for Hal?" Mike asked eyeing the body damage.

"Long story."

"How come you quit and go out on your own?" Blaster chimed in.

"Shorter story," Mark replied as he scanned the channels on the flat screen television.

"Amiela asked if you would be coming to visit while you are here this time," Michele added, wanting to be in the game with the older men. "Momma too."

"Not this time…In and out. Maybe when the contract is over…Be nice to see your family again. What's Amiela doing these days?…Finish school?" He stopped on the BBC News Asia channel as a story ran about the orphanage opening and shooting event.

"Didn't take long for that to go newsworthy," Mike noted.

"Never does…Blood always makes the news."

"I had a buddy working for Hal…he got me an interview," Roger said keeping on topic hoping to learn more.

"Hal likes those Secret Service boys. Probably 'cause he was one for ten years," Mark commented.

"Amiela is enrolled at Silliman University in Dumaguete now. She's studying to be a computer programmer," Michele said.

"Good for her. She'd be a good computer geek…and a pretty one at that," Mark said. "She's a sweet kid."

"She's twenty-two now. Don't think she would like you calling her a kid any more." Michele laughed.

"Damn, time flies. Bet she has a whole string of young dudes chasing her."

"Not interested in Filipino men…Says she's going to marry an American…go to the US and make a fortune so she can support Momma and Papa," Rodel said.

"Wish her the best," Zorro said as he studied the news footage. *Well shit!*

"Hey, man…that's you," Mike blurted out.

Mark started surfing the channels again. *Just what I don't need. Face time on BBC.*

"Seriously…how'd you come to work for Hal? Is it true he found you living in a teepee?" Roger continued his pursuit of anything about Mark's background.

"That was my father. Hal found me vacationing…Taking some time off from the rat race. That's it…That's all your going to get, give it a rest."

Roger and Mike exchanged looks.

"How come you quit?" Mike asked.

Mark stood up abruptly causing the two Americans to flinch. "It's late. Fast boat leaves at 0800. I'm hitting the rack."

After he left, Roger turned to Michele. "How long you two know Zorro?"

"Maybe five or six years. Pappa brought him home after a contract. He was hurt bad. Couldn't walk…serious concussion. He stayed with us for a few months," Rodel said.

"How come he couldn't walk?" Mike questioned.

"A bullet clipped his left thigh bone. Pappa said it was a good thing in hit the bone on the outside. Would have cut the artery in the inside."

"Saw a friend bleed out in Afghanistan…Really sucked not being able to do a damn thing," Mike said.

"Pappa had Amiela take care of him 'til he was able. He's the rich American she thinks to marry." Michele added.

"Don't know your sister but…I don't see him getting married again…Just don't see it," Crank interjected.

"I, for one, look forward to working with him. I learn everything he teaches me. Someday I might be a good operative like Zorro. That's what Pappa said," Michele added.

"Well watch out if he has Tola give you any lessons." Mike laughed. "Right, Blaster?"

"Damn straight."

PASAY, PHILIPPINES

Tong, a Triad gang leader, sat watching the news wearing only a pair of black silk loose-fitting pants. The many tattoos on his chest, back and arms denoted his standing in the family.

His group settled in Pasay due to it's proximity to the airport and the Manila North Bay seaport. Sent by Chang Wu to oversee the newly formed alliance between the Triad and the ZETA Mexican drug cartel, he considered it his good fortune and a promotion. Watching the news on the local television station, he could not believe his eyes when the clip came on about the incident in Cebu. *That's him! That's the man in the photographs.*

He immediately picked up his cell. When one of Wu's men answered he got straight to the point. "This is Tong. I am watching the local news. The man Wu is seeking is here in the Philippines."

"You are certain?"

"Ninety-nine percent certain. I only see him for a moment, but it must be him."

"I will have Master Wu call you back if you are positive."

"I am."

Twenty minutes later Chang Wu's ring tone sounded on his cell phone. "Yes, Master Wu."

"I am told you have seen the man I seek."

"Yes, Master. I watch the news and there he is...in a story from Cebu...What are your instructions?"

"Send someone to find him. Do not approach. I am sending five men."

"Yes, Master Wu."

"Do not alert him to our presence. Is that clear?"

"Yes, Master Wu. It shall be done. Should I not go..."

"No. You remain focused on our new business venture with the ZETAS. I want the money to flow immediately. Did you receive the shipment?"

"I have it secured in the warehouse as you instructed. The ZETA leader is setting up his distribution. I have made the first payment to the Chief of Police."

"Good. Keep me informed. The men will contact you when they arrive. Well done, Tong. You are proving to be a valuable."

BARNHARDT'S PRIVATE QUARTERS

Joris insisted his wife join him for a cup of hot chocolate before turning in for the night. He added enough sedative to her drink to insure she would not wake up before morning. Satisfied the drug had taken effect, he entered the walk-in closet and pressed a piece of molding. A secret door opened, revealing a room lit only by a single red light bulb.

He flipped a switch and the entire chamber became illuminated by studio lights. The acoustic flat black waffle board covered the walls and ceiling—a bit of overkill considering the three foot thick walls to the chamber were constructed to contain any sound emanating from the room. But Joris liked the look the waffling gave his productions and had always protected his dark secret with multiple layers of security.

Against the far wall, four orphans—two males and two females—sat gagged, blindfolded and secured to heavy metal chairs. A wicked grin crossed the Dutchman's face. He removed his robe and pajamas before neatly hanging them on a rolling clothes rack that had dozens of little wardrobe props waiting for his selection.

He opened a steamer trunk—the old style with hanging rods and cabinet drawers—and considered his attire for the session. Ultimately he decided on his personal favorite and put on the black leather pants, silver studded wrist cuffs and cross harness. Once dressed, he opened a drawer and removed a black skull cap. Placing it on his head concealed his identity completely—only his eyes, nose and mouth were visible.

Properly attired, he busied himself preparing the high tech video cameras—all nine of them—before testing the audio mics and adjusting the sound console. He finished with the stage lights. No expense had been spared. The final cost for his new playroom's equipment had exceeded a half million pounds. Joris smiled, satisfied all was ready.

Moving to the stage on one end of the room, he used the various monitors to adjust the positioning of the bondage racks, tables and suspension devices. Satisfied all was in order, he moved to the children and gently caressed each face. The orphans squirmed and struggled to free themselves, to no avail. Their actions brought a evil glint to Joris' eyes. *Ah...my little ones. You shall be my first...my very first stars here in Cebu.*

For the first time since entering the room, he spoke, "Tonight I will immortalize you...your performances will be seen by millions of satisfied customers. Now...let's see...who wants to be first?"

***

CHAPTER NINETEEN

BARNHARDT'S RESIDENCE
Bangkok, Thailand

Hans Schoeke and Rhino stood in the entertainment room surrounded by new computer equipment. Three house boys busied themselves carrying out the empty boxes and packing materials.

"Make sure to check every box for components before you dispose of them," Schoeke instructed.

"Yes, sir, Mister Hans. We finish I will come help you more," the oldest boy replied in excellent English. His eagerness to assist was evident. He studied computer science at night in the University of Bangkok South and felt he would learn something valuable from the eccentric man.

"Now what? You got the bloody room full a toys…time to rip out the old ones?" Rhino asked as he sat down on the edge of the pool table. He picked up the eight ball and rolled it down the dark blue covered table.

"Yes, yes indeed. But it will be a laborious activity. I must mark and notate in my laptop each and every cable as I do so. Maybe you would like to take a break? Francisca has been wanting to go to the mall...Would you take her for me?"

"Gladly. All these gizmos give me a headache."

Hans meticulously photographed each and every component in the security room before he detached it for the young house boy to remove. He entered the information into his laptop—using a special program he created just for such activities. His astute memory negated the need to do so but he was bent that way—*cross every T and dot every I at least twice* was his motto.

"Tija, make a label for this mainframe. Call it...for lack of a better name...call it the *mystery frame*," he instructed.

"Why mystery frame? All the others..."

"Because I have no idea what it does within the security system. In fact...don't remove it. I want to take a look at the hard drive later. There is an interesting encryption code. I don't have time right now to dechiper it."

"I will put it in this cabinet."

"Good. Very good," he said somewhat absentmindedly. *What does a encrypted mainframe have to do with this archaic security system? The whole thing is completely pedestrian. I could purchase most of the components at a Radio Shack.*

"Tija, be good enough to get me another glass of Thai tea...and see if Rhino and Francisca are back."

Darkness had fallen before Rhino and Francisca returned from the shopping trip. Both carried several bags from the parking garage into the elevator and on into the bedroom she shared with her husband.

"Just set them at the foot of the bed please." She laid back on the bed with her feet dangling off the edge. "I forgot how much walking is involved shopping in a mall. Hans normally orders everything online and has it delivered to our home."

"About done-in myself. The ol' arse...I'm sorry...my hip is starting to scream at me."

"No need to apologize. I have three children of university age, Mister Rhino...I've heard far worse," she said with a warm smile. "Tell me please...your name's not really Rhino is it?"

"No ma'am. It's a call sign. You know...like Zorro."

"How did you end up being called that?"

"Picked it up back in the days o' bein' in the South African Defense Force. Just seemed to follow me into the security business," he said as he sat down in a chair by the study table. "You mind? Oh man...becomin' a real pain in me arse."

Francisca picked up the small stool from the vanity and took it to him. "Come on now. No need for bravado...I won't tell anyone."

He propped leg on the stool. "Ah...thanks."

"How did you meet...Zorro...Steve...or whatever name he is using now? Did you work for Hal?"

"Never did. I've met the crazy Scotsman but never officially been on his payroll." He rubbed his thigh. "I met bro at one of the smaller De Beers diamond mines in Angola. He was head of security."

"Did you work for the mining company as well?"

"No…I was still a major in the SADF. My unit answered his call for assistance."

"With what?"

Rhino eyed Francisca for a moment deciding on how much to tell. "What the hell…I don't think he'll care. There was an assault by some bleks makin' a play for the mine…"

"Bleks?" she asked with a smile. "I don't understand some of your colorful language."

"A group of domkop natives. It was back in the Mandela days. Any way…according to Zorro's pass down, it started out 'bout a hundred Ubangies and by the time we got there it had more than doubled."

"Oh, my God. And how many men did Mark have on the security force?"

"That's the best part. I'll save it for last…After the twenty or so Angolan soldiers went down he called on the local kerels…ah…police. They sent a dozen men. When they arrived, the bad guys were drunk on beer they found in the canteen. The kerels were all hacked to death pretty quick…being out in the open and all. That's when bro made a open call on the mine radio for help."

"What's an open call?"

"A universal distress call going out on all channels…*Broken Arrow*. Zorro claims it started in the US military, but it went worldwide."

"Broken Arrow?"

"Your position is overrun. My unit was the closest to the mine. When we arrived we made quick work of it. What with our ground force and the helicopter gunships. I found him in the mine along with some of the employees. He'd made a stand at the entrance and the bodies were knee deep outside. There was a wicked klankie...ah...smell. Easily fifty bodies near the mine all bloated in the south Afrikaans sun and heat."

"He and his men killed fifty natives?"

"Ah...yes...the best part. When I asked him where the rest of his bloody security team was he answered...*What team*? Turns out...he was it. The mine was so small the De Beers people thought one man was enough with the Angolan troops stationed there twenty-four seven. Probably would have been, but...he was running out of ammo."

"Sounds like a movie. How did you stay connected with him?"

"I tracked down his employer from a card he gave me. I'd left SADF and was working for a global security group called Executive Outcomes. Getting some bloody wild contracts 'round Africa and Asia. Thought he might be looking for some work and I certainly needed someone with his skill sets."

"What do you mean?" Francisca was now completely caught up in the story.

"Special skills one needs to...you know survive...bad situations...meat grinder skill sets."

"You mean war skills?"

"Definitely," Rhino said as images from Kenya flashed into his consciousness—pausing his train of thought for a moment. His head twitched slightly to the left as he cleared his mind. "Turned out Zorro had gone out on his own the year before, but Hal's secretary hooked us up. Tracked him down in Bolivia. Got an invite to come over and draw a bigger check. But that's another story…I'm going to go check on Hans."

After he left, Francisca lay on the bed considering the story she had just heard. *There's a side to him I never imagined. Wonder if Hans knows?*

COSTA RICA
Montezuma Beach

Feng, his three remaining henchmen and Wong's eldest son sat in a local bar on the beach. A battered puke-green Suzuki minibus pulled up and the stranded cab driver got out along with the owner of the van—a smallish Japanese-Costa Rican. Both men's attire was soaked in sweat as they entered the shade of the palm thatched bar.

"Feng?" the driver asked as he approached the table.

The Triad leader lifted his hand slightly, "Do you have word of the Yakuza woman?"

"I do," the cab driver said as he sat down and motioned to the bartender.

"Go on," Feng said with impatient disdain for the man who dared to sit at his table without permission.

"She stole my cab a couple of days ago…"

"If you have information that leads me to her…I will see you have a new one."

The man's eyes lit up at the prospect. He studied the men at the table as the barmaid delivered his drink. "I learned she has a camp on a beach. How do I know you will make good on your promise if…"

Feng reached across the table with the speed of a cobra and grabbed the unsuspecting man by the throat. He jerked him onto the table as two of his men secured his hands behind him. "Do not insult me again. First you sit at my table without an invitation. Now you question my honor?"

"Ahhh…I…I…meant no disrespect," the cabbie said through clenched teeth—barely able to breath as Feng's grip tightened. "A surfer beach…a few kilometers…north…"

The Triad hit man eased his grip and nodded to his men to release the man as well. "What is the name of the beach?"

"Thomas knows which one. We could take you there." He massaged his throat and nodded to the owner of the van.

"Fine. If you are lying…or wrong…I will be very displeased. Finish your beer…Sung, bring the car."

COSTA RICA
Chikako's Hide

Chikako lay in her hammock putting another application of Chinese balm, aloe vera gel and emu oil on her knee. Satisfied with the treatment, she opened a bottle of colloidal silver and, using the dropper, placed a half dozen drops under her tongue. *One more day and I'll be…fifty percent.*

313

After allowing for the silver-impregnated liquid to be absorbed, she swallowed, and then took a long drink from her water bottle before lying back and closing her eyes.

A sense of foreboding rushed over her—a cold wave seemed to slice down her spine. She sat upright. *Someone is coming...someone dark.*

She swung her legs off the hammock and stood up. Hobbling few steps she was able to see both directions on the beach. No one could be seen other than the surfers on the breakers and a old man using a metal detector far down the beach to the south. *I see no one but...gotta go...gotta go now.*

She had her day pack and a shoulder bag in her tent for just such an occasion—bug out bags for immediate departure. She quickly gathered her camp stove, a pair of canteens and a third smaller bag with her spare ammunition and magazines before limping slowly into the jungle. She was gone in less than three minutes. *Move to secondary hide. Come back in an hour. If no one is here...I'll grab some more supplies.*

Using a freshly-cut palm frond, she expertly wiped her tracks for a hundred yards into the jungle and moved deeper into the wilderness park.

DIPITAN PORT, PHILIPPINES

Jesse had his bags and stepped off the ramp of the boat onto the wharf. He scanned the throng of men and women milling about the port. A man with a small sign held over his head caught his attention—hand-scrawled letters spelled *Jesse*.

"I'm Jesse. Who sent you?"

"I get a text last night to pick you up today. Where we go?"

"No idea yet. Waiting on a boat from Cebu. Need to shadow some people on it."

"Boat arrives in two hours. Come…I have a cab."

BOHOL SEA
Mark's Fast Boat

The trip from Cebu to Dumaguete had gone smoothly and after refueling, departed for Dipitan right on time. The sea had chopped up and the craft slowed from it's thirty-two knots to twenty to lessen the bumpy ride.

"What's our ETA?"

"1630…maybe 1700 hours," the captain replied.

"I'm going back to check on the clients." *Mighty good of Joris to charter this boat for his wife and kid. Still wondering why he didn't delegate his private jet.*

Entering the passenger cabin he found Tola and Dalisay chattering away like best of friends while Rutger sat staring out the portal. Michele was in the back asleep. *Stayed up too late listening to Crank and the boys tell lies I see. Well…no harm done.*

"Steve…come sit with me," Rutger excitedly called out.

"Sure thing little buddy. Dalisay, you good?"

"Yes, thank you so much. How much longer to Dipitan?"

"An hour…maybe a little more."

"I hope we can find a ride to my village quickly…"

"Berto called ahead…there's a driver with a van waiting. We should make your home well before dark."

"How kind of him. I am so anxious to see my family. Destiny has brought me home one more time. Do you believe in destiny, Steve?"

Tola looked to Mark after her question. A sly smile crossed her face.

"I don't believe in destiny or fate...or angels watching from above. I believe each choice leads to the next...Which in turn leads to the next...We control our lives."

"But...that's so sad...and lonely. You don't believe God directs our lives?"

"I believe there's a higher being...or something out there unseen that...that watches. But directing my life? No. I'm the master of my ship...sink or sail."

CEBU, PHILIPPINES

Tong's Triad underling made a call on his cell phone.

"Where is the American?"

"He is with a man named Joris Barnhardt. He just opened a new orphanage in Cebu. I suggest you start there."

"Text me the address."

DIPITAN PORT, PHILIPPINES

While Mark herded his clients and team to the waiting van, Jesse sat in his cab watching. *Damn son...what's up with the silver hair? Hell...you're as gray as I am.*

As the van pulled out, the cab driver did as well.

"Keep a safe distance, but don't lose them."

"I have them. While you were taking a piss I spoke to the driver…I work with him before. He told me where they go."

"You didn't tell him…"

"I just make small talk between drivers."

"Good man." *Only two other ops with you son…and one of them looks pretty green. But by the looks of your bags you came well weaponed. Sometimes…I wish…ahh to hell with that. Water under the bridge.*

RIZAL NATIONAL PARK

Everyone stepped out of the van into the oppressive heat.

"Thank you for stopping here. I want Rutger to know something about his Filipino heritage."

"Dalisay, you and Rutger stay with me. Tola you and Michele trail us. Look like tourists. I'll play the expat with family game…You know what to do Michele?"

"Everyone dies."

Mark grinned. "Everyone on the other team…You follow Tola's lead."

"Yes, sir."

The stroll through the park was uneventful other than Rutger climbing on every tree and rock he came to. His interest in the plaques describing the life of Rizal warmed Dalisay's heart.

"So he fought the Spaniards here?" the boy asked.

"No. This is where he lived while he resisted the Spanish rule. That's his house up there."

"Let's go. I want to see it!" He started to run off.

Mark jumped forward quickly and grabbed his hand. "Whoa there, pardner. We have to stick together."

"Okay, Tio. I'm sorry."

"Hey, little buddy, no reason to be sorry. Just stay close. Okay?"

"Yes, sir. Wow...look at that stream. Can we go look at it?"

"Of course we can," his mom answered. "But don't go running off again and don't get in the water."

"Yes, mommie...gee...look at the butterflies."

"You have a fine son there, Dalisay. His young mind goes bouncing around a bit, but he's a good kid."

"Do you have children?" she asked.

He felt a lump rise in his throat and he looked off toward the ocean. "Once."

She reached out and put her hand on his arm, "Oh...I am so sorry. I didn't mean to..."

A feeling of discomfort passed over him at her touch, but he did not remove her hand. "No harm done. We need to take a look at Rizal's house and get back on the road."

She saw the look of sorrow in his eyes. *What could have happened?*

DIPOLOG, PHILIPPINES

The route from the port in Dipitan traveled through Dipolog before the road to Oroquieta could be taken. As they passed through the narrow streets, Rutger was enthralled with the sites and sounds. Though Dalisay had taken him to visit her parents before he was now old enough to be interested in his surroundings. Passing by the city hall and the park he noticed a bird sitting in a small cage.

"Look," he said pointing at the multi colored bird. "That's a big bird."

"That's a Monkey Eating Eagle, the national bird of the Philippines. You will see more of them when we get home."

"I hope so. That one is so sad sitting there all alone."

"Think about it. Look how big he is…at least three feet tall and weighs what…fifteen or more pounds. The cage is too small. No way to fly around. Just sit there day after day," Mark said.

"Why?"

"No idea. People are cruel sometimes."

"How come you know so much Tio?"

"I don't know so much…Bet you know more already about computers than I ever will."

Standing on the corner across from the police station Mark noticed three men that looked out of place. He craned his neck as they drove past to keep them in view. *What are you mofos up to? I wonder if the police know you're packing? Definitely handguns under their shirts.*

Isagani took little notice of the white passenger van passing by other than it blocked his view for a moment. His attention was riveted to the comings and goings of the law enforcement officers and the lack of serious security around the building.

The cab followed at a reasonable distance to avoid detection. At a busy intersection the traffic delayed it in a swirling mass of motor bikes and trike cabs—each driver honking his horn incessantly as if that would clear a path.

"Close the gap, but don't get tagged," Jesse said.

"No problem. They will turn off on Oroquieta highway in a few minutes. We can make up ground there. Plus the road is a dead end."

"I'll need you to drop me a couple of kilometers before we reach the village then. This cab would be a red flag."

"As you say. I give you my number. You call me when ready for me to come get."

"I'll do that. What's with all the banners and decorations going up?"

"In two days the annual Golden Days celebration…Biggest one of the year. There will be parades with floats and music. Talent shows. There will be a Miss Dipolog competition. Last years winner was my second cousin. So much food one cannot eat it all."

"Filipinos know how to organize festivals."

"Everything is more fun in the Philippines. That's our national motto." The driver laughed.

COSTA RICA
Chikako's Second Hide

She staggered into her second camp and was relieved that neither of the two trips back to her beach property revealed any indication anyone had been there. *Maybe I'm wrong. Maybe no one is coming.*

Depositing her gear on the ground next to a fallen tree trunk and she sat down to rest her throbbing knee. *Short break. Then get organized.* Looking around she spotted a sloth hanging in a tree. The animal had been there all along, but did not move when Chikako came and went.

Okay. First things first. Get the hammock strung up. Fill the water containers.

Fifty feet from where she sat, a spring bubbled out of a rock wall and fell into a small pool before heading downhill to the beach. *Get this place ready and I am so in that pool. Feel nasty and sticky after humping all the gear.*

Back at the beach the Suzuki van, followed by the Triad's car pulled up on a rise above the surfer camp. The Triad, the cabbie and the owner of the Van stepped out.

"You are sure this is the right beach?" Feng asked.

"Several sources say she has a place here. I bet those surf bums can direct us to it," the cabbie replied.

"Go down there and find out. I want her in my grasp by nightfall. Go!" Feng ordered.

From his vantage point, the leader could clearly see several of the surfers turn and point down the beach. *I have you, Chikako.* "We go now," he said to his men. "Stay in the forest. Remember Master Wu wants her alive."

The men removed automatic weapons from the trunk as well as large meat cleavers—which they strapped around their waists in the leather sheaths—and melted into the jungle…

***

CHAPTER TWENTY

OROQUIETA HIGHWAY
Mindanao Island

Nothing more than a gathering of Nipa Huts, a small sari-sari store, a meat smokehouse and a community hut that served as the Catholic church every Sunday greeted Mark and the group when they arrived. The residents went about their daily tasks like their ancestors had for generations. They parked in front of the most modern and well-kept home—Dalisay stepped out, holding Rutger's hand and walked briskly to the front door.

"Momma...Pappa...I'm home. We're here," she called out.

A Filipina in her late fifties came around the west side of the structure wearing a palm leaf hat and simple floral cotton dress carrying a potted plant. Seeing her daughter and grandson she dropped the plant and rushed to hug them.

"Oh, my baby girl is home! Pappa! Pappa! Come quick, Dalisay is here."

A Filipino appeared at the door and hobbled out on two walking canes to great his grandson and daughter. "Come to me my little man. Come to me." He knelt down slowly and held out his arms with a huge smile on his face. "You have grown like a weed, Rutger. Look how big you are now."

"It's okay, Rutger. Go say hello to Pappa Luis," Dalisay said.

Michele and the driver began unloading the Barnhardt's luggage from the van while the family hugged, laughed and cried with one another.

"Very nice home. A little small for all of us don't you think?" Tola asked.

"Michele and I can sleep in shifts in the van with the driver if we need to. You stay with Dalisay and Rutger. We'll work it out," Mark replied as he scanned the area. Spotting a deteriorating structure on the hillside east of the village he made note of it. *Best vantage point I see so far. Have to check it out in the morning.*

"What about these?" Michele asked pointing into the van at the weapon bags.

"Keep 'em locked up inside. Just your pistol for now. The most dangerous thing I see is…that Carabao."

Michele and Tola looked at the old buffalo staked out to graze across the road and started to laugh.

"I anticipated a housing shortage and brought a pair of tents. I use them when I take the boy scouts camping. Nothing fancy but they *will* keep the mosquitos off," the driver said as he picked up a pair of suit cases.

"You're all right, Mito...don't care what Berto said about you," Mark replied. "We'll set a tent up in the back and one near the van. I'm probably dreaming...but any chance you have..."

"Air mattress? Yes I do. Four of them. I sleep on one in the van all the time," he replied.

"Dang dog...you're better than all right."

"Mark, Michele, Mito...come. I want to introduce you to my parents," Dalisay called waving her hand for them to join her.

Tola was already standing with everyone and Momma had her arm around her shoulders.

"Here we go, boys," Mark said.

Three kilometers west of Oroquieta, Jesse left the cab and without pause, walked off into the jungle.

"Damn...I'm gettin' too old for this shit," he said as he stooped over carrying his gear. *Nice and easy. No rush. Still time to get to the village and do a spotter's scan.*

Twenty yards into the tangled undergrowth he came upon a foot path that paralleled the road. "Now ain't that nice? Hope no one is out for a stroll. Definitely too damn old to do any snoop and poop roll into the jungle." He laughed at his reference to diving off a trail to avoid persons of unknown origin or intent.

He turned uphill and began to climb. *Oh man...I'm going to have to...stash some of this gear...and come back for it. If not...I'll be too crippled to function by the time I get there.*

As he walked he watched for a likely place to hide some things. He topped a small hill and could see the deteriorating stone structure Mark had noted earlier. He set down two of his bags and pulled a pair of compact Leica binoculars from his shirt pocket. *That may be home? I can see some rooftops below it. Has to be Oroquieta.*

Jesse noticed a small game trail intersecting the path he was on. *Wonder what's over there?* He picked up the bags and stepped off the path and on to the trail. In twenty paces he came to a fallen tree with a 4x2 open space under it. *Perfect. I'll stash two bags…sling the M14…throw some debris and come back.*

BARNHARDT'S ORPHANAGE
Cebu, Philippines

Crank knocked hard on Joris' private door. He had already rung the bell several times and could hear it ringing inside the residence. As he started knocking a second time Joris' voice came over the intercom speaker box.

"What is it?"

"It's Crank. We haven't seen you all day. Are you all right in there?"

"Yes, I am perfectly fine."

"Don't want to inconvenience you, sir, but I need a visual."

"I assure you I'm fine," Joris said with annoyance in his voice.

"Then you won't mind coming to the door," Crank replied with authority.

"Very well. Give me a moment."

Two minutes later the door opened. Joris, barefooted wearing a silk robe, stood in full view. His hair was disheveled, he needed a shave and looked as if he had very little sleep.

"Satisfied?"

"Yes, sir. Is there anything you need?"

"To be left alone. Good day," he said as he closed the door forcefully and locked it.

This is one weird duck. First he says he wants to spend time with the staff and kids...then he locks himself in his house for twenty-four hours. Be damn happy when this cluster is over. Crank mused as he turned to Berto. "Let me know if he pops out. Does Rodel have visual on the patio?"

"Immediately, Crank and no, he does not. But he is posted outside the security fence to the patio."

"Have you seen anyone come in or out of here today?"

"Only three refuse collectors. They removed some trash bags around 1100. Other than that...no one."

"All right then. Stay sharp."

Berto nodded, but a passing thought clouded his face. "Ahh...I don't know if it means anything, but the bags smelled...bad. And one of the men...I'd swear I saw him yesterday at the grand opening."

"How bad?"

"Like something was dead...Not real dead, but..."

"So there's varying degrees of dead now?"

"I, uh...I don't know. I mean, it smelled like...not too long dead...Before something has had time to swell up."

Crank considered the information. "What would a trash man be doing at the big shindig?"

"That's what I was thinking. It looked like they were having a disagreement," Berto said.

"Blaster and Dog will be coming on post in an hour. Add that intel to your pass down."

OROQUIETA VILLAGE, MINDANAO

The village residents finally departed leaving Dalisay and her family to some quality time. Tola had been accepted like a long lost daughter by the parents and was helping with the post-party clean up. Mark, Michele and Mito sat on the front porch drinking bottles of mango, coconut and banana juice.

"Only an hour of light left. Finish these drinks and we'll set up the tents," Mark said.

"I'm so full I can hardly move," Michele added.

"Best slow down on the leachon or you'll be bigger than a pig before we leave."

"Not as good as Pappa's, but sure was tasty."

"I'm going to sleep in the van. Already used to it," Mito said as he got up. "I'll get the tents and air pads ready for you."

"Michele...you familiar with a pump shotgun?" Mark asked.

"Pappa says I'm good...I prefer a M-16, though."

"No gottie M-16. I'll let you have the pump with the folding buttstock. Be easier to get in and out of the tent if the need arises." Mark stretched his arms and legs before getting up. *Ohhh...pretty certain the ribs didn't break back on the wharf...but damn...they're still sore as hell.* "Crank issued additional 9 mm ammo…right?"

"Two hundred rounds. Pappa had me bring two hundred from home. I have more than enough…"

"Ain't no such thing as too much ammo, kid."

Michele's shoulders slumped and he whisked some pebbles left and right with his foot. "I'll remember that Zorro."

Well before dawn, the village roosters began to crow. One thing not in short supply was roosters. Every home had several tethered or in cages.

Mark sat up slowly as a big red and black cock ripped off its first crow. "Well cocka doodle doo to you, too."

Stepping out of his tent and looking to the east he saw the sky turning light gray above the mountains. He had put on clothing suitable for the environment—all brought from Kenya and well worn—from his days working with the KWS Park Rangers. *Damn these boots feel good.* He flexed his ankles and toes before doing a couple of squats. The special-order rich brown leather packer-outfitter boots—customed made to Mark's specifications—showed hard use but he had cleaned and oiled them in Cebu before the trip. Reaching up to just below his knees they fit like a pair of old friends.

Not wanting to alarm the locals unduly, he only wore his Colt under his left arm. He carried the S&W Model 5906 and the 7" O&U to the van—descreetly stored in travel cases—and tapped on the window. "Mito. Rise and shine."

"Uggh…you get up too early," he replied as he unlocked the sliding side door. "I sleep some more."

"Suit yourself. I'm going to roust Michele then take a little walk about. Get the lay of the land so to speak."

"Yeah…okay," Mito said as he rolled over.

Mark set the gun cases on the floor and grabbed the hard case containing the super-secret BEF G3 carbine—given to him for his assistance in rescuing US Senator Breitbart and his daughter in Kenya the previous Christmas. He closed the door and tapped on the window again. "Lock the door before you drift off."

Mito's hand came up and fumbled around for the door lock. Once he saw it fall and heard the distinct click as the mechanism secured, Mark headed to the back of the house.

He was surprised to find Michele up, dressed and doing a series of Philippine stick fighting exercises. "Well done, young man. How about moving around to the garden side of the house? Keep an eye on front and back while I scout a bit."

"Yes, sir. Did you see that?" he asked as he pointed the eight foot bamboo stick toward the stone ruins on the hillside.

"Yup. Saw it last night."

"What do you think it is?"

"No idea. How about you scout it when I'm finished?"

"That would be cool. Sort of looks like an old chapel…minus the bell tower."

"I'll be back in thirty to forty. Keep a sharp eye. Don't be shy about firing a shot if there's a problem. Got it?"

"Yes, sir."

He grabbed the handle on the hard case and trudged up the hillside. Well outside of the village, he stopped on a ridge top overlooking a long narrow valley. On the other side, a rocky bluff had a field of boulders that had crumbled off a small outcrop. Mark looked around for any sign of other people. Finding none, he walked another forty yards past the crest and set the case down. *I've been wanting to check this baby out ever since Widowmaker convinced Dare Phillips to give me one. Damned nice of the BEF to be so generous.*

By memory, he rolled the seven wheels of the gun case's brass lock until they matched those of his Marine corps ID number. He pulled the top up to expose one of the most deadly weapons on the planet. The carbine looked, at first glance, to be Steyr AUG A2—but first glances can be deceiving. Designed by the Black Eagle Force resident genius, Blaze Hermann, it was an electromagnetic coil rifle capable of things no other rifle on earth could do.

Mark lifted one the two triangular-shaped battery packs from its recess. He opened the access panel in the weapon's buttstockand pressed the half-inch thick rechargeable unit in place until it snapped, and then closed the door. *So far so good. She even made it Marine proof.*

Its shape and the *This Side Up* decal made sure of that. He grabbed a magazine and glanced at the tiny depleted uranium double ojive ferromagnetic projectiles the carbine fired. They were about the size of a 16 penny nail without the head—sharply tapered on both ends. Sixty of them fit inside the custom magazine that was almost identical to a 20 rounder for a

M-16. *Not much to look at, but man...What they do is friggin' awesome.*

Mark lifted the rifle by its handgrip, slipped the mag into the well and locked it in place. *Almost ready to rock and roll. Decisions, decisions.*

The case had two sights nestled in the protective recesses. One was a Leupold Mark 4 scope in 4.5x14x50mm with a mil dot reticule. The other was a tactical EOTECH 552 with both day and NVG capability. He glanced at the distance to the boulder field and opted for the magnification. He slipped the Mark 4 onto the naked pitcatinny rail and threw the locking levers down, securing it for action.

Widowmaker Baker said the long range optics were already zeroed for 500 yards. All I have to do is press the activation button in front of the trigger guard. Sounds simple enough.

He pressed the activation switch and heard a slight humming sound as the sequential capacitors came alive. Electrons flowed from the device the users called a battery. In actuality, the power source was a proprietary ionic gel that stored the free electrons until needed, and not unlike a ultrahigh speed SD card, allowed them to recharge the firing capacitors in a rapid manner.

Taking a prone position, he looked around once more to insure he was alone. He spotted a basketball-sized rock atop a huge boulder and placed the crosshairs tangent to the upper periphery of it. *800 yards. They say this sumbitch is a flat shooter. Let's find out.*

Mark controlled his breathing. Once the target image was what he desired, he placed the pad of his trigger finger on the curved actuator and pressed. At exactly one pound of pressure the circuit completed. A titanium plunger pushed a single ferromagnetic projectile into the chamber and held it suspended there as the first drive coil created a hyper-intense magnetic field and repulsed the slender rod forward. A complex system of graphene nanotubes—filled with liquid mercury—were controlled by a tiny computer chip Blaze had designed. Carbon based graphene was a superconducting element.

Each successive set of coils wrapped around the lightweight barrel functioned exactly like the mag-lev trains at Disney World or the ultra-fast bullet trains in Japan. They alternately pulled, released and then pushed the projectile—accelerating it to an unheard of velocity of 12,000 feet per second.

All of that complex action was essentially invisible to the shooter. The bullet never made contact with the bore, resulting in minimal friction, no drag, no recoil and a funny noise that didn't even sound like a rifle firing.

Ponk.

Mark watched the target as a very brief blue plasma field was created by the hypersonic round as it ionized the atmosphere passing though it. What appeared to him was instantaneous impact on the small rock. It blasted apart and was reduced to a cloud of dust. A second later the sound of the rock exploding reached his ears.

Whump.

Holy shit. A big grin came to his face. He remembered seeing what happened to the kidnappers in Kenya, and the rebels who tried to overthrow President Mobutu there a few weeks later. They didn't fare much better than the rock. *Those boys weren't lyin'. This is a bad motor scooter.*

He picked out a couple of more targets to see if the first example was a fluke. It was not. He safetied the carbine, removed the magazine and battery pack. Once the gear was stowed back in the heavy duty case, he locked it and headed back to the village with a smile that didn't fade.

All the Nipa huts had little vegetable gardens, a hog pen and several chickens scratching about the fenced yards. Smoke from the coconut wood kitchen fires drifted lazily over the landscape in the soft early morning glow.

Gonna be a scorcher. Need to break out the mosquito control when I get back. Last thing I want is to catch malaria or dengue fever.

As he approached Dalisay's parents home he spotted Rutger holding a short length of bamboo imitating Michele's fighting moves. *That's a smart little goober. And from the looks of Michele's moves, he picked a good role model. Berto's kid is pretty good...and quick.*

Jesse knelt over a small fire preparing his morning coffee. On the move to the village he had discovered a fishing Nipa beside a stream and, realizing his limitations, opted to remain there overnight. The trip back to pick up his hidden bags had him down well after dark.

After a meal of canned corned beef and crackers—washed down with three cups of steaming hot Brazilian coffee from Cello's kitchen—he moved his gear to a small cave above the hut. Satisfied his hide was well camouflaged with brush, he picked up his M14, put on a belt with four magazine pouches, a small day pack with some canned tuna, more crackers and a two quart collapsible canteen. He tied a dark green bandana around his forehead and walked up the hill to recon the village.

Gonna be a hot one. My legs and back feel like I humped an elephant in here yesterday. It's definitely hell gettin' old.

"Michele...I'm back. How 'bout you scout the ruins? I'll keep an eye on the clients."

"All right! I can do that."

"Be ready to give a report when you get back. Take a good look around from up there. Details...note any special features to the building. Don't skip a good scan of this village either."

"Yes, sir," Michele said excitedly as he started off.

"Michele?"

"Yes, sir?"

"Take your shotgun...and get a canteen from the truck."

"Oh...yeah. Okay."

Man...good kid but greener than grass. What the hell...this may just be the perfect op to get some of the shine off his forehead.

"Tio Steve. Can I go with Tio Michele?" Rutger asked as he ran up to the Texan.

"Not this time, pardner. Michele needs to make sure it's safe first. Maybe later."

"Awww…shoot. I never get to have any fun."

"Sure you do. I saw you learning stick fighting…"

"Yeah. I get my stick and show you." He ran off—his little legs churning and his arms flailing.

"He really likes you."

Mark turned to see Dalisay and Tola behind him. "He's a bright kid. I couldn't help noticing…forgive me if I'm out of line here…but Joris doesn't seem to pay him much attention."

"Where's Michele going?" Dalisay asked avoiding eye contact.

"I sent him to check out the ruins. What was that place?"

"It was a Catholic monastery. The Japanese burned it during the war."

"I see. And no one thought to rebuild it?"

"No. It's full of multos. Before they burned it, they put all the men and boys from the village inside with the priests. The only men that survived were those who had run off to the mountains when the Japanese arrived."

"Ghosts?"

"That's what everyone thinks. I was not allowed to go up there as a child so I don't know. Gives me the creeps though."

Jesse found a good vantage point nestled in some trees with a in a trio of boulders offering protection. He leaned his rifle against one of the rocks and pulled his binoculars out. Below he could make out most of the Nipa huts but more importantly he had a excellent view of Dalisay's parents home—easily identified by the white van parked in front and the shiny metal roof. All the other buildings had woven palm fronds for roofs.

After scanning the village thoroughly, he scoped the stone ruins. He spied Michele below, climbing a washed-out roadway. *Huh...good I didn't make that my hide last night.* He held his view of the young Filipino as he entered the ruins and disappeared. *This'll do fine. Four hundred yards to the van. Down hill.*

CHAPEL RUINS

The inside of what had been the sanctuary was blackened while the other rooms were motley gray. Many of the walls had partially fallen in or out creating a jumbled pile of rubble. None of the roofing remained.

Michele wandered from one room to another—stopping briefly at each window or doorway to the exterior to view the surroundings. At the furthermost end from the village he discovered what was left of the bell tower, still two stories tall with the upper chamber collapsed inside itself—creating a path to climb and look over the wall at its highest point.

From the tower the young operative could see the entire village below as well as glimpses of the road winding back down the valley towards Dipolog.

I can see everything from here. Damn snakie, though...I hate snakes. He continually checked around his feet for the one thing that gave him the willies. Making his way back down he spotted the upper portion of a doorway filled with rubble. Cautiously he knelt and peered inside. Pulling his flashlight from a rear pocket he shined it into the dark space. *Wow! Look at that...some of the local kids are using this for a hideout.* Stacked against the walls of the room were numerous pieces of bamboo, several used motorcycle inner tubes looped together with a large leather patch secured in the middle. *Catapults. I remember when Rodel and I use to play war with catapults Pappa made us.* Stacked near another wall were a dozen six foot spears, a pair of rusty machetes and a trio of wooden crates. *Ummm...wonder what's in the crates? One thing's for sure...not crawling in there to find out. No way.*

Working through a series of small rooms along the west side he discovered a cistern. His light revealed water only ten or so feet below. In another room he found remnants of cooking pots—none of which were useable.

Taking one last look down at the village Michele could see Zorro next to the van looking up at him with binoculars. He waved his arm in long slow sweeping motions over his head. Seeing Zorro raise a clenched fist and pump his arm, he returned the signal before making his way down the hill as quickly as he could.

YACHT CLUB ISLE de SOL
St. Maarten/St. Martin

Thijs Vandeputte stepped out of the hot tub wrapping a towel around his portly waist and slipped his feet into a pair of embroderied beach sandals. He rushed to open his Skype program. *Damn! Why does he always call at the least opportune moments.*

Behind him, hands secured to a pair of large eye bolts, a ten year old girl struggled to free herself. It was evident she was not from the island by her light blonde hair and blue eyes. She was actually from the state of Minnesota, USA. Kidnapped only a week before, Thijs paid a hefty sum to obtain her and have her transported to his yacht.

The Skype signal ended before the irritated Thijs could activate his program. Once ready he called his partner back.

"There you are."

"Yes, here I am. What is it you want?" Thijs asked.

"Did you get the raw footage from last night yet?"

"Yes. The staff is processing it now."

"Some good stuff wouldn't you say?"

Always wanting applause. For someone so rich and powerful it is very unbecoming to seem so in need of adoration. "I haven't taken the time to look at it. I'll let you know once a rough cut is finished."

"Ah…of course. And what is it I see behind you, Thijs?"

The towel wrapped lecher looked over his shoulder as he answered, "A new plaything. Hoer training her now…She's a sweet little student…willing to learn…"

"Ha…that's why you have her tied to the pool?"

"I noticed you only sent four episodes. I assure you we could use much more…"

"All in good time, Thijs. The security group makes life difficult. But…I have a new team of Europeans coming in soon to replace them."

"Anything else?"

"No. I suppose not. I'll let you get back to your pleasures. Send me the rough cut of each episode as soon as possible. And have them throw together a compilation of the four. Do some fades and flash cuts…fast and dirty. You know what I mean?"

"I'll relay your message. Get some more episodes here as soon as you can."

"I'm feeling…invigorated. I am going to do six…maybe seven more tonight."

MALPAIS, COSTA RICA
Cabo Blanco Absolute Reserve

Without her red lens headband flashlight, Chikako would not be able to see anything at her second hide. The dense forest canopy obscured the night sky completely. She only flipped it on for a few moments if she needed to move about so as not to provide any clue as to her presence.

The day before, she had heard male voices in the direction of the beach talking in Mandarin. She knew the Triad had discovered her camp, but there was nothing she could do about it but wait. The knee was eighty percent recovered, but not up to any running through the jungle or close combat.

Unwilling to start her stove—tell-tale smell of smoke could prove fatal—she ate cold meals and denied herself the pleasure of a hot cup of tea.

Feng and his men sat up all night and all the next day watching her original campsite. It was brutal for the three urban goons. The insects—in particular the mosquitos—made the experience extremely unpleasant. They seemed to be feeding exclusively on their Chinese flesh.

Seeing the sun dipping into the Pacific Ocean horizon, Feng made a decision—one he would regret. He called out, "We go. She is not coming back."

Both men answered his call with relief and affirmation.

"Before we go…destroy her belongings."

They slipped out of the jungle began slashing her tent, smashing the coolers and anything else they could destroy with their meat cleavers.

One man walked around the tent enjoying shredding it with his razor sharp weapon. His disturbance of her nocturnal hunting brought a swift and deadly response by a three meter long female terciopelo—the common Costa Rican name for the fer-de-lance snake. It was olive drab with tan and rust blotches and she struck him in the leg just above the right ankle.

"Ahhh!"

"What is it?" the other Triad soldier called as he ran to his companion's aid. He knelt next to the stricken man writhing on the ground in agony holding his leg only to have the fer-de-lance inject her deadly venom in his left hand as well.

"Aeee!" He screamed as he fell back and fired a full magazine at the snake—missing it completely but managing to shoot his fellow Triad brother in the leg just above the two puncture marks.

Chikako sat bolt upright at the sound of gunfire and screams filtering through the jungle. *What the hell is going on?*

Feng slowly approached the men uncertain what was wrong. He stopped several feet from the dying men. "What is it?"

"Snake."

"It burns. We...we need...a hospital quickly."

"You will be dead before we arrive," the gang leader said without emotion as he pointed his suppressed 9 mm pistol at one, and then the other.

Pssst. Pssst.

DIPITAN, PHILIPPINES
Pulauan Port

Isagani and three of his MNLF soldiers rode in two separate trike cabs casing the port located in Barangay San Vicente. He made mental notes about the two lighthouses located on either side of the cove. *A couple of our RPGs will make short work of them both. Two men to assault the one on Tag-ulo Point and another pair to the one on the hill above. A great blow for Allah to disrupt all the sea travel in Dipitan Bay.*

The intense midday heat would drain the life out of those not native to the region. Only the air flowing over their bodies from the movement of the cabs gave any relief as it evaporated the sweat collecting on their clothing.

The port was seven kilometers from the Dipitan City proper and the piers were, for all practical purposes, poorly guarded—never more than a dozen bored and sleepy Philippine Army regulars. There were also an equal number of local law enforcement with a small detail of port authority officers. *I will have Jaco and ten men wreak havoc here while I take the remaining men with me to Dipolog.*

Satisfied with his reconnaissance the young MNLF leader ordered the return to his hideout between the sister cities. They stopped along the way at a local fish farm to purchase fresh bangus. The national fish of the Philippines was always a welcome meal. As the farm attendants prepared the filets, the leader mentally went over his plan once again.

Having procured the fish—iced down in cardboard boxes for the short trip—the trike cabs climbed away from the port through Dipitan and onto the Dipolog-Oroquieta National Road. The view of Dipitan Bay lay behind them.

Once they reached the crest of the mountains dividing the two cities, the view of the Sulu Ocean went as far as the eye could see to the west. Large white clouds moved slowly to the west casting dark shadows on the ocean as they headed towards Malaysia and Vietnam.

On a particularly sharp turn on the mountain road a passenger bus caused the trike cabs to swerve dangerously close to the edge of the road. Isagani grabbed the metal rod attaching the roof to the side car as the cab skidded—throwing gravel over the edge of the road and off into the jungle fifty feet below.

"Watch where you are going infidel!" he screamed.

The driver braked hard stopping on the narrow shoulder. He removed the key from the ignition and leapt off, running downhill as fast as he could.

Isagani jumped free from the side car and ran after him. The trike following his rolled by and the young leader jumped on. When it passed the running driver, Isagani struck him in the back of the head with the butt of his pistol—sending him rolling for several feet before he came to rest. Stepping off the cab Isagani ripped the key from the injured man's hand before stomping viciously on his neck. The sickening crack of his vertebra indicated he would not be getting up.

***

CHAPTER TWENTY-ONE

OROQUIETA VILLAGE

Everyone had gathered at the community building for the celebration of Dalisay's return. A pair of one hundred pound pigs—gutted, but still having its hide—were roasting over two separate fire pits. A half dozen men and older boys stood around in the shade of a tree drinking cheap Philippine beer as two men slowly turned the swine over the hot coals by hand.

A karaoke machine blared distorted music as several of the women and teenage boys sang one song after another badly out of key. The favorite tune seemed to be *Sinatra's My Way*.

God have mercy. Never cared for that song, even when he sang it. "Mito, need you to make a run...get more ice," Mark ordered as he checked the coolers.

"I will refuel the van as well. Anything else?"

"Three cases of Coca Cola, two cases of Sprite and some bottled water for Mark and Tola," Dalisay added.

"Here's five thousand pesos. I'll reimburse you if it takes more than that…You know what? Stop at that Jollibee we passed. Buy everyone an order of chicken. How many people are here Dalisay?"

"Oh, Mark, that's not necessary…"

"That's why I want to do it. Ain't no sense in it if it was necessary. I'll bet it's been awhile since some of these folks have had Jollibee."

"Some have never have," she replied as she put her hand on his shoulder.

Tola noticed the move and the look in her eyes before she looked away. "Rutger, how about you play soccer with the other kids?"

He sat on the three foot rock wall of the community building watching the others play. "I don't know if they would want me to."

"Only one way to find out…Go on now. I'll watch you."

It was all the encouragement he needed. He jumped off the wall and ran out to the other children playing.

"What else have they never done?" Mark asked.

"The people in this village are very poor. My parents have their home because of Joris. He only came here once but…but he has allowed me the money to build momma and pappa a better house."

"I could live here myself. Reminds me of how my grandparents lived in Texas. Raised most of their own food, never had a car or truck of their own…Just lived real simple."

"I miss it in many ways. If not for Rutger I'd be happy here. But he needs a good education."

Mito pulled up in the van and asked if anything else had come to mind before he departed, "I stashed your gear in the shed beside the well."

"Perfect. Double time it. We'll be out of ice in a couple of hours."

From his vantage point, Jesse could see most of the goings on at the community building. *Looks quiet. Think I'll catch a few winks.* Leaning back on his day pack the older Ingram gazed at the blue sky for a few moments before he dozed off.

ISAGANI'S CAMP
Dipolog River

Hidden in the jungle, the MNLF quickly built a crude camp—bamboo poles lashed together in lean-to fashion with green bamboo thatch roofs, small cooking pits, a slit-trench latrine downstream—to wait until the festivals. The stolen cabs were covered with brush just off the road.

"Small fires. Nothing to alert anyone we are here," Isagani ordered his men. *Tomorrow…tomorrow we strike.*

Jaco approached. "You wanted to see me?"

"You will take ten men and strike the targets we surveyed in Dipitan at exactly 1800. Our coordinated attacks will throw the infidels into a panic. After you have completed your work, ditch the cabs at the top of the mountain and follow the ridge back to this point," the young leader said pointing at a position on a map he had procured in Dipolog. "I will meet you there."

"I will not fail you, Isagani."

"I know you will not. Once we are all at the rally point we will travel here…to this small village. We can gather supplies…maybe a horse or mule to pack for us. We commandeer small ships and make our way back to Jolo."

"It is a good plan…"

"It is the plan shown to me by Allah in a dream. The infidels will know of his almighty power by our jihad. When we return to Takut Tangug, we will be heroes."

"We are low on ammunition, Isagani…"

"Strip the dead infidels. Take one of the passenger vans at the port. Fill it with all you can carry."

BARNHARDT'S ORPHANAGE
Cebu, Philippines

Crank gathered his team outside Joris' private quarters for a briefing. "Last day in Cebu, men. So far…so good. No rip tides or monster breakers. Let's keep it that way."

"I haven't seen Mister Barnhardt yet today," Berto said. "Just like yesterday. No one in or out but the trash crew."

"I'll do a visual on him when we're through here. We boogie board out of here at 1600 tomorrow. Don't let your guard down. On your toes, eyes wide. Got it?"

"Are you going to be joining us in Bangkok?" Blaster asked.

"No. Never work where you sleep and shit…When we get back to the big mango, Rhino will meet us at the airport."

"What do you charge to stay at your hotel?" Mike questioned.

Crank flashed his patented smile. "First we have to bleed together. After that…it's on me."

"Bleed together?" Blaster asked with a quizzical look on his face as he exchanged glances with Mike.

"Zorro tell you about Kenya?"

"Hell…he hasn't told us much of anything. What happened in Kenya?" Dog asked.

"I'll only tell you solid operators died. No place to duck dive, that's for sure. Think…fifty to one. Like that…A real tittie twister."

"I remember mainstream media talking about the military coup. Tried to overthrow the president…"

"Tried is the operative word, Dog…Tried. Until you catch a big one with me, Zorro or Rhino…the lotus blossom hotel is full up."

Roger and Mike looked at each other and shrugged.

"Any word from the man?" Berto asked.

"Not a peep. Doubt we'll hear from him…unless there's a tsunami. When we fly you could probably join him if you want."

"Rodel, Michele and I have another contract. Some movie people from England are flying in to do some filming at Bigfoot Studios here in Cebu. Biggest indoor water tank in the world. You hear of it?"

"Work is good. And no…don't keep up much with those movie girls. Let's break this cluster. Get some sleep," Crank said nodding at Roger and Mike.

BARNHARDT'S RESIDENCE
Bangkok, Thailand

Rhino and Keit were finishing a late lunch when Hans rushed in highly agitated.

"We must call Zorro."

"What's up?" Rhino asked.

"The computer mainframe…one of the mainframes…the one I could not identify as a functioning component of the security system. It's…it's…"

"Easy now mate. Take a deep breath. You look like the diggers 're comin' for you," Rhino said with a laugh.

"It's full of porno," the wild-eyed Hans finally stated as he paced nervously around the room.

"Lekker on…Let's have a look…"

"You don't understand…"

"Ja…I understand porno, Hans."

"This is child pornography, Rhino…The vilest form of child pornography."

Rhino and Keit exchanged looks in stunned silence. Hans walked in circles ringing his hands and mumbling to himself.

"Ag man bosbefok…don't you be makin' a flou of me."

Hans still wandered the room nervously.

"All right bru. Let's take a look…"

"I will not view it again. I'll open the encrypted site for you...but I cannot watch it. The faces on the little children..." He dropped to his knees. "Dear God in heaven."

"Keit, review the tapes. Go back...six months...no...a year. Log any suspicious activity. I'll take a look at Hans' findings."

CEBU, PHILIPPINES

Crank was refueling the stretch limo when his cell rang. Seeing it was Rhino he put the phone back in his pocket—deciding to call once he was finished.

Pulling away from the Petro station, he hit the callback button. Rhino answered immediately.

"You with Barnhardt?"

"No. I'm headed back to the orphanage though. What's shaking?"

Rhino began rattling off rapidly, "I've been tryin' to reach Mark. No answer. I called Maggie and left a message to..."

"Whoa there. Slow down. You okay? Is there a problem in Bangkok?"

"Dutchie mompie's into child pornography. Man...worst I ever seen. Snuff films...*Child* snuff films!"

"You sure?"

"No doubt 'bout it...Can you contact Zorro?"

"On it. Chill bro...I'll keep this on the low low 'til we get with the boss man. Suggest you do the same..."

"Hell *brak*! There isn't anybody to tell. It's just Hans, Keit an' me 'ere."

"Can you make copies?"

350

"I'm sure Hans can but…I'm not wanting any of this shit in my possession. Interpol would roast the balls of anyone with it."

"Do this…Make copies. Take them to the LEO that Zorro worked with on the hostage retrieval…No, hold off on that. Let's get Mark in the loop."

"God! You know I've seen some unbelievable stuff…but I…"

"Hang up. I'll get Zorro on the line."

OROQUIETA VILLAGE

Mark's satellite phone on the entry table of Luis' home rang. He had left it there to charge while at the celebration—it rang endlessly.

At the community building, the village residents were in full swing celebrating. The Jollibee chicken take-out orders had been consumed as soon as they arrived. Everyone then had heaping plates of leachon—roasted pig—pancet, fresh fruits and a variety of other native dishes. The light bulbs—dangling on bare electric cords throughout the structure—were on as the sun sank in the western sky. Most had been replaced with colored lights—red, green, blue and yellow—giving the area a festive atmosphere.

Some of the men and boys cheered on their favorite fighting cock in a small arena enclosed in bamboo. A half dozen of the losing combatants were hanging by their feet on the fence with their heads cut off. The village dogs jockeyed for position to lap up the blood as it pooled on the ground. One tan and black jumped up, snatched a dead rooster from the fence and raced off with two other mongrels in close pursuit.

"What are they doing momma?" Rutger asked pointing at the pit.

"It's a game. A really...terrible game."

"Why is grandpappa there then?"

"He doesn't know any better. It's...it's something he grew up with and he doesn't understand how...how..."

"Senseless and cruel it is," Mark interrupted. "You see a long time ago the Spanish showed up here and brought some of their culture with them. After four hundred years they left but cockfighting stayed."

"How come you know so much about everything, Tio Steve?"

"Cause I'm old, little buddy. Say...tell you what...it's time for me to take a walkabout. Want to go with me?...If it's okay with your mom, of course."

"Good. When you get back it will be bath time..."

"Why? Some of the boys I was playing soccer with told me they don't have to take a bath every day."

"Because I want you to be clean and safe. There are lots of things here that can make you sick. Your body is not used to them...Run along now. When we finish the bath you can read to me. I like to hear you read."

"Okay momma."

"We have to stop by the house first. I need to pick some things up before we go. Shouldn't be gone more than a hour."

DARK SECRET

COSTA RICA
Chikako's Hide

The smell of decaying flesh wafted into the jungle. Chikako sat motionless perched in a tree for several hours—watching for any sign that would indicate someone was waiting. Satisfied the camp was empty and unobserved, she climbed down carefully and slipped to the edge of the forest.

The sound of flies buzzing around their meal mingled with those of the indigenous bird life and the Pacific ocean waves rolling on the beach. *Two bodies. Tent destroyed. Everything else...destroyed. Their weapons are still there. Those could be useful.* She pulled a dark green bandana from her cargo pants and wrapped it over her nose and mouth.

As stealthily as possible she moved to the bodies, picked up the weapons along with their magazines, and slipped back into the jungle. *Strange...they both had single shots to the head.*

After careful inspection of each weapon, she laid them aside and made another venture into the camp. Finding a small shoulder bag the Triad had not destroyed she gathered up what items were still functional—a cup, a pair of two-liter water bottles as well as other small items. Satisfied nothing else could be salvaged, she took one last look at the bodies. *What the hell...why not?*

She carefully went through their pockets finding wallets, passports and a small amount of rumpled Yuan Renminbi—Chinese currency. *Hmm...Chinese boys. Definitely have to get the hell out of Costa Rica.*

Back in the forest she cut another palm leaf branch and used it to whisk her trail back to her second hide.

Back at her second camp, she used a length of olive drab paracord to tie one of the Mac 11s to a tree at waist level pointing down the trail. Using another length, she rigged a trip wire across the trail and secured it to the trigger. *Anyone comes around, this will slow them down. Need some sleep.*

The howl of a panther silenced the jungle. Smelling the kill, the big cat was checking for competition.

OROQUIETA VILLAGE

Mark and Rutger sat on an outcropping some fifteen feet above the road.

"How come you have so many guns?" Rutger, asked looking in particular at the short barreled O&U shotgun on Mark's hip.

"I need them for my work."

"My father doesn't need any guns for his work."

"No he doesn't...But he needs someone like me who does."

"Why?" Rutger tossed a stone onto the roadway.

"Sometimes there are bad people who will try to take advantage of other people...like your father. It's my job to see they don't."

"I see...Wow! Look at that. What is it?" the boy asked, pointing up at the sky.

Mark glanced up to see a Chrysopelea paradisi floating by before landing in a tree. "That's a flying snake..."

"Aw, snakes don't fly."

"That one does. Actually it flattens out its body and glides from tree to tree…or to the ground."

"Can it kill you? I mean is it poisonous?"

"Not as poisonous as some. Its fangs are back in its mouth rather than near the front. They mainly use constriction to kill their prey. Bats…other small reptiles. But if you didn't get medical attention pretty quick it could kill you."

"Damn. You know so much…"

"*Damn*?"

"I'm sorry. Please don't tell momma I said that."

Mark reached over and ruffled his hair. "Our secret, little buddy. Just between you and me." *Josh would be about his age now.* A glimmer of sorrow flashed across his face before he could turn to look where the snake had landed.

"What's wrong…you mad at me?"

"No. Absolutely not. We should be getting back, your mom will be wondering about us."

DALISAY'S HOME

Tola stood on the porch with Mark's satellite phone when they returned.

"Someone trying to call for many times." She handed the cell to Mark.

"Where is everybody?"

"Mito and Michelle are out back, taking a shower. The family is inside."

Mark walked back to the van before checking the call list. *Umm...Crank and Rhino. Wonder what's up?* He hit the recall feature for Crank first.

"Zorro...we have a problem..."

"Joris? Is he secure?"

"We have him in his private quarters. No way to tell this but straight up...Looks like the sack of shit is a pedophile."

"What?"

"Call Rhino. He and Hans have the details. What do you want me to do with him?"

Mark was stunned by the news. "Hang tight. I'll get back with you."

He called Rhino straight away.

"Damn bru...I've been waiting..."

"Details."

"Hans found some videos. Child porno...snuff videos as well."

"Put him on the line."

"Hans here."

"Secure the data. Hold on to it 'til we are all back in Bangkok."

"I will do as you order. Francisca and I are leaving tonight. We cannot stay here any longer. Rhino will have what you want."

"Understood."

"Steve...everything all right?" Dalisay asked.

Mark turned to see her standing with Rutger a few feet behind him. "Yeah. No big problem. Just some unforeseen…uh, anomalies. We may need to leave a little sooner than expected."

"Oh no. We have members of our family coming day after tomorrow. Surely…I mean if it's not big problem…we could stay a few more days. Please?"

Mark considered the request and weighed it against the news. *Hell…another day or two won't change anything.* "Yeah, sure. Couple more days."

"Oh thank you so much. He hasn't seen his whole family now in two years. They will be delighted to see how much he's grown."

They turned and walked back to the house as Tola moved closer to Mark.

"We go?"

"Soon. We know now why Dalisay wanted you around Rutger every minute. Joris is a pedophile."

"You will kill him?"

"Depends. Have to sort this all out. The sick fuck has half a dozen orphanages in as many countries. Certain to have associates involved at each…"

"If you kill him it will end. There will be no one to…"

"Not so. The one thing I learned in Kenya about ivory poaching is cutting off the head of a snake…does not insure the beast dies." They stood in silence.

The village had gone to bed and only the hamlet mongrels were still up, scavenging for scraps.

"I need to call Crank again. Stay close to those two. Don't tell them…"

"I no tell."

Jesse watched the event below him with keen interest. *Something's not right. Mark's body language is all wrong. Is it here and now…or is it on the other end of the phone call?*

BARNHARDT'S ORPHANAGE
Cebu, Philippines

Crank paced back and forth by the limo. He could see both Roger at the front door and Mike at the side patio from his position. *This is the weirdest fuck yet. I sure wouldn't want to be in the Dutchman's shoes.* His cell vibrated.

"Go."

"Who's been in and out of his private quarters?"

"Just the trash crew."

"Anything odd in their business?"

"Berto says they show up everyday and roll a buggy inside. When they come out there was several large plastic trash bags. They have a foul odor…"

"Here's what you do, Crank. Tomorrow you follow the trash crew until they are well away, then land on them and inspect the bags. If what I think is in there…get plenty of photos. The bags and the crew."

"Then what?"

"Get some answers from the crew…Don't care how. Record it."

"If there are bodies?"

"Secure them on ice…literally. Don't want them to deteriorate. Detail Berto and Rodel to do it. We'll get the local law involved after you have the evidence."

"What about the trash guys?"

"We want to give 'em up to the justice boys…after Joris is on the plane. Send Blaster and Dog with him back to the big mango. Tell the bastard you have some other work that requires you to stay." Mark paused. "On second thought…Keep the crew until I call you. I'm stuck here for a couple more days."

"Done and done. I had a gut feelin' about this sick bastard."

"So did Tola. Water under the bridge now…Focus on the present. Hell, Crank, I took this gig to span the gap 'til Nicaragua. Seems like there was a bigger purpose."

"Ah…don't go getting all psychic on me. It is what it is and you…well, we just stepped in it. That's all."

"I gotta call Rhino back. Get your end squared away."

BARNHARDT'S RESIDENCE
Bangkok, Thailand

Rhino, Hans and Francisca were eating a late meal when Mark called again.

"What's the plan?" Rhino asked.

"Roger and Mike will be landing on you tomorrow night. Check with Crank for the details. He's staying in Cebu to tie up loose ends."

"What do we do with the sick fok once he's here? Can I filet him and slow roast him on the spit?"

"I wish. Act like nothing's changed. Tola and I are out of here in a couple of days. Wait for me to get there."

"Cut the trip off...Get your scrawny arse back here..."

"He's been at this a long time. I can feel it in my gut. Another couple of days 'til all the karma in the world lands on his worthless head isn't going to matter."

"Maybe, but I have to nod and smile till you get here. That's going to cost extra. And if I have to shake his hand you will never be out of my debt."

"You're starting to sound like Hal. Bottom line, this is one more lesson in never divide your forces. Crank's in Cebu...you're in Bangkok...and I'm in bumfuck Mindanao."

CANOAS, COSTA RICA
Panamanian Border

Chikako stepped off the public bus and fell in line with all the other travelers. She considered the eight dollar fare a bargain and a great cover for her extraction from Costa Rica. The mix was half expats or tourists and the others were Panamanian or Costa Rican. The Canoas was a well traveled crossing. When she stood in front of the Costa Rican security guard—his uniform shirt soaked in sweat from the midday heat—she handed him her papers.

"What is the purpose of your visit to Panama?" he asked.

"I need to renew my tourist visa."

The man casually viewed them—seemingly more interested in her figure than the documents—before returning her passport and motioned her to move on.

On the Panama side, the same question and casual inspection occurred before she was allowed to board another bus. The sign on the front of rickety vehicle read *David.* It was a quaint village in the mountains and a normal destination for those spending twenty-four hours or more before returning to Costa Rica and have a new fifty-nine day visa issued.

Buddha is with me. I don't see any other Asians. I'll get to David and contact Hal.

The bus pulled out and began its laborious journey through the mountains. All the windows were down, but the light breeze that blew through them did little to ease the stifling heat. Next to her a Panamanian woman breast fed her baby. Across the isle an old man rolled a cigarette and lit it before exhaling a pungent cloud of smoke.

Perfect. A bus ride next to a nasty chimney....Joy to the world.

***

CHAPTER TWENTY-TWO

DIPOLOG RIVER
Isagani's Camp

Daylight filtered through the trees as the men prepared a breakfast of dried fish and boiled vegetables. The thin smoke drifted upwards and dissipated in the foliage above.

Isagani still sat on his small prayer mat. *Today...we strike...* His visions of grandeur were interrupted by Jaco.

"We are out of fish, rice and..."

"Take two men and go to the market in Dipitan. While you are there do one more inspection of the police station and the docks."

"What about the airport in Dipolog?"

"I will send someone else. Go now. Be back before dark."

OROQUIETA VILLAGE

Jesse ended his vigil when Mark left his tent. It had been a long night, made all the harder for the lack of activity. *Back to the fishing hut and get some hot chow...and definitely coffee. Catch a few winks...a cold bath in the stream.*

The short hike seemed longer after sitting on the ground overnight. He had only stood occasionally to stretch to loosen aching joints and muscles. Jesse carried the M14 across both shoulders with a hand on the barrel and the other on the buttstock. The sound of a breaking stick caused him to pause and slowly drop to a squatting position while moving the rifle to the ready. *Easy...probably just a critter looking for breakfast.*

Moving behind a boulder with a fallen tree resting on it, he peered at the hut fifty yards below. An adult Filipino and two boys moved about preparing to go fishing. *Good news, bad news...no hot chow this morning. But at least I wasn't shacked up in there when they showed up.*

Watching them brought back a flood of memories. Images of a fishing camp on Devil's River near the Texas and Mexico border flashed by in a montage: *Mark and his older brother Seth splashing in the river as ten and twelve year olds would—dunking one another and throwing water into each other's face with cupped hands skimming over the surface of the crystal clear river. All three of them sitting on rocks with fishing poles in the afternoon sun. Hell of a place for two boys to learn how to camp and fish. No telling how things would have turned out if...There are no what ifs...*

A hour passed before the three were settled in and focused on the task at hand. Jesse left his rifle and gear behind the rock and moved down to the small cave where the bulk of his supplies and gear were hidden. Using natural cover between himself and the river, he worked his way over the top of the hill before dropping it all.

Just have to make do at the observation site. Cut some brush and build a hide. Hunker down for the day and sleep.

JESSE'S HIDE

The heat precluded any real sleep. The constant swarm of no-see-ums caused him to drape a small towel over his face adding to the uncomfortable conditions. Unable to take it any longer, he sat up slowly and looked out through the brush he had cut.

Movement on the trail to the ruins caught his eye immediately and he scoped it to see Mark returning from his rifle orientation session. *Son, you turned out to be a fine looking young man. What the hell you got in the case?*

Jesse followed him all the way back to the house and noted that the case was secured in the van. *What else you got hidden in there?*

Satisfied nothing was amiss, the elder Ingram rummaged through his supplies and pulled out some food and a water jug. *Here I am eating canned shit while son number two is probably chowing down on left overs from yesterday's feast. Oh well...tuna and cheese dip...or cheese dip and tuna...that is the question.*

CEBU, PHILIPPINES

Long Chi Mein—leader of the Triads sent to capture Mark—sat in a battered delivery truck with a faded sign that read *Fernando-Gonzales Plumbing.* Positioned to have a clear view of the entrance to the Barnhardt Orphanage he waited for his target to appear. His cell rang and he saw it was Tong in Pasay.

"Hello."

"Do you have him?"

"No. You are certain this is where I will find him?"

"The newscast identified him as the head of security for the owner of the orphanage. I do not know where else he could be."

"Wu is not a man to be disappointed. Use your resources…Find out."

"My resources?" Tong asked.

"You said you have the Chief of Police in Pasay on your payroll…let him do the inquiry."

"How do you intend to get him back to China?"

"Wu will arrange it. My job is to capture him. Your job is to assist me…Assist!"

"Yes, right away."

Long Chi hung up just as Crank arrived. Using a pair of binoculars Long watched the operative closely as he walked around the SUV. A cargo truck with sign that read *Medical Waste Disposal* pulled up and blocked his view. Four men got out and rolled a large gray cart away from the truck. *Why would a truck for Medical Waste be stopping here?*

Within a matter of minutes the men returned with it filled with black bags and rolled it into the truck. As they departed, the SUV pulled out after them. Both vehicles disappeared from sight and Long returned his vigil to the orphanage.

GOTHONG LINES CONTAINER PORT
Cebu, Philippines

Crank eased the black GMC to a halt a good distance from the row of shipping containers where the medical waste truck had stopped. He, Roger and Mike watched as the men downloaded the truck's cargo into a forty foot rusting container.

"Dog…hand me that case on the floorboard," Crank ordered as he reached back.

Mike handed him a small Haliburton case. Crank opened it to reveal several suppressors—each in a individual slot in the foam interior. He selected one and closed the case before drawing his pistol and attaching it.

"Don't use your weapon unless necessary. I'll take the shot if needed," Crank said as he put the vehicle into gear and rolled forward.

"What do you think is in there?" Roger asked as he checked the chamber on his Beretta pistol.

"We'll find out in a minute. If they scatter…pick one. We want witnesses…Got it?"

"No problem, Crank. I take it we should have suppressors?" Blaster asked.

"Always a good idea. Hit Hal up. He'll charge you an arm and a leg, but they'll be disposable and can't be traced back to you if you have to ditch 'em."

The garbage men were busy with their work and did not realize the threat until Crank slammed on the brakes and leapt from the vehicle. "Hands where I can see them!" he yelled.

Roger and Mike followed a moment later as the others began to run in different directions. Blaster landed on the nearest and immediately pinned him to the ground, face down.

Dog sprinted after another one and slammed him to the concrete with a jolt from his stun gun.

Crank picked the one he considered to be the boss, and face planted him on the deck with a .45 round to his right leg.

Pisst!

"Ahhh…my knee! You blew off my knee!"

"Nearly. Still looks attached, but you struggle and I'll cap it again," Crank said with a wicked smile.

After cuffing the three with flexible ties and placing them face down in the cargo section of the SUV, they inspected the container.

"Damn…this some rank shit," Roger said as he held his arm up to his face—attempting to breath through his sleeve.

"Smells…dead. I know dead when I smell it," Mike added.

Crank pulled a folding knife and sliced open one of the bags. The little hand and arm fell out into view. "Aww, dear God!"

All three men stood in uneasy silence. Crank cut open more bags exposing other tortured and mutilated bodies of children.

"This is sick," Mike said in practically a whisper.

"No…this is fucked up, man," Roger added.

"All right...use your phones. Get photos. We gotta get out of here before anyone comes along," Crank ordered as he stepped out of the container. Walking to the far end, he bent over and threw up. *Act like nothing happened. Easy for you to say, Zorro...*

OROQUIETA VILLAGE

Tola led an old horse around the streets with Rutger on its back. The smile on his face was priceless.

"Look at me! I'm a cowboy," he called out to anyone and no one in particular.

Dalisay walked alongside ready to catch him if he fell. Mito had his head under the hood of his van checking fluids while Mark and Michele sparred with bamboo poles at half speed.

"Like that, Zorro. Slap forward with your left hand...then twist up with your right. See...the lower end catches my stick and flips it up."

"Sweet. I could learn something if I hung around you for a month or two."

"No way. You'd be really good in a few weeks. Bet it's all that other martial arts stuff you know."

Out of the corner of his eye Mark caught a flash of light, a reflection off Jesse's binoculars. *That's odd.* Not wanting to indicate he saw anything, he continued sparring, but kept a close watch on the area he thought the light had originated from. After several minutes he wrote it off. *Only once. Seeing spooks everywhere...all the time it seems.*

Jesse pulled back into the shade when he saw Mark look up. He leaned to his left and used the boulder to brace himself and shield his binoculars from any sun that could cause a flash. *Whew! Thought he nailed me for a minute.*

Mark's cell started ringing. He disengaged from Michele and walked to the front porch and retrieved it from the small round plastic table. He sat down in a position that allowed him to scan the hillside from which the reflection had occurred as he answered.

"Go."

"You sittin' down?" Crank asked.

"Matter of fact I am."

"We grabbed up the garbage men. They were hauling the bodies of dead kids to a shipping container at the Gothong port. Mutilated bodies."

Mark sat starring at the mountainside. Images of little bloody and torn bodies flashed through his mind. A sense of rage began to creep into his heart. *Breathe, damn it. Not going to fix this right now. Breathe.* "How many?"

"I don't know. I cut open a half dozen bags...none over ten years old...boys and girls." Crank's voice cracked.

In as even a voice as he could muster, Mark lined out his plan and instructions. When he finished there was a long pause. "You still there?"

"Yeah, boss, still here...What if I just cut off his dick and stuff it in his mouth?"

"Hold on…tie your emotions up. You have to keep him from knowing we're wise to his activities. When I get back to Bangkok I'll call you and we lower the hammer on this sick sack of shit in both countries."

"You remember the slaughter in the Congo?…The village?"

"Yeah. Never forget it."

"Like that…but only little kids. Dumped like trash…If your plan doesn't work…don't get in my way."

"I won't."

Dalisay walked up with Rutger and Tola. "Time for snacks. Care to join us?"

"No…No thanks. Tola…a word," Mark said stoically as he left the porch and walked into the street.

Tola joined him. "What's wrong?"

"Crank just found evidence…Joris *is* a snuff pedophile."

"Oh…that sorry bastard…no wonder Dalisay not want him alone with Rutger."

"Assuming she knows something. Dig around. See what she tells you."

"Done," Tola said as she turned to go. She paused and looked back. "We still going to stay tomorrow?"

"Yup. Crank's going to put Joris on his plane today. Rhino is going to pick him up in Bangkok. We got no air transport 'til he's down at home," Mark replied as he mulled over the turn of events. "I need to call Rhino…right now."

Tola continued on into the house, stopping only at the door to look back for a moment. *Karma is coming.*

Mark dialed as he walked down the street, forgetting about the incident on the hillside altogether.

"What's the latest?" Rhino asked.

"Fill you in later. Need you to get a turn around on the jet as soon as you can. Have it pick us up here in Dipolog as planned only sooner...day after tomorrow."

"Can do. Hans and Francisca left today. He said to keep the fokin' check. Wants nothing to do with Barnhardt. Especially his money. I have a couple of USB sixty-four gig flash drives and the covert main frame."

"Hide the flash drives somewhere in his office. Put the mainframe with the other equipment Hans replaced. Clean 'em. In fact, clean everything you touched that's computer related."

The day passed slowly in a haze of cooking fires and sweltering heat. Mark stood in the shower stall for a overly long period of time letting the cold water wash over him. *How? How did I miss this? There were clues...Dalisay not wanting Rutger...*

BOOM!...BOOM!

The sound of two large explosions yanked his consciousness back to the present.

BOOM! BOOM!...BOOM!

Three additional smaller explosions occurred quickly after the initial two. Mark stepped out of the stall wrapping a towel around his waist and looked to the northwest. Large clouds of black smoke began to rise above the mountains. A series of other explosions kept rolling in.

DIPITAN PORT, PHILIPPINES

Jaco's men executed their roles with precision. The two-man teams assigned the lighthouses destroyed the huge light globes with single rounds from their RPGs. The three men detailed to hit the fuel storage tanks set off their explosives, triggering all the others to attack.

Jaco and two men sprayed the entry guard shack and the main barracks with their rifles. Jaco fired his M203 grenade launcher, and then reloaded and placed another round into the upper room of the harbor port authority building. The explosion detonated the propane tanks in the small kitchen adding to the devastation.

Men and women not killed outright by the initial explosion ran to the shattered glass windows and leapt out—their bodies in flames—and dropped to the ground three stories below.

The men attacking the northern lighthouse encountered a group of soldiers and were immediately engaged in a firefight. Those assaulting the southern lighthouse made their way towards the rally point only to encounter several policeman. They cut the surprised and dazed law enforcement officers—armed only with 9mm handguns and .38 special revolvers—down quickly.

The two men stopped only long enough to strip the dead of their weapons and ammunition before fleeing into the jungle. Once in the cover of the forest, they looked down on the main complex of the port. Massive flames rose where the fuel dump had been. Thick black smoke towered several hundred feet above the carnage.

Jaco and his two men covered the three who had blown the fuel depot as they stole a delivery truck and raced for the gates. A soldier staggered to his feet in the parking area and strafed the vehicle as it passed. His fire killed one and critically wounded another before Jaco ended his life in a hail of lead.

"Let's go!" he screamed at the two men beside him. They ran to the shattered guard shack. "Get their weapons!" He yelled pointing at the dead soldiers.

The truck screeched to a halt only long enough for them to jump on board. To the north they could hear the firefight going on between their brothers and the Philippine Army soldiers.

The driver asked, "What about our men to the sou…"

"No time to divert. They are on their own," Jaco replied. "Go! Go!"

The truck drove off, the engine straining to pick up speed as the driver pressed the pedal to the floor.

"How bad is he?" Jaco asked looking at the wounded man.

"He needs medical attention," he replied.

The truck slid to a stop as the two insurgents from the south lighthouse stepped onto the roadway waving their arms. In a blur of movement they were on board and the vehicle raced on.

"Allah Akbar!" Jaco screamed, raising his rifle over his head and slamming it into the roof of the cargo truck.

The others followed his lead and chanted as the truck raced along the winding road.

DIPOLOG AIRPORT

Isagani fired the first shot—a RPG round into the control tower—to initiate the precision assault. The tower exploded in a ball of fire and smoke. He could hear the blasts at the port and reveled in the beauty of his plan and it's execution. Having expended his last grenade, he tossed the launcher to the ground and brought his M16 up to his shoulder, firing short bursts into the backs of three soldiers standing thirty yards away transfixed on the control tower's destruction. They fell like sacks of rocks without knowing what hit them.

A half dozen men raced into the terminal building yelling praise to their god as they swept the crowd with automatic fire. Men, women and children fell in the deadly barrage of hot lead. The screams of the dying and those attempting to escape were barely heard over the noise of the weapons.

A security guard fired his aged revolver and killed one assailant before going down himself. Another guard threw down his pistol and raised his hands only to be cut in two by AK fire. A mother huddled over her two children and a baby. One of the terrorists emptied a magazine into them all.

The explosion from the fuel dump shattered every window within a hundred yards. The burning jet fuel melted vehicles nearby. A breeze from the ocean blew the choking black smoke across the site, blinding the killers and their prey equally.

Isagani ran to the downed soldiers he had just killed and ripped a pair of goggles off one's head. He put them on—his eyes already tearing from the acrid smoke. A siren wailed in the distance. He turned to see a fire truck racing in his direction.

Firing three quick, but well aimed shots, he killed the driver. The truck swerved hard and plowed into the terminal building adding to the death toll inside.

BOOM!

A smile crossed his lips as he heard the bomb explode at the police station in Dipolog. *Havoc and mayhem runs loose on the infidels.*

The surviving rebels gathered in the parking lot, spraying any moving target. Again, men, women and children were slaughtered indiscriminately. A Dodge passenger bus with *Santa Maria Louisa Hotel* printed on the sides attempted to flee. It was stopped when the driver slumped from his seat with a gapping bullet wound to his head.

"Pick up weapons and ammunition. Behead the wounded. Quickly!" Isagani ordered.

Five men jumped on motor bikes and raced around the lot firing as they went—stopping only to gather weapons. The majority of the radical Islamists climbed into the passenger van. They knocked out the side and back windows to clear firing ports. Isagani climbed aboard last chanting, "Allah Akbar."

OROQUIETA VILLAGE

Mark stood watching the dark clouds of smoke rise higher in the sky. Mito and Michele joined him.

"What do you think it is?" Michele asked.

"No idea...but it ain't good."

"Industrial accidents maybe?" Mito suggested.

"In a rats ass. One maybe…two…no way. Looks like Dipitan and Dipolog. What do you think, Mito?"

"Yes it does. We should be far enough away…"

"Don't think so. Even if we are…we need to prepare for the worse…make sure everything is…"

"What is it? What happened?" Dalisay called from the front porch.

Mark turned to see her, Tola and the entire family looking at the smoke. Dalisay instinctively reached for Rutger and pulled him to her. Tola broke her gaze on the black cloud and looked to Zorro.

"Get everything you need for a overnight camp out. Necessities only…One bag," Mark ordered.

The family seemed mesmerized and did not respond.

"*Dalisay*! Did you hear me?"

"Yes…yes I did. What do you mean by necessities?" she replied without looking away from the ominous cloud.

"Tola, take over. Do it now. You, Rutger and your parents. Chop chop! When you're ready, put the bags next to the front door."

Villagers stood outside starring as well. Some walked into the street and talked excitedly with one another.

"Camp out where?" Mito asked. "This road leads right back to Dipolog."

Mark turned and pointed. "Up there. The old mission."

Jesse could not see the thick smoke on the opposite side of the mountain, but the explosions and the movements below told him something was wrong. *This ain't good. Ain't good at all. Have to chance it and do a look see.*

Mito, Michele and Tola loaded the bags into the van. Dalisay and her family stood on the front porch huddled together in a state of shock.

"Mito...you and Michele get this gear up to the old mission. Then get back here."

"Let's roll, Michele," Mito ordered.

Fifteen minutes later the van reached the last bit of the old road that was passable and halted. The two got out and started hauling as many bags as they could carry up the trail and into the ruins. The men made two trips, and then Mito drove back down to the home.

"Mito, go over to the community center. Gather up all the propane tanks. Michele...scrounge around...find us some water containers...at least twenty gallons worth. Rinse 'em out...then fill 'em up. Add ten drops of this for every gallon. Let's go boys...move it."

Michele studied the two ounce bottle of Ster Bac 07 for a moment before asking, "What is this?"

"Water purifier."

Dalisay approached Mark. "What is going on, Steve? Why all this?"

"Every now and then you get a gut feelin'...I got one. May turn out to be nothing...may not."

SECURITY HOUSE

Rhino entered the living area to find Roger, Mike and Keit discussing the turn of events.

"One screwed up first contract is all I have to say," Roger barked.

"Agreed. This is one nasty mutha," Mike added.

Keit sat quietly listening to the other two men

"Suck it up, moffie pies," Rhino ordered. "When Zorro gets back, the screw will turn and shithead will be sorry he was ever born."

"And just how will that be?" Blaster asked.

"No fokin' idea, but I know Zorro…Dutchie is going down hard…Dante's Inferno will seem like a paradise compared to what is about to happen."

***

CHAPTER TWENTY-THREE

MALINDANES MOUNTAINS
Zamboanga del Norte, Philippines

The insurgents left a cave that had provided shelter from a pre-dawn thunderstorm. The long night following their successful attacks was marred by the suffering of the wounded and dying.

"Move in threes. Keep a good fifty meters between the cells. If the military sees a large group, it will be bad for us," Isagani ordered the group as they stood in the light drizzle.

"I will take point," Jaco said.

"Good. There is a small village one day's march. We will use it for our supplies and celebration of our great victory," Isagani answered. "Move out."

The men divided up as their leader instructed and began the rugged march across unknown territory. Several men slipped and fell on the rain-soaked earth.

Only two hours passed before one of the men misjudged his footing and tumbled down the mountainside clawing, at the brush and rocks to catch himself. It was to no avail and he disappeared over the edge of a hundred foot fall. "Aiiiee!" was the last sound he made. The jungle claimed his body at the base of the cliff with a bone crunching greeting.

Isagani moved back to the site of the accident. *Careful. Don't want to die now.* "The two of you wait for the next three and join them. Watch where you walk. There are no virgins waiting for a fool."

Seven hours later, the rebels sat on a hill overlooking Oroquieta. No one else had suffered a mishap, but all were exhausted from the journey.

"Jaco, take five men and move down to that hilltop, the one above the Nipa fishing hut. Wait for my signal then move in. I will take the others and cut off any escape on the road."

Jaco pointed to those he wanted and stepped off without reply. The thought of sleeping on a pad in a hut was enticing after the cold rock floor of the cave.

"The rest of you...come with me. Once we secure the road we will move in and take Allah's blessings."

The others followed him without hesitation. They too had visions of comfort and pleasure running through their heads.

OROQUIETA VILLAGE

The day had been a joyous one for Dalisay and her loved ones. The extended family had arrived at noon and a second celebration ensued. As always the residents of the village joined in—any celebration in the Philippines is a much appreciated break from the monotony of daily life.

"Michele, go relieve Mito. Keep a sharp eye," Mark said.

"Yes, sir."

Dalisay visited with relatives she had not seen in years but noticed Mark's changing of the guard. She excused herself and left the crowded community building to join him. "Still have that feeling?"

"Yeah, I do."

"Why don't you come join us for a while? Some of my uncles served in military and want to meet you."

"Maybe later. The news said the explosions yesterday were terrorist attacks…"

"Very sad for the families there, but who would care to harm us here? This is just a simple village. They have nothing to gain by attacking us."

Mark's satellite cell rang. "It's Rhino. I need to take this one," he said as he walked away.

Dalisay stood watching him for a moment before turning and rejoining the festivities.

"Go."

"Barnhardt just got up and saw the news. He's going bonkers to find out how you all are."

"Put him on the phone."

"I'm on the roof. Thought I should talk to you first. Joris said he tried his wife's cell with no success."

"All the normal lines of communications are down over here. Call me back when you have the sack of shit standing by and I'll get her on for them to chitchat...How are the boys holding up?"

"Good as could be expected. We're all keeping as far away from him as possible."

"Find out the status on the Dipolog airport. If it's closed, we'll need a fast boat out of here. If the port is shut down you'll just have to beam us up, Scotty."

"Get back to you on that. Did you tell Missus Barn..."

"Hell no. Not going to until..." his cell beeped informing him another call was in coming. Checking the number ID he saw it was Hal. "Gotta go. The crazy Scotsman is calling."

He switched over to the other call. "Hey, big dog."

"See you started another war."

"Bite me. What's up?"

"Just calling to see if you were still able to answer. The main stream media claims the attacks in your neck of the jungle were mussie terrorists. Are you up to your A-hole in ragheads yet?"

"Nope...While I have you on the line...what financial advisors do you have in your pocket in Bangkok?"

"Why? You have a hot investment lead? You wouldn't cut your ol' buddy out would you?"

"Not for me. Hell, I don't know any PC way to say it... so gonna just throw it...the Dutch client is a serial pedophile..."

"What? You pissing down my back now?"

"Wish I was. Rhino and Hans found rock solid evidence in Bangkok and Crank confirmed it in Cebu."

"Have to admit you lost me. Why the need for financial advice?"

"I'm taking him down soon as I get back to the big mango. His wife doesn't know…"

"You sure about that? Hard to get anything past a woman. I know…I've tried."

"I'm pretty sure she's an innocent victim in all this. When I take him down, I want to make sure she has the keys to his empire."

"I have a guy in Singapore. I'll text his number to you."

"Thanks. Any word on the Chinie men?"

"That reminds me…your little Yakuza called from Panama. Says they tracked her down…"

"Is she all right?"

"Do I detect a bit of interest? Is there more to the *help a maiden in distress* than you told me?"

"Cut the crap. Is she safe?"

"I had a pair of ops in Panama City. They picked her up in David last night."

"Give her my number…"

"You sly dog you. Hard to keep secrets from an old wolf you know. She asked for your number. Told her I'd have to ask."

"Yeah…yeah…give it to her. Put it on…"

"Your tab? Consider it done. This must be some kinda woman. You haven't shown this much interest in a split-tail since Lydia…"

"Gotta go." Mark hung up. *Running solo is hard enough without the Triad on your ass.*

The sound of Michele's shotgun firing one round echoed back to the village followed by half a dozen AKs firing on full auto. *Gut feelin' never lets me down.*

Mark ran to the community building and without expounding on his actions grabbed Rutger. He ran toward the van yelling, "Get out! Everyone run for the trees!"

Panic gripped the crowd and froze them in place. Tola took Dalisay by the arm and started after Mark. "We go."

Mito had the doors open by the time Mark arrived and he set the boy inside. "You stay right here. Understand?"

"Yes, Tio."

"Tola, get her in the van. Mito fire it up. Pull over and load up Momma and Pappa."

"On it."

"What about the rest of my family?" Dalisay asked.

"We'll come back for them if we can. Go Mito!" Mark pulled the case for his S&W 9mm and a canvas ammo bag from the van and slammed the door. After it drove off, he laid them on a rock in front of the house and put on the Bianchi shoulder rig, checked the pistol magazine and slid it into the well-worn leather holster. Next he pulled a magazine carrier from the bag that held five extended twenty-five round magazines and slung it over his shoulder.

He checked the chamber on his Colt as he started down the road toward the gunfire—keeping to the side of the road and moving from cover to cover—weapon at the ready. *Always pick out your next cover before moving.* The words of a grizzled Marine sergeant played through his mind as he moved.

Another pair of shotgun blasts indicated Michele was closer and the ensuing AK rounds that followed told him there were at least a dozen gunmen on the young operative's ass.

Coming to a curve in the road Mark knelt and peered around a stone cistern. A tango ran across the open roadway fifty yards away.

Bamm!

A single well-aimed shot sent him tumbling face forward onto the hard-packed earth where he skidded to a stop in a kneeling position. *Should have used your friggin' prayer rug, raghead.*

"Fall back, Michele. I'll cover you," he called seeing the young man would be overrun in short order if he did not move.

Michele fired two shots before turning and running in a crouch toward him.

"Zig zag, kid. Zig…zag!"

The insurgents leapt into the open and followed, firing wildly as they ran. Mark pulled his 9mm and using both handguns fired at the charging men. *When laying down cover fire it's not so much about hitting a target as throwing enough lead downrange to cause the enemy to duck.*

In the brief moments of Michele's retreat, three rebels went down to Mark's fire. The others dove behind a rock wall allowing the young man to run and fall panting on the ground beside him.

"Well done. Reload," he said as he continued to fire with the Smith and Wesson. Half a dozen bullets cracked by or impacted the cistern, causing him to duck behind it.

"I hit two…I hit two!" Michele said excitedly as he fumbled to load the 870 pump.

"Breathe kid. You have to breathe. When you're loaded…move back to…" Mark quickly glanced behind. "Move to that pickup truck. Get behind a tire. I'll move when you're set."

Michele jumped up and sprinted as he thumbed another round into the magazine.

Mark laid down controlled fire until he heard his call.

"Ready."

Before moving, Zorro dropped a magazine from each pistol and slammed a new one home. He fired three rounds from each and ran evasively to the truck. Rifle fire kicked up dirt around him, impacting the truck as he slid behind the front tire.

Michele returned fire and dispatched the rifleman with a load of 000 buck to his left arm—shredding the flesh and shattering the bone just above his elbow.

Mark took a quick look into the cab and saw the keys in the ignition. "Gonna to fire this bitch up. When I start rolling, jump in the back. Stay low. Lay down as much fire as you can."

"I got it…loading."

A lull in the gunfire was all he needed. He yanked open the passenger door and had the engine running in a heartbeat.

Throwing the vehicle in gear, he popped the clutch and laid the gas pedal to the floor. Michele rolled inside truck bed, and then rose to a kneeling position—firing as fast as he could.

Mark twisted the wheel to the left and began an evasive driving maneuver. The swerving of the truck threw the operative onto his side saving his life as a volley of shots flew by his last position. A couple of rounds clipped the top two inches of the tailgate punching nice .30 caliber holes through both sides. Another one shattered the rear window—throwing a blizzard of safety glass cubes all over the interior. Mark reacted with a swift reversal to the right.

Jesse had been sleeping when the first round was fired. He woke up and rubbed the sleep from his eyes as he heard the 7.62 rounds in response. *Oh, shit!*

He grabbed his rifle and moved some of the brush aside in front of his hide. Looking down he could see the Muslims advancing on the lone shooter. He fired twice—hitting both targets with the suppressed M14—before he heard the sounds of boots on both sides of his position. Carefully he pulled his rifle back into cover and unholstered his 1911 and thumbed the safety off. *How many mutha fuckers are out there?*

Two men passed his hide not more than fifteen feet on either side. Both were intent on covering ground to join the fight and missed him in their haste. *Damn...that was close. Let these jack wagons get on down the hill. See how many more there are.*

In less than a minute, five of the advancing men were in plain view below his position. *Keep moving. Just a little further. Pick your scrawny asses off, one, two, three.*

Isagani blew his whistle in three short bursts—signalling his men to cease fire. In rapid succession the remaining combatants blew one blast to let their leader know how many were still in the fight.

Seething rage washed over the young leader's face when he discovered eight or nine of his force were down. From his position he could see the rusted red Isuzu pickup racing up the roadway and the inhabitants of the village running wildly out of the village into the forest. Looking along the path the pickup was driving, he spotted the white van parked on the hillside below the stone ruins. "Regroup! Rally on me!"

The battle-hardened rebels fell into formation for a final assault on the little hamlet. Two men moved among the dead or dying and collected their ammunition before passing it out to the living.

Jesse picked the farthest target—who was lagging well behind the others—and placed a 7.62x51 Winchester National Match round squarely between his shoulder blades. The man crumpled silently to the ground like a rag doll. His companions continued to advance without realizing he was no longer with them.

Turning to the other end of the advancing line he dropped another without any recognition by the group. As he selected his next target, movement caught his attention. Off to his right, well in advance of the others, another man moved effortlessly toward the village below.

Jaco had taken the southernmost position in the advance. He had not seen his men fall.

His unexpected appearance caused Jesse to hold his fire. *Easy now, or I'll be up to my happy ass.*

CHAPEL RUINS

Mark parked the pickup behind the van and jumped out. The side door to the van was open and inside he saw the G3 rifle and several bags of 9mm, .45 ACP and 12 gauge ammo.

"Get your scattergun ammo. Some of the 9 mil as well if you can carry it," he said in a calm, even tone. The initial rush of adrenaline had passed and his Zen meditation allowed him to focus.

"I got it…we sure kicked their asses, didn't we, Zorro?"

"The fat lady ain't sung yet…'Til she does, we are in a world of hurt."

"But I did good? Right?"

Mark paused and looked at him directly. He had seen the same thing in the eyes of young Marines in Afghanistan and knew they were looking for reassurance. "Yeah, you did great. Hell of a fine show, Michele. Now get moving."

"Yes, sir." He straightened his shoulders and swaggered away.

Entering the ruins, Mark found Tola and Mito positioned to cover them. Both were focused on the village below and the advancing enemy.

"I count…maybe thirty," the retired Filipino Marine said.

"Mito, you have the only rifle…I want you up in the tower. Tola, hold your fire unless they shoot at us. Michele and I are going back to the van and get the rest of the ammo."

"We only brought five of the propane tanks up here."

"I saw the others. Good a place as any for 'em. Go, we're waiting on you."

Mito took off immediately and once he was in position Mark made his move with Michele close behind.

"Take one of these tanks…" Mark said as he handed a half-full cylinder of propane to the younger man. "Put it in the cab of the pickup. Make sure Mito can see it from the tower."

Michele nodded. Mark moved the other bottles into the front seat of the van before dragging the remaining supplies out.

Their climb back up to the ruins did not draw any fire. The Muslims were far too busy looting the homes and sari sari store to notice them. Not so for Isagani and Jaco. They stood studying the old mission. Jaco handed the worn Chinese pocket binoculars back to his leader.

"I see four with weapons."

"As did I. It will be dark soon. We rest tonight. Tomorrow we take them."

"Why not just leave them, Isagani? Assaulting them will…"

"You question my leadership?"

"No, of course not…I only offer a suggestion."

"Good. They killed our brothers. They are infidels. We shall take retribution on them before we continue our journey."

Jaco knew it was unwise to argue. He turned to join the men at the store as his head exploded, throwing bits of brain and blood on Isagani. He fell to the ground and crawled behind a fence. *Where did that shot come from? Someone killed my most trusted follower…and made no sound.*

Jesse turned his rifle on a man exiting Dalisay's home. The man stood on the steps drinking a cold bottle of Coke when the round cut through his throat—severing the esophagus and his spine just below the skull. He fell backward into the open doorway—his body involuntarily twitched as life drained onto the concrete slab.

Mark and Michele staggered into the ruins under the strain of the loads. Both men dropped the bags once inside and sat down, breathing heavily.

"You should see this," Tola called out. She handed him a pair of field glasses.

"What's goin' on?"

"See the man down in the doorway of Dalisay's home?"

"Yup."

"And there's another one down in the street. Thirty meters to the west."

"Got him."

"They both dropped a few seconds apart. Not a sound…just dropped like a sack of wet rice."

Jesse lay scoping the Muslims. *That's enough for now. Take too many down and they'll figure out where I am. No way to evade 'em on this muddy ground.* He wiped his forehead with his dark green bandana. The heat and the recent rains made the landscape as humid as a sauna. *Ha...like my old ass is going to evade anyone.* He lay laughing softly to himself as darkness began to fall on the village below.

BARNHARDT'S RESIDENCE
Bangkok, Thailand

Joris stormed into the security house like a bull on a mission. "Where are my old computers?"

"We put them in the storage room in the parking garage," Rhino replied.

"I need one of them tonight. It has sensitive business data on it."

Yes it does you sick fok. Rhino thought before replying, "They are all there. Hans had the units labeled just in case you needed any one in particular."

"Is the security system functional. I thought that man Hans was going to be here to demonstrate where my money went," Joris said in a perplexed and angry tone.

"He showed me. I can show you when you're ready. What's Val cooking up for dinner?" Rhino countered.

"I gave him the night off. You'll have to fend for yourselves...and the kitchen in my home is closed for tonight. I don't want to be disturbed."

"No problem Mister Barnhardt. We're big boys. Anything else?"

Joris stood clenching his jaw for a moment shifting his weight from one foot to the other. "No. Nothing."

After he left Roger was the first to speak. "I'd like to knee cap that bastard right now."

"Doubles on that," Mike added.

"Hold it. Zorro's about to give a lesson to that sick fok…and you don't want to be in his way when he does," Rhino said flatly. "Keit, make a run for some take out? What do you girls want?"

OROQUIETA VILLAGE

The valley below and the hillside where the chapel ruins stood were dark. Only the hillside on the far side still showed any signs of light as the sun set. In the village below the terrorists continued to ransack the deserted homes.

"Call me if anything changes. I'm going to check on the family," Mark said as he got up from his watch position.

"Yeah, boss," Tola and Michele said in unison.

He patted Michele on the shoulder as he passed. "Well done young man. Well done."

After he left Michele turned to Tola. "Does that mean he thinks I'm a good operative?"

"Must. Never heard him tell anyone else that"

In the base of the old bell tower, Mark found the family huddled together in one corner. Rutger was sound asleep in a sleeping bag with his grandmother.

"What's happening down there?" Dalisay asked.

"Looting. Everyone okay in here?"

"We will need more water soon."

"There's a well in another room. I'll put Michele on it…"

Four teenage Filipino children entered the room through a side window. Mark wheeled, pulling both handguns from their shoulder holsters in blinding speed. Seeing they were unarmed children he lowered the weapons.

"Any more out there?" he asked.

"Just us. I don't know where anyone else is…everyone ran out of the village and we came here because it's our hideout," the oldest boy said.

"Your hideout?"

"Yeah, you know…our fort."

"What's your name?" Mark asked as he holstered his pistols.

"Francis."

"Can we stay? Please?" the youngest girl asked, nearly in tears.

"Of course you can," Dalisay said taking her in her arms. "Are you hungry?"

"Yes, and I'm thirsty too," one of the boys answered.

"You know any secrets about this place?" Mark asked.

"Well…we keep our stuff in that room down there," Francis said pointing at the collapsed doorway leading to the items Michele had discovered earlier.

"What kinda stuff?" Mark asked as he moved to the opening.

"Our slingshots, catapults, shields, swords…stuff like that."

"Show me." Mark handed the boy his flashlight.

Once inside the chamber, he illuminated it in a sweeping motion and came to rest on the catapults.

"Are they still good?" Mark asked with a bit of anticipation.

"Sure…We shoot rocks all the way down to the village. Scares people when they land on their roofs."

"Bring one up here."

Once out of the semi-hidden room the teenager demonstrated how they set them up.

"What's the biggest rock you ever shot with this?"

"Oh…maybe the size of a basketball."

"How far did it go?"

"In the air?"

"Yeah."

"Half-way back to our village."

"Follow me and bring that with you," Mark directed as he turned and headed back to Tola and Michele.

Isagani blew his whistle three times, again calling his men. It was just after midnight and he wanted to set perimeter guards.

In five minutes the remaining men stood with him inside the

store. Finishing a head count, he realized another three men were no longer with him.

"You and you…down the road eight hundred meters. You take up guard on that stone ruin. Kill anyone who tries to leave it. The rest of you…sleep," Isagani ordered.

"Wait…I want three men to go up that mountain and find the shooter. He killed Jaco. I want his head on a stick by dawn!" Isagani said through clenched teeth.

Jesse watched as three of the Muslims started toward him. *Guess I wore out my welcome. Time to go.*

Francis and Michele had the catapult standing and pulled the motorcycle inner tubes back as far as they could before releasing the basket ball sized rock. The bands snapped forward propelling the orb into the night sky. The full moon offered just enough light to follow its progress. It impacted on a large boulder a little more than half way to the closest house.

"See. I told you," Francis said with a big smile.

"Let's try one more about like a baseball. I bet I could hit Dalisay's home from here," Michele chimed in.

"Find me a rock that weighs about the same as one of those half-empty propane tanks," Mark said.

Both young men hefted a tank.

"These are lighter than the rock we just fired," Francis said.

"You two are my mortar team. Get some stones and practice on different ranges. Be quick…Only a few hours 'til dawn," Mark ordered as he started the climb to Mito's position.

His satellite phone rang as he reached the upper level of debris. He held up one finger to Mito.

"Go."

"Zorro…it's…Chikako."

A rush of emotions flooded over him as he stood in the moonlight. Time slowed down and the sounds of night in the Malidang mountains faded.

"You okay?"

"Yes. I hurt my knee several days ago, but other than that…I'm okay. Where are you?"

"Philippines."

"On a sail boat?"

"I wish…I'm on Mindanao…Zamboanga del Norte."

A long pause ensued before she spoke again. "Hiring any help?"

"I'd give my left nut if you were here right now…"

"Easy bad boy…You may need both some day."

Mark could not help but laugh. The absurdity of his present situation and the unexpected call caught him off-guard.

"I meant I could use your skill sets right now."

Her words came out in a rush. "You're in trouble? What's happening? I'm sorry to call you if…"

"Slow down. Just a bit of unexpected difficulty."

"Tell me where…I'll be there."

"This will be over before you can get here. Hal told me you're in Panama."

"Yeah. Panama City."

"I'll have to call Rhino. He'll make the ticket happen for you. I keep a place in Brazil. Ain't much, but it's a safe haven. When you get there you'll need to contact a woman named Marta Maria."

Again, a long moment passed before Chikako spoke. "Someone special? I'm sorry I shouldn't have asked that."

"Just a long time friend. Marta will make sure you're settled in 'til I can get there. Can Rhino reach you at this number?"

"Yes, but I can get my own ticket. Have your friend send me an address…Thanks."

"Be there when I tie up loose ends…call you when I'm headed your way."

After saying good-bye he hung up and stared at the night sky for a moment—Mito waited patiently.

 Mark turned to him. "Get something to eat. I'll stand watch for a couple of hours."

"I'm good. You should…"

"I could use the solitude. Call you in three to four."

"You're the boss. Hey…what's up with the propane tanks?"

"Hot 5.56 makes propane go boom…From up here you got a line of sight on 'em."

Two hours passed and from his position Mark had seen the tangos enter several of the houses and the lights go out. *Everybody has to sleep sometime. Give 'em another hour…I'll go down and visit.*

BOOM!

Mark looked to the hillside across the valley and saw a huge ball of fire below the ridge line. *What the hell?*

Jesse stopped dead in his tracks and looked back. *Found my little surprise did you? Teach you to go messin' with a man's possessions. One claymore plus one phosphorus grenade makes a hell of a wake-up call.*

Isagani peered out the window of a home he had chosen for his rest and watched as three human forms in flames ran down the mountainside. *When I am finished with the infidels in the ruins, I will find you. Then, I kill you very slowly.*

Mark watched the burning men as well. Their screams were distant, but definitely blood curdling. *First the flash of light. Now this? Don't believe in angels but whoever is up there…you're a friend of mine.*

He climbed down the rubble inside the tower and entered the room where Tola, Michele and Mito sat watching the event. "Mito, take the tower. Tola, go comfort the civilians. Michele, draw water…add the 07 purifier. May not have another chance come dawn."

"What do you think happened?" Michele asked.

"Not sure, but it thinned the odds."

"Who's out there?" Tola asked.

"No idea. I saw a flash of light earlier about that same location. Then there's the dead mussies you pointed out."

Ingrham

"Whoever it is better identify themselves if they come in here. I'm shooting anyone I don't know," Mito added.

"Keep your eyes on me, then. I'm going out...Planned on going into the village, but that little show over there will have the goat fuckers on alert," Mark said as he readied himself.

"What you going to do?" Michele asked.

"Set a couple of surprises. Find me some paracord. I'll signal with my flashlight before I start back. Mito...like this," Mark said as he flashed his illuminator with a red lens cover. "I'll hit you a couple of times with two flashes as I move around. When you see three...I'm coming in."

"Got it."

"That'll have to do," Mark said softly to himself as he placed the last bit of grass on the paracord trip wire. Observation from the old mission reveled two foot paths or animal tracks leading from the village up the hill. He turned toward the bell tower and shielding the flashlight from the village below, signaled he was coming in. *Both trails trapped. If the skanks come up using the trucks for cover...Mito will light 'em up with propane. Then there's the catapults.*

Dawn broke like every other day only it seemed more precious to Michele. He had trained with his father and brother just for such a situation. The reality of death lurking so close made this morning seem different. He checked his 870 one more time—easily the twentieth time since he ran to the ruins with

Mark. He wore Zorro's shotgun rig and had fifty 12 gauge rounds at hand. "What are the green one's again?"

"Flechettes. Save 'em for close in."

"Yeah…right."

"You focus on the old roadway, Michele. Tola and I will cover the approach up the hill," Mark ordered as he laid his spare magazines out within easy reach. *Never enough ammo. Down to three grenades now. Someone needs to invent lighter grenades.*

They all could hear Isagani's whistle from below. Three sharp tweets.

"Won't be long now. Pee if you need to," he said.

Jesse paused upon hearing the whistle as well. Unsure how many men might have come up the mountain after the first three caught on fire, he had kept on the move. He looked up and saw a stand of trees amongst a jumble of boulders. *Good a place as any.* Turning to his right, he began to climb.

Once in the trees he found a spot that gave him good visibility of the south end of the village and the hillside below the mission. *Damn I could use a cup of hot Joe right about now.* He laid out his poncho and placed his day pack on a rock ledge then set his rifle down on it.

Mark counted twenty-plus men working their way toward their position. "Mito…Tola hold fire 'til my signal. Michele, you and Francis get that first propane tank ready."

Ingrham

He pulled the G3 rifle from its case and loaded it. *This will give 'em an oh, shit moment…*

***

CHAPTER TWENTY-FOUR

MISSION RUINS

"Launch a tank boys," Mark said quietly to Michele and Francis.

They pulled the catapult bands back as far as possible and released. The steel canister flew forward and clipped the top of the stone wall—tumbling end-over-end before it hit the ground only forty feet outside the ruins. It bounced erratically down the hill coming to rest near a pair of rebels.

"Elevation damn it! Elevation!" Mark yelled as he sighted the G3 rifle on the stationary target.

Ponk. A faint streak of blue light briefly appeared in a line directly to the propane tank.

BOOM!

The cylinder exploded instantly, throwing a ball of fire and hundreds of jagged steel projectiles in all directions. The closest two rebels turned to run and were engulfed in the flames as well as impaled by the searing metal projectiles. One fell and lay burning—a piece of shrapnel slicing through his chest. The other stumbled down the hill, screaming in agony.

"All right boys...adjust...don't want the damn tanks in here...downrange...downrange."

"We got it," Michele called back.

The insurgents opened fire. Most of the rounds impacted the stone walls and bounced off harmlessly. Some came through the windows and ricocheted around the rooms where the defenders waited for Zorro's orders to open fire.

"Send it."

The second tank flew clear of the wall and sailed far down the hill—floating slowly like a ruptured duck. Mark tracked it with the G3 and just before it hit the ground—he fired.

Ponk!

BOOM!

The hypersonic steel projectile found its target ten feet above the ground and sent the fireball and ragged steel shards flying over a fifty foot radius. None of the insurgents were hit but the realization that they could have been slowed their progress.

"Twenty degrees to your right. Shorten the throw. On my command..."

The two adjusted as best they could to his orders for a change in direction and distance.

"Only three more tanks," Michele called out.

An AK 47 round deflected off a window sill and tumbled erratically as it sliced into Michele just above his waist. He fell to one knee before rolling onto his side, holding both hands on the wound.

"I'm...I'm hit," he called weakly.

Mark looked back to see the young Filipino down. His shirt was already soaked in blood. *Oh shit!* "Francis, get pressure on the wound."

The teenager stood frozen in fear. Playing war was far different than what he was caught up in.

"Francis! Pressure now!" Mark yelled.

The boy looked at Michele, and then knelt and pressed on his hands. "He's...bleeding too much."

"Tola...Mito...open fire," Mark ordered as he moved to the fallen man. He tore his own shirt off, pulled Michele's hands away from the wound and packed the wadded makeshift bandage against it. The dark color of the blood told him either a kidney or his liver had been hit. He knew the boy was dying and there was absolutely nothing he could do about it.

"Hang in there kid."

"I did good...didn't I?"

"You did great...A real number one operative."

"Tell Papa...I did...Momma?...Mommaaa..."

He breathed a final sigh. Mark looked down at his face and closed the dead boy's eyes. A hard lump grew in his throat and tears rolled down his cheeks.

Tola and Mito rained fire down on the advancing force.

The cacophony of the sounds of combat was distant for Mark. *Son-of-a-bitch...he was just a kid.*

"Zorro...they are closing," Tola called out.

Wiping the back of his hand over his eyes, Mark moved back to the G3 and looked for a target. A Muslim attacker dropped behind a boulder and fired a long burst.

Mark returned fire at the base of the rock.

Ponk.

The hardened steel projectile punched though as if the stone was so much Styrofoam—burning a smooth inch-wide hole all the way through the six ton boulder. It impacted the attacker's body and vaporized it into a pink cloud.

Blap.

His head flipped some fifteen feet into the air before it dropped back down, bounced twice and rolled downhill.

To Mark's left he saw a attacker blown upward and backwards by one of his grenade traps. The man's body tumbled down the hill—one leg hanging by a just a tendon below the knee the other gone altogether.

Jesse had a ringside seat to the battle below. He loaded the M79 grenade launcher—lovingly known as the Blooper by men who served in Vietnam—with a fragmentation round. *Wish I had a range finder...just have to lob and pray.*

Bloop.

The recoil of the single-barreled weapon was light—about that of a 20 gauge shotgun. Jesse watched the deadly projectile arcing in the morning light as it traveled toward the rebels.

It fell short, and exploded harmlessly, but the attackers knew when it landed on their flank. Two men turned and sprayed the jungle—a worthless waste of ammo. *Okay...Let's try this* he thought as he loaded another frag round and brought the barrel up to lock the action. He adjusted rear sight elevation and pulled the trigger again.

Bloop.

The round seemed to take forever to land.

BOOM!

The grenade exploded between the two insurgents, but neither was killed—only stunned and knocked off their feet. One man was hit in the arm, the other had a short piece of wire embedded deep in his thigh. They scrambled up and ran to the center of their advancing line.

Blue streaks of light from the G3 tagged one, then quickly caught the other as they ran.

Ponk!...Blap!...Ponk!...Blap!

Both men exploded in twin geysers of flesh and blood.

Jesse couldn't believe what he was seeing. From his position, he could not hear the slight supersonic crack of the coil rifle, but the results were clearly visible. *Jesus! What the hell kind of Buck Rogers weapon is that?*

He laid the M79 down and picked up his suppressed M14. Seeing several of the attackers surging forward, he picked the one in front and dispatched him.

The effect on the others was immediate. They all began seeking cover.

Mark had noted the grenades being fired on the Muslims from a position to his east. *Who the hell is out there?*

A pair of terrorists charged into the room where Mark, Francis and Tola were positioned. They had been dispatched by Isagani before the assault began and had traversed the jungle on the west side of the ruins to flank the defenders.

Both wildly sprayed the room with their AKs as they ran in screaming, "Allah Akbar! Allah Akbar!"

The steel jacketed projectiles ricocheted around the stone room. One caught Francis in the left leg just below the knee.

"Ahhh!" the young boy screamed as he fell.

Mark wheeled, drawing his O&U 12 gauge from its holster in a lightning blur. Falling back and onto his right side, he shot the closest man with a *mucho gaucho* round. The two fifty-eight caliber slugs impacted center mass. One ball hit his heart the other his right lung with the seven strand connecting wire slicing through his sternum.

Nineteen flechettes impaled the second attacker from crotch to neck with his second shot. Both jihadis crumpled under his accurate fusillade.

Two rounds had found Tola—one to the right thigh and the other in the left arm above the elbow.

"Fuck!" She fell back against the stone wall, lost her weapon and grabbed her arm. "I'm down!"

He dropped the empty shotgun as he rolled over and pulled his 1911, and then quickly stood up. He took a quick peek through the back door from which the men had entered and rushed across the room to her side.

"Hang in there," he said as he assessed the wounds. Neither were immediately life threatening—he turned around to Michele and removed his belt—*Won't be needing this any more, my friend*—wrapped it twice around her leg and made a secure tourniquet.

"Get me up…"

"First, your arm."

He pulled a blue bandana from his pants cargo pocket and wrapped her arm tightly—picked up her weapon, dropped the nearly empty magazine and reloaded it before handing it to her.

"Okay…easy does it now," Mark said as he lifted her to a position at the window. "Conserve your ammo."

"Put my mags on the ledge for me."

After he followed her request, he called out, "Mito!"

The silence told the him what he suspected. "Mito! Answer up, man!"

"Looks like it's you and me, Zorro," Tola said with a forced smile as she fired semi-auto at the remaining attackers.

"My leg," Francis called feebly.

"Jesus…when it rains it fuckin' pours…Dalisay! Get in here! Stay low. Do it now!"

A moment later the frightened woman crawled into the doorway. "Oh, my God!"

"Get Francis out of here. Take him back with your family."

"I…I…"

"Now, Goddamn it!" Mark yelled as he took his position at the wall. He pulled his hide-out weapon from its waistband holster—a Remington Model 51 .380 caliber pistol. "Take this." He handed it to her.

Dalisay reached out and grabbed the weapon with trembling hands. "I…I…I hate…guns."

"These ragheads get past us, you'll be thankful you have it…Now get Francis out of here."

A constant roar of gunfire made it hard to think, but she managed to do as he ordered. As she dragged the boy out of the room, her last sight was Mark and Tola firing at the enemy. *Dear Lord…protect them. Bless them with your…*

A half dozen rounds impacted the wall next to the door, cutting her prayer short.

Isagani was the first to hear the sound of the approaching blades.

Whomp Whomp Whomp

He immediately turned to the north and in the distance he could see a pair of incoming *Cobra* helicopters. Both were military surplus given to the Philippine Army by the United States, but still very serviceable and headed his way.

Tweet! Tweet! Tweet!

He blew his whistle to alert his men. When they looked back from their fighting positions, he used his hands and signaled them to disperse into the jungle.

Immediately the remaining few began to scurry for the forest to the east and west. Isagani quickly made his way east using whatever cover was available to avoid the streak of blue light that disintegrated his men as they fled.

Jesse had heard the choppers incoming long before anyone else. The familiar sound was ingrained in his mind from days in Vietnam. *Yeah, buddy! Come on in!*

He pulled a fresh M-14 magazine from a shoulder bag and, after tapping it on the heel of his boot, he locked it into the well with a sharp click. He rocked it back and forth to insure it was properly seated. Before he could re-engage, all the attackers had faded into the forest.

I'll just hunker down here...take a shot if it doesn't give away my position.

A sense of deep relief rolled over Mark as he picked up a visual on the helicopters.

"Dalisay...Tola needs you," he called out

She appeared at the doorway on her hands and knees and cautiously peered around the corner. At the sight of Tola slumped against the stone wall, she jumped up and ran to her.

"Let me see," she said fearfully.

"I'm good," Tola said, and then passed out.

Mark moved to the door and looked at the rest of the family huddled in the far corner. "Stay here. Keep down. I'll let you know when to come out."

Most of the villagers had returned to their homes and were assessing the damages. Mark stood in a clearing with the commander of the helo force.

"How'd you know to come here?"

"Several of the residents called for help on their cell phones. We got here as soon as we could," Captain Royial replied.

"We have wounded. Can you get them back to Dipolog?"

"Of course. My men will assist any way we can. By the looks of it you made a good showing here today."

"Two dead…two wounded. If you had not arrived…it could have been whole different story."

Rat tat tat tat

Both men looked up the mountain to the east at the sound of rifle fire.

"You have any special forces guys operating around here?" Mark asked as he lifted his binoculars.

"No. Why do you ask?"

"Someone has been helping us…made a huge difference. Got no idea who, but I owe 'em a case of beer at least."

"None of our forces have left Dipolog or Dipitan except us. Too busy holding the positions and weeding through the population to insure no one else is there to wreak havoc."

"Damn strange then. Know who these assholes were yet?"

"Muslim National Liberation Front. This is the furthest north they have been active in a long time."

"Is the airport open yet?"

"Tomorrow morning."

"Good. I need to get some clients out of here and back home."

Jesse lay in wait, expecting the dying insurgent's last burst of full auto fire to attract some of his brothers. Only the sound of the wind was audible. Sure enough, a rebel crept out of some dense brush and scanned the terrain.

Isagani paused and studied his dead brother. *Your virgins await you.* That was his last thought. A 175gr HPBT round moving at 2580fps round from Jesse's suppressed M14 impacted his forehead. His dreams of becoming a war chief dissipated with the pink and gray spray of his brain matter painting the foliage behind him.

BARNHARDT'S RESIDENCE
Bangkok, Thailand

Dalisay insisted on Tola staying at the residence until she healed. After seeing she was a comfortable as possible, considering her injuries, Mark met with Joris and went over the details of the events.

"That's it in a nutshell. As promised...your family is safe."

"I am forever in your debt. I will have the bonus check cut this afternoon. Who do I send the money to in the Philippines?"

"Just give it to me. I'll deliver them to Berto's and Mito's families."

BARNHARDT SECURITY HOUSE

Mark finished the debrief, leaving the men sitting silently reflecting on the encounter on Mindanao.

"How did Berto take the news?" Roger asked.

"Like any father would."

"Change of subject…what's the plan for sick dick?" Rhino asked.

"I'll set a meet with Virote. Contact Interpol. Have Crank drop the bomb in Cebu…Suggest everyone get packed. When the shoe drops, we'll be out of here."

"What about Missus Barnhardt and the kid?" Mike asked.

"I have an associate en route to replace us. Should be here tomorrow. 'Til then, Keit and I stay."

"What do we do?" Blaster questioned.

"Take your money and run. You two need to report to Hal and get geared up for Nicaragua."

"Then, I take it we did good enough here?" Dog asked.

"Hell…Zorro would have you on a spit, turning over hot coals if you didn't." Rhino laughed. "What's the gig in Nicaragua pay, anyway?"

"Less than here…more than the lotus blossom hotel," Mark said with a huge grin.

"Hey…I'm done at Crank's Shangri-La…for now. I'm closing on a hundred percent recovery. I need to start makin' some dough."

"You're in Rhino. Should be a piece of…"

"The hell you say! You're starting to sound just like the crazy Scotsman…And you know I don't much care for cake."

They shared a hearty laugh as Roger and Mike looked on sharing a confused look.

BARNHARDT'S RESIDENCE

Mark approached Dalisay and Rutger sitting in the rooftop garden. The boy was feeding broken crackers to the koi in the pond. She was reading a book about a security operation in Kenya. Since her experience in the Malindang mountains, her interest to know more about the shadowy world in which Mark worked was peaked.

"What are you reading?" he asked.

She closed the book and tried to hide the cover. "Oh, just something I picked up. How is Tola?"

"Doing good," he replied as he took the book from her. "Keit delivered her daughter a short time ago and they're catching up. You should try to meet her before she leaves." Mark thumbed a few pages of *Blood Ivory*, and then looked at the author's bios. "One of them was there. And most of the others…are dead."

"Really? And how do you know this?"

He returned the book. "I know the guys that lived."

"I see. About Tola's daughter…she can stay here as long as her mom does. What's this?" she asked, pointing at the laptop and a USB flash drive in his hands.

"Rutger, come here, little buddy."

When the boy stood beside him Mark ruffled his hair before saying, "The guys are playing a video game over at the security house. They asked me to let you know in case you wanted to join them."

"Can I momma? Can I?"

"Yes you can, but you come back for your nap when I call you. Understand?"

"Yes, momma," he said as he ran for the lift.

"Now what is this all about?"

"There is something on this memory stick you need to know about…It ain't pretty. I'm going to leave it with you. When you've seen enough…You'll find me downstairs in the kitchen with Val."

Mark placed his laptop on the table along with the flash drive and joined Rutger as the elevator arrived.

Dalisay turned on the computer and loaded the tiny drive. Her heart sank when the images came up. "Oh, my God!" She recognized the physique of her husband—the man who had drugged and raped her following the beauty pageant so many years before—although his face was hidden under a leather mask. Tears welled up as she covered her mouth and then closed her eyes tightly…

Mark was in the kitchen, quizzing Val to determine his involvement or knowledge about Joris' actives.

The sound of a single gunshot coming from the floor above caught him off-guard. He immediately drew his Smith and Wesson and ran to the stairs, taking them two at a time as he raced up. At the head of the stairwell, he paused and scanned the hallway before proceeding.

He peered into the master bedroom and found Dalisay standing over Joris—lying on the floor wearing only powder-blue silk pajama bottoms—bleeding from a gunshot to the groin and his hands held up in a defensive position. He was pleading for mercy.

"No! Don't...please!"

Before Mark could react, she emptied his Remington 51 into her husband's chest and head. The big man's body shook from the violent impact of the Federal Hydra-Shoks at close range—and then lay still.

"Put the gun down, Dalisay."

She dropped the weapon from her trembling hands—it landed on Joris's blood-spattered torso with a thud. She leaned over his body and hissed, "You sick evil bastard! You'll never hurt anyone ever again...May you burn in hell."

****

TIMBER CREEK PRESS

PREVIEW FROM

TIMBER CREEK PRESS

NICARAGUAN HELL

by

DORAN INGRHAM

CHAPTER ONE

AMERRISQUE MOUNTAINS
Nicaragua

"Range…550…Wind, one-quarter factor right," DeLeon, the muscular former Colombian DEA sergeant and spotter for Mark Ingram said quietly.

"Target?"

"Fifth rider…Grey horse…Range 525…"

Mark Ingram—wearing a ghillee suit—lay on his poncho under the cover of a low dog seed tree branch between two boulders. His M14 National Match rifle—lovingly referred to as Betsy—was resting on his hydration pack and aimed at the advancing column of men. He made an adjustment to his Nightforce 5x25x56 B.E.A.S.T. scope. Satisfied with the doping, he slowed his breathing, let a breath out half way—and squeezed the trigger.

Colonel Alfredo Hernandez Sacasa never heard the sound of the shot. The 175 grain M118LR MatchKing 308 round impacted his chest just below the neck throwing his lifeless body onto the rump of his mount. The animal felt his rider shift on his back then heard the report causing it to bolt forward as the dead man slid off, hitting the rocky ground and tumble down the mountainside.

The men under the colonel's command scrambled for cover and began to fire wildly—without any clue as to where the shot came from.

"We go now, Zorro?"

"Yup...only getting paid for El Bastardo Negro...Got no quarrel with the others."

Both men eased back from the shooting position and began packing their equipment. A single round impacted the tree above them causing them to hug the ground.

"You think they know where we are, Zorro?"

"Nope...if they did, there would be more than just one round. Let's get out of here before they figure it out."

With their weapons and equipment collected, they scrambled down the backside of the mountain to three tough mountain mules they had tied to a picket line.

In a matter of minutes they rode off with DeLeon leading the pack animal.

"Who hired us to kill the scourge of Nicaragua?" he asked.

"Hal took the contract..."

"No, I mean who hired Hal."

"Hell…have no idea. Don't care," Mark said before taking a swallow from his CamelBak drinking tube.

"He had a family. I saw them on the news…"

"Don't care."

***

ZORRO'S RULES

1. Anyone and everyone who stands against us... Dies.

2. There is no such thing as too much ammo.

3. Always bring a gun to the fight. Better yet bring two.

4. When in doubt shoot first. There are no second place winners in our line of work.

5. The faster you eliminate the bad guys the less you get shot.

6. Wear body armor. It may be heavy and hot...but it beats the hell out of being dead.

7. Bullets are better than rocks. Grenades are better than bullets.

8. Study Sun Tzu's Art of War. It's the bible for our line of work.

9. Make sure your weapon fires every time. If angel dust makes your gun jam you're dead.

10. Carry locked and loaded at all times. Cycling rounds will get you killed.

11. Never work for free. Even a plumber gets paid to make sure the toilet flushes.

12. Never make it personal. Clouds your judgement.

13. Profile at will. Helps identify the enemy.

14. Someone is always looking for you.

15. Avoid physical contact with the enemy. Especially rolling around on the ground.

16. If all you have is a handgun... Make sure the caliber starts with '4'.

17. If you think someone is following you... They are.

18. Believe nothing. Verify everything.

19. Learn to say no.

20. When a contract is over walk away.

21. Unless you're working in Switzerland... The Geneva Convention is not in play.

22. When it hits the fan, keep these four rules in mind:
    1. If it moves... Kill it.
    2. If you think it moved... Kill it.
    3. If you think it is going to move... Kill it.
    4. See rule number one.

TIMBER CREEK PRESS

www.ingramcontent.com/pod-product-compliance
Lightning Source LLC
Chambersburg PA
CBHW051513250626
47156CB00001B/72